RED FLAG

City of Angels/Dead on Arrival
CODA Book 1

by

Steve McManus

Cover design by Denis Lenzi
Author photo by Brandon Reece
Book design by Steve McManus

First Print Edition: August 2015

ISBN 978-0-9964485-0-5

Visit stevemcmanus.com

For Kellie and Paloma, Theresa and Kevin, Mike and Sheila.

Special thanks to Sheila Rees (without whom…), Leslie Johnson and Diana Finch.

If you enjoy this book please return to your point of purchase and rate it.

RED FLAG

CHAPTER 1

Danny Kasho walked briskly out of the bulging semi-circular atrium of Van Nuys Courthouse West as if he'd been prematurely disgorged from the pregnant belly of Lady Justice herself. He nonchalantly swept some presumptuous fool's notepad and Diet Coke can off one of the waist-high marble walls flanking the stairs and claimed the end spot as his, laying his charcoal leather Louis Vuitton messenger bag on top, careful to keep his courtroom drawings flat inside and eyeing the people coming out of the building as he loosened his tie with two fingers. Only one of the two exit doors sandwiched between the employee and public entrances was in use today and the general egress was especially slow.

He posted a quick update to his blog: *Court adjourned for the weekend. Lawyers and judge debating Byzantine*—which was hard to type with his phone's meddling autocorrect—*rules of law. Trial starts Wednesday. Prosecution has to be praying Patron plays let's make a deal before then.*

At one time or another, either for a story or a serviceable bathroom without a line, Danny had been into nearly all of the buildings that comprised the innocuously-named Van Nuys Civic Center—the unremarkable east courthouse for civil and family cases, the slightly taller glass-fronted west courthouse for felonies, misdemeanors and traffic violations, which looked across the plaza at the backside of the Valley Municipal Building with its Art Deco friezes, eight-story tower and rosette stonework. It was a shrunken version of LA's famous city hall downtown and an outpost of civic services found there, containing field offices for the mayor and the city attorney and legal or financial departments of a dozen local agencies, as well as being the headquarters of the Council of Governments for the San Fernando Valley cities. Rounding out the judicial/municipal ecosystem was an LAPD police station and a jail and a great many bail bondsmen and lawyers with storefronts in the surrounding streets. Van Nuys Courthouse West was always a busy place, especially when a high-profile trial like this one was underway.

Danny blogged for a regional crime news website called City of Angels/Dead on Arrival—CODA.com, which had been a fledgling upstart when he joined in 2010 as a paid intern for a dime above minimum wage. He bought a used police scanner off Craigslist, borrowed a camera from a neighbor, maxed out a credit card for a laptop and a Dictaphone and dove into the darkness, mortgaging his life on his eventual success, or at least comfortable self-sufficiency, preferably sooner rather than later. He ran up the miles on a pre-owned Honda and brought back nightly tales of felonies and felons young and old to fill CODA's daily output. Tips started paying his rent and he became a regular at most of the forty superior court locations spread out around LA, and had been to Van Nuys many times over the years. Viewers around the country had too, beginning in 1993 with the Menendez brothers in their ugly sweaters, post-parental shotgunning. Or with angry former TV star Robert Blake, white-haired in a pallbearer's suit, acquitted in 2005 of shooting his wife in their car outside one of Danny's favorite Italian restaurants in the Valley which had since undergone a radical and disappointing renovation. Blake's karma had been suitably shitty ever since.

The standard group of court reporters was emerging piecemeal into the thickening crowd in front of the building. They all knew each other but the different mediums were clubby—TV hung with TV, radio with radio, print with print. Bloggers like Danny were the free radicals undermining the system, the information hunter-gatherers who owed nothing to nobody.

Matronly Martha Simmons from the local CBS station pinched her glossy smoker's lips together as she hurried past in her kitten heels and peach Ann Taylor pantsuit. "No door duty today Danny?"

"You know I was just looking for that citizenship merit badge, Martha. I'm a people person. I'm a helper."

"Keep looking Danny, keep looking. And aren't you aiming a little high?"

"I'm sure I don't know what you mean."

Martha chuckled, "You will Danny, you will."

Except for when she was being cryptic with him he liked Martha—he'd gone drinking with her before and she was the real deal from back in the day, two or three decades ago. She was teasing him for being publicly castigated by an overzealous sheriff's deputy for holding the courthouse door open when they were all here yesterday. Reprimanding him right in front of everyone, a jury of his smirking peers but not, thank God, the object of his affection.

So today he changed his plan of attack, which was first, get here super early to grab one of the coveted seats in the back of the sixth-floor courtroom so he'd be among the first out the door, then bound down the stairs to avoid waiting at the elevators and nab the end spot at the marble wall nearest the doors, regardless of whether some fool left a Diet Coke and a notepad there in a queenie passive-aggressive attempt to reserve the location. Both items were so much litter in the dry plaza grass now. Shame on them. Yay for him.

And Phase One of Operation Voelker accomplished.

Milquetoast Eric Garvey from NBC followed close behind Martha. He was shucking off his sport coat with the cheesy elbow patches, eager to find a way through the spectators, participants, lawyers and journalists in transit, and people just loitering about on smoke breaks. Eric was jumpy, peering over heads to see what the hold-up was—maybe he was looking for a bathroom without a line. He was always squinting even when it wasn't this sunny out. Even when he was indoors. Even probably when he slept in his bedroom curtained with his collection of bad ties, of which he seemed in innumerable supply. "Kasho you make a better doorstop than a writer."

"Oh hey Mr. Magoo, have you ever seen your own eyes? Has anyone?"

"I can see how many people aren't reading you perfectly well."

"They're too busy gawking at the ties your mom bought you for Christmas twenty years ago."

Danny checked the exiting crowd and accidentally made eye contact with diminutive moon-faced Carlos Esquivel who was shooting the cuffs of his crisp little suit elaborately to draw attention to the animated face of his new watch. Carlos never seemed to be holding anything and barely carried a microphone even when he was on camera. He was an ex-morning anchor at his station recently demoted back to the field and he wasn't taking it well.

"So this is how you make a living Kasho," he tried to quip. "I forgot to tip you yesterday, let me see if I have some change. Can you break a single?"

The joke wasn't so funny coming from wee Carlos. "Up your wife's allowance chico, she isn't paying me enough for my services. You keep her on a shorter leash than she wants me to."

Wee Carlos started to retort but the exiting push of reporters and spectators swept him along like a little duckling. Dickhead.

One of the female Fox reporters who came and went in different flavors but who all had similar smiles as if they'd just bitten into a habanero chili pepper, something inhumanly spicy which had them right on the verge of screaming hysterically, was the apparent owner of the dispatched Diet Coke and notepad. This one was skinny and Asian and in her yellow and white cowlneck mini dress resembled a banana split on legs as she spun her stick-figure arms around herself in a windmill of bewilderment over Danny and his stuff occupying the space where *her* stuff was supposed to be.

He pointed helpfully toward the lawn. "That yours?"

She gaped at him. Her makeup-caked eyelids snapped like the jaws of a deep sea-dwelling fish hauled up out of the dark into a bright world of searing ambivalence. "What…the…*fuck?*"

Life is like a toilet bowl, Danny's shrug seemed to say. You're constantly confronted by assholes.

The Foxtress made an indignant noise in the back of her throat and clicked away to find a section of wall low enough for her to cross over onto the grass in her mini-dress and eighteen-inch nightclub heels. She was probably three feet tall without them.

At last Carrie Voelker from ABC strode out of the courthouse and the mid-morning sunshine tightened into her own personal spotlight. She gifted Danny with a dazzling smile as the wind played with her shiny blond hair in slow-motion, and while she passed in her black contoured boot-cut pants he indulged in a nice long look at her finest asset. She was her station's newest court beat appointee and by far the best they'd ever had. The best anyone had ever had, with all due respect to Martha Simmons in her heyday. Even the chirping of the birds sounded like whistled catcalls from construction workers.

Danny grabbed his bag and pushed off the wall with a glance at the Foxtress who was tip-toeing through the crispy grass with her preposterous heels in one hand and her tiny nose wrinkled as if she was having to navigate a minefield of dog shit on top of everything else.

Carrie Voelker waited a few steps away so he could catch up. "Guilty as sin but will Charlize get him off again—this time for good? We'll be live at five."

"Is that how you're going to position it?" Danny smiled, pleased as Patton driving through France. Mission accomplished.

"I'll find some way to keep it from looking like a foregone conclusion," she said. "What about you?"

"I'm going with the classic Greek tragedy—Man murders Wife, Man fakes death, Man runs off with Hot Secretary."

"*Executive* hot secretary. I didn't know CODA was into the classics."

"We are when they look like Charlize Patron. Besides, ridding yourself of wifeypooh so you can hook up with the help is so old it's practically biblical."

They'd talked exactly once since pre-trial hearings began three weeks ago but he'd caught the occasional thrilling furtive glance from her. They'd smiled at each other and rolled their eyes at the necessary banality of courtroom proceedings and he'd been instantly smitten nose to toes. But whenever they had a spare moment either some advantageous interloper cut in or an overzealous sheriff's deputy broke up the party and he'd been unable to reconnect with her. Hence today's imperative success of Operation Voelker.

They stopped in the shade of a tree on the grassy pedestrian mall between the San Fernando Valley Constituent Service Center on the corner which contained more municipal government service branches and looked like a retail outlet, all tinted glass and earth tones, and an ugly federal building sheltering the local chapter of the IRS. The federal building was a plain concrete box with rows of narrow windows like arrow slits from which the taxmen and women could monitor the merchants in the temple—a smattering of ten by ten canopy tents set up in the plaza with vendors selling purses, jewelry, and clothing off draped folding tables. The food carts were good in a pinch but sometimes came back on you later. After Inglewood one side of the federal building had been cordoned off for repair but Danny noticed the tape was gone now so the tax collectors must be finally back to code.

Like a wartime news reel narrator he said, "But now—will true love prevail and Patron's mysterious memory problems persist? Or will she finally come to what few senses she has and do her part to give Slick Nick first degree with special circumstances as a parting gift for their weeks of coital bliss on the beach?"

Carrie added, "For which she'll earn herself a minimal sentence and eventually disappear into free obscurity, which once again proves that a woman's emptiest head is still smarter than a man's smallest head."

"Assuming her IQ is bigger than her breasts."

"Right? It's hard to look remorseful with the size boobs he bought her. Maybe she can act sorry for *them.*"

Danny liked talking about boobs and little heads with Carrie Voelker. This was going better than he'd expected. He stole a glance at hers as she removed her blazer and folded it over her purse, a Jurassic-sized pearl-colored faux-leather tote with a double handle and pockets on the outside, her fashionable version of his carry-all Louis Vuitton messenger bag. Like everything else about Carrie Voelker her breasts were, in Danny's learned opinion, absolutely exquisite, and decorated today by a long beaded necklace that drew his eyes helplessly down into their warm snugness beneath a raspberry pleated chiffon top with spaghetti straps. She was 5'9" or so, on the underside of 30, with straight white-blond hair and a degree of tan that looked egregiously healthy on camera and off. She'd mentioned that her station was grooming her for an anchor position but he hoped she stayed out in the field so he could see her from time to time. No offense to Martha Simmons but next gen eye candy was in the tour rider.

Carrie took out a compact and deftly started reapplying her lipstick, turning toward him to shield herself from the hot wind tugging at the trees and the tent tops. "Got any plans for the not-long-enough Labor Day weekend?" she asked into her compact's mirror.

He wished that was an invitation to share some Prosecco and a Jacuzzi. "Work, hopefully."

"Aww. All work and no play? You guys have it so tough."

"Who?"

"You sketchy independent contractor stringer-types."

"Oh, you mean everyone who lives hand to mouth outside the lucrative cushy tushy cottony double-ply world of TV?"

"Exactly! All you guys who'd be cleaning pools otherwise. Having to chase news all night it's amazing you can get up for court in the morning. I'd still be in my PJ's." Carrie smacked her lips and beamed at him.

Danny started to stare so he pretended his phone had buzzed with a new message, wondering what *pajamas* entailed for Carrie Voelker. He pictured silk and teeny tiny amounts of it. "Work is better than no work when work equals pay. And I'm not a stringer, I'm gainfully employed. I don't live in my parents' basement either."

"Well you've got that going for you." She put away her gear and checked her phone. "Let me see your drawings. I always see you drawing but never get to see the actual drawings. Let's see if I could pick them out of a lineup."

Danny hesitated, then smiled almost bashfully. "Okay, sure."

Their fingers touched as she took the spiral-bound 9x12 drawing pad. He watched her leaf through his sketches on the heavyweight acid-free white paper, pleased to be the occasional center of her attention. He thought he'd gotten good likenesses of ex-investment banker Nick Mendoza, 54, physically fit but only 5'6", with a full head of jet-black hair plugs—in his drawings Danny left extra space between the tufts to illustrate it. Mendoza's tan had faded since he and his girlfriend Charlize Patron were arrested without incident in Cabo San Lucas last year, three months after the body of Dina Mendoza, Nick's wife of eleven years, was found in the master bathroom tub of their Tarzana mansion with two supposed suicide notes taped to the mirror, one hers, one his.

Dina had drowned in three inches of water from a combination of Absolut and oxymorphone—both bottles were found conveniently within reach and empty. Nick Mendoza's rambling suicide note—the verbatim contents of either note wouldn't be revealed to the public until trial but portions had been leaked to the press within hours—allegedly alluded to having discovered his wife's body, about blaming himself for not realizing how seriously depressed she was, and of being too distraught to carry on without her. There was a vague reference to ending his life with one of his many firearms in a particular area of the desert so for five days military personnel, law enforcement and hundreds of hope-filled volunteers combed a wide swath of the high desert between Edwards Air Force Base and Barstow, but came up with only animal bones and the conclusion that the man's remains might never be found. It was wide-open, harsh land, and a despondent man so inclined could easily be swallowed up by it.

But when the authenticity of Dina Mendoza's handwriting on her suicide note was called into question, and the autopsy eventually concluded bruises on her body were consistent with having thrashed and kicked inside the infinity tub, and the cause of death was ultimately determined not to be drowning but mechanical and positional asphyxia, detectives broadened their net and quickly snagged on Charlize Patron.

Charlize was 25 and petite, a waifish 5'2", and had once been a pretty brown-haired girl from Rancho Cucamonga before she underwent about a thousand cosmetic surgeries to more accurately conform to Nick Mendoza's fantasy specifications of what his augmented blond girlfriend should look like. Nick had hired Charlize as his personal secretary soon after they met in the Polynesian bar of Trader Vic's in Beverly Hills and she was promoted to executive secretary within days. Nick gave her a private phone which he paid for and she answered 24/7. Less than a year later Dina Mendoza was dead and Charlize and the supposedly auto-deceased

Nick were beginning a permanent vacation in Mexico. But ignoring his admonitions of secrecy, Charlize texted her friends all about her trip (her defense was already postulating that by calling it a *trip* Charlize had indicated her belief it was a temporary indulgence and that she didn't know anything about Dina Mendoza's death and therefore was almost as much a victim of the crime as Dina Mendoza was). Charlize's friends said as much to the police when investigators came looking for her after Dina was found and Nick was not.

In court Charlize was trying her best to come across as naïve and impressionable while a defense-approved make-under transformed her formerly lascivious beauty into a false dowdiness. She had demonstrated a willingness to make home movies of the pair's athletic sexual escapades, which naturally found their way to the internet and into the prosecution's case (CODA provided links but for legal reasons did not store copies of the videos on their servers). Charlize sat demurely at the defense table with her legs primly crossed and no longer spread, her hands limp in her lap as if she had palsy instead of running them over her skin per Nick's off-camera direction, but to the surprise of everyone she had so far declined to remember certain key details of her lover's whereabouts on the day Dina Mendoza died. If the prosecution didn't turn her their case was open to speculation, and in LA speculation went a long way.

Danny's drawing of Charlize was all lips and tits and reminded him of something his father might have drawn for the summer tourists—it was too much of a caricature. He'd have to redo parts of it when he got home before he uploaded the drawings to his Investment in Murder blog about the Mendoza case.

Looking through his drawings Carrie Voelker's parted lips moved like exotic plumage as she murmured, "We spend so much of life on the seedy side of it, don't we?"

As if she was sharing a secret with him, like what color underwear she was wearing. The tag of Carrie's top was sticking up and Danny wanted to reach out and tuck it back in so he could touch her bare back and the small mole under her right shoulder blade. "Clean only pays the bills for cleaners."

She turned to a page with smaller drawings of the lawyers and presiding judge. "I thought of you this morning when I heard about the fire in Malibu."

Danny was about to remark what a coincidence it was that she was thinking about him this morning because *he* had been thinking about *her* when his phone buzzed for real and the text on his lockscreen stopped him pre-gush.

Get up Corral Cyn ASAP.

The sender's name gave him goosebumps despite the heat and he momentarily forgot Carrie's admission of being practically infatuated with him.

He blinked—she'd said something. "Sorry, what?"

"These are really good," she said again. "You're a real artist."

"I like amenities too much to be an artist."

"Are you going to post these?"

"Yeah." Reluctantly he forced himself to add, "Speaking of which…"

"Seedy Greek tragedies won't wait." She closed the drawing pad and handed it back to him. "See you later Danny."

"I'll be watching you tonight Carrie," he said in his best Vincent Price.

"I can never have too many weirdoes in my life," she sang over her shoulder. Her heels clacked along the walkway in time to the swaying of her hips as she went to meet her crew at their blue and white news van, parked with the others along Van Nuys Boulevard displaying all the variety of local news—Martha's blue and white van, Eric's white and blue van, and wee Carlos's blue and white van. They were even all the same thinnish European-looking modified Ford.

Despite the urgency he took a moment to savor the miracle of bio-engineering that was Carrie Voelker, like every other right-thinking man in the plaza was getting whiplash doing too, thanking her and her parents and whatever mitochondrial mojo had gone on behind the scenes to create her splendidness. Then he walked quickly in the opposite direction, following a walkway between the Valley Municipal Building and a day care to where his pre-owned 2014 Accord which replaced his original Honda was angled into a spot at an expired meter on Sylvan.

He stuffed his tie into the pocket of his court suit jacket and laid it in the back seat, then removed the license plate-size News Media Official Parking Permit and the old cell phone recharging cable from his dashboard, the end of the cable that went into the car's lighter nicely obscuring the parking permit number. A friend at a TV station had gotten it for him a few years ago and he'd been forging the annual expiration sticker ever since. It would pass a visual inspection but not a computer check and he tried to use it only when necessary.

He replied to the text *On my way* and tapped his phone to bring up freeway traffic conditions.

Corral Canyon was in Malibu, and today Malibu was burning.

CHAPTER 2

He made the westbound Valley crossing on the 101 bathed in eerie golden sunlight which highlighted the vibrantly glowing screens of the hulking five-story tripedal media tower squatting over the most gridlocked freeway exchange in the country like a giant invading robot from a planet of merciless advertisers.

There were four such towers around LA, each shaped like a giant bee skep some five stories tall with huge wraparound LED screens. Video played constantly but silently—billboards with audio played on the lower screens closest to the traffic, the sound beamed directly into passing motorists' phones and car stereos from whichever screen was nearest the vehicle, an intrusion which had led to numerous but so far unsuccessful lawsuits. Only an antiquated car stereo or the monthly opt-out fee could alleviate the din, and the waiver didn't even cover all kinds of ads, exempting politicals and whatever else the tower vendor as mass aggregator decided drivers really couldn't do without hearing.

The first tower went up in 2016, hunkering over the 105 and 110 interchange in South LA. In a vain attempt to placate outraged residents—the towers went up so fast because they were mostly empty space apart from the composite skeleton and the screens—the vendor attempted to humanize the behemoth by nicknaming it Anna and giving it a whimsical social media stream. Bella, the second South LA tower located just east of Anna over the junction of the 710 and 105, and the third tower Carla at the massive East LA interchange near downtown, seemed to go up simultaneously, with accompanying PR blitzes, media feeds (Bella was a romantic, Carla somewhat snide being closest to metropolitan downtown), resident protests and lawsuits.

Delma, the fourth and newest tower, went up last year over the 101 and 405 quagmire in the Valley, and was known for issuing practical tips for better living during the precious few hours per day her audience was not locked inside their vehicles within range of her highly-attuned sensors. She and her siblings were still operating despite the class action lawsuits pending against the vendor and the city from thousands of residents incensed by the towers' obnoxious height and glare, fully convinced they'll somehow have the monstrous things uprooted and disassembled and the pieces cast off into a molten lava pit somewhere.

Danny knew better. Never mind the huge upfront investment made on constructing the towers out of super-expensive composite material covered in hand-sized photovoltaic cells. Never mind that the cash- and water-strapped city received nearly half of the ad revenue owing to the structures being erected on city land. Delma alone broadcast to over 400,000 vehicles every day moving at an average speed between leisurely strolling and quadriplegic standstill. At peak times it could take an hour to traverse the junction. Priceless quality eyeball time. The president herself credited the pioneering towers erected in the Boston-Washington Corridor of the Northeast megalopolis with aiding her historic election bid.

The only thing keeping a fifth LA area tower out of Hollywood was the fault line which the state geologists couldn't get around and which was under increased scrutiny after Inglewood—San Francisco had so far thwarted efforts to build similar towers in the Bay Area, claiming seismic concerns—while the noisiest preservationists were bought off and shut up. The sisters were here to stay.

Whenever traffic stopped Danny scrolled through his phone, reacquainting himself with names and faces of contacts he hadn't had a reason to look at in months, and posting pictures of the smoke plume rising silently over the mountains, a massive column of static grays and whites cleaved by crosswinds at thirty thousand feet as glimpsed between the water conservation billboards with their wide LED screens issuing constant reminders—*Stop making a splash, conserve water! Think outside the sink! Save the flow conserve H2O! Save water—it's not just a drop in the bucket, it's the law!*

He thought again about Carrie Voelker thinking about him this morning and how little she'd been wearing at the time.

Operation Voelker was going swimmingly, spawning a pleasantly giddy flutter in his belly reminiscent of the Saturday morning of Labor Day weekend last year when a wildfire started in the woods off Little Tujunga Canyon, a hairpin road favored by motorcyclists twisting up and over two mountain summits through Angeles National Forest northeast of LA. A bucolic little horse-friendly suburb called Lake View Terrace, where Rodney King was beaten by police in 1991, lay at the south end of the canyon behind the empty basin of the Hansen Dam, and new housing developments sprawled like a fungus through the Antelope Valley on the north. Not much in between unless you were on an ATV or a horse. It was the fourth suspicious fire in Angeles National Forest in as many weeks.

At the initial press conference an LA County Fire Department arson investigator named Mike Cruz declared that the so-called Dillon Fire had been intentionally set, describing "unnatural burn vectors" resulting from the use of a "flame-propelling device." A reporter asked him if he'd ever seen anything like that before. Cruz said he had, but moved on to a question from another reporter who wasn't on the same page who asked something Cruz could defer to another official to answer. The press conference ended without Cruz saying another word. He hadn't said anything officially about it to anyone since, referring all questions to the fire department public information officers.

At the time Danny was going through a dry spell of noteworthy offenses and offenders and was slumming it through the churn of short distresses, homicides and almostcides—almost homicides—predictable by their economic location around the city. He was itching for something deep to jump into so he made his way to the Dillon Fire's incident command post which was organized in a gravel turnout less than a mile from the fire's point of origin and proceeded to gather hours of interviews with anyone at the scene who'd talk to him—residents, firefighters, victims, battalion chiefs, arson investigators like Mark Pavelko from the U.S. Forest Service who was genial and forthcoming and turned into a terrific source. Everyone but the reticent Mike Cruz who automatically deflected reporters to fire department public information officers ensuring everyone got the same thing unless they had a source inside the investigation.

Danny scoured previously published sources—articles, blogs, official investigative reports, news releases and Forest Service incident reports, hundreds of photos and videos. The specter of arson was raised repeatedly as it often was during California's ever-lengthening fire season, stretching across the calendar year like a snake trying to catch its own tail, fueled by the new normal of mega-drought. But drilling down using Cruz's keywords he was able to isolate seven wildfires in just the previous seven weeks with references to unusual scorch marks or burn patterns.

He replaced the detailed Los Angeles and vicinity map pinned to a wall in his bedroom with color maps of four parched Southern California counties and plotted the eight wildfires on them with red plastic thumb tacks, backtracking from the Dillon Fire through the epic conflagration called the Box Fire which had erupted on Wednesday August 22 in Angeles National Forest, a fire that would ultimately take six weeks and some 150,000 acres of national forest to wrestle into containment, back to the inauspicious spark that started the firestorm, a smoldering grassy mound of earth surrounded by the suburbs of Thousand Oaks in Ventura County which burned less than an acre on Saturday July 14 and took only fifteen minutes to contain and extinguish. The so-called Hillcrest Fire was the first confirmed wildfire with the telltale scorch marks, which made it significant in both location and catalyst, though no one had been able to develop anything significant from it.

A firefighter who'd been among the first at the scene of the Dillon Fire told him that he personally saw a polystyrene foam drinking cup standing unscathed atop a charred trash can behind the fire line. Danny was split over whether it was meaningful or one of those casual coincidences that reminds you that Mother Nature is the ultimate prankster. When he asked Mark Pavelko about the cup the Forest Service agent blamed an inmate crew for littering, but the more he downplayed the significance of the cup the deeper Danny's teeth sank into the soft underbelly of its significance—until he became convinced the person who left the cup was the person who burned everything around it. And a drinking cup might have DNA on it.

Finally Pavelko asked him not to post anything about the goddamned cup.

Danny balked in graphic, anatomically-challenging phrases, citing everything from the US constitution to Roe v. Wade.

Pavelko offered unparalleled access in exchange for his concession.

Danny conceded.

Red Flag, his definitive blog about the wildfires, was born.

First he created the *de rigueur* sobriquet. Authorities may have been reluctant to even acknowledge a single suspect was behind the wildfires, but with four blazes back to back in Angeles National Forest and the overall westward creep toward greater Los Angeles, in a post on September 7 Danny christened the suspect the Angeles Arsonist. The nickname stuck like sticky tree sap. Pavelko was ambivalent about the moniker; he told Danny that they called him the Bug within the task force, with as much derision as two meager syllables could allow. Bug, short for Firebug. Danny didn't like *firebug* because it inferred a helplessness in the face of one's nature or urges, and while he'd met a few such helpless wretches over the years they paled in comparison to the sheer number of offenders who were just smart enough to willingly and consistently make bad choices.

The federal task force—technically called a fusion center in their press releases—was a direct result of Danny's public connection of the prolific spate of wildfires. Investigators and special agents were drawn from multiple agencies—the US Forest Service, Cal Fire, police and fire investigators from LA, Ventura, San Bernardino and Kern counties, the Office of the State Fire Marshal, Office of Emergency Services, FBI, ATF. On and on the acronyms went. Exact figures weren't disclosed but there were estimated to be between twenty and thirty investigators dedicated to identifying and capturing the so-called Angeles Arsonist.

But eight more wildfires burned into November. Red Flag's readership grew exponentially as the number of devastated acres soared. The online map looked great and was interactive with photos and video and stats and links to related interviews. The last confirmed fire was the sixteenth in just four months, the Los Liones Fire in Pacific Palisades behind the famed

Getty Villa museum, which burned close to 60 acres on Saturday November 3. There was no damage to the museum but nearby neighborhoods and a church were evacuated. Local news broadcast dramatic footage of stranded hikers being airlifted off the trail below Paseo Miramar with the wall of advancing smoke behind them.

After that fire the Angeles Arsonist retreated into hibernation as winter weather balmed the scorched earth he'd left behind. Crews mopped up and waited. Families grieved the loss of houses, the decimation of land. A firefighter's family mourned a loss much greater. Investigators solicited tips and chased leads. Danny did too, interviewing anyone he could find with a connection to the fires and adding to the maps in his bedroom, trying to flesh out the phantom by the few facts he'd left behind.

The Angeles Arsonist had averaged a major fire a week from July 14 to November 3, an unprecedented pace of destruction. Eleven fires had been set on Saturdays, five on Wednesdays. The schedule had to be indirect evidence of whatever passed as normal life confining the guy—a job, a family, things that forced him to at least partially conform to society's shape like tough dough molded in a pan. With few exceptions he seemed fond of a general geographical profile investigators had come to rely on—perhaps, Danny suggested in a post about the eleventh fire, the devastating Chalk Fire on September 29, *too* heavily. It was true most of the wildfires were started off rural roads, often in a turnout or bend at the opening of a canyon. Since fire spreads faster uphill than down the steep terrain offered his fires a head start. It was agreed that the suspect was a white male but from there the profiling fell apart. Some armchair geniuses believed he was employed, others that he was unemployable. He was married. He was divorced, and bitterly. To some he was in his early twenties, to others over forty.

Other than his race the only point of agreement was on the device—a military-grade flamethrower, possibly surplus, possibly homemade. A devastating weapon in the hands of an arsonist wandering far and wide across the extra-dry late summer mountains around Los Angeles. Today's fire in Malibu accompanied by Mark Pavelko's text—*Get up Corral Cyn*

ASAP—begged the question Danny and everyone else had been waiting to ask since last November:

Is the Angeles Arsonist coming back?

As he neared Malibu the giant plume began to move, bubbling and rolling upward on itself, dark smoke crowned by light across craggy mountain tops. The Accord's air conditioning cooled the smoke smell seeping into the cabin through the vents as Danny followed Malibu Canyon down to Pacific Coast Highway.

In some ways he had anticipated Pavelko's text. Yesterday the National Weather Service issued a Red Flag Warning for the region, with forecasters predicting temperatures in the upper 90s, winds of 20 to 40 miles per hour with local gusts up to 60, and a relative humidity of only 10%. By noon Santa Ana conditions were being reported in the Antelope and Santa Clarita Valleys with sustained northwesterly winds at 30 miles an hour. Firefighters were on standby across the county but Malibu was the first to explode.

Traffic slowed well before Pepperdine University even came into view. Danny inched around the scenic private campus onto the coastal highway where red, lemon and white fire engines from companies all over the southern half of the state were lined up on the shoulder. Adding insult to injury during the emergency a crane truck was blocking a lane, positioned to hoist up a car that had left the road and was visible in the tree tops of the property below the embankment. Eastbound traffic was compressed into one lane and westbound drivers were enticed to slow down and stare.

At the intersection of PCH and Corral Canyon Danny encountered his first organized resistance—a sheriff's roadblock on the corner where the old BeauRivage restaurant used to be. He'd been there on a date just a few days before it burned down in June 2012 from an electrical short in the attic. The relationship hadn't gone anywhere either but it had sure looked promising on that wine-drenched night by the sea.

One of the uniformed deputies at the roadblock examined his license, laminated media pass and CODA ID. Paused about fifty times to listen to the radio clipped to his tan-colored shirt. Danny eyed the flat body cam clipped to the cop's uniform and tried not to fidget and sure as shit didn't play any reggae.

"Go as far as the RV park," the cop finally said to him.

"And then what?"

The cop stopped to listen to his radio for about twenty minutes. "And then stop," he said after so long that Danny had almost forgotten what he'd asked.

"What's happening at the RV park?" he asked.

"Nothing, which is why you're going there. Or you can turn your vehicle around and leave the area."

The cop held Danny's credentials daintily by two fingers as if he might release them to the whim of the Santa Ana wind. Danny poured on the obsequiousness and answered, "Yes sir. Thank you. I appreciate it."

He took his things back greedily and passed over the RV park in the large switchback, cruising nice and slow until he reached the entrance. He parked beside three or four other cars with single occupants and probably authentic media passes slanted on their dashboards. Journalists too sedentary or obedient to do anything but wait until the story came to them gift-wrapped. No cops here though, they were too busy to babysit reporters.

Danny kept his engine running.

After five minutes that felt like five years of indentured servitude under a sadistic feudal lord a fire truck finally came lumbering up the road, screening him from view at the roadblock. He stepped on the gas and willed the underpowered Honda to embrace its inner funny car and give him high octane G's to press him back into his fabric seat. The motor whined agonizingly through the twisty ascent up the mountain as he checked the rearview mirror for a pursuing set of police lights that never came.

He aimed his ultra-compact Sony camcorder out the window. Nobody was evacuating yet from El Nido, a tiny, dense cluster of houses with ocean views clinging to the western side of the ridge, but it was a different story further up Corral Canyon at Malibu Bowl, a community of about a hundred houses, some on their tiptoes at three stories to peer over one another and the top of the mountain ridge at the ocean. The line of fleeing vehicles packed like refugees, some towing horse trailers, eventually forced Danny to squeeze into a vacated space on the side of the road behind a news van whose crew was sheltering inside from the heat and wind.

He texted Pavelko that he'd arrived and arranged the media parking permit and cell phone charger on his dash, then shouldered his messenger bag, grimacing at the added weight of his laptop which he couldn't leave behind to melt in his car, and doffed his official CODA baseball cap. CODA's body outline logo was emblazoned on all of their merchandise—sales from their popular online gift store helped subsidize the endeavor given the vagaries of online ad revenue.

He walked near the houses to avoid traffic; the road was too narrow for sidewalks. The wind howled up the canyon, blasting sand and grit into his nose and mouth. Within a minute his shirt was soaked through with sweat. After ten more his phone buzzed and he stopped beside an official-looking white Toyota pickup parked in the driveway of a presumably empty home, with a lightbar and a red stripe down the side like the Cal Fire supervisors' trucks which were common sights at wildfires. Danny turned his back to the wind and shaded the display with his hand so he could read it in the hostile sunlight. It was a text from Pavelko saying he was coming down to get him.

"Oh sweet Jesus." Danny gratefully sat down on the curb and drank half a bottle of water with loud frog-like gulps. A long black Mercedes sedan rolled past with two white-haired passengers sitting rigidly in front. The back seat was filled with suitcases and duffel bags full of the five P's of evacuation—pets, papers, prescriptions, pictures, PC's—in the form of portable hard drives. Anything you could carry that was irreplaceable should your house and all the rest of your belongings be about to cease to exist. Wildfire evened the economic playing field—the only difference between the rich and the rest was how quickly and comfortably they could recover. Otherwise fire was an equal-opportunity destroyer.

He was blogging that thought from his phone when he looked up and saw someone sitting at the wheel of the pickup, watching him. "Hey."

"Hey yourself," the driver said.

Danny tapped his phone to record video and stood up. "Mind if I ask you a few questions?"

"You a reporter?"

"Yeah." He crouched by the open passenger window and presented his ID with his elbows on the door to keep his phone level. "Danny Kasho, CODA.com. What's your name?"

"Tillson." He was a big guy with a prominent ridge over his eyes and a thick, flat nose that made his nostrils flare. A double chin pressed against goggles looped around his neck. He wore his dark hair long in back over the collar of a standard yellow wildland firefighting jacket. A detailed topographical map was spread across the dashboard. Food wrappers and soda bottles had collected in the passenger footwell. His jacket and spruce green Nomex brush pants looked practically new; evidently he hadn't been tapped for duty yet.

Danny was satisfied with the imaging on his phone. "You working the fire?"

"I'm a volunteer firefighter. They need all the help they can get up there." Tillson's voice was high-pitched and boyish, as if his vocal cords hadn't matured along with his body.

"It looks pretty bad."

"Active perimeter of thirty miles. Fifteen hundred firefighters. Zero percent containment. It's bad alright."

"You been up there yet?"

"'Course I have. What TV show do you work for?"

"It's online, CODA.com. What's your first name?"

Tillson hesitated. Opened his mouth, then snapped it closed with a toothy click.

"For your permission to quote you," Danny explained.

"Carl."

"What do you do when you're not volunteer firefighting, Carl?"

"Wait for the next season like everyone else."

"Got any thoughts on how it started?"

"Looks deliberate to me. Know why?"

A red LA County Fire Department Ford Ranger squealed to a stop and honked. Mark Pavelko beckoned through the open window.

Danny tapped his phone. "Thanks for your time, Carl. Good luck." He grabbed his messenger bag and hurried over between passing fire engines and evacuees.

Mark Pavelko's dark hair curled up from under a black and orange San Francisco 49ers cap. In the grating Chicago accent Danny remembered he said, "Looks like somebody's luau got a little out of hand. Wanna go get some?"

They shook hands through the window. "Love me a good luau." Danny walked around the front and got in, grateful for the air conditioning and shade.

Pavelko executed a tight three-point turn while holding his badge out of his window to stop traffic and they headed up the winding ridge road toward the fire.

CHAPTER 3

US Forest Service Special Agent Mark Pavelko drove with his right hand and worried his ear lobe with his left as they ascended the uppermost cutbacks of Corral Canyon. He wore a gold wedding ring and a silver watch on the inside of his left wrist. Ray-Ban aviator sunglasses were looped around his neck on a neoprene strap and rested against the chest of his sea green Forest Service polo shirt which was spotted with dark islands of sweat.

A two-way radio propped in the console had someone else's name taped to the back of it and squawked with information relayed from around the firefight. Communication was always a challenge at major events like this and could—in crucial lapses—be almost as dangerous as the fire itself. Hand crews, engine crews, air crews, support crews and supervisors all fought for space on the crowded radio channels for everything from bulldozers to bathrooms.

"What do you say Danny?" Pavelko said. "That's what you wear to a luau? The world is round Mr. Shiny Shoes, don't be such a square."

"I was in court, I can't be looking like I joined your men's group out in the woods for bear hugs and brewskies."

"Finally getting those traffic tickets cleared up?"

"I was trying to get out of jury duty."

"It's our civic obligation. This is the land of milk and honey and jury duty, you frigging freeloader."

The road's usual sweeping views were blocked by the dense smoke billowing out of the canyon. Danny videoed a red Air Crane helicopter chugging past at low altitude, a gangly aircraft that looked like a gigantic stick insect, modified for wildland firefighting with the addition of a hose dangling umbilically from a water tank in its belly. He recalled that it was leased from a company in Oregon and cost something like $8000 an hour to operate.

He said, "Speaking of milk and honey you look like you're eating well."

Pavelko patted his belly jutting over the lap belt but didn't smile. "It's not the hotel food, I promise you that."

"Looks like you got yourself a pretty good luau going here today."

"Hope you brought your appetite. You're not a frigging vegetarian are you?"

"Strictly omnivorous. Thanks for calling me. I almost couldn't get up here."

"You took long enough."

"I was getting my shoes buffed."

"They locked it down a couple hours ago—some of your contemporaries beat you here before they did."

"So drive faster. This isn't your car, who cares? Go all TJ Hooker with it."

"Only if you climb out on the hood. LA County has nicer trucks than the Service, this is a pleasure to drive. Like a Sunday out with the kids."

"Speaking of which how's your family?"

Pavelko tugged his earlobe. "My family? My family is perfect. Everything's perfect. My girls are gorgeous. Emma and Addison. They're eight now. I'm trying to watch my mouth."

"I noticed."

"Did you? At least it's a habit now. Almost anyway. Their mother wants me to so, you know. I'm working on it. Like I don't have enough frigging challenges in my life. I'm taking them back to Chicago."

"To visit your old stomping grounds?"

"For good, I think."

"Really? Got homesick?"

"Something like that. Time for a change."

"Do you have to spend a lot of time away from them?"

"Too much. That's going to end real soon."

They stopped at another roadblock and parked on the dirt shoulder behind a red heavy-duty Type III wildland fire engine, its raised chassis and four wheel drive optimized for rough terrain.

"Good thing you wore your shiniest shoes," Pavelko said, "we're walking from here. Man, you are a disaster on the road. I thought you were a commando journalist, ready for anything."

"Anything except a camping trip. I didn't bring any s'mores either."

"You didn't see the smoke this morning?"

"I didn't want to assume."

"You didn't want to get your hopes up you mean. Keep boots in the car, bud."

"Yes sir."

"That goes for s'mores too. Love those frigging things."

Hot minutes passed trudging under the midday sun into the violent death of a landscape. Danny took pictures and video as Pavelko listened to his radio, huffing and puffing under his extra weight. Grit was sandblasted into their faces and Danny wished he'd brought his court tie to cover his nose and mouth like a metropolitan Tuareg.

Firefighters in yellow jackets and overpants, hardhats and equipment web belts carried chainsaws, shovels, and axe-like tools called pulaskis at shoulder arms like rifles as they tramped past the incident command post which was arrayed between Corral Canyon and a dirt fire road rising on the edge of a ridge. A group of stocky red four wheel drive fire engines and a big LA County Fire Department incident command truck were parked amidst official vehicles, ambulances, and the personal vehicles of battalion chiefs and supervisors who'd rushed to the scene from their homes early this morning. Speakers at the ICP broadcast the chaotic traffic clogging the radio channels. Portable showers and a mobile kitchen unit with long plastic dining tables were already set up in this makeshift, temporary village for the firefighters. Danny counted six local TV news vans. A pair of Wide Load tractor trailers, empty of the dozers they'd transported which were out clearing fire lines, were parked near one of the big white coroner's trucks he'd seen before at major events when there were multiple fatalities.

He took pictures of it and looked at Pavelko. His question was drowned out by a yellow and white Firehawk helicopter thundering by on its way to do a water drop. "Was somebody caught in the fire?" he repeated, loudly.

Pavelko nodded toward a group of reporters gathered for a briefing with an LA County Fire Department PIO in front of the incident command truck. "I'll be back in a minute."

While Danny was grateful that Pavelko had helped him get this far, he didn't think a public information officer briefing really warranted *Get up Corral Cyn ASAP.* This merely put him on par with his contemporaries. Sure that was something, he thought as he hurried over to join the briefing, but it wasn't *ASAP*, one of his most reviled acronyms. Right up there with LOL and ICYMI, or prefacing a tragic headline with SO SAD.

A detailed topographical map of the area was taped to one of the two slide-outs protruding from the side of the command truck, built on a 40-foot Freightliner chassis with room for six inside. Danny worked his way around cameramen and a guy holding a boom mic, stepped around flats of bottled water and leaned his Sony camcorder in over the shoulder of a shorter reporter, half-thinking it was wee Carlos Esquivel but knowing the only way he could have beaten him here was with a jet pack. The short guy turned to see who the encroacher was and Danny flinched—it wasn't a guy at all.

It was Ursula Ruda.

He should have recognized the khaki safari vest with its many pockets bulging on her petite frame. She wore rectangular glasses with red clip-on lenses that tinted her brown eyes black and a nylon Tilley hat that shaded her shoulder-length auburn hair which she wore straight over her ears to hide the flesh-colored hearing aid nestled in her left one. Ursula was the only notable writer at Crime Time, which was the only notable local competition to CODA. Danny called it Dime Time because generally speaking their reporting wasn't worth one—Ursula Ruda being the notable exception.

He moved a few inches to the side. "Hey there."

"Nice shoes," she said.

"We missed you in Van Nuys this morning. Didn't you get the invite?" He noted the same old DayGlo charity bracelet whose fad had come and gone around her wrist.

"No deal, no point".

Danny recalled the immaculate splendidness of Carrie Voelker's finest asset. "I beg to differ."

"Go beg somewhere else."

"I will, as soon as I'm done here."

"Why wait?" Ursula pushed her little black Sony digital recorder toward the PIO as the fire captain updated the fire stats, speaking loudly and clearly for the mics held in front of him.

The Backbone Fire had broken out around eleven o'clock last night. In its first hour it had consumed approximately 2200 acres, or about 37 acres per minute. Winds from the north-northeast blowing consistently at 30 to 40 miles per hour with gusts approaching 70 were contributing to the fire's rate of spread. Flame lengths of 200 feet had been seen as the fire crested the ridge on the other side of the canyon. The huge convection column was spiraling some six miles into the sky. Storms of embers and flaming brands were observed spotting as far as a mile in advance of the fire. Even utilizing what natural boundaries they could incident commanders weren't close to getting a box around the fire. Some were predicting it would go all the way to the beach like previous bad fires in the area had. One crew had already been overrun but survived uninjured. Nothing so far was slowing the fire's advance toward the exclusive ranch homes around Malibu Lake where engines and crews were building up for a defensive fight.

Danny thought Backbone was a good name. He blogged the name and figures from his phone as other reporters asked routine clarifying questions he didn't need. Ursula was listening intently as if it was the first time she'd ever heard them.

Pavelko rejoined him without the borrowed radio. "Come on."

"Stay off my story," Danny said to Ursula.

"Find one and I will," she replied.

He felt her eyes on his back as he followed Pavelko toward the dirt fire road—when Ursula Ruda stared at you she could resemble an owl. A troublesomely sexy little owl. Made you nervous and turned on at the same time.

He and Ursula had both had pieces competing for best online investigative series at the prestigious LA Press Club SoCal Journalism Awards Gala at the swanky Biltmore hotel downtown in June. They knew each other distantly from working around town but had seldom talked. Just noticed each other. Ursula had come to the awards gala dressed as her hot doppelganger, her hair cropped tight like a flapper's, wearing a little black dress that was fitting a form nobody knew she had. They were already drunk when they hooked up in a handicapped stall of a bathroom while an honorary award was being presented a few minutes before their category.

Danny's winning plaque rested on the floor against the side of his desk at home and Ursula hadn't spoken to him since. Normally that wouldn't bother him except he couldn't stop being bothered by it. Especially when he saw her.

That was the Ursula Issue.

"You hear some firefighters were overrun?" he asked when he caught up to Pavelko.

"Lucky for them they got their shelters deployed in time. Those things are rated for twelve hundred degrees but at five hundred the glue holding them together starts to break down. If the fire burns over you quick enough you'll survive. If it slows down or intensifies, you won't. Either way if you've gotta get into one something has gone seriously frigging wrong. You know what LCES is?"

"Lookouts, communications, escape routes and safety zones. Standard safety protocol."

"Words to live by. This fire's a real bad bitch right now."

"Is it like the others?"

"Answer's a definite maybe."

"Well that's quotable."

"Hey, who else is giving you a lift into the definite maybe? Did I cut in line?"

Adding to the challenge for investigators was identifying genuine Angeles Arsonist fires from other suspicious blazes which were often quickly and erroneously attributed to the same suspect, bogging investigators down in fallen power lines and careless campers and at least one copycat arsonist out in Riverside. No one was eager to jump to conclusions with this much at stake.

The shell of a car burned bone-white slumped a hundred feet up the fire road. Danny zoomed in with his camera and got a shot of the plate. A brown sign for Backbone Trail, a sixty-mile hiking trail through the Santa Monica mountains, was scorched but still upright; the gate had been swung open and locked for emergency vehicle access.

"911 call came in last night about 11:30," Pavelko panted as they hiked up the dirt motorway, both of them wincing into the wind-blown dust and sand. "First responders arrived ten minutes later to an uncontrolled blaze and that car burning behind the fire line."

Danny's feet were killing him. It felt like he was walking on ball bearings. He could feel every single loose stone through the soles of his court shoes. First fire of the season and he was in his Cole Haan wingtips instead of his Timberland hikers. Unbelievable.

"Smell that?" Pavelko asked.

He had to pause to suck air in through his nose, he was breathing too hard to use it. "Gasoline?"

"The nose knows."

"So much for the luau."

The fire road was dug into the side of the hill over steep drops into dense thickets of shrubs and trees which had already been reduced to wasteland. Blackened stumps of manzanita and sage clawed like fingers out of a decimated terrain broken by occasional green sprigs which had somehow survived the onslaught. Smooth rocks jutted some thirty feet out of the top of the ridge. The mesmerizing ribbon of flame at the bottom of the canyon was barely a mile away.

An inmate hand crew, a dozen men of a variety of ages and ethnicities in distinctive orange gear, stood off by themselves with a Cal Fire captain in yellow. The con crews went through the same basic training as the professional Type 1 crews, which included the Hotshots who sometimes flared tragically into the public eye. But there were no guards, and the inmates carried the same hand tools as the professional firefighters that could be brandished like weapons in the hands of rebellious color-coordinated serfs. They were a self-policing, self-reliant group of outcasts that only needed enough hard work and empathetic authority figures to break their resistance to falling into line, an obvious model for non-violent prisoner rehabilitation staring the state and taxpayers in the face. But out here the cons knew their place—if there was a line or a priority the professional firefighters came first.

Pavelko nodded to a steely-faced county fire captain observing firefighters and sheriff's deputies who were erecting a tent over an unnatural splash of color tangled in scorched shrubs.

Danny's excitement choked in his throat like a half-chewed piece of meat.

Singed red fabric clung to a charred, discolored torso enmeshed in burnt tree limbs like a spider clutching a grotesque, partially-cremated prize. Bare arms were bent skyward with fists clenched like the desiccated remains of a boxer belatedly daring life to fight before it left. Most of the visible skin had oxidized into blotchy, brittle black tissue that looked like tree bark. Teeth leered in a horrid smile out of a face stripped of its humanizing features.

Danny took pictures automatically, trusting his camera to compensate for his trembling hands and fighting the impulse to gag. He instinctively recognized the humanoid shape of the thing—the midsection covered by apparently non-flammable red shorts, the purple Ugg boots melted around the stumps of feet. Only the most cosmetic elements of life remained. Who was this person? he asked himself to keep his brain from seizing up like an engine that had run out of oil. What were the steps they'd taken that led them to this mockery of life, these base human secrets of vulgar muscle and fat exposed to strangers? They had been burned so thoroughly it was as if someone had tried to smite the cosmic energy of life itself.

Someone.

"You all right?" The muscles worked in Pavelko's jaw.

"Yeah." Danny felt suddenly lightheaded. He cleared his throat and said with more conviction, "Yes."

"Suppose I should have warned you."

"I'm fine. Who is it?"

"We don't know yet. Come on, watch your step." Pavelko led them up a grassy fissure that served as a natural path between the rocks and was strewn with litter, plastic wrappers, smashed green and brown beer bottles. "Interesting place to start a fire, eh Danny? Surrounded by all these frigging rocks."

Danny traced carvings hewn into the walls with his fingers, primitive shapes and initials like stone age graffiti etched as if into the bark of a petrified tree. He had no idea this place was here, this remote, rugged tiara over Malibu's expensive dress. The rocks tapered near the end, briefly shading them before they came out onto a rocky plateau affording a breathtaking panorama of the mountains and the wildfire down below. A fleet of drones deployed to survey the fire, the big eight-rotor octocopters government agencies preferred for law enforcement and general surveillance, buzzed autonomously around the smoke which was so close it looked like you could reach out and cup some in your hand like dry ice. The drones were part of the Fuego—Fire Urgency Estimator in Geosynchronous Orbit—alert system which combined drones, manned aircraft and infrared imagery from a dedicated satellite to detect fires in the western US within three minutes of their ignition.

A tall man in navy blue cargo pants and a yellow Nomex work shirt with the sleeves rolled up stood on the plateau with his back to them, surveying the inferno with his hands clasped behind his back.

Danny shaded his eyes. Across from them rose another outcropping of rocks not as high as the one they stood on. Several investigators and coroner's technicians were gathered around the chest-high entrance to a cave. A small campfire ring had been carved out of the ground, a shallow stone bowl filled with ashes and chunks of burned wood. A blue and white cooler was upended nearby with a smattering of plastic cups. The last reach of sunlight fell upon a spill of gray limbs on the rock floor just inside the mouth of the cave.

They were surrounded by corpses. Wholesale slaughter had happened here. A massacre—and Danny decided on the spot to use that in the title of his Red Flag update, which was going to be epic. The Backbone Fire. *Massacre in Malibu.*

Below the outcropping a woman with a ponytail and a dark blue ATF t-shirt was bent over, photographing something on the ground marked by a little yellow flag. An impression in the dirt maybe. A ruler was laid on the ground beside it for reference.

Pavelko touched his elbow and he lowered his camera.

"Danny I believe you know Captain Mike Cruz. Mike this is Danny Kasho, the reporter we talked about. The one who christened our Bug for us."

Cruz turned around slowly, as if stirred by a distant noise. He was in his mid-50s, an imposing man a couple inches taller than Danny, who at six feet was substantially less than Cruz's heavyset frame. Cruz wore his polarized wraparound sunglasses up on his sun-reddened head which was beaded with sweat. His moustache had so far retained the flinty hue which had fled his hair, which he wore longish and combed-back like a Western movie actor. His gray eyes cast a disdainful look at the body outline logo on Danny's hat, the press lanyard hanging around his neck, his dusty sweat-soaked suit clothes and not so shiny shoes.

"Good to see you again sir," Danny said and gulped the rest of his water.

Cruz stared blankly at him, then at Pavelko. "What's this all about, Mark?"

Pavelko drank from his canteen. "We agreed we're going to need the public's help. Mike—meet the public."

"Here, Mark?"

"Right here, Mike."

Cruz started to say something, then stopped and frowned as if Pavelko had just remarked a non sequitur such as the commuter train schedules in India.

"We agreed he's reading his own clippings," Pavelko said, "which means he's following Danny's blog like everyone else is. Scrolling through the comments, seeing what people are saying about him. Maybe he's even posting comments himself."

Danny's fingertips tingled. So the Backbone Fire *was* connected to the others. The Angeles Arsonist *was* back. He'd often wondered if the suspect was reading Red Flag but it never occurred to him that he might be an active member of the posting community too. He licked his lips. "How many victims are there?"

Pavelko wiped the sweat from his eyes. "Three females and one male in the cave. Looks like they died from smoke inhalation but obviously we don't know yet. Plus the burned body down on the motorway."

Danny said to Cruz, "An informed and vigilant public can only help. He *is* one of us. Somebody knows him. Somebody's his neighbor."

"Your hope for a headline isn't a good enough reason," Cruz said calmly, like a teacher rehashing the same arguments for a new class of dumbshits.

"We've got five good reasons right here," Pavelko said. "All in various shades of dead. Enough is enough—we need a different approach. This is what we talked about." He tipped his chin at Danny. "This is who he is."

"This isn't a media ride-along, Mark."

"We said we want to take away this guy's hiding places. Danny here's got a nice bright spotlight he can shine for us. We let his blog take point. We give him some stuff, maybe we can draw him out. I think the Bug's itching to talk to somebody. To brag."

"So you keep saying."

Pavelko took his cap off and scratched his head. There was an ugly purplish-yellow bruise on his forehead. "Well Mike, you of all people should know how it feels to be the lone voice in the wilderness."

Cruz curled his lip and glared at Danny. "I don't recall agreeing to *give* anybody anything."

"So you'd rather wait for the next one?" Danny asked. "And the one after that, and the one after that?"

"Are we satisfied with point of origin?" Pavelko asked, redirecting the conversation.

Cruz waited an admonishing beat before answering. "The first one's outside the cave entrance. You can see the scorching on the rock. Flames ignited the shrubs, smoke filled the cave and killed the four victims. Second one's by the edge. Scorch marks on the ground, spotting several feet away which started the fire on its path around the west side of the rocks. Third is the single victim—he or she was sprayed with flammable liquid and either jumped or fell into the foliage, which ignited the fire that climbed the ridge on the east side. Both fires combined on the north side of the rocks and started down into the canyon."

"How popular is this place?" Pavelko asked.

"Students, local surfers, they all know about this place. We've had to put out fires here before but nothing like this. This fire should not have been that intense that fast, even under these conditions. Those kids should have been able to escape. He waited outside the cave to see if any of them tried. One did and was set on fire."

Cruz's detailed, dispassionate delivery was almost unnerving. Danny hoped the wind noise wasn't interfering with his recording.

Cruz glanced at him, hesitating a beat before adding, "He's back Mark."

Pavelko chewed his lip. "Agreed. And he just hit the big leagues in a major frigging way."

Danny flushed with excitement—Red Flag had just hit the big leagues too.

"So what is he going to do for us?" Cruz jerked a thumb at Danny. "What do you propose *you* give him, Mark?"

It was the first hint of a breach, the first indication that Cruz might acquiesce, with just enough prodding, just the right kind of incentive.

Danny's pulse was racing from something other than the hike in. Nobody else was this close. He was inside.

Pavelko was obviously prepared for the question. "Like we discussed, we say that we know how he made the flamethrower. We know how he's starting the fires, we know why, we're tracing parts and suppliers. More than that—we know *him.* We know he's older, professional, he's a firefighter—"

"He's a fanboy not a professional," Cruz objected tiredly. This was a point they'd obviously gone over many times already. "He hasn't been hired by any fire department anywhere. He might work for a tangential agency but he's no firefighter. And he's still young."

"Playing Bob the Builder with a flamethrower isn't a young man's game, Mike."

"So he's matured past the point of matches. He's still acting out of an anger he's too immature to control."

"Since when is age synonymous with control? He's in control as much as he wants to be. Especially after chilling out for nine months—"

"Ten months," Danny said. "November third was the last one."

"Then I'd say he's got more than enough control," Pavelko continued. "And he's hiding in plain sight. Somewhere."

Cruz clucked his tongue. "This isn't getting us anywhere. This isn't investigative, and *this* isn't the place or the time." He aimed a thick finger at Danny. A class ring glittered on his fist. "Tell me you understand Mr. Pavelko's murky arrangement since I myself do not."

"Perfectly," Danny replied. "According to you two the Angeles Arsonist could be anybody. Thanks, that's really Pulitzer material. Does everyone on the task force think he's someone totally different? And what parts and suppliers have you actually tracked down?"

Pavelko coughed into his hand.

Cruz's eyes narrowed. "Mister…?"

"Danny Kasho, CODA.com."

"If you'll excuse us, we have work to do here."

"Thanks for the reminder Mike," Pavelko said as Cruz turned back to face the smoke. "C'mon Danny."

They went back down between the rock walls to the fire road. The wind had shifted and brought with it the awful reek of a body's worth of burned skin and organs. Danny opened a new water bottle, confident Ursula and everyone else hadn't been able to get past the command center. This was epic hugeness.

"You got some gems here today," Pavelko said to him, as if reading his mind like a ticker tape.

"I got a bunch of conflicted investigators, that's what I got."

"Sure, but don't write that."

"Seriously—is there no consensus on the task force? Is there no fusion? You guys aren't anywhere with this?"

"According to Red Flag you'd know if we were."

"I pride myself on my sources. What was the ATF agent photographing on the ground? Boot prints?"

"Boot prints? What boot prints? I'm talking about you being close enough that the ground's still warm under your shiny shoes."

"I appreciate that."

"And I appreciate your discretion." He coughed again. "And I'd appreciate seeing what you're going to post about this. About what we talked about up there."

This was the price of Pavelko's deal—an oversight committee. "Okay," Danny said.

"Okay what?"

"I'll send it to you before I post it."

"I appreciate that. Don't say anything about any boot prints for me."

"What boot prints?"

"Attaboy. Deputy Brown here will escort you back to your car. I'll call you later."

They shook hands and Danny followed the uniformed deputy back up the fire road. The burned body had been shrouded from view mainly because of the news helicopters overhead, for which he was grateful. He wouldn't have the chance for a second look, a clearer picture. He wished he could move the image to a memory stick and forget he'd ever seen it at all.

He quickly texted an update to Red Flag—*Malibu fire dubbed Backbone. Intentionally set. Out of control and growing.*

The Angeles Arsonist is back.

And he'd just killed five people.

CHAPTER 4

Even in late summer the shower couldn't get hot enough to scrub away the death coating Danny's skin like the ash covering his car after Deputy Brown dropped him back at Malibu Bowl. As he drove the rest of the way down Corral Canyon the ash blew away almost as if it had never been there, leaving him to think about the resilience of the corporeal stuff, the muscle, the bone, the teeth. How hard it was to really destroy all traces of a human being.

After the last granules of sand swirled down the drain he turned off the water and stepped out of the shower. The whine of the old building's pipes made him think of the residents of Malibu Bowl, if they'd dismissed the anguished wails carried on the midnight wind from the cave a mile and a half away as coyotes instead of people dying.

He grabbed his towel off the radiator and wrapped it around his waist, leaned on the sink and looked at himself in the medicine cabinet mirror as he brushed the grit off his teeth. Danny was dark-haired and thin, not exactly graceful but possessed with a certain economy of motion. His hazel eyes were gold-green when he was happy and brown when he was not and, he'd been told, betrayed a melancholy that belied his thirty-eight years. More and more as he got older he saw his father Paul Kasho staring back at him in his posture, his crooked nose, the slightly incredulous furrow of his brow. His brother Victor and sister Cynthia looked more like siblings than he did. They were both sandy blond and dimpled, and their eyes—Cynth's blue, Vic's brown—were the same shape, one slightly rounder than the other in a permanently dubious wink. Danny was his father through and through despite having spent his whole life trying not to be.

His roommate Garrett was upstairs, the bass from an ominous thunder effect he was working on reverberating down the walls and rattling the ice in Danny's Tanqueray and lime juice on the tile counter. Garrett was a one-man audio company that did sound design for commercials and film—"the just-right sound from airplanes to zebras." He was a youthful forty-five and a long-time resident of the four-story 1927 Villa Carlotta apartment building on Franklin Avenue, a busy east-west artery crawling along the base of the Hollywood hills. Danny had been introduced to Garrett through a friend in 2010 and lucked into the apartment when Garrett's roommate at the time abruptly moved out to get married, thus circumventing the year-long waiting list. He got the job at CODA in the same week and settled happily into both as if his wandering was over.

Hi all. I ran into Gary Calder the other day and he said to tell everyone hi. Also someone called to tell him your father is ill. I thought you might like to know. Love, Mom.

Vanessa's emotional stonewall had always been as thick as English masonry and her email to her three children was typically ambivalent, as vague as if the conversation had taken place at a great distance and been hard to make out. Twenty-six years of silence and suddenly *your father is ill.* What did that even mean? Danny knew she hadn't asked the right questions of whoever Gary Calder was, he didn't recognize the name but he was intimately familiar with his mother's passive ways of illustrating the distance between their life and his. She probably hadn't asked Gary Calder any questions at all, whenever *the other day* even was.

When he read the email yesterday his first impulse had been to call her, still a natural reflex after all this time. Vanessa thought reporting violent crime for a living in light of what happened to their family was a decision impaired enough to suggest Danny was blessed with the same latent crazy gene as his father. It had been a reporter after all who'd first coined the nickname Killer Kasho in 1993. Literally overnight Danny's hated middle school nickname *Cashew* had morphed like an irradiated butterfly and he too became Killer Kasho, the rotten fruit of Paul Kasho's loins.

Victor and Cynthia had both contacted him after Vanessa sent the email. Cynth called and left a message, then emailed; Victor sent a text full of WTF's and excessive abbreviations and exclamation marks. They both wanted to know what he thought they should do if something happens. *If something happens.* He could already hear the responsibility being assigned. If dad dies in prison, who will bring him home?

Last night he'd typed the name into the Department of Corrections and Rehabilitation website inmate locator. There was only ever one Kasho—Paul Vincent, CDCR#B61209, age 68, admission date 10/15/1993, current location Solano, a medium-security prison located in a fertile agricultural plain halfway between San Francisco and Sacramento. Danny hadn't checked his location in a long time—he was somewhere else before Solano. They moved prisoners around like cattle from place to place, prison to prison. Always in the interior of the state, never close to the water. Having grown up seaside, living somewhere far from the ocean was punishment heaped on punishment.

Your father is ill.

Danny took a deep sip of his gimlet and examined the blisters on his feet. This was a major setback in convincing himself that the bulk of his childhood happened to someone else.

In the summer of 1993 he'd had a summer job at the hotel on the island off Calendula as an all-purpose gopher for the well-heeled set installed around the pool. Some of the regulars had taken to teaching the twelve year-old boy drink recipes, many of which he'd somehow retained over the years. The gimlet was to be prepared as Raymond Chandler's detective Philip Marlowe drank them in 1953, half gin and half lime juice, though Danny readily substituted a wedge of lime and tonic when Rose's lime juice wasn't in the cupboard.

He pressed the sweating glass to the red soles of his sore feet and closed his eyes. He saw stainless steel tweezers probing the cracked and blackened skin of the burned body by the cave, separating individual strands of purple Uggs which the inferno had fused to the flesh. In the years since finding his first dead body at age twelve he'd seen a number of corpses through his work at CODA, some of them minutes-fresh and *in situ*, but never before had he seen a human being reduced to the brittle-looking husk in purple Uggs snarled in the burned vegetation.

He wondered who the person was, he or she, and who was going to miss them, and what living with the knowledge that they'd died in the most pain and suffering someone could die in would do to their friends and relatives. Knowing that their last moments alive had passed in incomprehensible agony, like his last few minutes with his dad, sobbing in his arms in their living room before the police came to take him away.

He carried his smoky wadded-up shirt through the high-ceilinged living room with its persimmon walls densely draped with Garrett's collection of swap meet paintings to the compact single-load washer/dryer stack in a nook off the kitchen. His slacks and coat would have to be dry-cleaned. The Cole Haans were probably beyond repair but he'd let a cobbler decide. He started a load and brought a fresh gimlet back to his room, pausing to watch Carrie Voelker's segment on the Mendoza hearing with the sound down, imagining her mouth issuing gasps of pleasure instead of coherent syllables, with a not as serious look on her face. Intent, focused, but not serious.

Since they weren't on the ground floor he and Garrett left the French windows overlooking Franklin open virtually all the time, except when it was windy or during the seasonal late winter cold snap. The building didn't have air conditioning, making floor and ceiling fans critical to surviving the ever-lengthening summer. Through the open windows they'd both actually heard the rumbling shockwave of the Inglewood earthquake coming a half-second before it punched the building and every drinking glass they owned exploded onto the kitchen floor.

The magnitude 6.3 quake rocked for 20 seconds at 7:12 AM on Thursday April 20 2017 along the Newport-Inglewood fault line, which began a few miles offshore and ran through Long Beach all the way up to Beverly Hills beneath nonstop population, and killed over a hundred people in 1933 when it last seriously shrugged. The epicenter was actually two miles northwest of Inglewood in Ladera Heights but it was Culver City, on the other side of the bumpy ex-oil scrub land of the Kenneth Hahn state recreation area, that bore the brunt of it. Most of the twenty billion dollars in damage and all three fatalities occurred there, including effectively shutting down production at Sony Pictures studios for a month. The ensuing two-day ground stop at nearby LAX had caused epic diversions to area airports—satellite pictures of the airliners wedged in beside each other across Southland tarmacs looked like triangular blossoms along paved stems.

While the quake didn't cause the widespread damage of Northridge in '94, Northridge happened seven years before Danny moved to LA. Inglewood was his first serious earthquake, exponentially stronger than the common tremblers familiar to longtime residents, and had pretty well frozen him in place for a solid minute or so before he swung into action and ran down into the street with everyone else to get reactions and shots of the damage to the four-story turreted former hotel Château Élysée across the street, which had developed an extremely photogenic crumbling gash in its western freeway-facing side.

Like every other news outlet CODA had immediately swung into crisis mode and contributors like him who still had a phone signal kept reporting until their phone battery died. His kit included a backup charger and he lasted two days, right up until the power came back on in Hollywood and survived the surge of everyone plugging their stuff back in at the same time. Now every single glass he and Garrett owned was either plastic or acrylic. The environment paid when the environment played.

This evening the breeze was very warm and very dry, a classic devil wind carrying the smell of smoke on its wings. He plugged his phone into his desktop computer to charge and sync, then unpacked the contents of his messenger bag. He got the Louis Vuitton for a steal at the Melrose flea market one Sunday long ago. It had sturdy silver hooks on the outer flap which secured his standard J-kit for the journalist on the go—notebook, pens, drawing pad and pencils, flashlight, his old-fashioned but indefatigable Dictaphone, extra rechargeable batteries for all, Leatherman multi-tool, sunscreen, CODA baseball cap, pocket binoculars, snack bars, ibuprofen, bottled water.

He fished a thumb tack out of a drawer of his Ikea desk and pressed it into the map of LA county on the corkboard. Sat back and sipped his drink and stared at the location of the Backbone Fire, way up among those strange etched rocks. Not an easy in and out, just the one twisty road,

Corral Canyon. No through and through like Little Tujunga. Setting the fire late at night instead of early in the morning. The unusual ignition day of Thursday instead of Saturday or Wednesday.

The victims.

Arson was a non-confrontational crime—whatever happened after the flames took hold, the arsonist was typically long gone. But this time he'd stayed to ensure the people died. That terrifying evolution made Danny wonder what had happened in the man's life to provoke the change, or if it was a proactive choice to commit mass murder in a geographical cul-de-sac given how much law enforcement was patrolling the lonely rural roads he preferred. With a flamethrower a firebug could burn anything he wanted at any time, but the Angeles Arsonist had exercised—on his own or under duress—ten long, excruciating months of restraint between the end of the great fire siege of 2018 in November and the Backbone Fire. Wildfires of the size he was adept at setting were not minor events hidden in the news. He'd either chosen completely different locations like carports or abandoned buildings and left none of the telltale scorch marks or he'd been inactive, waiting for the big show in late summer and early fall, when California was at its most dried-out and the smallest spark could ignite the greatest inferno—and provoke the biggest response. He was continuing to move out of the hinterlands into populated areas and was *intending* to kill now—there was no collateral damage anymore. All at once he'd destroyed five lives and all of law enforcement's assumptions about his M.O. He was paying attention. He was experimenting and evolving and the task force charged with arresting him couldn't even agree on who they were looking for.

Dozens of stories had come and gone over the past ten months with varying degrees of resolution. Only Red Flag remained constant, simmering lowly as the weeks turned into months. Danny had stared out his windows at rainy winter Hollywood—the last time he could remember it raining—and thought about him, out there somewhere in the drizzle too, in control or forced to appear that way, waiting. Waiting until it was time. When it was just right. When the devil winds blew in his favor again.

Mark Pavelko was right—he probably *was* reading Red Flag.

On his way home Danny had texted the tag of the burned car to a carefully-cultivated friend of a friend named Michelle, who was blessed with loose morals and a supervisor job at the Holiest of Holies—the DMV. They'd met at a party a few years ago and he made sure they stayed in touch, sometimes texting her when he didn't even need anything just to keep the connection alive. Michelle usually replied quickly one way or another, being an inherently lonely person eager for interaction, but she hadn't yet tonight.

He put his headphones on and started going through the audio and video he'd recorded, jotting notes on a yellow legal pad. Fortunately wind noise hadn't interfered much at all. He listened back to his brief interview with volunteer firefighter Carl Tillson and wondered if he'd been put to work yet or if he was still maintaining his lonely vigil in his pickup. *Looks deliberate to me. Know why?* Danny smiled. Because the Bug was back, that's why. The Angeles Arsonist had set fire to Malibu's crown. And Danny was the only person outside of law enforcement who knew it.

But not for long.

MASSACRE IN MALIBU was the title of his first significant update to Red Flag since January, when one of the hikers rescued in the Los Liones Fire in Pacific Palisades had suddenly remembered seeing a white truck leaving the vicinity of the fire. It was a surprising recollection at the time, coming nearly two months after the incident. The hiker even suggested a partial tag, as if the details had resurfaced under hypnosis. A lot of drivers of white pickups were stopped, wasting a lot of time and resources, but the search proved fruitless and was eventually dismissed as a misguided and dangerous effort to meet the expectations of morning news programs eager to jump on rumors spilling out of the investigation at the time.

Today Danny made it official: the Backbone Fire had been set by the Angeles Arsonist. Five bodies had been found at an alleged party cave at the top of Corral Canyon—one had suffered severe burns. The victims were young and may be from the Malibu area. After ten months the Bug was back. With Mark Pavelko in mind he noted that investigators believed they were closing in on the suspect through the parts he'd used to build his flamethrower. He said that investigators had a clear impression of who they were hunting—his age and station in life, and that he was close to the firefighting community. He would be discovered through his own specialization.

Danny had no second thoughts. The ruse didn't have to work, it only had to work for now.

He cropped and posted five of the seventy photos and videos he'd taken, but none of the female ATF agent photographing the boot prints. One of the two shots he got of the burned body was too graphic to use but the other would be okay with a standard warning NSFW (one of his favorite acronyms). The text of his post automatically reformatted itself into CODA's boilerplate style thanks to an active template created by CODA's content manager Serge "Suge" Litvinovs. It was vital for any business interacting electronically with the public to have a prickly resident computer tech genius on staff and Danny tried not to bother him unnecessarily.

After proofing the entry online he sent the unpublished link to Lucinda Baskin. Lucy was CODA's managing editor and oversaw all the blogs, directing the news and feature reporting of the more than two dozen writers. After a moment he sent the link to Pavelko as well, uncertain what he'd do if Mark sent back notes as if he was his new editor.

Lucy had submitted Red Flag to the Press Club for consideration last March, long after the arson investigation had fallen off the news cycle and detectives were in the grind of chasing leads and tips and falsehoods like the hiker's miraculously recovered memory. Danny's entry was a series of six articles focusing on the eleventh fire, the devastating Chalk Fire which broke out near the geometric master-planned community of Stevenson Ranch north of LA in the early morning of Saturday September 29. The fast-moving flames rained embers down onto the first rooftops less than three hours after ignition. One firefighter died, over twenty were injured, and almost every house west of Poe Parkway was damaged or destroyed.

Damage was in the hundreds of millions. A year later they were barely starting to rebuild, such was the insult to injury of so-called insurance.

Danny's interviews with firefighters were a captivating mix of nobility of effect and practicality of cause—some were from firefighter families and grew into it, others just needed a job. His interviews with impacted homeowners, including adults and children who'd lost prized possessions that were priceless on their individual pained sliding scales of pain, were heart-wrenching and contributed to the overwhelming flood of charitable donations in the wake of the disaster.

City of Angels/Dead on Arrival ended up beating out Ursula Ruda's site Crime Time for best website of a news organization exclusive to the internet, so the other contributors, Lucy, Suge, manager Ronald Schiff and publisher William Craig had all been as pleased as he was. CODA started in 2008 on the rebellious whim of Craig as purely crime reporting but had since grown to include other local and regional news, politics, even a little sports and entertainment. Because of its success this year there was a renewed push to change the name to something less noir-sounding and more evocative of the broader infotainment reach of the organization, but Danny hoped William Craig kept it as is. CODA was like a pirate flag in a sea of generic news acronyms. A picture of the gang taken at the awards gala hung on his bedroom wall beside Cynthia's family. The plaque leaning against his desk reminded him not to get comfortable—get close. The blogosphere was a meritocracy. Posting bullshit could only last you so long.

He flipped the laundry into the dryer and finished up the courtroom drawings from the Mendoza trial. Handwritten notes to himself described what was happening so he could caption them properly for his blog. He fixed Charlize Patron's sketch to make it less vindictive, softened her like the pliable dough she wanted to appear to be. Drawing was a guilty pleasure Danny had inherited from his father. Dozens of color drawings, mostly landscapes from Calendula—the marina, the hotel, imperious from its cliffside perch on the island, the forest of old cars with two small bicycles on their sides on the ground—clapped against his walls when the ceiling fan was on high.

His hometown occupied the southern cup of Camino Bay, which was shaped like a curly parenthetical bracket a little over halfway between LA and San Francisco. Small beach towns with nautical names dotted the coastal highway up to the city of San Sebastian on Camino's north end. The moist western slopes of the rugged Santa Lucia mountains checked Calendula's spread to the south and east and helped keep its climate mild. Summers were warm, breezy and dry, winters were overcast and wet, with fog banks typically a thousand feet thick. It was scenic as hell. Danny was a good artist, not as good as Paul but good, and his own quiet contentment at the scraping sound of the colored pencils on the paper—thick, high quality eighty-pound bond he knew his father would approve of—always shared space with the shame of the man he wore like a birthmark.

Paul Kasho had been head of the art department at foodmaker Sibelius Industries, a sizeable employer in Calendula. He had designed the famous smilin' pie logo for their most popular product, individually-wrapped baked fruit pies which became the company's bread and butter. Danny grew up seeing the animated smilin' pie commercials during Saturday morning cartoons and in his lunchbox at school. All the kids had them so you traded for whatever your favorite of the six flavors was—apple, blueberry, grape, cherry, pineapple, and mixed berry medley. Whenever the commercial aired Vanessa would cheerily sing *"Cha-ching! But not for us!"* Danny knew it got on his dad's nerves and thought he found some kind of reward in the smilin' pie's popularity, especially since he'd conceived the logo in only a few minutes on his lunch break one day.

During the summer Paul drew caricatures of tourists and sold them along with sketches of waterfront Calendula. He was an unofficial tourist attraction and it was not uncommon for customers to come directly to the house. The day after a promotional air tour of vintage biplanes touched down in Calendula in the summer of '93 a French pilot named Félix Robitaille came to get his portrait drawn by the renowned local artist and vanished. The next day Danny was biking through the forest of old cars, an undeveloped parcel of land between the marina and the airport where trees and grass had grown around and up through dozens of rusted out, abandoned cars from another era. A single dirt path wound around earth-toned rusted shells of grown-over wrecks disintegrating among the waist-high grass under a canopy of trees that filtered the sunlight into long dazzling shafts and it was there, drawn by the sound of flies, that Danny found Robitaille's body hidden in the high grass with the telltale necklace clutched in his hand.

Once the Mendoza trial drawings were finished Danny scanned them into his computer, downsized and color-corrected them, then uploaded them for inclusion with his post.

Lucy replied: *Good work Danny*. Her standard response to her troops in the field. He published the update without waiting for Pavelko's input, if there was any. Drawing boundaries already.

Malibu-related stories were getting a predictable spike in views, particularly pieces about celebrity residents who didn't have enough to contend with from the wildfire being further inconvenienced by the single-vehicle accident he'd seen on PCH. The coastal artery had been closed to all but emergency vehicles for hours, only reopening for commuters in time for rush hour early this morning.

Red Flag readers had already begun commenting on the return of the Angeles Arsonist and extending their sympathy to the families of the five cave victims. Locals tried to describe the fire's smell to readers who didn't live here. Danny scrolled through the comments but he didn't know what red flags he was looking for. He doubted the detectives monitoring his blog did either. Members of social news sites were scouring user-posted images, trying to crowdsource the problem of sifting through so many thousands of pictures and videos posted by people who believed they possessed potentially case-breaking data. Unfortunately the internet egged on the groupthink over collective intelligence as everyone making up the hive mind searched for anything suspicious in the widest definition of the term, outing innocents, wreaking havoc. It was the web at its most destructive.

Danny realized the apartment had fallen quiet. He poured his drink into a plastic cup, left their door unlocked and climbed the access stairs at the end of the hall up to the roof. Garrett and a half-dozen other tenants were arrayed on folding lawn chairs looking west over Hollywood at Backbone's giant plume backlit by the setting sun. A cooler sat in the shade of a beach umbrella weighted down against the wind by sand bags.

Garrett was draped over a yellow lawn chair as comfortably as if it were an Eames lounge. He was a little shorter than Danny, his arms sleeved with tattoos, tussled dark hair and a soul patch below his amiable half-smile. "Dr. Kasho I presume. Thought I heard you bustling around. Can I interest you in our Labor Day specials? We've got bottled water and bottled water lite in the cooler. Also some nice screw top chardonnay but I know you're a wine snob."

"And you're a beer snob. I'm good." Danny indicated his cup. He greeted his neighbors as he eased into a chair, elevating his feet on the cooler with a sigh and taking in the hazy red brushfire sunset.

"You missed Karen and Gina," Garrett remarked. "Gina asked about you."

"Which one is she?" Danny rubbed his eyes. It was as if the fire victims had left granular-sized pieces of themselves behind to irritate his eyes, force him to think about them.

"Dark hair. *Actress.*"

"Hot," clarified Todd, one of their fourth-floor neighbors and, as its oldest tenant, the unofficial mayor of the 48-unit building.

A skinny 20-something woman in shorts and a tank top named Shirley interjected, "We were just talking about how the fire started."

"We heard it was a campfire," her spectacled husband Francis added. "But now everyone's saying it was intentional."

"That it was *him,*" Shirley added.

Francis and Shirley lived on the second floor and Mayor Todd called them Freddie and Flossie after the Bobbsey Twins because they looked like siblings and dressed in similar clothing, as if their shorts and shirts were homemade from the same swatches of curtain fabric.

Garrett noticed the faraway look in Danny's eyes and aimed his plastic cup of wine at the plume. "Same guy?"

Danny sipped his gin and juice. "Looks that way."

They drank in silence for a minute before Garrett sighed and said, "Makes for a nice sunset though, doesn't it?"

CHAPTER 5

Online he liked to call himself Fireman666. If the username was taken he'd immediately try to contact whoever had it and demand they give it back. If the usurper replied (which sometimes happened) it invariably provoked a volley of emailed threats and curses until they inevitably stopped responding, leaving him pacing furious circles through his things until his anger and dissatisfaction dissipated. When the frustration got too bad he'd go for a drive. Otherwise he'd stay in and work and stew over things.

He was home tonight, sitting on a green molded plastic chair in his underwear, his wide back rounded like a landfill as he hunched over the table, frowning in concentration. His tongue lapped at the sweat blooming over his lip. Furry breasts sagged onto an inverted papasan of stomach squeezed against the table where the bare humps of his elbows rested as he stripped the end of a piece of copper wire with a short-bladed knife as if he was peeling an orange. His legs were crossed at the ankles and his feet tapped in time to the cadence of the news as if it was a catchy song. His thoughts jumped and twisted like the flames on TV. They had preempted every show on every channel except the Mexican ones, who stuck to their carnival-like game shows and soap operas no matter what was happening.

Metal glinted meanly in the close shadows, out of reach of the bare light bulb hanging over the table. The room was infused with the complicated redolence of body odor, sweat, oil, grease, gasoline, the pungent cat piss reek given off by the white pellets of ammonia-based fertilizer packed like a confectionery into glass Mason jars standing in neat rows on a wooden shelf supported by L-brackets. Inside other jars ball bearings and carpet tacks malevolently reflected the flickering glow of the TV. He was unfazed by the potentially lethal mixture around him. The jars and drums were like friends who wouldn't turn their back on him, wouldn't turn against him, wouldn't fail. They didn't ask for answers, just ignition. They were the ultimate problem-solvers. The greatest levelers.

He put down the knife and copper wire and took a long, noisy pull on his can of lukewarm Bud, closing his eyes as he tilted his head back to swallow. The fold of skin in the back of his neck was slick with moisture. It was so hot it felt like something had heaved itself up on top of the city and died. 106° downtown today. Hotter where he was with his windows closed to avoid the snoops. Hotter still out in the canyon where the fire was.

He wiped his mouth with a thick forearm, crushed the empty in his fist and tossed it toward the open bin where it bounced off the clutter at the top and clanked onto the floor with the other crinkled cans. Fluctuation, he thought as he stared at the crumpled aluminum carcasses twinkling like sparks in the changing light thrown by the TV.

The thought went nowhere. He went back to scraping the end of the wire.

Once upon a time the strength of the memory alone was enough to tide him over for days. Sometimes weeks. But eventually—then sooner, and sooner—he'd wake up hung over, or still drunk, with the creeping anger on the move like an aggressive tumor, like mom shuffling around in her housecoat, and the memory of the event faded from view like a pale body into a muddy river. That was one of his most primal images from childhood but he didn't know why. He'd never asked mom about it—couldn't ask her something like that—and as far as he knew all her other children were accounted for. None had drowned. And *he'd* never killed anyone like that.

When he was eleven he'd started a fire at the back of an abandoned house with old clothes he'd found and a can of lighter fluid he'd shoplifted. It was a crack house, everyone knew that, and they found the remains of one of them in the smoking ruins the next day. At first he was terrified and prepared stories to get himself out of it when they came to accuse him. But when he realized he wasn't going to be caught—he wasn't going to be arrested for anything at all—he calmed down and settled into the awareness of his newfound power with the same secret wonder he'd felt when he was five or six after the first time he scraped a wooden match down the side of its box and released a prematurely sexual eruption of endless opportunity. He'd been around fire for as long as he could remember. Ultimately squatters got what they deserved and so did crackheads. It wasn't *his* fault they were there.

But down deep in a burgeoning second self that he didn't bring to school or to the family room or to church or to the 7-11 for mom's cigarettes he'd known perfectly well that the house wouldn't be empty. He'd known the rotted old wood would go up like a Fourth of July sparkler. And down deep—but not too far—he knew that he'd have been bitterly disappointed otherwise. He'd recognized early on the utter disregard he felt towards everyone around him, the fundamental disconnection from them, and he grew from the realization. He became better because of it. So anything less than having the police and firefighters and reporters sifting through the smoldering debris would have been a disappointment. Anything less would have been like the rest of his life and that wasn't going to be good enough.

Eleven had been a liberating age for him.

He closed his eyes tight and shook his head violently from side to side, his cheeks flapping noisily and sending gobs of sticky white spittle flying, forcing himself to think of nothing more until the end of the wire was exposed about an inch. Then he laid it with dozens of others similarly prepared and picked up a fresh one. He didn't know how many would be enough but he had a feeling he was almost there. The designs were all in his head so inevitably there was some fluctuation. How successfully you dealt with the unforeseen was a measure of how hard you'd be able to kick against the pricks. The bosses. The judges. The ex-wives.

A 9/11 poster taped on the wall of the burning twin towers fashioned into upraised fists admonished to *Never Forget.* He couldn't agree more. He was living proof. Never forget that when you pushed people, sooner or later they pushed back. And it *always* came as a surprise. America had gotten a taste of it and eighteen years later they still called it a tragedy. *He* called it an education. He called it *enlightenment.* He called it the equal and opposite reaction to an unfair action. He wouldn't go so far as to root for them—hell, the next thing they blew up might be under *his* ass—but he wasn't surprised like everyone else was whenever blood ran in their streets instead of some distant place they'd only ever see accidentally while waiting for the start of the next game show.

People pushed back.

Things were getting so bad at work the pressure was squeezing his head in the familiar vice. He was out of sick days and he'd already used up his vacation days for the year. He'd asked about short-term disability but they said no outright. They didn't even think about it. Didn't even listen to him, as usual. So he distracted himself with plans of a different sort—he became a toymaker. It was easy to find instructions online—harder to find good ones, but they were out there. He set off three in remote places to test them. They'd worked—one of his toys had almost killed *him*—and then he put one right behind his ex-wife's house. It went off in the middle of the night as loud as anything. Scared the shit out of everybody. He was one of the first people there, went to her sympathetically, comforted her, vowed to have his high-placed law enforcement friends make her case a priority. He borrowed her flashlight and showed her where pieces of scorched, twisted metal had bit into her house but—thank God—failed to penetrate the walls. Showed her how close she'd come to dying tonight. She'd watched him with wide, deliciously terrified eyes in the flimsy nightgown she'd been wearing in bed, hugging herself, shivering from the pre-dawn air and her fear. Nobody called the cops.

His thoughts came to rest on the laptop's screen glowing at the other end of the room like a squirrel having climbed down from myriad branches to scent the wind before stepping onto open ground. He glommed his internet signal off a neighbor's WiFi. One day when he was looking through the window he saw the network name and password on a bright yellow sticker affixed to the modem. It had been months and the guy still hadn't realized it. If they ever came about the stuff he looked at online they'd break down the wrong door. Nobody ever gave him credit for how smart he was.

The web page on the computer auto-refreshed every few seconds as the string of pearly comments grew longer and longer and longer. Everyone had something to say. Everyone shouted their opinion into the din of a nation of experts, tried to insert themselves into everyone else's lives as if they were each other's proctologist instead of shrink. It was typical—and there was no reason to put up with typical anymore. He'd had *years* of typical—a *lifetime* of typical—and it had brought him here, to the very edge of something he was only just now beginning to see the shape of. It was the true shape of himself, the imprint he'd leave upon the earth and everyone on it.

His best-kept secret were the two Hims, This Him and That Him. That's how he knew himself. Sometimes he'd talk out loud about how inferior This Him was, a posturing runt compared to That Him, how This Him should be more like That Him. That Him didn't say anything. That Him never did. This Him covered up for That Him, always had, with school, work, women, mom. This Him took all the shit in the world for That Him, who never said thanks, never showed his appreciation for nothing. Just did his own special thing. This Him went along for the ride. And This Him enjoyed it. More than anything he did. But This Him had a feeling, a notion indistinct in shape but clear in course that the day was coming when there'd be only one Him. A Super Him, godlike and powerful and feared. He deserved this.

Everyone was talking about Danny Kasho, who was doing a lot of talking about *him.*

He stood up so quickly that he knocked the chair onto its back and he began furiously jabbing the knife into the table top as fast as his arm could piston, *thok thok thok thok thok* like a woodpecker into the mottled surface which already bore hundreds of pits and gouges from previous such assaults and trembled under the barrage like a submissive partner.

He stopped as suddenly as he'd started, breathing hard and sweating even worse than before. The blade quivered in his fist and it took him a moment to remember what he'd been doing with it. How many seconds has passed? Had it been a minute? More?

His black eyes focused on the clock—a gift from mom, of course—sitting glumly in a corner, its mechanism dismantled and its hands broken like a thief's, then up to the color photocopy of a man's face held against the wall by a fork buried up to its tines in the powdery plaster. He had a whole stack of photocopies—all of the same picture of the man. He hung one of them at a time and used the fork on it when he felt like it, until the paper was ripped, the face disfigured and torn as if dogs had attacked it, or a berserk chimpanzee. A whole section of his wall had been slashed and dug into as he hacked through picture after picture. Sometimes he burned them and left the ashes to blow away outside. This copy was new and still mostly unscathed, the paternal smile of the man untouched, for now.

There were only four beers left in the fridge. He popped one, gulped half of it and brought it back to the table. He wiped the foam and spit from around his mouth and the sweat from the back of his neck. He sat down and picked up another wire, different than the ones he was working on. Thin and transparent fishing line, trailing off into the shadows. He wrapped it around his finger like a piece of dental floss until it was taut, then plucked it with his thumb.

Something metallic snapped in the shadows like the jaws of a mechanized pit bull.

He allowed himself a little smile. Then he laughed—a high keening sound like a whimpering mutt. Like a laugh track encouraging a positive reaction to something that wasn't funny at all.

Everyone was talking about Danny Kasho. But for once—soon—they'd be talking about him. *This* Him. This ascendant Super Him who would be the very last word for a great many people. The closing argument in a world full of talking heads. The last voice ringing in their ears was going to be his.

CHAPTER 6

Danny was at his computer, finishing a live chat about the return of the Angeles Arsonist hosted by an east coast news website. Since he wasn't on camera he was comfortably shirtless in swim trunks. His phone, camera, camcorder, stapler, and a little jade Buddha with a jewel in its belly all doubled as paper weights to keep his notes from blowing around under the fan.

After way too much screw-top chardonnay last night he'd retired around midnight and drawn until he fell asleep to the sound of his original police scanner, which looked like a walkie-talkie with an elongated flexible antenna and broadcast the constant chatter of the city's teeth feeding on itself. The average Angeleno might be alarmed to know how many mentally ill naked people were wandering through traffic at any given hour. He'd started a new drawing of the house he grew up in, leaving the usual details of the weathered sea-gray two-story house and detached garage purposely vague because after all these years some details were still tender. The last things he remembered were the sound of his pencil clattering distantly to the floor and rolling under his bed, and Vanessa's voice whispering the word *ill* in his ear like a lullaby.

What made Paul Kasho more ill than someone who killed five people with a flamethrower, he wondered as he browsed the growing comments and shares on Red Flag. Nothing popped out but he was satisfied with the greatly increased traffic. The comments section was a thriving social ecosystem all its own, all he had to do was add the water and air of fresh information.

His phone buzzed with a new message. It was Michelle from the Holiest of Holies—the tag came back for a 2017 Acura hybrid registered to a Katie Anne Martyn, 21, white female. Danny replied *No you*, an inside joke between them as pale a reflection of true affection as the incidental brush of Carrie Voelker's fingertips.

Michelle replied immediately: *Drinks Sunday? I got Monday off.*

Danny hesitated, then replied *Perfect. Call you in the afternoon. Thanks again.* Michelle had dark hair. A single mom, wide hips, around 40. Lived somewhere like El Monte, but the north side of it, which wasn't so bad. She was enthusiastic and genuine and not enough of anything to be anyone's everything.

He started at the source and found Katie Anne Martyn in his first search. She was a student at Pepperdine University. Blond and pretty, her youthful exuberance was irreconcilable with the twisted limbs and charred flesh less than four miles from her campus. Instead of waking up in her dorm she slept zipped up in a thick plastic bag in the county coroner's refrigerator downtown, awaiting autopsy thirty miles from the bed she was supposed to be in. All five of them were.

Three females, two males. Two couples and a third wheel. If one Pepperdine student had driven up to a party cave, he thought, she went with friends. Probably friends from school. Their absences had probably already been noted on their individual social streams but not yet connected in the larger one. Chances were Pepperdine was missing five students, not one.

Two couples and a third wheel.

He wondered if someone was missing. Someone who had intended to be there but wasn't. Someone who'd survived because of it. Someone besides the killer who knew what happened.

He created a new Gmail address and pointed it at a cutout webmail account, cleared his Facebook cookies and signed up as a female named Claire Coogan. Alliteration in a girl's name was cute, and cute got you in the door. He spent half an hour crafting the profile, uploaded a photo of a girl from Google Images who looked like a Claire Coogan after stripping it of any metadata, and started Liking and Adding Friends. Then he waited for someone in Katie Anne Martyn's social network to take the bait.

Mark Pavelko called.

Danny silenced the police scanner. "The federal government is an early riser."

"We taxpayers don't pay us to sleep. I pay for my own exhaustion. I get screwed twice over. You sound chipper."

"I'm working. It's 8:30, I've already done an interview. I don't get paid to sleep either."

"Well take a break from your press junket and come over and meet me at the hotel. It's a frigging special agent convention here in scenic Agoura Hills. Complimentary WiFi and continental breakfast, woo frigging hoo."

Danny started gathering his things. "Where are we going?"

"It's a surprise. Get moving, we're already on the clock."

He entered the hotel address into his phone for driving directions and scanned the morning news on his desktop as he packed his J-kit in his messenger bag. The Backbone Fire had so far consumed 5500 acres and four houses. 2000 firefighters were already committed with less than 10% containment. Changing wind vectors had forced flames into the mouths of all the major coastal canyons in the Malibu area. Fire crews were massing on PCH in preparation for what one incident commander described as the "fight of their lives." The smoke could be smelled as far south as San Diego, where other fires had erupted north of the city near Escondido, inaugurating this year's fire season in earnest.

Pavelko was waiting outside the entrance of the three-story sandstone-and-green Hampton Inn dressed in jeans, a fresh Forest Service polo shirt and his sweat-stained 49ers hat. The hotel was busy—news crews with a fleet of colorful station vans and white network satellite trucks were using it as a base of operations too.

He directed Danny back to Kanan, a twelve-mile winding road cut through the mountains west of the fire. He propped his phone in the door pocket and they wheeled out of the parking lot. "What, no shiny shoes today?"

"Going commando," Danny said. In his Timberlands, just in case.

"I didn't ask how it's hanging, I asked about your shoes. Those look like new boots."

"They're not."

"Well they're practically new."

"They're not either."

"What are we listening to?"

Danny checked his phone. "Lee Scratch Perry."

"Sounds like reggae for drunks instead of stoners."

"How are things going on the task farce?"

"We've taken over a conference room. No windows and too much hot air. It's like trying to work in a sauna."

"Is your room nice at least?"

"Sure. They don't call it a suite for nothing."

"Did you read my post?"

"Sure."

A few seconds of drunk reggae bopped past.

"And?" Danny asked.

"It was fine."

"That's it?"

"Sure."

"Nothing else to add?"

"The prose here and there needs some work but I wouldn't want to step on your artistic toes, I know you artsy-fartsy types are sensitive about that. Your readers are an opinionated bunch though aren't they?"

"They've all got one, like an asshole and an appetite. So that's it?"

"What's it?"

"That's all you have to say?"

"About your post? Yeah, why?"

"'Cause you're an opinionated bunch of something too."

"Whatever gave you that impression? And if I got an opinion about something you'll know it, believe me."

Traffic slowed on Kanan and formed up into a shiny metal snake motoring past large estates hidden by tall trees and fences with street names like Castle View Drive and Hunt Club Court on the left and the dry bones of the mountainside rising to the right. *Conserve Water—Conserve Life!* urged an oversized billboard. *If the grass is always greener, you're doing it wrong* affirmed one of the many environmentally-themed bumperstickers coating the back of the car they were following.

Danny thumbed his phone to record. "So how does a troublemaking kid from Chicago become a special agent for the Forest Service?" He angled the phone toward Pavelko like a microphone.

Pavelko eyed it suspiciously. "'Cause my modeling career never took off."

"Completely understandable but I'm confident there's a better answer than that."

"Can't you just sit back and enjoy the scenery? Quietly? Like a normal person? Or a dog? Haven't you got this already? I didn't know this was our first date."

"I've been woefully lax on your background check."

"What, I have to pee in a cup too?"

"Only if it's yours."

Pavelko made a face and sighed. "You want to know why I joined the Forest Service?"

"I do."

"'Cause of the bunnies."

Danny paused his recording. "Look you son of a bitch, be serious."

"I am serious."

"Bullshit you are. Bunnies?"

"Swear to God, man."

"Bunnies."

"Hop hop."

Danny stared at him. "Does that stem from some major childhood trauma or something?"

"You gotta understand I'm from a crazy family," Pavelko said. "Lots of kids. It's why I love mine so much. I just love them. My grandmother used to tell me that whenever I got a shiver it's 'cause a frigging *ghost* just passed through me. Believe that? Telling that shit to a little kid! So one time they took me and my brothers up to Manistee National Forest in Michigan, across the lake from Chicago and up north a ways. We get there and a fire had just swept through, and all I remember—I was just a little kid, like five or six—all I remember is this lifeless silence. Not a peep, chirp, howl, nothing. Just wind. Like everything had died. And I thought it was so unfair to the animals when you only have so many places you can go, and you can only move so fast. I cried and cried. That was the sort of luck we enjoyed on our family outings."

"So you became a cop instead of a travel agent?"

"Suffice to say it made a lasting impression, but no. That was more of a job opportunity than anything else. Busted my ass into Chicago PD, then a lateral transfer to San Fran. Eventually, I don't know, I guess I had enough of knocking on doors, wearing out shiny shoes trying to solve the murders of people nobody cared about. Thought I'd try something else. The bunnies caught in the burn that day must have stayed with me and I signed up with the Forest Service in 2010. It's almost like the Foreign Legion the way it attracts misfits. Makes men out of boys. And it isn't as buttoned-up as Cal Fire."

"Because you're a punk rocker at heart."

"My mom made me take piano lessons. 'Cause you know, nothing attracts chicks like endless hours of scales and Bach."

"You just impressed me there with that."

"Figured I would. For some reason I haven't forgotten how to play, though I don't get much chance to. There's one at the house."

"A piano?"

"Yeah, an upright. I don't think the girls even see it as an instrument anymore, it's just the thing the picture frames sit on."

"They don't know enough about their dad's many talents." Fathers, it seemed to Danny, were just as inclined to keep secrets from their children as from their wives or anyone else. "Did they ever catch whoever started the Manistee fire?"

"Oh I don't know. I doubt it. And you know, that's arson. It doesn't have a high closure rate. It's a hard crime to prove. So much evidence goes up in smoke, cases can take years. San Fran homicide did way better numbers, especially when I was there. But nowadays with the drought, the endless summer's gone bad. It's been too hot and too dry for way too long. Keeps us busy."

"Do you travel a lot?"

"During the so-called fire season, yeah. My mom lives down here actually, so I get to see her when I feel like making myself nuts. She retired here of all places for her golden years. Told you I had a crazy family."

"Maybe she just wanted to be closer to her favorite son."

"Yeah I don't think so. Anyway I've spent most of the last year down here because of this guy, the so-called Angeles Arsonist according to hack blogger Danny Kasho."

"Got to admit it's catchy."

"Oh it caught all right."

"His real name will be a revelation and a letdown."

"Names are interchangeable anyway. Every day brings a new asshole du jour."

"You should get a real job and go work for Hallmark. Surround yourself with all the cute little pink bunnies you can stand. What do you do when you're not on the road?"

"I work out of Vallejo, on Mare Island just north of San Fran. The office is right next to a golf course, how cush is that? Just perfect. But you gotta be good at interfacing."

"Interfacing?"

"There's your euphemism of the day. On some of the big campaign fires that spread across multiple jurisdictions you get everybody from local and county fire and police, Forest Service, Cal Fire, Bureau of Land Management, Bureau of Indian Affairs, Office of Emergency Services, Edison, FEMA, NIFC, NICC, FBI, ATF, DHS. OSHA investigates whenever firefighters are killed. Everything from the SPCA to the FAA gets involved. List goes on and on."

"The alphabet soup of modern bureaucracy."

"And it tastes like ass, I'll tell you that. Interfacing with all those agencies is something else I'm working on, besides my frigging potty mouth."

"Punk doesn't pay anyway."

"That's some consolation, partner."

At Triunfo Canyon Road they both looked to the right toward the unseen canyon where the Shiloh Ranch Fire blackened forty acres on Wednesday October 31, 2018. The fifteenth wildfire set by the Angeles Arsonist was stopped before it reached the homes entrenched along the bottom of the canyon but the Halloween horror was palpable for residents watching the flames bear down on their homes, with the disaster of Stevenson Ranch barely a month old.

"It was your wife, wasn't it?" Danny said.

Pavelko looked at him. "Was what?"

"Why you moved to San Fran."

"You sure you don't have this already?"

"I'm sorry, I forget her name."

Pavelko looked out the window. "Linda. Her name is Linda."

"What does she do?"

"She shops, doesn't she. It keeps her happy. And if she's happy, I'm happy." His smile seemed forced. "The girls are the best parts of us. If they learn anything bad it's because we teach it to them, whether we realize it or not. They're big girls now, Emma and Addison. But not too big—they still make me birthday cards."

"When was your birthday?"

"Tuesday."

"Aww. Happy belated."

"Thanks, that sounds almost heartfelt."

"How'd you and Linda meet?"

"She was going to Roosevelt University in Chicago. I was a rookie cop already divorced and thinking of becoming a lawyer—"

"So much for punk rock."

"And what can I say? I wore her down. When she graduated I left the city I was born and raised in and moved to San Fran with her. Pretty town—you been?"

"I think it's the only other place in the country I could live."

"Well don't get ahead of yourself, this country's bigger than you think. See it from the road, the way it was made to be seen. And don't discount Chicago."

"The weather discounts Chicago."

"Winter, construction and summer—the three seasons. But you gotta go, it's a great town. I'm taking the girls there soon. After I'm done with this. They've never been there either, and that's not right. That's where I'm from, so that's where they're from too."

"Linda's from San Francisco?"

"Yeah. My Bay Area babe. Now what about you, Mr. Shiny Shoes? What's your story besides the one you're writing? I should take over your blog for you, make it a little snappier. You got a girlfriend?"

"I'm inbetween right now."

"A girlfriend sandwich! Lucky wiener."

Danny's thoughts fell to Carrie Voelker, whose beauty was as above him as his lust was beneath her.

"Where you from again? Someplace up north right?"

Danny stopped recording. "Calendula."

"I know Calendula, I've driven through there a bunch of times. Ate at the hotel on the island there once. There was a bad wildfire near there a few years ago but I didn't work it."

Cynthia, Victor and Vanessa had all mentioned the smoke blanketing the city. Hearing the event referenced by an unrelated source made Danny ashamed that he hadn't been more empathetic at the time as they had after the Inglewood quake. Empathy within the Kasho family had been in short supply for twenty-six years, as if their cherry hearts had all grown hard pits in their center. Everyone but Cynthia's.

"Your family still there?" Pavelko said.

"My brother and sister are. And my mother." Paul Kasho had always been the ghost, the empty chair at the dinner table, but now he was flesh and blood again. And *ill.*

"What about your dad?" Pavelko asked as if he'd seen the contents of Danny's thoughts on a billboard.

"He left when I was twelve." His stock reply sounded like more of a lie now that Paul could be leaving him again, for good. Again. Scared and in pain and alone. He didn't understand the point of the curtain call yet, whether the man even deserved one, but he couldn't keep putting Cynthia off. Someone would have to do something in case something happened. Some sort of plan had to be in place.

Pavelko clucked his tongue. "Tough age to lose your dad."

"You're kind of on the cusp of manhood. You need all the help you can get."

"Let me tell you, that cusp keeps right on going. Even after you have kids. How long you been a writer?"

"Ever since I was a kid. I'm just lucky to be eking out a living at it."

"Why cover crime? Why not Hollywood beauties?"

Danny shrugged. "You want to save the bunnies. I want to give them a voice."

Pavelko gave a little smile, a genuine one. "Good answer."

CHAPTER 7

They turned onto Mulholland Highway and drove a mile to the Seminole Overlook, a roadside turnout with a scenic view of the mountains and the highway unspooling below. A pair of motorcyclists were standing by their bikes after taking pictures of Backbone's monstrous plume rising behind the southern ridge, mutating into a living thing like a massive horse's tail swishing away the fly-sized helicopters and orange Superscooper airplanes buzzing around it.

"Devil winds, that's what they call them." Pavelko checked the silver watch on the underside of his wrist and leaned on the descriptive marker which explained the volcanic origins of the landscape, burning today as if to bolster the claim. "Firebugs can't resist them. Stirs them up like locusts. Rubs them till they can't frigging stand it anymore."

"One thing readers always ask is why fires are so bad in Southern California."

"You tell them it's because California was forged by fire. It evolved with it. It evolved *because* of it. Wildlife and wildfire go hand-in-hand. They coexist in a balance only nature can achieve. The only thing different now is the amount of people in the way. It's called the wildland-urban interface. Write that down."

"I got it, professor."

Pavelko gestured with his water bottle. "These mountains are covered in chaparral—shrubs, chamise, manzanita, scrub oak, sage. Chaparral has a crown fire regime which means when it burns, the entire system burns, right down to the dirt. Tell your readers that nine out of ten wildfires are caused by humans, not lightning."

"It's obvious you love what you do."

"Not bad for a Bridgeport punk, huh? I'm not a patient person by nature and arson is a slow, careful kind of investigation, trying to narrow down the point of origin to as small an area as possible. Something the size of Backbone, you're looking at ten square feet or smaller."

"That's amazing, shrinking an inferno down to a single spark." Danny said the line into his phone so he'd remember to use it in his post when he went through the recording later. "How do you know where to start?"

"Structure fires start at the hottest place. Wildfires start cool and get hotter as they spread out in a V fanned by wind, terrain and fuel, fuel being anything that can burn—trees, bushes, houses. You learn how to read the angle of char on trees to see which direction the fire came from and how fast it was going. Sometimes they go by so fast the front of the trees facing the fire aren't burned so bad, the backsides are. The big fire leaves little fires behind to go back and burn what they can." Pavelko made the peace sign with his fingers. "The base of the V is your point of origin. By then you're down on your hands and knees looking at unburned blades of grass inside a grid of square foot quadrants. They aim at the ignition point after they fall backward, like getting your legs knocked out from under you."

"You look at individual blades of grass in a wildfire."

"That my friend is what I do. I find the unburned blade of grass pointing toward the truth. No matter where it's pointing." Pavelko took his cap off and scratched his head, showing off the ugly bruise on his forehead. He checked the time again and replaced his hat. "What's happening now is the Santa Anas are driving the fire toward the coast where it's being met by an on-shore flow. The opposing winds are stalling it in the canyons and causing rolling wind eddies that lift embers way up off the ground and carry them far and wide. Adds to the fire's speed, spotting so far ahead of itself, and canyon walls are steep so a lot of it's inaccessible, tough to fight. We're mostly doing indirect attack using fire roads and clearing new lines by digging out the fuel before the fire can get to it. It's not satisfactory but for what we've got on our hands and where, it's the way to go. You fight the fire you have, not the one you think you have. And you live out here with your fingers crossed. Defensible space Danny, it's all about defensible space." Pavelko frowned at the plume and was silent for a long minute. Finally he asked, "How many fires you think this Bug's set?"

"Seventeen including Backbone, but probably more."

"Why do you think more?"

"Because arsonists like to set fires."

"Not too complicated is it? For reasons I am not at liberty to discuss—you understand—we're focusing on five of them, including Backbone."

Twice in as many days Danny was getting stuff nobody else had—not the networks, not locals, not Ursula Ruda, nobody. This was all his. One year to the day after meeting Pavelko at the Dillon Fire in Little Tujunga Canyon, the Forest Service special agent had turned into a genie, granting wishes for exclusives for the price of an oversight committee. "Which ones?" he asked.

"The Box Fire at Mount Wilson. Multiple points of origin, each twenty or thirty feet down from the road. That fire started in a way it wouldn't naturally have been able to, allowed it to back downhill and really start cooking up."

"That's how you were able to determine so quickly that it was intentionally set."

"Remember who made that announcement?"

"Not off the top of my head."

"Some reporter you are. You should have this stuff memorized."

"That's what computers are for, so my highly advanced brain is free to concentrate on the big issues of the day."

"The Dillon Fire in Little Tujunga Canyon," Pavelko went on. "The Bug drove in from one direction, started the fire and kept right on going. On top of everything the guy's lucky—that's a popular road with drivers and motorcyclists looking for a technical ride. But until they saw smoke nobody reporting any suspicious vehicles—the most tips we got were about a bunch of frigging Lamborghinis out there that day."

"And your average 'Ghini driver only burns money."

The two motorcycles sneered loudly away down Mulholland and Danny thought about the ease in which an arsonist could operate—drive in, set a fire, drive away. If not for the inescapable encumbrance of the flamethrower—Vietnam-era flamethrowers could weigh seventy pounds fully loaded—arsonists were malicious phantoms coming and going as breezily as angry embers carried on the wind.

"The Chalk Fire." Pavelko shook his head. "To this day I am amazed we didn't have more fatalities right at the start, the way that fire came over the ridge at those houses. Then the Brown's Creek Fire outside Porter Ranch a week and a half later. If it had been set any farther south those houses would've gone up just like Stevenson Ranch."

"I remember the horses." Danny had posted a shot of the blackened corpses of horses trapped at a nearby ranch by the fast-moving flames of the thirteenth fire, which started on Wednesday October 10, before the scope of the disaster of the Chalk Fire had even sunk in, their skinny legs bent skyward like the arms of the body in the bushes below the Malibu cave. It had been too risky to try and save them by opening the corral gates—they would have run wild and panicked among the firefighters—so they'd been left to die where they were. No houses had been lost but the mandatory evacuation had sent residents fleeing under the watchful eye of news helicopters. The panic in the city had been tangible.

"Two direct assaults against massive residential communities." Pavelko sighed at the smoke plume. "And now Backbone. Five dead and not a single one of them collateral damage. He went right out and murdered them. What led him to this, Danny? That is the frigging question we ask ourselves. What led him to this."

The silence that followed was prickly with possibility. Danny finally prompted, "You have a suspect?"

Pavelko checked his watch again. "At this point I'm going to ask you to turn off your phone."

He held it up so Pavelko could verify it.

"We're about to go a little over and above the usual rules of confidentiality, Danny."

"I think we already have. Remember yesterday at the cave? That might take some explaining someday."

"You know as much about it as anybody on the outside and you do good work. But you're still a frigging reporter."

"You could say that a little nicer. How many awards have *you* won?"

"Does attendance count?"

"You said you need the public's help. I have a direct line to them. I have them on speed dial."

"Yeah? Under *Public* or *Them?"*

"I've already agreed to help you and Cruz—"

"And yourself, don't forget that."

"Of course, otherwise what's the point? What else didn't you tell me yesterday?"

"Besides everything? Don't get ahead of yourself, junior."

"My phone's off."

"Officially."

"Officially."

"I'm serious Danny. This conversation never happened."

"My phone is literally and figuratively off. Come on, Mark. Jesus."

Pavelko drank some water and began to speak slowly and carefully, brushing over the identity of the person the way Danny might start a courtroom sketch, as a vague shape to hastily define, then coax the details out of until the image was able to breathe its own name.

"There's a person of interest who's been present at a lot of the fires," Pavelko said over the sound of the cars behind them accelerating between the curves on Mulholland. "Gets there early, makes his presence known. Always knows just what to do, where to look, whatever. Whatever it is, he's got the answers. He's the first to declare it's arson, and the first to declare it's the *same* arsonist."

The tips of Danny's fingers tingled. He blinked twice like shutters banging in a high wind. "It's *Cruz?"*

"Hey—it's not *anyone* yet. We need to be clear about that Danny—nobody's accusing anyone of anything and neither will you. Believe me, Mike Cruz—and this *is* for the record—is one of the best arson investigators I have ever seen. I admire his work. He's a brilliant investigator."

"And he's right."

"Yes he is—all the time with this case in particular. Instinct is one thing but too much of it…too much of it starts to look like something else."

"What about the DNA on the cup from the Dillon Fire?"

"The cup. Personally I don't put much stock in the cup. But Mike does, which is probably a smart move considering the DNA on it isn't his. That's about all we know about the frigging cup. But what else do we know? We know there were no fires prior to July last year, right? Know what else happened that summer? Mike's wife Jackie died of cancer. Four months from diagnosis to death. Two weeks after her funeral the first fire was set at the Hillcrest Open Space Preserve in Thousand Oaks."

The preserve was a treeless hump of earth in the middle of the west valley suburbs in Ventura County. There was a hiking trail and panoramic views at the top and on July 14 soon-to-be telltale scorch marks around an empty, graffitied five million-gallon water tank nestled into the open space. No one in the nearby houses recalled seeing a vehicle coming or going on the access road, just the smoke from the flames suddenly blotting out the morning sunshine.

"What about the boot prints the ATF agent was photographing at the cave?" Danny asked.

"What ATF agent? What cave? All kinds of people were taking all kinds of pictures of everything."

"What was it?"

"It was a crime scene Danny, and a frigging complicated one."

"Why would Cruz leave boot prints?"

"Who says they were boot prints?"

"Why would he let something like that be found?"

"What does *let* have to do with anything? They were made, they were found."

Danny's mind was racing. "Where was Cruz Thursday night?"

"As a matter of fact he was in Malibu, surveying county fire readiness in advance of the Red Flag Warning. Prepositioning, he said. Said he could smell the fire coming and wanted to make sure they were prepared. Believe that? He could *smell* it."

Danny rubbed the shell of his phone, wishing he was recording this. "So what do you want from me?"

"Well Danny, you and your little blog have gotten quite a promotional uptick from your unparalleled access. Not to mention the quality of your sources."

"And the quality of my prose."

"Makes for a nice break from posting cat videos on YouTube eh? Red Flag is your ticket in."

"To what?"

"Interviewing Cruz."

Danny made a face. "I've tried. Everybody's tried. You don't get anything that isn't in the press release. He won't talk to me. He doesn't talk to anybody."

Pavelko checked the time again. "I think he will, under the right circumstances. I think people like him love to talk, love to impart their knowledge and their opinions. I say if he wants to be heard, let's give him an audience and see what he has to say."

"How?"

"We're going to get you a seat at the master's ball."

Danny became aware of a growing midrange whine coming from over the embankment on the other side of the road. "The what? What's that noise?"

The impossibly close red belly of a huge DC-10 roared low and slow over the embankment in a dangerous terrain-following flight path just 200 feet above ground at only 160 miles per hour, its three howling jet engines drowning out the buzz of a white twin turboprop Beechcraft escorting it like a pilot fish.

Danny yelped with exuberance, recording the flyby on his phone as he flashed back to a similar moment in his childhood, the infamous summer of '93 when he was twelve and the Calendula summer was hot and limitless and school in the fall an infinity away and he'd watched the approach of the fleet of seven vintage biplanes of the air tour with all the other kids out on the breakwater. He'd been looking forward to it ever since it was announced in the spring in front of a festive crowd, as if their city's Olympic bid had won. By the time the planes came roaring into town that August day Calendula was dressed in the peach and white tour colors, every home and business sporting bunting, flags and streamers. The planes had looked low enough to reach up and touch as they passed. Danny had tried but the flying machines slipped through his fingers two days before all the innocence of the boy did too, like life itself might be doing right now to his father.

"Who says the Forest Service doesn't have good toys, huh?" Pavelko whooped.

The aircraft duo banked to the right and just before they sank out of view Danny saw the expulsion of orange retardant from the big jet's belly. "Awesome."

"At twenty-six grand an hour with a three-hour minimum it better be. She is one expensive date. Nice line, right on the money. Those boys are sharpshooters." Pavelko leaned on the marker again. "Mike's annual fire department charity barbecue at his house is tonight of all nights. Jackie used to organize it; he's kept it going in his own way. Bad timing with Backbone but there it is. You're going."

"You think so? He likes me all of a sudden?"

"Who can say no to good press?"

Danny bristled. "I can't agree to good press, just press."

"That's what I mean. Just do what you do Danny, but try not to be irritating. Ask questions, get him to open up. See what he has to say, that's all. Nothing sneaky, just be a frigging reporter."

"And then report back to you."

"And in the meantime you enjoy your all-access pass, which is good for you *and* your press junket."

"Why are you asking me?"

"Is there someone else you want me to ask instead? We don't have the manpower to drill down into all the fires we attribute to him so we're outsourcing some of the work. I thought you'd be up for it."

"A federal task force doesn't have the manpower?"

Pavelko squinted. "It's more of a task force within the task force."

"You two really don't like each other do you?"

"Don't even go there Danny. There's nothing personal about this. No one's out to slander the man. This is just business. This is *our* business. All I want to do is cross Mike off the list, that's all. I want that more than anything. And I'm asking for your help to do it."

"You should put me on the payroll."

Pavelko held out a thumb-sized USB drive.

Scowling, Danny pinched the thumb drive between his fingers like a dead bug he'd extracted from his lunch.

Pavelko clapped him on the shoulder. "Good man."

"So this was the field trip? You brought me all the way out here for this?"

"What, the plane wasn't good enough?"

"Seriously Mark."

"Seriously this was part one. I promised you all-access, now we gotta get moving." Pavelko went back to the Accord.

"Where are we going?" Danny asked.

Pavelko opened the passenger door. "To where the Bug called in his latest fire."

"Wait, what?"

"Oh I've got your attention now?" Pavelko smirked. "And we're listening to something else on the stereo. Scratch Mr. Lee if you please."

"What do you want, Bon Jovi? I can't help you bro."

Pavelko's grin showed his teeth. "Sure you can Danny, sure you can."

CHAPTER 8

Pavelko acquiesced to Bob Marley but just barely.

Without lights and siren they had to endure the gridlock on PCH with the rest of the coastal highway drivers with Danny's mind spinning so much faster than his wheels. He was dying to know what Pavelko meant about Cruz calling in his fire. Called who? 911? Someone on the task force?

Mike fucking Cruz?

Pavelko had grown increasingly anxious since they left the Seminole Overlook. His phone hardly stopped buzzing and he became impatient with traffic, fidgeting and grinding his teeth and muttering at the cars ahead of them to *move.* It was pointless anger on a canyon road where it was impossible to pass—and the line of cars stretched all the way to the sea. They were obviously late and Danny knew he was going to go over like a lead balloon with whoever they were meeting. Presumably other investigators. Maybe Mike Cruz. He wanted to ask Pavelko if there wasn't a more colleague-friendly way of bringing him in—something more akin to *interfacing* instead of an unexpected knock on the door in the middle of the night.

Pavelko's thumb drive felt like incriminating evidence of a conspiracy, like something a police dog could detect and have Danny pulled roughly out of line. Access for info—that's what this boiled down to. Either way he was going to beat the shit out of TV—and Ursula Ruda. Mike Cruz the legend. Mike Cruz the imposter. Danny marveled at it. The initial accusation hadn't fit Paul Kasho either until it was seen the right way, like a tailor-made suit, clothing that couldn't be worn by anyone else. A sentence customized for the offender.

But Mike fucking Cruz?

"They're using Pepperdine as a staging ground," Pavelko said after a long silence, as if he'd run out of internal monologue and finally had to say something.

The mention of the school gave Danny his opening—Katie Martyn's social network had been accepting Claire Coogan's Friend invitations all morning. "Have you identified the victims yet?"

"We're still contacting the families."

"But you know they all went to Pepperdine." Rolling the dice.

"Save it. The parents shouldn't hear it from you first."

The ocean came into view and while they were stopped Danny photographed the plume with his phone through the rear window. It was low and to the east, dripping dirty tendrils of ash across Malibu and out over the sea. The shot looked good so he posted it to Red Flag. He wanted to say so much more—the weight of Pavelko's bargain was already a burden. He scanned the comments and wondered if Mike Cruz was lurking there like a virus. And how long he'd been there.

LA County Sheriff's deputies were diverting traffic around a gas station on the corner of Pacific Coast Highway and Heathercliff over which one of their quadcopter drones was hovering. Pavelko held his badge out the window and made Danny drive down the center lane which was exciting. A deputy waved them through the intersection and they pulled into the gas station driveway. Pavelko instructed Danny to park brazenly on the sidewalk which was even more exciting. Even with all the cops he still locked his doors.

A group of day laborers watched from a distance, having been displaced by the police activity from their usual spot on the sidewalk between the gas station and a Best Value hardware store next door. They were suspicious of the police and wary in general, but work might come regardless so they stuck around at a discreet but curious distance, halfway to invisible.

Two men and a woman stood around a white Ford extended cab 4x4. Mike Cruz was sitting sideways behind the wheel with his legs dangling out the open door. The sight of him brought a nervous flutter to Danny's stomach as he and Pavelko walked over. He saw a trio of evidence technicians working on a public phone shielded from the intersection by a stand of palms and the fuel price display. Wondered if he could get away with a shot but held off for now—there was a drone overhead and he didn't know whose.

"Sorry I'm late." Pavelko didn't sound like he meant it. "Danny Kasho, this is Travis Salk and Igor Adjani, LA County Sheriff's Homicide, and Tracy Orman, ATF. Danny's the journalist we talked about."

Danny took *journalist* to be an upgrade from Pavelko's introduction of him to Cruz yesterday as a mere *reporter.*

Detective Travis Salk was broad-shouldered and thick-necked, all torso, sweating through his white dress shirt. The tips of his full moustache were going gray and he glared at Danny behind a pair of mirrored Oakleys.

His partner Igor Adjani's complexion could pass him off as a native in a variety of Los Angeles communities. His eyes were deep-set and dark, his narrow face creased on either side of his mouth. He wore a neat moustache the same jet-black color as his eyebrows. His tie was red with blue checks; Salk's was navy with pale blue dots. Adjani wore a big watch on his right wrist but held his pen in his left hand. All he said to Danny was, "Your phone's off right?"

Tracy Orman was a slender woman in jeans and tan cowboy boots and was writing in a notebook in a black vinyl zippered enclosure she had open on the hood of Cruz's pickup. She wore a dark blue ATF t-shirt and a baseball cap with her sunglasses perched on it. Danny recognized her as the female ATF agent from the Malibu cave yesterday and put her age somewhere around his—mid to late thirties. Perhaps the most perfect blossoming age of a woman. Tracy regarded him dispassionately from under brown bangs before returning to her notes.

Keys jingled in a pocket of Mike Cruz's khaki cargo pants as he climbed out of the truck. He looked down his nose at Danny for a long minute with his mouth working around a wad of gum. Danny met his gaze, thinking it was impossible to sustain two lives forever—while you were attending to one invariably the other was slipping. This had been going on for fourteen months already. This man might have murdered five people two nights ago and here he was, first among equals, with peers who didn't know they were chasing him.

"Seems you've gotten yourself embedded," Cruz said as he chewed. "What was your name again?"

Danny humored him. "Danny Kasho."

"Cash what?"

"Cash…oh."

"With all due respect to our esteemed colleague from the Forest Service, Mr. Cash Oh, this isn't a bus ride for tourists."

"I understand."

"Whatever you think you see here doesn't belong to you."

"Thanks for the opportunity to help."

"Oh don't thank me." Cruz smiled emptily at Pavelko.

"Interfacing, Mike, better interfacing," Pavelko said. "Tell me about the 911 call."

Travis Salk said, "The caller left the receiver hanging which is how it was traced, but the phone wasn't secured and it's been used since. We're printing it anyway."

"We're assuming he didn't hang up on purpose," his partner Igor Adjani added.

"Igor and I checked the security cameras but they don't reach to the phone," Salk said.

"No way you could see the fire from here." Pavelko was looking across PCH at the mountains. "What is it, about five miles that way? You couldn't even see the glow from here at night with the hills."

Salk said, "In other words the caller knew both that a fire had started and that there were possible victims because the caller started the fire."

Pavelko chewed his lip and looked at Cruz, then at Danny. "So the Bug picks up the phone after killing five kids in a frigging cave. Why? Buyer's remorse?"

"No such thing," Cruz said. "There's nothing accidental about him. He sets each fire knowing the moment it starts to live on its own it's out of his control. That's part of the thrill."

"So's calling 911," Igor Adjani said.

Danny recalled the map on his wall he'd been studying since meeting Pavelko yesterday. "But Corral Canyon dead-ends up in the mountains. If there's nothing accidental about him he must have known they'd be up there." He looked at Cruz for a reaction but got none—Cruz's expression could have been etched in stone.

Pavelko took his cap off and scratched his hair and his bruised forehead slipped in and out of view. "That's a real good point, Danny. Where did he find them?"

"Maybe here," Salk said. "Which is why he called it in from here. Which is what we've already talked about while waiting on you, Marky Mark."

"Igor you got the call?" Pavelko asked, ignoring the gibe.

Adjani put his phone on speaker. Danny surreptitiously thumbed his own phone to record. He could tell by the posture of the investigators that they'd already listened to it while they were waiting for Pavelko. And him.

911 what's your emergency?

Yes. I'm calling to report a fire. Corral Canyon Road. There are possible victims.

How many victims? What's your name? What's on fire? Hello? Sir are you still there? Hello? Hello?

No answer, just the intermittent fuzz of cars passing on PCH picked up by the phone receiver twisting in the wind by its cord.

The recording stopped.

The drone breezed past overhead.

First impressions—the caller was male. He spoke quickly, the pitch of his words heightened by excitement or tension and oddly muted as if he'd been cupping the receiver with his hand to try to disguise his voice. He was flesh and blood and vain enough to make a phone call, voluntarily revealing previously unseen features of the invisible man. As Adjani replayed the call Danny couldn't help but wonder what Mike Cruz sounded like when he was excited.

He asked him, "I'd like to know how you feel hearing the suspect's voice after fourteen months."

Cruz popped his gum. "You said you weren't here to ask questions."

"How about tonight then Mike?" Pavelko suggested. "Danny could come to the fundraiser and ask his questions there."

Muscles worked in Cruz's jaw. "That'd be even worse Mark. Why don't you tee up a good idea for a change, like buying this young man's bus fare back to band camp?"

Salk and Adjani snickered. Orman didn't look up from her notebook.

Danny said, "I'll do a write-up on your charity too. Guaranteed you get a boost in donations. Who can say no to good press?"

Pavelko said, "And who can say no to money for the orphans, eh Mike?"

"What are you, his agent?" Cruz snapped. "I said no. I said no to this whole idea of yours. No to my house. No to tonight—*especially* tonight! However you want to run the Forest Service's side of this investigation is up to you Mark, but don't push your Hollywood ambitions on the rest of us."

The pitch of his voice rose along with its volume but Danny wasn't fooled—the sound of an arsonist in the throes of a fresh firesetting wasn't to be imitated in the façade of his professional life. Cruz was the epitome of self-control. Danny waited on Pavelko, who was looking at Cruz the way he might look at one of his daughters during a tantrum—without anger, just patience seasoned with disappointment. Salk, Adjani and Tracy Orman busied themselves, this being not much of a spectator sport. Danny got the impression they'd seen it before.

Cruz shifted his weight from foot to foot as radios squawked and two news helicopters thudded into view overhead, attracted to the clot of policemen.

"It'll just take a few minutes," Danny said to him.

"No it won't."

"For charity," Pavelko said, then slower, "For *charity,* Mike."

Cruz huffed and fidgeted and finally sighed heavily as if he was being forced to submit to a colonoscopy. "Got a pen?" he muttered.

Travis Salk snickered. "There goes the neighborhood."

Danny held up his phone. Cruz leaned into it and recited his address, his sweaty upper lip curled with irritation.

"Good deal," Pavelko said cheerily. "Danny, meet you back at the car."

Adjani handed Danny his business card. "Since we're going to be bumping into each other," he said humorlessly.

It was the affliction of inclusion—if Danny accepted it he was accountable, just as if he'd signed a contract. His feet on the ground here might very well force his presence in court later in front of his smirking peers. He imagined the unpleasant change in Carrie Voelker's tone like the hard rush of cold seawater through a breached hull.

But he took the card just as he'd accepted Pavelko's thumb drive and slinked back to his car parked on the sidewalk and surrounded by cops. He entered Adjani's contact info into his phone and dropped the card in a trashcan, and photographed the gas station and the locals and the drone and the day laborers watching the scene. He was wheeling and dealing now. He was at the mouth of the cave where the dragon slept, smelling its awful stench and stepping on the cinders of those who came before, but confident nonetheless. He had a trick up his sleeve—he was the invisible man too.

After a few minutes Pavelko came over. "So what do you think? Good job on tonight by the way."

"You were right."

"About what?"

"About the arsonist making contact. Now who's being uncanny?" Danny turned his back on the gas station to make sure he didn't glance at Cruz. "He's kind of a dick isn't he?"

"Yeah but don't write that."

"I can't tell if the caller was him or not."

"Wow, it's like we have real jobs after all. We not meaning you obviously. But you see how complicated this is."

"Almost as complicated as task forces within task forces."

"Yeah but don't write that either."

"Speaking of which—"

"I appreciate your position Danny, I really do. And I trust you appreciate mine. We do have a deal in place already don't we?"

"What about the call?"

"Its existence okay, but not a transcription."

"It's three sentences!"

Pavelko chewed his lip. "It's arrogance Danny, that's what it is. His Achilles heel is his arrogance. I'm going to be here a while so you're on your own getting out of here. But mark my frigging words Danny—he reaches out like that once, he'll do it again. It just added to his thrill. He's gonna want to get as close as possible to crossing that line. And look at you figuring out he followed the kids up there."

"You hadn't thought of it?"

"You got a faster mouth than me."

"That'll be the day."

CHAPTER 9

Danny was at his computer, trying and failing to not think about Karen and Gina who were lounging at either end of the sofa in the living room as casually as if they lived here. They were in matching tans, ponytails, short cutoff jean shorts and bikini tops, painted toes and ankle tattoos. Effortlessly seductive the way young beach-raised girls could be.

After he got back from Malibu he'd done minor updates on three ongoing stories—a decomposed Jane Doe found in Griffith Park, a fatal hit and run in Sherman Oaks, and a fatal arson in Compton, then he'd gone up the street to the grocery store. When he came back he found Karen and Gina thumbing their phones and leafing ambivalently through some of Garrett's audiophile magazines on the coffee table, utterly unattended while he did some work before they went out for dinner—some of the deeper bass pulses from the ominous thunder effect made the iced tea shudder in Danny's sweating glass. Danny had to summon all his intestinal fortitude not to drop onto the sofa and join the girls. He was awed by how much of a geek he was. Two beautiful young unattended women were on the other side of a thin wall from him. His door was open, and yet he wasn't stepping through it.

Instead he was sitting alone in his bedroom trolling through Mike Cruz's online footprint.

Cruz was a 32-year LA County Fire Department veteran from Davis, California. He graduated from the Fire Academy in 1987 and became a Fire Suppression Aide on a Helitack crew—firefighters who were delivered by helicopter for the initial attack on a wildfire—at Fire Camp 8 in Malibu. Every couple years he transferred to various fire stations and camps around LA County, and was promoted to Fire Fighter Specialist and Fire Captain along the way. He had even been an instructor at the Recruit Training Academy.

Cruz was also an inventor. In 2003 he patented an adjustable-stream drip torch that had been adopted by some fire departments in California and Arizona for prescribed burns and backfires. With such proven mechanical aptitude no wonder he was so quick to deduce what kind of device the Angeles Arsonist was using.

A notable stain among the commendations and accolades was a 2008 tragedy where three firefighters died battling the Lancaster Quail Complex fire near tiny Gorman in the northwest corner of LA county—just a few miles down the I-5 from where the Angeles Arsonist's second fire at Fort Tejon would break out ten years later. Cruz had made a questionable judgment call for the firefighters to shelter in place—and something had gone seriously frigging wrong, as Pavelko would say. The final incident report faulted contradictory radio traffic and the firefighters' own decisions. Cruz wasn't held responsible but he was transferred from field command and hadn't risen above the rank of captain, as if he'd hit a glass ceiling.

Danny studied pictures of the man throughout his career—Cruz crouched over charred wood, studying the inside of a torched carport, speaking behind a bramble of microphones at a press conference. His face hadn't changed much over time despite the years of exposure to sun and wind. There was an intransigence to him like the hotel on Calendula's island, a constancy imposed by sheer fortitude. Residences on the island showed the wear of being subjected to salty seaside wind but somehow the hotel's turrets, low-pitched pediments and ornamental pilasters appeared unaffected by erosion, as if time itself steered a wide berth out of respect. Danny saved a high-res version of Cruz's formal LA County Fire Department portrait, smiling stiffly in his short-sleeve midnight blue uniform shirt in front of the flag and one of those indeterminate Sears backgrounds, then turned his attention to Cruz's dead wife.

Jackie Waller married Mike Cruz in 2013. She was an interior designer of some renown with two kids from a previous marriage. He was childless after his first marriage dissolved in 2007. Through her husband Jackie got involved with the LACoFD Widows and Orphans Memorial Fund and hosted her first fundraiser barbecue at their house in September 2014. The annual events were covered by local press and each pulled in tens of thousands of dollars for families of fallen firefighters. There was a picture of Jackie holding an oversized check—Danny thought she looked like the actress Ali MacGraw, long brown hair parted in the middle, silver bracelets and dangly hoop earrings. He thought she was elegant-looking. Like any lucky man Mike Cruz had married above his station. Jackie made only a brief appearance at the 2018 event, just long enough to greet a few friends and convey her appreciation before she was assisted back to her room where she died in bed a few days later on Sunday June 24. Her obituary described her battle with lung cancer as "short but valiant." She was survived by her husband Mike, son Jack, 21, daughter Julia, 20, and parents Leonard and Amanda Hoover.

Four months from diagnosis to death is what Pavelko had said. How valiant could you be with 120 days of pain left to live.

Two weeks after Jackie's funeral the brushfire broke out at the Hillcrest Open Space Preserve in Thousand Oaks. Since that inauspicious start Mike Cruz had been a highly visible presence in the media. He couldn't save his wife but he could be an investigative hero now. But why the ten months of inactivity between the Los Liones Fire in November and Backbone? What had he been doing all this time?

A knock on his door interrupted his thoughts. Gina the hot actress was looking in at him.

"Hi," she smiled.

Danny spun around in his chair so fast he almost tipped out of it. "Hi yourself."

"Am I disturbing you? I know you're working."

Gina wore a glittery ring in the button of her flat belly. She was barefoot and brunette and her cherry-red toenails and fingernails went spectacularly with her peacock bikini top. Danny judged her breasts to be the exact size of his open hands. He snatched up his lucky pen and rolled it between his fingers. "That's okay. Really, come in."

"I thought I'd see if you wanted to come with us," Gina said. "We're going to get something to eat if Gare ever takes a break. Thai, maybe."

"I would love to—seriously, believe me I would—but I've got a thing tonight I've got to go to."

"Really?" She made it sound like a dare. She stepped into the room, bringing her perfume with her like a security detail. "Gare said you were a nightcrawler. Or was it night owl?"

"Hey—I give a hoot, so give me wings at least." Danny self-consciously watched her investigate his bedroom, the drawing pad on his unmade bed, the sketches of Calendula whispering on the walls under the fans, the photos and notes and maps and pushpins, the lights and microphone, the sound-absorbing triangular foam tiles nailed to sheets of pegboard bundled in a corner. His chest of drawers was half-open and he was relieved to see no underwear had been left leering out at her. From a woman's perspective it must look more like a college dorm than a grown man's bedroom slash office.

"Are you working on your blog?" Gina asked as she inspected the pictures on the walls.

"Yeah. Getting ready for a dinner meeting tonight with the Angeles Arsonist task force investigators."

Gina cocked her head at a color drawing of a stocky biplane banking over sailboats moored in Calendula's marina and her ponytail brushed her bare shoulder. "This is so cool."

Danny didn't know if she meant his proximity to law enforcement or that drawing in particular. Garrett had met Gina and Karen while working on an indie film a few weeks ago. One of the reasons Danny so admired his roommate was that to Garrett, anything was seducible. He barely had to try. People were helpless to like him. Especially excruciatingly beautiful young tanned actresses with ankle tattoos.

"These fires are your story aren't they?" Gina asked.

"What do you mean?"

"Gare said you gave the arsonist his nickname. The one everybody uses now. But he used a pretty word for it."

"For nickname?"

"Yes."

"Sobriquet." Gina smiled and Danny felt like he'd tickled her, his fingers rubbing over her ribs below her breasts.

"He said you used to come home smelling like smoke," she said. "And that you don't smoke, which is good. I like that."

"I absolutely do not smoke cigarettes. Never touched them. But last year I did have some monster dry-cleaning bills from going out to the fires. I try to dress smarter now, be more prepared. Usually fail."

Gina pursed her full lips. She was wearing shiny gloss instead of lipstick. "What's this year going to be like for you?"

He wondered what her mouth tasted like when she wore the shiny gloss. "It's looking real good so far."

She smiled. "But…?"

He sighed theatrically. "Indeed. But." He wished the but came with two t's and belonged to her.

"But you gotta get ready for your dinner meeting." Gina made *dinner meeting* sound like *empty night without a full body massage with copious amounts of baby oil…and me.*

"I do," Danny nodded glumly, surrendering to the guillotine of responsible abstinence.

"Okay then. Another time?"

"Yes please. Seriously—*please.*"

"Seriously okay," she smiled. "Have a good night, Danny."

"You too Gina."

She left his door open behind her. He closed his eyes and flared his nostrils at the lingering scent of her and marveled at himself. He was a veritable supernova of poor choices.

He took a moment to corral his thoughts, then checked into Katie Martyn's Pepperdine network. Her wall was full of jokes, remarks and growing telltale concern about her silence. Some of Claire Coogan's new "friends" were curious about who she was since no one seemed to recognize her. Others either had her confused with someone else or were just looking for friends no matter who they were. Either way their acknowledgment granted him deeper access.

After nearly an hour of cross-referencing Danny felt confident that he had the names of two more of the cave victims—Lisa Higgins and Neil

Weber, who along with Katie Martyn were inexplicably remiss in the digital corroboration of their lives. In one picture Lisa Higgins was wearing purple Uggs. Danny thought about how much Gina and Karen could be like Katie Martyn and Lisa Higgins. How much their boyfriends—unless they didn't have one, particularly Gina, which would be excellent—could be like Neil Weber. Death like that for kids that young was as capricious a fate as contracting a fatal superbug from a zip line.

For his Red Flag update Danny began to elaborate—the five victims killed at the Malibu cave were Pepperdine students. The initial 911 call about the burgeoning Backbone Fire was believed to have been made by the person who started it. After fourteen months the Angeles Arsonist had contacted the police to taunt them—a frightening indicator of his future behavior. Danny had listened to his recording of the 911 call over and over on his way home, convinced he'd be able to hear something in the arsonist's fourteen words that would lead him to divine his identity.

Yes. I'm calling to report a fire. Corral Canyon Road. There are possible victims.

Despite repeated listenings the man in the recording gave nothing away except his gender and his dangerousness, both of which were already common knowledge. It was just a noisy recording of a noisy call and would have to stay that way for now. But he'd finally spoken, just like Pavelko said he would.

Danny uploaded the video of the DC-10 flyover, which was very loud and very awesome, then cropped and posted a picture of the investigators and evidence techs at the gas station. Mike Cruz was looking at the camera—at him—as if he wasn't listening to what was being said. As if he didn't need to.

He proofed his update online, emailed Lucy the link—and after hesitating a moment, Pavelko too—then scrolled down into the comments. There was nothing noticeably unusual but it was noticeably busier. Readers were discussing Red Flag being an almost real-time window into the investigation. Danny thought that was true—technology could belittle journalism into mere play by play. You had to dig deeper. Get closer.

A member called UCANBRN2 was arguing with another member, a regular commenter called CrmnlyMandy, who had taken to calling serial arsonists "neurotic bedwetters." Back and forth they went. Danny could always spot the opinionated ones right away, but any increase in traffic was welcome—according to the site stats which he had access to, Red Flag was again CODA's most-viewed blog by far. Traffic was traffic.

Pavelko called. "Do reporters think of their questions beforehand or make them up as they go?"

He was on speakerphone and Danny wondered who else was listening. "Both."

"What are you going to ask him?"

"I'm going to start with what he thinks about Mark Pavelko's allegation that he's a neurotic bedwetting firebug."

"Sounds good, that's what I'd do. Know where you're going?"

"I have my own personal satellite array in the palm of my hand. Let me guess, you have a big paper map you can't fold back up."

"I got Trace, she looks like she knows what she's doing. Gonna wear your shiny shoes again?"

Therefore Tracy Orman was obviously in Pavelko's task force within a task force. "Only if you wear your skinniest thongs."

"If nothing else there's always tons of food so if you're wise you'll take some meat off the bones tonight and put it on yours," Pavelko said. "Unless you're a frigging vegetarian, in which case I'm sorry for you in more ways than one."

They hung up. After a moment Danny referred to one of the pictures he'd taken at the Chalk Fire last September. Mike Cruz was addressing reporters from a podium set up outside the incident command truck. Just behind him and to the side, Mark Pavelko was frowning intently at his back, his head cocked and eyes narrowed as if he wanted the next question Cruz answered to be his.

Danny added Jackie Cruz's burial date—June 30—to his master Red Flag calendar. He couldn't recall anything that stood out good or bad in his personal life last year. His stories had become the framework of his house and he an unrestful spirit passing between its rooms, until *your father is ill* had grounded him like an electric shock.

Twenty-six years hadn't eroded the afterimages of his father. And he was still alive, *ill*, an aging man with no privacy and no contact except for the uneducated psychopaths he was confined with. Events were shifting the axis of Danny's resentment of him, pulling him closer to the persistent grip of reconciliation. He felt keenly that he was running out of time. He was going to have to reach out and see if there was anything left of the man who raised him, who'd shown the beginnings of the world to him, and ask him why he did what he did. Why the risk of a communal punishment his family would have to bear for the rest of their lives hadn't been enough to stop him that day.

CHAPTER 10

Mike Cruz's two-story ochre-colored Mediterranean was situated within earshot of the Rose Bowl, above the Brookside Golf Course which straddled the Arroyo Seco's dry concrete chute on a quiet, shady street of three and four-bedroom Spanish style houses built in the 1920s and 30s.

The gated mission-style entrance was open to a cozy front courtyard. Crickets chirped in the bushes nestled at the bottom of bright windows and strummy music from the backyard quivered on the smokeless wind. Danny took pictures without the flash and reflected for a moment on how easily abnormality hides in plain sight, in rank and file middle class homes and routines and jobs and families, respectable lives built like buildings landscaped with falsehoods that withered and died the second they stopped being fertilized with their owner's bullshit.

He climbed the stone steps to a plastic pineapple affixed to the door knocker. The sound of voices came from inside and he was about to open the door when it swung open. A guy half the size of the house with a red and white Hawaiian shirt and matching red moustache filled the frame like fleshy caulking.

Big Red looked Danny up and down with boozy eyes. "Help you?"

"I'm here for the party."

"What party?" The big guy was incredulous. "There's a party here? Who invited you?"

"Mike Cruz. And Mark Pavelko from the Forest Service."

"Who?"

"Mike's best friend."

The man grunted. "Thought I was." He shouldered his way past with his entourage, another man of equal build and wardrobe and two women in blouses and flowery sarongs. The tipsy women leaned on the men and giggled like younger women than they were as they teetered down the stairs.

Cruz's off-white living room was full of big dudes wearing Hawaiian shirts, Bermuda shorts, plastic leis and flip-flops, drinking bottled beer or cocktails out of pineapple cups with straws and Polynesian garnish. Slack-key guitar warbled out of recessed speakers. A carpeted staircase rose to the second floor above the living room's plaster ceiling which curved down to meet the walls. To the left of the door was a setting with chairs by a bay window which looked out to the street. Firemen's wives in colorful tropical blouses, shorts and sarongs sat in armchairs flanking a fireplace containing a plant instead of wood. A chain of little cardboard palm trees was hung from the mantle. They looked at Danny as if he was here to deliver food.

"Looking for this, guy?"

A blue plastic pail was held waveringly at his chest by a muscular guy in a yellow fire helmet and a Gold's Gym tank top. His eyes were watery and the beer in his plastic cup looked flat.

Danny said, "Am I looking for your bucket? I don't think so, no."

The guy puffed up his sizeable pecs. "Well you ain't going any further without putting something in it."

The guy balanced himself against the wall and the pail turned enough for Danny to see *DONATIONS* written in Sharpie on a piece of masking tape. All he had in cash besides the $50 he carried around in case a low-level bribe was necessary was a single $20. "Is twenty enough?"

"It's never enough, but if it's all you can give," the guy swept his hand like a gate opening, "enter if you dare."

Danny dropped the bill in the pail. There was a lot of cash in there, bigger bills than his, some checks.

Through an archway to the right was a formal dining room where a Hispanic woman in an apron was replenishing food in silver chafers on a bamboo-trimmed table. Another woman worked in the kitchen which featured granite countertops and an island big enough to double as a wet bar for the adjoining family room, where the flooring turned to terra cotta tile and shelves displayed photographs, awards and mementos spanning Mike Cruz's life and career. Both women were dressed in jeans but wore makeup and jewelry too as if they might get to attend the party, like seat-fillers at an awards show.

A somber group of guests reclined on the leather sofas by a second fireplace and a huge flatscreen TV which was showing live coverage of the

Backbone Fire now that night had fallen. The dark hills highlighted clusters of embers waiting for dawn to renew their storm, as bolder flames jumped in a dance punctuated by the occasional erupting tree.

At the top of the screen was the standard red *Breaking News* banner. Another one at the bottom declared—*Official: Two firefighters confirmed dead.* Backbone's body count was now up to seven.

He blogged the update from his phone and wandered down a hallway off the kitchen lined with photographs, framed still lives of Jackie and the kids, Jack and Julia. Most of the pictures portrayed the three of them on vacation—Jackie and the teenagers skiing, on a beach, beneath the Eiffel Tower. Cruz was either the unseen cameraman or absent altogether, as if the trio was a complete unit and Mike was just a mid-life addendum to keep their mom happy. After Jackie left so did they—the kids didn't appear in any pictures as the adults they would be now. The photos could have been snapshots from someone else's life.

Vanessa hadn't taken many pictures of the Kasho kids growing up. Cynth told him there was next to no evidence on display at her house to indicate she even had a family, except pairs of Victor's tennis shoes on the mat by the back door. He reminded himself that he *had* to reply to her email. To Cynthia and to Vic.

Your father is ill.

So what? Every killer dies too. But it was an empty statement, like condolences for someone you didn't like.

The bathroom was at the end of the hall opposite a lamp-lit den with overstuffed leather chairs and crowded bookshelves. A lone spotlight shining on a framed photograph of Jackie Cruz made her smooth face look like a holograph, a disembodied 3D head mounted like a curio in the bookshelf. The word *Mother* displayed in woodcuts and plastic tags and miniaturized license plates and key chains and mugs presumably brought back from their many trips. Maybe it had been an inside joke to them at the time. Maybe Jackie and her kids had laughed whenever they got one, wherever they were. Maybe Mike had laughed too, if he was there. *Mother.*

Danny wondered if the bedroom upstairs was a kind of shrine to her, if Cruz still slept on his side of the bed Jackie died in.

Through the sliding glass doors at the rear of the house which were open to the backyard came the mouthwatering smell of fresh meat cooking. The yard was densely landscaped with mature trees and a high fence. Tiki lamps marked a perimeter around guests sitting at round metal folding tables beside a glowing asymmetrical swimming pool. On the far side was an outdoor kitchen with grill, fridge, fire pit and elevated wooden deck.

Mark Pavelko saw him from the deck and came over, chewing something off a skewered kebab. He was the antithesis of tiki in boots, jeans, a polo shirt and his 49ers cap.

"Luau?" Danny smiled.

"You thought I was making that up didn't you. Come on, I could piss more effervescent beer than this but the food's frigging gourmet. This is like my eightieth plate."

"Were you able to develop anything from the cave? How are those boot prints coming?"

"What boot prints?"

"The ones I'm not supposed to mention accidentally."

"All right, all right. We identified them from the tread as Thorogood size 12."

Pavelko spoke low, his lips barely moving like an untalented ventriloquist; Danny had to strain to hear him over the party noise. "Thorogood as in George?"

"As in a brand of firefighting boot that hasn't crossed over into the fashion world as far as I know. The guy's a gear junkie. But don't post that, obviously."

"I'll add it to the list of redactions." Danny made a mental note and thought that between the brand and size of the arsonist's boots and the sound of his voice they were putting flesh on the bones of the ghost at last. Boot prints and a phone call. As if the arsonist was secretly begging to be identified. To finally be *credited* in public. "Does Cruz wear size 12's?"

"Gee, why don't you go have a peek in his closet and find out? While you're at it why not ask him if he's made any calls from gas stations lately?"

"What makes you think the prints are bona fide?"

"Incongruity."

"Like the cup?"

"If you say so."

"Have you identified the burned body?" Danny wondered which parents had just lost their daughter and how fast he could track them down for a reaction.

"Neil Weber. What, you didn't know that?"

"I knew the name. I thought the burned victim was female."

"Because of the purple Ugg boots, right? Rookie."

"Maybe he borrowed them from Lisa Higgins."

Pavelko looked at him sharply. "You better not be posting their names. We haven't even finished the notifications Danny."

"I'm not the only one on the story Mark. Someone's finding out as we speak. Like you said if he's reading Red Flag he's reading it for the same reason everybody else is. Deal or no deal I can't be left behind. The clock is running."

"So let it."

"Not when it's my living. I just don't want you to be surprised."

"You kidding me? I love surprises."

"Famous last words."

Pavelko led him over to where Mike Cruz, wearing a long grass skirt over shorts, was cooking at a smoking silver propane grill. He had a coconut shell bra tied around an ugly flesh-colored t-shirt. The brightly-colored garland around his neck matched the plastic carnation clipped in his longish silver hair.

"It seems you and your benefactor both misunderstood the dress code," he said when he saw Danny. "Why am I not surprised. You're not a vegetarian are you?"

"Why does everyone think that? I come from a long line of carnivores," Danny said.

"Then you're welcome for what you're about to receive. Have a Mai Tai and make yourself scarce."

At the mention of *Mai Tai* the concoction recipe passed before Danny's eyes like the incandescent bulbs of the old Times Square news zipper: *1 ounce each fresh lime juice, VSOP rum, dark Jamaican rum, 1/2 ounce orange liqueur, 1/4 ounce each almond syrup and sugar syrup, 2 cups crushed ice, shake well, pour unstrained into double old-fashioned glass, garnish with mint sprig. Should be color of amber not crayon.* He couldn't remember who told him that. He could tell these were watery just by looking at them, and pulled a bottle of water from a cooler instead. Some of the hotel regulars around the pool that summer of '93 had told him to make himself scarce too. He'd been looking in from the outside his whole life.

Pavelko got him set up with an overloaded paper plate of ribs, kebabs, corn on the cob, baked beans and coleslaw, more food than he could possibly eat in one sitting, and they climbed onto the elevated deck behind the grill where a mixed group of people in plastic chairs sat in a semi-circle. Mark made the introductions—Pete Costner from Cal Fire's arson team for southern California who Danny had interviewed before about the two fires in Angeles National Forest, Box and Rincon, Dennis Abner and Candrea Rooney from the sheriff's department arson/explosives detail—the bomb squad, and photogenic ATF agent Tracy Orman.

Danny shook hands with everyone but Tracy who gave no indication she was aware he was even here. "I didn't know there was a dress code." He bit into the topmost hunk of meat on his skewer. Tender as Gina the actress's skin probably was.

"Yeah Mike takes that stuff pretty serious." Pavelko took a chair beside Costner and retrieved his bottle of beer. "As you can see from *his* wardrobe malfunction."

"Summer casual's turned into Hawaii Five-Oh No Not Tiki," Costner agreed. He was in his late 30s, muscular and windburned. His loose shirt with its cheesy tropical sunset print was unbuttoned halfway and he was leaning forward in his chair with his elbows on his knees as he peeled the label from a bottle of Budweiser. Cal Fire was the California Department of Forestry and Fire Protection, a state-level fire and emergency response department that contracted with local governments and agencies for wildland fire protection and management. It had dozens of aircraft and hundreds of engines positioned around the state and rarely did a major wildfire not involve them directly.

"I just saw that two firefighters died." Danny felt guilty saying that with a mouth full of food. Pavelko was right—this was gourmet.

"They were overrun by the fire," Pavelko said. "Crashed their engine trying to get out of the way. Heat was too intense for a rescue effort."

"They're facing everything you don't want to face out there," Costner said. "Wind, heat, drought conditions, slope, dense fuel load of dried-out vegetation. It's less than ideal."

"Chalk up two more for the Bug," Dennis Abner added quietly. He was in his late forties, clean-shaven and with male-pattern baldness. He wore wire-framed glasses and his jutting chin pushed his mouth slightly off-center in a disapproving skew.

Danny was thinking about the 911 caller mentioning possible victims. Now there were two more that he'd caused, and he wondered if that was still less than the Bug was hoping for.

Abner's partner Candrea Rooney was a petite woman with short businessy blond hair and a mouth which was formed in a mirthless smile. They were both dressed in jeans and Hawaiian shirts with multicolored flowers, his blue, hers red. Only one of the seventeen fires—Los Liones in Pacific Palisades—was in LA city jurisdiction; sheriff's departments across four counties were shouldering the bulk of the investigation.

Candrea Rooney sat beside Tracy Orman on the wide deck railing. They stopped talking as soon as Danny sat down. Tracy had chosen jeans and a powder blue cotton shirt rolled up at the sleeves. And cowboy boots. And a bottle of Bud Lite over the watery Mai Tais. She wore a gold necklace with a little cross on it. Danny wanted to know what her deal was.

"Sad frigging day for the crews," Pavelko said. "But tomorrow's forecast is better, isn't that right Abby?"

"Winds will be somewhat down and humidity somewhat up," Abner said, "so the forecast is better, somewhat."

Danny took out his phone. "Okay if I get this?"

"Well that didn't take long," Cruz snorted from the grill.

"Have the names of the firefighters been released?" Danny asked.

Pavelko answered, "Captain Jason Hertzog and Specialist Brian Rollins, LA County Fire."

"I'm sorry." A moment of silence set to an inappropriately buoyant party soundtrack passed with Danny wishing he could ever listen to someone else's tale of loss without being reminded of his own.

Pete Costner said, "Hertzog was a veteran. Rollins was just a kid."

"Did any of you know them?"

"Not personally. But we're all in the fraternity of pain today."

"You feel it whether you know them or not." Dennis Abner squinted at Danny through his glasses.

"Were you always interested in arson?" Danny asked him.

"I was a detective first. I've always been interested in solving puzzles. This came about as a natural extension of that. I think I'd be wary of someone with an abiding interest in fire becoming a member of the detail."

"I think I would be too." Mike Cruz joined them, swirling his watery Mai Tai with a curly straw. Tracy Orman moved her feet off a chair and Cruz sat down with a crunch of grass skirt.

Danny scoped out Cruz's feet, exposed in all their ugliness by his flip-flops. Could be size 12. But what did he know other than he wore 10½. He put his plate down and angled his phone toward him. "You started out as a firefighter right?"

"They're all detectives who turned firefighter, I'm a firefighter who turned detective." Cruz took a drink and smacked his lips with satisfaction. His flinty moustache was wet along the bottom. "But I'd agree with Abby about enjoying solving puzzles."

"I enjoy catching people who kill firefighters." Costner had gotten the beer label off and was carefully flattening it on the armrest of his chair.

"Is that your background too?" Danny asked Tracy Orman, but she looked elsewhere, ignoring him. "The 911 call's a game-changer," he tried.

"Is it?" Cruz said.

"The suspect is obviously reaching out," Danny said. "He wants to be heard. He's got something to say."

There was another awkward silence.

"So why does someone commit arson?" He hoped Tracy Orman would answer—or even Cruz—but professorial Dennis Abner took it.

"By and large for the same reasons as most other crimes. Money, anger, revenge, attention—except that an arsonist can start a hundred serious fires before he's caught. They're usually only charged with the last fire, the one that got them caught."

"This guy could face the death penalty now," Costner said.

Danny refined his question. "What makes someone become an arsonist?"

"Generally speaking there are four types of arsonists. Psychological types." Abner counted them off on his fingers, "Curious, expressive, delinquent, pathological. Curious firesetters are typically children with low impulse control, little supervision and a budding fascination with fire. Simple means of ignition with everyday household items. They're embarrassed and remorseful when confronted and can be dissuaded from such behavior in the future—every arsonist is a firesetter, but not every firesetter is an arsonist."

Danny made another mental note to use that line in his post. He glanced at Cruz, whose attention seemed to be occupied by the glowing pool, an expensive form of rebellion now that full pools garnered homeowners an extra water tax on top of all the other new water taxes. Many owners had allowed theirs to go dry, leaving the concrete pockmarks to crack and grow weeds amidst the graffiti and skateboarders, California's new drought generation. But not Mike Cruz, evidently able to weather the cost like most homeowners could in this part of town.

Dennis Abner went on, "Expressive types are under stress, be it real or imagined, and seek to vent their frustration by setting fires. Why some turn to fire instead of shoplifting or vandalism, we don't know."

Pete Costner said, "Why they can't just pick up a guitar, write a mopey song and get laid, we don't know either."

"Delinquent types set fires for vandalism or revenge," Abner continued. "They enjoy the power from getting a big reaction or response, like the arrival of the fire department. They may stay to watch the fire or return later to smell the smoke. They set fires for jealousy, boredom, revenge. They have comfort zones and often live in the community they target. Crap home life, likely juvenile criminal record. Press coverage, news conferences, everything's an ego stroke to them."

"Some of them want to look like heroes," Pavelko noted.

"Last and the very least in terms of the number of them, thank God," Abner touched his pinkie, "the pathological pyros."

"Real sickos," Candrea Rooney nodded. She had a slight sibilant lisp.

"Everything from firefighter groupies to people who get sexual release from firestarting. Obsessive-compulsives operating nocturnally, setting fires quickly and easily, without any concern for whether the property's occupied or not. Some of them come back, try and insert themselves into the investigation, others turn themselves in just to talk about it."

"This guy doesn't sound like a pyro," Danny said.

"Because he's not," Mike Cruz said.

"You get some intersectionality, some cross-behavior," Abner said. "People aren't machines. But generally speaking, four types."

Pavelko sighed around his beer, "But unfortunately academia doesn't take us any farther than our belief that he's a firefighter."

"Not all of us believe that," Cruz said. "For all we know he's just someone who built himself a flamethrower. Or acquired one. We don't know it's homemade. We don't know how he got hold of it. Or even what *it* is, exactly. We're all just speculating."

Danny wanted to ask about the boot prints but couldn't throw Pavelko under the bus like that. "At least you have his DNA," he said.

Dennis Abner sipped his drink. "There's some ambiguity about that."

"Nothing ambiguous about it," said Cruz. "A soda cup found perfectly unscathed atop a charred trash can? Since when does divine intervention extend to garbage? It was put there *after* the fire burned past by the person who *started* the fire. The same person who called 911 to let us know he'd been at the Malibu cave. Like he's Kilroy."

The man in the Gold's Gym tank top and fire helmet beckoned to Cruz from the back of the house.

"But as we like to say in the law enforcement business," Cruz said as got to his feet, "we'll match him when we catch him. The old-fashioned way," he added over his shoulder as he stepped down off the deck. "By not leaving it up to the kiddies."

"You're such a charmer Mikey," Costner grinned. "Isn't he a charmer? He's a charmer."

"Old school charm," Abner said.

Costner cupped his hands around his mouth. "Hear that Mikey? Even Abby says you're old."

Cruz made a comment about them to some guests near the back of the house before he went in and the guests laughed.

"What is it you call the suspect on your website?" Candrea Rooney asked Danny. "It's a website, right?"

"The Angeles Arsonist. And everyone calls him that now, not just me. My blog is called Red Flag, on CODA.com—City of Angels/Dead On Arrival."

"Sounds charming," Rooney said dryly.

Dennis Abner glanced at Pavelko as if for a cue. "Mark says you two have spoken."

All at once Danny realized that these five investigators from four different agencies comprised the task force within the task force—and Mark Pavelko was its prime mover. "We have," he said.

"We need to be clear," Abner said, "nobody's making any assumptions, and neither will you."

"I'm not."

"'Cause not everyone thinks you're a good idea," Pete Costner said.

"What else are you going to do? The guy just killed seven people. The city's on the edge of panic again, right where it left off last November. Red Flag has gotten over two million hits since *yesterday.*"

"*And* it won an award," Pavelko said.

"And I look forward to writing all about the Bug as soon as you kiddies arrest him. But if you want me to help you need to help me by giving me information."

"Keep in mind you're just a tool," Tracy Orman said.

Her voice was a husky alto and Danny thought she may have been a smoker once, before her career in arson investigation. He smiled at her for finally acknowledging him at all. "Thanks, Tracy. I've already gone out and said your little posse here is closing in on him which is obviously bullshit. It's only my reputation—my whole goddamned *livelihood* I'm risking here. You want my help, I need more than you've given me. What about the boot prints I saw you photographing?"

"What boot prints?" said Orman, Pavelko, Abner, Rooney and Costner in unison.

Cruz emerged from the house with the man in the fire helmet. He returned to relieve his backup at the grill, which was giving off a lot of smoke.

Danny said, "My readers are already crowdsourcing it anyway and the clues they have are bullshit. Give them something to work with."

"You're going to have to give them something," Pavelko said. "And you never know—Red Flag could bag another trophy."

Danny swore under his breath and got up. "What I'm going to bag is another water. Anyone need a refill?" He aimed that question at Tracy Orman. With the slightest tip of her chin she sent his best intentions packing, so he stepped down off the deck and threaded his way around the pool.

* * * * *

Beer bottles floated in the coolers like bodies after a storm. Danny was going to have to go inside for water but decided to blog a little something first, so he found an out-of-the-way spot by Cruz's garage and took some pictures of the party from there.

There were probably thirty or forty guests inside and out; the property could easily accommodate twice that. He could see it all done differently, from a woman's perspective, with Jackie Cruz's refinement and taste. Before the disintegration into Mike's mostly male, mostly departmental friends who came to put the present at bay for a while by ruminating on the past over watery drinks and Tiki music.

"Hey buddy." The Gold's Gym guy with the yellow fire helmet was stuck in a doorway on the side of the garage with bags of ice in his arms. His face was bright red and a vein coursed up his forehead. *"Door."*

Danny pulled open the door which was held by a stiff self-closer at the top. A set of keys on a red and black D.A.R.E. keychain jingled in the handle.

"Thanks buddy. We got thirsty people to rescue." The man staggered toward the house. He tipped and his plastic helmet clattered onto the walkway, then he righted himself and kept going around the corner.

Danny braced the door with his foot and looked inside. A bare bulb glowed from the ceiling with a pull-chain which had been lengthened with twine. The narrow storage room had been sectioned off from the rest of the garage by unfinished drywall with a door cut into it, allowing space for a white chest freezer—the Gold's Gym guy had left the top up over bags of ice and packs of meat—and shelves with old cans of house paint and pool conditioner. A skimmer stood in the corner beside a long pair of gardening shears.

He made sure that he wouldn't be locked in, then released the door and tried the interior door. The handle was locked. He checked outside again—no guests were nearby, so he pulled the D.A.R.E. keychain out of the handle and went back to the interior door, sort of wondering what he was doing and sort of going out of his way not to. He fumbled with each of the keys in turn until the lock clicked from its housing and he pushed open the interior door. Except for the shaft of light dribbling a few feet over the concrete floor from where he stood the garage was pitch black. He felt around on the wall and found a switch and fluorescent lights ticked on over built-in cabinets, red Craftsman tool chests, shelves of metal and rubber parts, containers of screws, washers and bolts, a rectangular wooden work table.

He made sure the door was unlocked and opened the exterior door a crack. No one there. He slid the keychain back in the handle and let the door close, went back inside the garage and closed the door behind him, and started taking pictures with his phone.

On the table were a boxy blue welder, a spool gun in its open foam-lined case, cutting torches, nozzles, a clear face shield and goggles, goatskin gloves. A dull aluminum canister like a scuba air tank stood beside it. Beneath the table sat an air compressor, a fire extinguisher, a Shop-Vac and a trash can. Slender metal pipes of various lengths stood in a row against one wall where tools in graduating sizes hung neatly from nails inserted into pegboard. Patriotic artwork shared space on the walls with photos of Cruz hunting with buddies, all woodland camo and apex post-killing grins, deer in Wyoming, elk in Montana, insignias and patches from LACoFD and other fire agencies, an *I'm the NRA and I Vote* sticker. Metal shavings twinkled in the shadows. A thick black binder lay on a shelf built over a minibar fridge, beside a laptop, spiral-bound notebooks and a broadband scanner. Like Danny, Cruz monitored police and fire radio channels—he was among the first to arrive because he was always listening.

He stepped gingerly over to the shelf and briefly considered the laptop. He lifted the stiff cover of the black binder with the edge of his thumb. Inside were clear plastic sleeves, twenty or thirty of them. He glanced over his shoulder at the closed door, then lifted his hand and opened up the binder. The first plastic sleeve contained several 8½" x 11" sheets of paper. The top one was a DMV-style photograph of a young white man with a Marine Corps haircut and poor rural anger in the tight set of his small mouth and slightly lopsided blue eyes. Below the photo in typeface was *Akon, Marvin, DOB 7/14/89,* followed by brief biographical info and a summary of priors—in Mr. Akon's case assault, possession, and arson, highlighted in yellow. There were scrawled handwritten notes in the margin. Danny took a picture of it and turned the next plastic sleeve. Another photograph of a man. This one was older, black. *Armstrong, Lemarr. DOB 4/27/72.* Mr. Armstrong's many priors included attempted murder and arson, highlighted in yellow. A line of thick black felt marker was crossed diagonally through the sheet, apparently negating it.

Danny lifted the next sleeve. *Carroll, Walter.* The next was *Daniels, Charles Ray.* And so on alphabetically. Sleeve after sleeve, face after face, man after man, white, black, brown. Each accompanied by a short biographical synopsis Mike Cruz had gleaned from who knows where. Some had more notes than others, more pages tucked neatly into the clear plastic sleeve. Some photos were official-looking DMV-style head shots, others looked like they'd been taken surreptitiously, without the subject's awareness. Most had the black felt marker crossed through them. He thumbed through to the last sleeve. No black marker strike through the photo of the chunky face of a white man who looked familiar, something in the dark eyes, the flat nose—

He froze.

Keys jingled at the exterior door.

He listened to the Gold's Gym guy lumber back into the freezer room, wheezing and cursing, and hoped he was too drunk to notice the strip of light visible beneath the interior door. Tried to think of what to say as an excuse when he did. Came up empty. Better it just didn't happen. He closed the binder and tiptoed over to the door, staring at the handle and listening to the man heave bags of ice out of the freezer then burp loudly as he struggled with the door. The exterior door swung shut behind him and the party noise became distant again.

Danny commanded his heart to slow the fuck down, switched his phone to video and panned around the room.

Annotated USGS maps with their colorful swirling topographical lines were taped onto wall-mounted dry-erase boards with landscape photos and satellite imagery, handwritten notes on white paper, schematics of something mechanical—gaskets, tubes, labels like F-4 regulating valve and D-12 igniter clamp screw, arrows connecting it all into a cohesive whole. In some places the drawing was done in pencil, in others ink, perhaps reflecting Cruz's confidence in the accuracy of those sections. The workshop was not so unlike Paul Kasho's over the garage of their house in Calendula. Cruz's smelled of oil and grease, the viscera of machinery; Paul's had had an earthy smell from the natural ingredients he used to make his own inks. Although devoted to different disciplines, both places offered the same kind of insulation from the outside world. The same environment for poisoned thoughts to grow like mushrooms.

The maps covered five Southland counties—Los Angeles, Ventura, San Bernardino, Riverside and Kern. Other maps presented smaller areas within each for detail, with scores of red and yellow pushpins dotted across them, each wrapped with a tiny sticker labeled in precise script with a handwritten date in blue or black ink. It reminded him of his Red Flag map at home. The easternmost red pin was in San Bernardino National Forest. The label read 8/4/18.

He knew the date—the Cedar Crest Fire, the third fire. He worked his way roughly westward through some of the red pins. 8/8/18—Cajon. 8/18/18—Rincon. 8/22/18—Box. 8/25/18—Delta. 9/1/18—Dillon. 9/15/18—Weldon. 9/29/18—Chalk. 9/19/18—Channel. 10/10/18—Brown's Creek. 7/28/18—Tripps. 10/27/18—La Barranca. 7/14/18—Hillcrest. 10/31/18—Shiloh Ranch.

8/29/19—Backbone.

His fingertips tingled. They were all here. Every fire attributed to the Angeles Arsonist was here. But those seventeen fires weren't the only red pins and there were dozens more yellow pins.

Danny's eyebrows jumped up his forehead like startled cats. There had to be a hundred pins across the maps.

The exterior door unlocked with the sound of a hammer being cocked.

Right away he knew it wasn't the ice man again. He looked around frantically but there was nothing big enough to hide behind or inside of. The interior door handle began to turn and as the door swung open he slipped behind it like a stagehand almost caught in the spotlight. The knob stopped an inch from his crotch and he held his breath. He was done. His mind fizzed with the humiliating apologies he was about to start blubbering.

He could hear breathing on the other side of the door which moved as lazy as the tip of a cat's tail. He could smell barbecue and beer. At any second the door would be pushed open all the way into him and the trespasser uncovered. He knew the person on the other side of the door was wondering why it was unlocked and the lights were on.

Long seconds passed with his heart thumping loud as a drumroll before an execution, surely loud enough to be he heard. His chest began to burn. In a few seconds he'd gasp and suck in air. He had no excuse for being here, no story, no defense. His eyes began to water as his lips quivered.

Mike Cruz muttered, "Larry you dumb ass." He turned off the lights and closed the door behind him. The light went off in the freezer room and a moment later the exterior door opened and closed.

Only then, alone in absolute darkness, did Danny finally exhale.

CHAPTER 11

"…There were pieces of Beemer all over the place. Kid's lucky to—"

Detective Travis Salk stopped in midsentence as Danny returned to the deck with a dripping bottle of water he'd plucked out of a different cooler. Bottled water had become a party's most expensive supply but manufacturers and retailers insisted the 300% spike in cost was market forces, not price gouging. Danny's phone was in his shirt pocket and it was recording, live-streaming to the cloud which burned through battery power but made the device safely expendable, should shit unexpectedly go south as shit was wont to do from time to time.

"Homicide's here Danny," Mark Pavelko grinned as he sat down. "How many parties can you say that about?"

Danny avoided making eye contact with him or Cruz. "I helped a guy get some ice from the garage, then took care of a couple things." He was confident in his lie's scaffolding of truth. He'd been gone fifteen minutes. Pete Costner had left. So had Dennis Abner and Candrea Rooney; Salk and Adjani had taken their chairs. Tracy Orman was texting on her phone. She'd switched to water.

"Crime never stops huh," Pavelko said.

"I'd have to go live in MacArthur Park if it did." Despite it being a Los Angeles Historic Cultural Monument the park near downtown lacked the clout to keep its lake's fountain operating because of its primary use as a well-established homeless encampment of tents, boxes, bags, umbrellas, grocery carts, a jamble of limbs and litter and radios in a half-dozen languages. Danny asked the detectives, "Have you identified the cave victims?"

Salk and Adjani had loosened their ties and were halfway into their beers. No one said anything for a long moment, the awkwardness heightened by the swinging tiki music and party lights and sporadic male laughter from around the pool.

Adjani said, "N.O.K.'s were today. One of them got it over the phone."

"The ass-end of investigations," sighed Pavelko. "Comes with the badge."

Danny asked, "Was it Katie Martyn's parents? Or Lisa Higgins'?"

Salk took a long pull on his bottle. "You want to impress us, don't pretend it's not the Information Age and everybody thinks they've got a right to everyone else's. Impress us by knowing when to keep your fingers off the keys without having to be asked."

"It's not up to me. The clock is running."

Pavelko snickered. "I already hate that frigging phrase."

"Speaking of running." Adjani rubbed his cheek. "We met one of your contemporaries today."

"Who?" Danny asked.

"A girl about this tall," Salk yawned, "short hair. Little sunglasses. What size are those coconuts Mike? C's?"

"B's," Pavelko said.

"The hell they're B's!" Cruz thundered.

"Hers are like yours," Salk said.

"She must have done track at school," Adjani said. "She had one foot in ICU before security even saw her."

"Not to mention her exit."

"Hurdles or something," Adjani mused.

Danny grimaced. "Her name is Ursula Ruda. You should arrest her. It wouldn't be her first time."

"Who is she?" Salk asked.

"She writes for a news website like CODA but not as good. At all. I forget the name of it."

"Competition nipping at your heels Mr. Cash Oh?" Mike Cruz drank, obviously pleased. "Where are all the *real* reporters? Doesn't anyone work for newspapers anymore?"

"Ursula Ruda," Pavelko yawned. "Sounds exotic. Travis you got me yawning now."

"She's not exotic," Danny said. "Who was she there to see?"

Adjani said, "Let's just say visiting hours are over."

"Permanently," Salk added.

"Pass that along for us." Adjani stood up. "Mike—thanks for the invite. We'll talk tomorrow."

"Company kills, as they say," Salk agreed. "Adios amigos, Marky Mark."

They shook hands with Cruz. "Thank you boys for stopping by. Next time I promise—more food and less reporters."

Mark Pavelko and Tracy Orman followed Salk and Adjani past Cruz, venerating him like a tiki god and interfacing with guests around the pool on their way out. Cruz's tipsy smile looked pasted on his sweaty face. Coconut boobs heaved with shallow breaths, his eyes focused on something no one else could see.

It took him a minute to realize Danny was still there.

Cruz turned sharply in his chair and stared at him as if he was a trespasser caught lounging on the family sofa watching TV.

In an even tone of voice with barely a hint of the defensiveness the comment warranted Danny said, "I've got fifty gigs of video and photos, over a hundred hours of interviews, I've done local, network, cable and radio interviews, internet chats, my blog's got two million hits in two days, *and* I won a fucking award."

"So what?"

"So spare me the real reporter shit and talk to me." In your true voice, he almost said.

"*Talk* to you? If you don't mind me asking, since it *is* my house—why the hell are you here?"

"To get some answers from the old man of the mountain who won't talk to anybody even though he knows the most about the suspect. You were the first to identify the device, the first to connect the fires—"

"You're not owed anything, Mr. Cash Oh." Cruz turned back around to face his pool and his party. "The problem with your generation is you feel you're entitled to answers just because you have questions. The real world doesn't work that way. The only thing you're entitled to do is die."

"And here I was thinking Mark's the one who should work for Hallmark. Okay then—I've never interviewed anyone with coconut boobs before and I'd like to cross that off my bucket list before the Grim Reaper crosses me off his. That better?"

Cruz tugged off the carnation clipped in his hair and struggled out of the coconut shell bra. There was an irritated rustle of grass skirt. He shook the remains of his drink at him. "You've got this long."

Danny took out his phone and pretended to turn it on, as if it hadn't been recording the whole time. "First let me say you have a beautiful house."

"Thank you. That's all Jackie of course. I haven't changed anything. That was her thing, making things better. I just wrote the checks."

"She could have helped with your costume."

"Yes, well, nothing's been the same since she left." There was a sourness in Cruz's tone as if Jackie had dumped him, not died.

"I lost my dad when I was twelve," Danny offered, "and it still feels like I've misplaced something important."

"I think Mark has misplaced his mind. You were all his idea, you know that right? Nobody else thinks it's a good one. But that doesn't bother you."

"I'm not in the business to make friends."

Cruz scoffed. "What business? Banner ad sales? How is increasing your readership good for this investigation? How is getting you more interviews good for the people who've lost their homes and their belongings? Their children? Their *fathers?*" He leaned on the last word to show how not special Danny's loss was in the grand scheme of loss.

"An informed public is good for you and for them and for everyone else too."

"That's what press conferences are for. You should attend them like the real reporters do. Publish what you're given, let us do our jobs and stay the hell out of the way."

"What you've been holding back is exactly what we need out there to find him, flush him out. Somebody knows him. Somebody knows what kind of boots he wears."

Cruz shook his head. "Mark really has told you too goddamned much."

"I haven't posted anything he hasn't approved, just like we agreed."

"It's only a matter of time."

"Right—until the Bug goes and starts another massive fire. Where's this one going to be?"

"As generous as Mark is being to you, at some point we'll have to account for your presence in court, did you ever think of that? Did *he?*"

"Mark's right—the media can apply pressure through an informed and vigilant public. Someone's living next door to this guy. Working with him. Watching him come and go. Wondering about him. The Angeles Arsonist *is* one of us."

The diminishing ice swirled in Cruz's plastic cup and he muttered, "He may not be as far removed from *us* as you think."

Danny's fingertips tingled. To Mike Cruz there was only one club and you were either in it or you weren't—*us* meant firefighters. Self-incrimination marched in lockstep with the craving for fame—Cruz couldn't help himself. "You know him the best of anyone—who is this guy?"

Cruz showed his teeth. "Why, he's Felix of course."

Danny blinked. His mouth gaped like a yawning flytrap. "Felix? Felix *who?*"

"Do they not teach science in grade school anymore?" Cruz sighed. "Do you not have any idea what a DNA molecule looks like?"

Of course, Danny thought with chagrin. "Felix the Helix."

Cruz clapped his hands loudly three times. "Congratulations. But you're not quite *Jeopardy!* material are you. Do you think our Bug's a dangerous man? A serious man?"

"Extremely both. Especially if he's close to the firefighting community. It's already been fourteen months and—" Danny almost said *a fucking hundred*—"who knows how many fires."

Cruz shook the last of his drink. "So what makes him special? Since our Forest Service friend considers you to be such an expert."

"The complexity of the device," Danny said at once, desperate to keep his window of opportunity with Cruz open. "Most arsonists compose theirs with simple items, like match sticks wrapped with a rubber band around a burning cigarette. But you said—I remember the quote—that as soon as you saw the burn patterns of the Box Fire, you said they were too far and too *directional.* Since fire climbs faster uphill than downhill something had to have *propelled* the fire."

"I said that?"

"It's a decent paraphrase."

"It's nothing I couldn't have gotten from a *newspaper.* Not good enough, rookie, and your time is up."

"The device is what's going to get him caught—I believe that. That's what I wrote."

"You wrote what Mark approved you could write. That doesn't say much about the free press does it? It doesn't say much about your journalistic integrity does it?"

"He has to have some place to put it together. Somebody lives next door to his workshop. Somebody knows." He wanted to ask Cruz about his garage. He wanted to gain some kind of insight into Paul Kasho through the two men's insulated retreats. He wanted to know what whispered thoughts began to scream in the countless hours when yours was the only voice, when your personal opinion was the sole arbiter of what was real and what was not, what was valuable and what could be dispensed with.

But Mike Cruz said nothing.

Danny said, "We know he sets fires on Saturdays or Wednesdays, always early in the morning so they'll grow as the day gets hotter. Backbone was started late on a Thursday night. Something has changed to make him act outside of his comfort zone."

"No, he's simply become more comfortable. He just took the map people like you draw of comfort zones and burned it on our doorstep and you say he's incapable of changing? Incapable of evolving?"

"Starting one of his fires at night instead of in the morning? Murdering five people with his flamethrower instead of an assault rifle and then call 911? Yeah he made some changes on his own—but something forced him to. Is he acting out of grief? A desire for recognition? Revenge? He wouldn't tamper with something this important to him without an irrefutably good reason to." Danny didn't know if he was hitting anywhere closer to home with Cruz than where he sat on the deck. "What do you think?"

Cruz finished his drink and turned his empty cup upside down on the arm of his chair. He gazed at the two stories of French windows glowing at the back of his house. The cleaning ladies were moving around inside unoccupied rooms with rags and black plastic garbage bags. "Mr. Cash Oh, a word to the wise—you should at least try to live up to your own pretense."

"Pretense? What pretense?"

"You haven't asked a single question about the memorial fund."

Danny cleared his throat and thought, shit. "I'm sorry—I got so caught up. I donated at the door."

"We appreciate that. What we don't appreciate is spying."

Danny's skin prickled. He'd been busted in the garage after all. And now he was alone with Cruz with no defense but a cell phone broadcasting into the ether for posterity. "I'm not spying—"

"I'm spending less time trying to catch the suspect than I am trying not to be framed by him. I'll speak to Mark directly when it's time, I don't need to go through his secretary. You're nothing but a salesman so spare me the pitch and ask your question."

Danny sat forward in his chair. "You're the inventor—how does someone build a flamethrower?"

"There's nothing inventive about it, you can find the instructions online. Or haven't you looked yet?"

"I can't make heads or tails of schematics, I'm more the artsy-fartsy type. How would you do it?"

"There are any number of different ways. The fuel's a cocktail of kerosene, gasoline, and diesel. There are other combinations, even homemade napalm, but that's not what he's using. Two tanks—a big one for the fuel, a small one for the propellant, a compressed gas such as nitrogen. Two grips and two triggers, perhaps from legally-registered firearms. The rear trigger allows the nitrogen to flow through a pressure regulator to the top of the fuel tank, pushing the fuel down into the gun through the hose. The front trigger turns on a battery-powered spark plug at the nozzle, igniting the flowing fuel and creating the fire stream. Two point five gallon capacity. Just over fifty pounds fully loaded. It can shoot a fuel stream thirty yards for eight to ten seconds."

"Where would he get everything?"

"Gasoline and diesel come from places called gas stations. Camping stores carry kerosene. Nitrogen can be purchased from any welding supply store. The device can be assembled with parts from any decent hardware store. All over the counter stuff. All it takes is some research, some time, and some determination." Cruz licked his lips.

Danny imagined him standing in front of the schematics in his garage with his chin upraised, nostrils flared with pride, scrutinizing the diagrams like a general inspecting battle plans. "That's what he's using?"

"That or something like it. Now if you don't mind Mr. Cash Oh," Cruz took a cigar from his shirt pocket, "I'll enjoy the rest of my party without you at it. Drive carefully."

Danny turned off his phone. "Thanks for your time." He left the deck and quickly made his way around the pool and back through the house. The Gold's Gym sentry in the yellow fire helmet dozed in a chair in the empty living room. "Night Larry."

The man stirred and smacked his lips. "I'm fine," he slurred, and dropped his chin back to his beer-sticky chest.

CHAPTER 12

He was familiar with this corner of Hollywood at the gnarled foot of the famous hills, though he hadn't been here in years. There used to be a video rental store in the mini-mall across Bronson from the grocery store where he was parked, but the space was empty. *For Lease* signs were taped up in the windows that were once smothered with movie posters. Next door to it was a pet shop, a Chinese take-out place, a laundromat, and a liquor store. Fine-tuning life's essentials down to a four-pack.

Thirty seconds after he turned off the engine the minivan was too hot to sit in. He didn't want to waste pricey gas by running the air conditioning so he got out, briefly savoring the unmistakable seasoning of smoke on the hot wind, and went inside the grocery store. He scooped up a hand basket and it bumped against his thigh as he carried it around, pretending to be doing some light shopping like everyone else. His busy eyes roamed behind mirrored sunglasses with arms that squeezed his temples.

The store was bright, crowded and loud. It was cool to the point of cold in here and the sweat coating his skin quickly dried. Like This Him and That Him—hot and cold, with barely a razor blade's width of separation. People pushed carts up and down the aisles as lazy as honey bees, as if they were strolling past the walls of a gentle maze of tall pre-packaged hedges. The shelves of colorful logos in near-perfect rows were almost sensory overload today, as if they could induce some kind of consumer coma.

Surrounded by all this food he realized he was hungry—starving, actually—but he hadn't made a list and without a list he couldn't buy anything. He only had a few bucks on him anyway. He went and stood by the cold beer in the liquor department, staring at his reflection in the foggy refrigerator windows, a cubist rendition of himself in different colored beer labels. He wanted to feel like Clark Kent or Peter Parker but instead he felt naked as a jaybird, as mom used to say when he helped her bathe. She was the one in the tub but he had to be naked too, mom having vulnerability issues and wouldn't—repeat would not—have her own son feeling high and mighty over her. No sir. So he'd helped her when her other children didn't have to, her mottled flesh like the tips of his fingers after having been submerged in the dirty water too long, until he finally moved out at 31 to marry his first wife. That lasted all of a year and then he moved back in to his old bedroom. His bed hadn't been made in the year since he last slept in it, the sheets unwashed for even longer than that.

As he studied his reflection in the refrigerator windows he once again went over every millisecond of Thursday night. In hindsight he couldn't see anything he'd done wrong considering he'd been operating without a plan which was like shopping without a grocery list. Without a plan he shouldn't have been operating at all. But there were one or two things he could realistically improve on.

He'd been delayed leaving work, which was the first thing he hadn't anticipated. He'd tried to get out of it but everyone was watching, and it *was* overtime. They had arbitrarily changed the schedule again and suddenly he had to work the late shift Friday which spoiled his refueling plans to be ready early Saturday morning. So he had to do it that night, which was why he was at the gas station on PCH filling up the red plastic cans to load the tanks when the two cars had driven in one after the other—a fancy red BMW electric and a white Acura hybrid with window tints.

The Acura stopped on the other side of the pump he was using. The doors of both cars burst open and five or six people spilled out, a mix of males and females that looked like college students. The girls were pretty, synthetic blondes in shorts and skimpy tops, ponytails and hoop earrings, wearing disdain like perfume. He well imagined the derisive comments mom would make about them. He didn't make eye contact. He stared at the digital pump gauge tick speedily upward while his anticipation built and let his thoughts return to the first fire that he'd really planned out and prepared for. The first one that ever really meant anything. It was in elementary school.

There had been smaller fires before in secluded places, derelict lots and undeveloped tracts. He stole the ace of spades Zippo from mom's boyfriend at the time—the one he'd heard her confide to that she'd given birth to *him* out of spite to her then-boyfriend, his own unknown father—and then applied the flame to alcohol-soaked rags he'd collected from the school's art supplies. He even pulled the fire alarm, unleashing a klaxon wail of euphoria. *And* helped teachers direct panicked children to the nearest exit. He'd watched enthralled as the firefighters tramped into the school like giants in helmets, oxygen tanks, hoses and axes—it was right before gym class, he'd timed it perfectly—and was struck dumb by all the awe and reverence a boy could feel. He knew right then and there that he was going to be one of them someday.

They called him a hero. They even gave him a plaque which he still had in one of the cardboard boxes he kept in the back of one of mom's closets, still in its original bubble wrap since she refused to hang it up or otherwise display or even acknowledge her son's accomplishment. He checked on the boxes whenever he visited her. The packing tape remained undisturbed—which to this day surprised him. Boundaries had never been important to mom, so leaving them there was like baiting her. He pretended he didn't know what he'd do if she ever opened them and saw the stuff he kept in them, but he knew. He'd fantasized about that in typically minute detail for decades. Ever since he was a child really, already the unwanted spiteful derailer of mom's happier life.

As he matured simple mechanisms begat more complicated ones. At first the designing was almost as fulfilling as actually using them, when they worked. He'd suffered his share of fizzles and once burned his hand pretty good when a small incendiary bomb went off prematurely. He had to reposition his bed to cover the hole in the floor. His mom punished him for weeks even after her boyfriend, who was a contractor, had repaired the hole and taken the opportunity to knock the wind out of him with an adult-strength punch to his soft stomach accompanied by the advice not to cause any more trouble like that for mom. His *girlfriend*, he called her.

The flamethrower was a natural evolution, not just the right tool for the job but in fact his masterpiece. It was an extension of him, proof positive that he could truly take any thought he wanted and make it real. Make it *actual*. He could turn the word *flame* into a stream of fire hotter than hell itself. And he had no doubts he was going to wind up there, in mom's particular hell. For as long as he could remember she'd always said there was a special place there waiting just for him. She said he never did anything right and she was usually right. Except for two things—about her becoming a millionaire through her eBay second-hand clock business, and about his ability to make That Him possible.

Not just possible—real. Actual.

Dangerous.

Wheezing through her mouth mom barked, *Are you fighting the fire or trying to start one of your own?*

He looked up and saw the male driver of the BMW facing him in the space between the gas pump and a trash can, just a few feet away. He wore knee-length surf shorts with shark fins on them. His tank top revealed too much of his tanned muscular torso. He had a fake smile and a gap between his front teeth and was the sort of prick who'd picked on him growing up and bossed him around now. The prick's pal leaned on the Acura as it was refueled, preoccupied the glowing face of his watch. He had short hair and a long neck and a lean swimmer's physique, and wore red lifeguard swim shorts and a tank top with a cross and the words *GET RIGHT* on it. The girls had gone inside the convenience store with the third male and for the moment the three of them were alone outside.

The gap-toothed prick spoke to him. "Hey guy, I said are you fighting the fire or trying to start one of your own?" He was slurring his words.

He ignored the prick and stared at the gas pump, thinking he should just cut it off now and leave, but he only needed a little more.

"Hey, did you hear me? I asked you a question."

"Ease up dude," his friend said to his watch.

"I'm just asking, that's all. I mean look at him. He looks like a man on a mission, and you gotta respect that. You gotta give props where props is due."

He suddenly remembered how he was dressed—navy blue t-shirt, yellow Nomex pants with reflective silver trim held up over his jeans by suspenders, his boots. He'd subconsciously slipped on the gear after work.

Mom's questions were a lot like that—insults barely concealed by an inquisitive smile like a mound of dirt hiding a roadside bomb. He was suddenly uncomfortable.

He answered, "Fighting it." This Him's voice sounded timid and weak and he hated it. Wished he could cut it out of him like a malfunctioning organ. Maybe that's what it was going to take for there to be only one him. One voice to rise above all others.

"What?" the drunk prick said to him.

"I said fighting it."

"Right on," said the prick's friend, grinning at his watch.

"What are you doing with the gas tanks?" the prick asked.

"Nothing." He realized now, staring at his frosty reflection in the beer cooler door, that he should have said he was filling up a car that had stalled somewhere. It was simple and it would have ended the dialogue right there. But he always only thought of the best lines after the fact.

"What do you mean nothing?" the drunk one asked. "I thought you said you were a firefighter." The prick stepped over the raised threshold dividing the pump and looked in the back of his truck, at the mass covered with a tarp.

"Hey, get away from there." He jammed the nozzle back in the pump, spilling gasoline on the pavement. "Get away from there."

"Alright guy, geez. Don't get your panties in a wad." The prick held up his hands and for a minute looked like he was about to fight. The driver. The leader. The Big Man in Charge.

He felt That Him stirring, a growing pain at the base of his skull that always announced That Him's awakening like the accidental pluck of a tripwire.

He thought about the utilitarian black 9mm Glock 19 in the glovebox, fully loaded with a 15-round magazine plus one in the chamber for 1.8 total pounds in the hand around the contoured polymer grip, and how simply he could solve this situation before it turned into a problem. But it would spawn other things, other problems, and it might ruin everything else, at least temporarily. Right now temporary was too long. He simply had to get out, get away, stay in control.

"What are you going to burn?" the guy with the watch asked.

"It's for a prescribed burn." Technical terms ought to end the conversation.

"Fighting fire with fire, I get it. That's cool."

"Well it sounds like a shart of an idea to me," laughed the prick as he went back to their side of the pump. "Whatever guy, good luck. I'll look for you on TV—I'll say that's him! That's the hero! The toasted marshmallow!"

He felt his face flush as he stowed the gas cans in back—making a point of locking the pickup's shell. He was relieved the engine started right away and he sped out of the station. At the first light he made a hard right and braked for an immediate left across oncoming traffic into the empty parking lot of a real estate office, long since closed for the day. From here he had an unobstructed view of the gas station on the corner, the two cars and the people. The females and the other male had come back out and had joined the assholes at the BMW and it took him a minute to realize he knew what he was doing.

Exactly what That Him *intended* him to do.

The decision had already been made, and when he realized that his chest relaxed and he calmed his breathing while his eyes blinked like the cameras of an assault team doing recon, which is how he thought of himself in almost any given situation. Constant preparation for a plan that hadn't yet been executed but could be at any time.

At night it was easy to keep the two pairs of taillights in sight on PCH. Three miles later they turned off the coastal highway onto Corral Canyon and headed up into the mountains. He hung back. There was no traffic on the canyon road and the moon reflected enough light for him to see so he turned his headlights off to be invisible.

He felt as if everything had been leading up to this. Life before now had been a trial run for this and what he'd become after this. What That Him already was. Supreme. Godlike. He drove faster not from fear of being caught but out of eagerness for the experience. He'd waited his whole life and every passing second added months more.

He came around a bend in the road and saw the interior lights of the cars a couple hundred feet up ahead. He stopped suddenly, waiting and watching and checking the rearview mirror. No one was coming. No one was going. He forced his eyes wide and when they'd dilated enough he spotted the pinpricks of light bobbing along the black landscape. Flashlights on a footpath.

He found their cars parked in a shallow turnout of a gated entrance to a dirt road used by firefighters as a natural fire break. The engines were ticking like dry bones tapping together. Bulbous silhouettes of high smooth rocks were tinted blue-white by the moon which seemed to smile at him. He'd never seen it look that way before.

You wouldn't know there was anyone out here at all.

He got out, opened the back of his truck and within five minutes had the flamethrower fueled up—a process he was adept at even in the dark.

He heard a man's voice and flinched, sloshing gasoline onto the ground. He ducked behind his truck with his heart pounding. His gun was inaccessible from here because the interior light would come on as soon as he opened the door. And then he'd have to use it because if he didn't he'd be forced to explain what he was doing here—and what the thing on the ground behind his truck was for. It was so quiet out here. The others would hear the shot. They'd come to check it out, and then he'd have to shoot them too, running around in the dirt like frightened rabbits. This is not what he wanted.

He peered through the dusty window of the pickup shell and saw the drunk prick weave around the gate blocking the motorway and lurch over to the red BMW, which chirped and blinked its lights when he was close enough to it. He got in and the engine whined to life and the rear wheels spun and the car accelerated through a U-turn, spitting gravel off the side of his pickup, and sped away down Corral Canyon.

The prick hadn't even seen him, him and his truck and the thing on the ground.

Silence and solitude returned like whispers of encouragement.

He waited another minute or two until he was confident no one else was coming back to the other car. Then he tugged on his jacket and gloves, helmet and heat shield, taking care to leave no skin exposed. He put his arms through the straps and heaved the heavy tanks reeking of gasoline onto his back, cradling the three foot-long tube connected to the tanks by an umbilical hose as he hiked up the road in the Fireman666 exoskeleton toward the smooth rocky humps barely visible in the darkness. This Him was behind the wheel tonight. That Him was just along for the ride.

When he reached the rocks he couldn't see them.

He could hear them though—the intermingled clatter of dance music and voices. Laughter, as if they were mocking him, playing hide and seek. Seething with frustration, he was almost ready to go back and burn their car and wait for them to come see what happened when he realized the noises were *above* him. He looked up, his range of motion severely limited by the equipment, and noticed the skinny offshoot of a path between the towering outcropping rocks. Litter had been left like a trail of bread crumbs.

He could barely squeeze through with the tanks on his back. He'd never experienced anything like the moment he stepped out onto the rocky plateau, momentarily screened by a tangle of dry bushes not ten feet away from them. Most of the light came from flashlights laying on top of a cooler and the glowing face of a digital boombox. Behind his goggles he panned across the scene from left to right and back. A bare-chested man—the prick's friend who'd been preoccupied with his watch at the gas station—was bent over the wan light of a feeble campfire, blowing on it and talking absently to two females sitting on blankets with their arms around their knees and plastic cups in their hands. Inside the cave, the mouth of which was around six feet wide by three high, more flashlights shone up the rock walls and left the two people laying together on the floor in shadows.

The memory came prickling pleasurably under his skin like a chemical reaction and made him audibly gasp in the grocery store. Another shopper gave him a look. He lowered his eyes and moved on from the beer fridges.

One of the females outside the cave had made a sudden noise and the man at the campfire looked up and saw him resplendent with all the merciless power boiling in the tanks on his back like venom that had to be purged from swollen fangs. The prick gulped "Hey?" just as the women started to scream.

He squeezed the rear trigger half a second before the front trigger and loosed a blinding yellow-white stream of fire straight into the bushes, a tinderbox of parched vegetation which exploded in an immediate wall of acrid smoke. He knew they were screaming but he couldn't hear them over the roar of the flamethrower and his own sustained shouting, deafening in the face shield and helmet, like the bawling of a performer reaching the end of all he has to give to an audience.

The flames immediately started to breathe on their own under the nurturing wind, crackling and hissing and moaning, and soon the smoke became too much even for him. He climbed back down to the dirt motorway, his knees wobbling, shaking and unsure, then terrified.

Already warming to his flames, the earth seized his feet as if by molten roots spewed from its core, and like a billboard lit up over a traffic jam he was forced to come to grips with the fact that he'd just done something he couldn't come back from.

This was different than the usual post-fire—suddenly wanting to take it back, to drive away and leave everything as it had been but wasn't anymore and never would be again. They would have been if not for that goddamn switch being flipped like an ignition switch. Sometimes you didn't know a wall was a gate until you broke through it.

A howling figure launched off the plateau over his head and crumpled onto the ground in front of him in a cloud of dirt and smoke.

For a moment he was too stunned to move. He recognized the bare-chested man in the red lifeguard shorts. He was wearing purple boots and had burns all over his arms and chest. Moaning and crying, the man dragged himself up and began to limp down the dirt road in the direction of the cars, swearing at the pain and pleading loudly with God, who obviously was no match for Fireman666 here tonight.

In a heightened state of arousal he trailed the man by only a few feet, easily within range, and after a few steps the man seemed to sense him and turned and saw him and his bleeding lips fell open and before he started screaming the fire stream caught him like the flaming talons of a great hellish owl that practically split him in two. The man became a swirling, shrieking, penta-limbed ball of fire that cartwheeled into the bushes and it all went up together, the newly-born flames reaching into the night sky like an animal testing its legs before it started to run.

The flames got so high so fast that they almost trapped him and he had to move quickly, ducking from the intense heat on both sides of the path.

He had enough fuel left to burn their car. He was out of breath and sweating profusely when he got behind the wheel of his truck after stowing the gear in back, easier with the lighter weight of the empty tanks. The mountaintop was already beginning to glow. He wanted to watch but he was sure he heard helicopters thumping toward him, dogs barking and baying at his scent, sirens, wailing cacophony encircling him like sharks, and mom's voice behind it all, accusatory and unending. His hands shook his car keys in a merry jingle. He drove with his windows down so the thumping air could drown out the screams and the fleeting stink of guilt seeping out of him like a pungent curry.

By the time he'd driven four miles up the coast—careful not to speed, PCH was popular with the cops—he had calmed down enough to think, to listen to That Him, who told him to park near a gas station in Malibu, which he did. He waited, listening for instructions, encouragement, praise. Maybe even envy. But That Him was quiet for a long time.

Eventually That Him told him to take the Glock out of the glovebox.

He did.

That Him told him to close his eyes.

Confused, he did.

Now kill yourself, That Him whispered over and over and over again, in one ear then the other. *Kill yourself for what you've done. Raise it, squeeze it, kiss the shit goodbye.* Then shouting, *Blow your brains out! Kill yourself! Kill yourself! Kill yourself!*

He started to cry.

Kill yourself!

No!

Kill yourself!

Instead he got out and hurried over to the payphone at the gas station and called 911. You didn't need a quarter to dial 911.

He actually *called* 911.

Who knows what the hell he said. He hadn't planned for it so he wasn't prepared, he didn't have a script. He remembered the dispatcher was female and he wondered what she looked like. It was like he'd called her at home late at night to talk dirty to her. In hindsight he was glad it hadn't been a man, that might have thrown him off. But it was something to plan for if he ever did it again. You never know what you might get.

If he did it again. Leaving the phone hanging like that. *X marks the spot. Come find them. Come see what I did.* It was exciting for sure, but as This Him always said risks like that were like unprotected sex with a hooker. He wanted to smile but the flicker of pride was too akin to happiness and he didn't know happiness, not really, and there was so much yet to do, but he'd driven away giddy, positively elated for the first time in as long as he could remember, his teeth reflecting the oncoming headlights.

That Him didn't make another sound.

He felt like he didn't breathe again until he got back home and dead-bolted the door. He sank to his knees and almost threw up, gagged and coughed and spat onto the floor but didn't puke. Then he undressed and laid in bed clutching the Glock to his chest, staring at the cheap stippled ceiling and listening for the sounds of cops at his door. He wasn't going to go to prison. He'd lived in their cages of one kind or another his whole life, theirs and mom's, and if it came down to it—*if it came down to it*—he was not repeat *not* going to live out the remainder of his life in another one.

But once again no one came for him. It was as if he'd been given immunity by the whole world.

For the sake of appearance he plucked something off a fluorescent grocery store shelf and dropped it in his hand basket. Moved his head this way and that, pretending to scan the abundancy. He found what he was looking for at the far end of an aisle. Danny Kasho had something in his hand, an item of food—no, his phone. Paused in mid-shop to deal with whatever couldn't wait, as conditioned as one of Pavlov's dogs—ring his bells and he'd sit up and pay attention.

Pay.

Attention.

He walked down the aisle and stopped a few feet away from him. Looked out the corner of his eye at Kasho in his black tank top and blue shorts, flip flops and a baseball cap with the body outline logo of his stupid website on it. He hadn't taken off his sunglasses. He had fair skin, as if he didn't spend much time in the sun. He was carrying a hand basket full of Red Bull, power bars, a six-pack of bottled beer. He smiled at whatever he was looking at on his phone and muttered *Bullshit* just loud enough for him to hear.

Unable to resist, he bumped his basket against Kasho's, anticipating the moment of shocked recognition, the *What are you doing here?* But Kasho just murmured an apology and turned away. He didn't even look up at him.

He left the store irritably and went and sat in the microwave oven on wheels. Watched the wind pull at the awnings of the store. Kasho came out a few minutes later, still engrossed with his phone, hurrying up the sidewalk toward his building as if he had wings like one of mom's china angels she kept in her living room. He knew where Kasho lived, he'd even gotten into the lobby and knew which floor he was on, but he'd heard people coming down the stairs so he left. This Him was still a chicken shit in some ways. Always had been. But that was changing.

He pictured himself seizing Kasho, twisting him round by his head until it popped off his spinal column and he could shout his confessions right into his ears. Then he could chew his ears off and swallow them and his secrets too.

The urge for confrontation was swelling past the shallow internal levee of self-control, the pressure rising like the force of the wind which had blown him back into Hollywood tonight, to the sidewalk outside Kasho's apartment building with shit blowing all around him as if a tornado was whirling up the street.

He stared at Kasho's door and though about the parade they'd give the firefighters who died. And what a dead reporter deserved.

CHAPTER 13

Danny scowled at the high-res pictures of Mike Cruz's workshop artfully panning and zooming Ken Burns-style across his desktop monitor, the equipment, tools, schematics, plans, mysterious black binder and all those goddamned pushpins glaring balefully under his phone's flash like nocturnal predators disturbed by a researcher.

Garrett was out; the apartment was as quiet as it could get over the sirens and car horns of a Hollywood night. Danny could smell the smoke through his open windows as the ceiling fan cooled the sweat on his bare chest. When he got home clutching a wad of junk offers of water reclamation from the mailbox—he wasn't ready to drink his own pee no matter what flavor they said they could make it—he could still smell Gina in his bedroom. At first her scent was a depressingly lusty leftover as if someone had borrowed his bed for sex during a party, leaving him with damp sheets and a used condom to dispose of. But then her fragrance brought a much-needed smile to his lips with the blossoming hope that someday he'd have damp sheets because of her. Or Carrie Voelker. Or almost anybody for that matter. It had been too long. Way, way, way too long.

Conversation recorded from Mike Cruz's deck played back through his speakers, the voices of the task force within a task force—Mark Pavelko, Dennis Abner and Candrea Rooney, Pete Costner—then Travis Salk and Igor Adjani and Cruz himself, all warmed by a parametric EQ plug-in, the same software Danny used on his own voice when he was doing interviews from here.

Who were the men in Cruz's binder? Suspects? If so, of what? He wanted to assume the binder's contents dealt with the Angeles Arsonist but how would he know, the binder wasn't labeled. His cursory search for Marvin Akon resulted in just one relevant hit, his arrest in 2009 for setting a fire in an apartment complex in Redlands, a former citrus capital a few miles west on the 10 freeway from where the future arsonist had been born. Cruz was an arson investigator, maybe it was his little black book that wasn't meant to be seen by anyone but him. Nothing was cryptic when you knew the code.

Danny groaned into his beer. He couldn't be entirely sure he hadn't touched anything inside Cruz's garage and had already fabricated a story to frame hapless helmeted Larry, but defensiveness wasn't sneaky. Once the conversation was taking place the accusation was as good as made. Investigators were notoriously difficult people to try and sneak shit by.

This is all over the counter stuff, Cruz intoned over the tiki music. *All it takes is some research, some time, and some determination.*

And some serious skill with a welding torch, Danny thought, sipping from a sweating bottle of Stella Artois. The weight of the device likely explained why the fires had all been set near roads—walking any distance with that much weight on your back had to be a challenge, even though he'd hiked up the fire road to the cave in Malibu. But what did he know—the monkey on *his* back weighed exactly the same as the skeleton in his closet.

Emails and texts from Cynthia and Victor were multiplying like the questions he had for Vanessa, timeless questions, the same questions he'd always wanted to ask but never could, and now had to.

Mark Pavelko had called while Danny was westbound on the 134, aiming for the 5 south and the Los Feliz entry to Hollywood by Griffith Park, an undeveloped island of rugged black hills surrounded by the city lights like a lava flow cut off by the sea. They were still doing earthquake repair and retrofitting on the overpass at night but it didn't hold him up long. He drove with his music off to better focus on the buzzing in his ears: *He may not be as far removed from* us *as you think.*

He let the call go to voicemail; Pavelko didn't leave a message.

Instinct is one thing, Pavelko had said, *but too much of it...too much of it starts to look like something else.*

I'm spending less time trying to catch the suspect than I am trying not to be framed by him, Cruz had rebutted.

Danny minimized the photo, opened a subfolder of his prodigious Red Flag notes and a new Google search.

Mark Pavelko's career entailed far fewer spotlight moments than Cruz's. His name came up only occasionally, related to fire investigations around the southern half of the state. Danny found one photograph of him at a 2015 wildland firefighting conference in Sacramento. According to a Forest Service questionnaire he browsed online Pavelko's arrest/prosecution/closure rate was high enough to be notable. Similar to Cruz, Pavelko always seemed to know what to do. And there were plenty of mentions in Red Flag, he noted sourly. For someone quoted so often he should have had deeper background on his source by now.

He scrolled through the audio files from the Seminole Overlook, jumping forward incrementally till he found the exchange he wanted.

There's your euphemism of the day.

It was your wife, wasn't it?

Was what?

Why you moved to San Fran.

You sure you don't have this already?

I'm sorry, I forget her name.

Linda. Her name is Linda.

Danny paused the recording. Mark Pavelko's voice was higher-pitched than Cruz's, at least on the phone.

Linda Pavelko was not hard to find. A June 2019 article in an excruciatingly snotty San Francisco high society magazine featured photographs of the blond and blue-eyed socialite at her home in the exclusive Pacific Heights neighborhood. She looked as unblemished and strategically-coiffed as a politician's wife. They called the area where she lived the Gold Coast—billionaires lived there, not Forest Service agents' wives. The article described her as a "philanthropist and patron of the arts" who was "blossoming after a painful divorce last year." Further searches revealed Linda was the daughter of actor Nelson Fisher, a staple of the small screen in the 80s and 90s and an apparently highly successful investor since then, which no doubt accounted for the foundation of his daughter's patronage and philanthropy.

Danny sat back in his chair. For a few seconds he was aware of nothing but his immediate environment—the fans whirring, Garrett's thunder rattling the treble clef statuette on his bookshelf, the blaring horn and siren of a fire engine caught at a standstill in the congested intersection at Franklin as honking cars inched out of its way.

Mark Pavelko the ex-cop from Chicago had landed a rich man's daughter from San Francisco, got a taste of the high life, two kids and a divorce. He still wore his wedding ring like costume jewelry. Still talked about his family as if it was a cohesive unit. He was talking about taking his daughters back to Chicago and Danny wondered if he even had the legal right to. As if wealthy Linda Fisher from San Francisco wouldn't have already staked out her territory with high walls and machine gun nests manned by daddy's lawyers. They may be Mark's offspring but they were her kids. Pavelko was fighting above his weight class.

The audio recording from when he'd rejoined the group on the deck looped back to the beginning. Detective Salk was saying something. It was faint but audible enough for him to catch the words this time.

"*…There were pieces of Beemer all over the place. Kid's lucky to—*"

Salk had stopped suddenly—as all conversation had when Danny returned. He paused the playback and searched for car accidents within the last week involving BMWs that were serious enough to warrant a trip to an ICU. In all of Los Angeles there was only one that made the news, on PCH Thursday night—the remains of which he had driven past yesterday on his way to meet Pavelko at the top of Corral Canyon. A CODA contributor named Evan Gottlieb had posted it. The single-occupant, single-vehicle accident had been called in at 10:45 PM. The driver, a 22 year-old male identified by Evan in a subsequent update as Derek Cavanaugh, was transported to UCLA Medical Center in serious condition.

The problem with your generation is you feel you're entitled to answers simply because you have questions, Cruz said on the recording.

Danny sat up, put his beer on a coaster and murmured, "Yes we are."

His search for Derek Cavanaugh revealed a handsome, shaggy-haired young man with a wide smile that displayed a gap between his front teeth.

He was a student at Pepperdine University. Danny logged into Claire Coogan's Facebook account and found him there too—he was in Katie Martyn's social circle. His status had evolved from the lost to the found—right down to the room number at the hospital to send cards and flowers, his wall garnished with digital get-wells like fake flowers at a headstone.

Danny clicked a bookmark in his browser, entered his password at the prompt and was presented with a directory of CODA contributors' folders. He scrolled down to Evan's. The PCH crash was his newest entry so its subfolder was at the top. More pictures of the crash scene were inside. Cavanaugh's crimson BMW 3 Series electric coupe was a mash-up of metal and plastic and glass resting at a downward angle in the trees. Its front had accordioned and the airbags deployed. In the lights of emergency responders pale dirt could be seen dusting the lower sides of the mangled auto body.

Cavanaugh had enjoyed freakishly good luck Thursday night to have come out of that mess in serious instead of critical condition or in a body bag—given the severity of the wreck it would have been the most likely outcome. Danny stared at the dirt on Cavanaugh's Beemer and pitied poor Ursula Ruda for having to resort to sneaking into the hospital for a ghoulish picture.

In his post he wrote *If the arsonist is as close to the firefighting community as some investigators suspect, he might be capable of wreaking far more havoc—and taking more lives—before he's caught. It's already been fourteen months and by some estimates over fifty wildfires.* He thought for a moment then added, *Other investigators suspect over a hundred.* To bolster his pretense he donated a paragraph to the LA County Fire Department Widows and Orphans Memorial Fund. He didn't have to try hard to be sympathetic—the two firefighters that died today likely left behind families now shattered like wine glasses in an earthquake.

He closed with: *Investigators have spent the last fourteen months sifting through the ashes of this man's compulsion. They see his face in the bodies twisted on the smooth rock above Malibu. They hear his voice summoning his audience in the 911 call. He's as flesh and blood as the lives he has taken, and I feel like I'm getting to know the human behind the horror too.*

His phone buzzed with a text. He expected Pavelko again but it was Lucy Baskin.

Heard poss deal for Patron?

He frowned—he hadn't heard anything new about the Mendoza trial. He replied *Nothing yet* and was bothered to distraction by the thought he was missing something. Precognition had become his Holy Grail ever since his father killed a perfect stranger in their house, the belief that there was always a clue beforehand, a red flag that could be recognized and a disaster averted and otherwise normal families kept intact. He found only one source mentioning a supposed plea deal for Charlize Patron—a Reuters stringer named Gibson who he knew from around town. He assumed that's where Lucy got it. One source wasn't enough so he didn't post it on Investment In Murder, but he wondered if Carrie Voelker had heard about it and was taking it seriously, and then began the inevitable spiral of self-doubt beginning with the obvious—what if Gibson's right?

As the raw audio files, pictures and video copied over to Pavelko's thumb drive he grew increasingly angry. At Pavelko, at Cruz, at the task force within a task force, at the whole goddamned mess. Pavelko's deal was for him to help draw the Angeles Arsonist out of the shadows using the only tool he had. It was time to stop being a tool and without thinking of checking with Pavelko first, he described a flamethrower built to Mike Cruz's specifications. He didn't mention the Thorogood brand boots but Googled them to get an idea of what they looked like. Some styles looked like militarized Doc Martens. He was beyond reporting now, beyond commenting. He was actively engaged, setting traps and tripwires.

His phone rang. It was Pavelko. Passive-aggressive Mark Pavelko who wanted him to be sneaky, just not *sneaky*. Danny rubbed his eyes—he couldn't keep putting him off like Cynthia and Victor and Vanessa and Paul Kasho. Everyone around him needed answering.

He picked up.

"Where you been?" Pavelko asked. "I've been calling. Come on down."

"Down where?"

"Downstairs."

Danny blinked. "You're here?"

"Yeah. Let's talk." Pavelko hung up.

He was sheltering in the alcove of the building's front door with his shoulders bunched and his hands wedged into the pockets of his jeans. Wind-whipped litter and leaves hissed sideways through the air behind him.

Danny resisted the wind tugging at the heavy door as he peeked around the edge of it. "What's up? Where'd you park?"

Pavelko nodded up the street where passing cars were dodging fallen palm fronds. "Got a lift with Trace. Christ Danny, you gonna invite me in or what?"

Danny hesitated, then pushed open the door. Pavelko slipped inside, close enough for Danny to smell whatever he'd been drinking besides the beer and watery Mai Tais at the barbecue. There was no sign of the beguiling Tracy Orman so he closed the door quickly, bolting it too which would piss off any resident who'd nipped outside for a quick keyless errand, but tonight devil winds trumped convenience.

Pavelko climbed the steps into the cool, dimly-lit lobby. "This place is a trip." He flopped heavily into a brown leather armchair under an antique floor lamp with a lighted onyx base and a silk shade with dangling gold fringe.

During the day the majority of the light came from a picture window which looked into the courtyard, the wall sconces with their bordello-red low-wattage bulbs installed more for decoration than illumination. The comforting historical mustiness was infused with the smell of years' worth of incense and whatever other combustibles drifting down from the apartments above.

Danny perched stiffly on the slender arm of a Victorianesque serpentine-back walnut frame velvet sofa as if to indicate the brevity of the meeting. "A lot of this stuff is old movie props from the 40s."

"Got a view?"

"A bit."

"Nice."

Each time the old building creaked Danny looked hopefully to the stairs for company but they remained alone in the lobby beneath the low inlaid ceiling. "Sounds like the wind's trying to rip the trees out."

"It could you know," Pavelko said. "Trees in LA don't have deep roots 'cause the whole ecosystem is artificial. It only exists 'cause people water their lawns. Used to anyway. Something to it right? The most artificial place on earth has shallow roots. I mean no shit, right?"

"I thought Vegas was the most artificial place."

"No, Vegas is honesty. Vegas is truth. Vegas is what you could get away with if you could get away with it all the time." Pavelko yawned at him like a cat. "So what'd you find out? I know you looked around. You were gone long enough."

Danny wondered if Cruz had noticed too. "How did you know where I live?"

"I looked you up. It's easy."

"Yeah? Well I looked you up too. You didn't tell me you were divorced."

Pavelko's fingers tugged on the lamp fringe. "What did you just say?"

"Last year your trust fund baby of a wife Linda divorced you yet you're still talking as if your family's together. You're not being honest with me."

"Honest? How long have we been dating?"

"Forthcoming, or whatever you want to call it."

"We're not talking about me. Me and my family aren't any of your business, Danny. Your business is the business I gave you—what did you and Mike talk about? Did you record it? Where's the frigging thumb drive?"

Danny tossed it to him. Pavelko missed the catch and the inch-long plastic drive bounced off the cushion beside him and clicked onto the tile floor.

"Is that everything?" Pavelko said.

"Nope. Mike said he knows that you think he's the arsonist. And he seems to think *you* are."

"And what do you think about that?"

"I think the two lead investigators on the task force have it in for one another. This isn't a fusion center, it's a fission meltdown."

"That's very clever Danny."

"I'm not cut out for spy games, especially when I can't tell whose side I'm on."

"Ah, so we're back to this? You're not a spy you're a businessman. It's quid pro quo. Did you or did you not learn anything of value?" Pavelko gave each word its own weighty independence, like separate blows to a skull from a hammer.

"I looked in the workshop in his garage."

"The door's locked. How'd you get in?"

"Does it matter?"

"Yes and no. Anything interesting in it?"

Danny shook his head.

"Is that a yes or a no?"

Pavelko had to be recording them. "It's a no. Just tools and welding equipment. He's an inventor. But he's got maps of the fires."

"Which fires?"

"Mark—"

"Which fires Danny? The man's an arson investigator. He's worked more fires than you've banged chicks."

"That's very clever."

"Which fires?"

"The fires set by the Angeles Arsonist. Felix the Helix."

Pavelko stared at him, then snickered when he realized what he meant. He snapped his fingers on the fringe and the lamp wobbled on the floor.

"You don't look surprised," Danny said.

"'Cause I'm not. And you shouldn't be either. I told you about him."

"You sure did. You told me all kinds of things about him. Nothing truthful about yourself however."

"My problems are my problems!" Pavelko's shout reverberated around the lobby. His face twisted with anger, made even uglier by the bruise on his forehead. He blinked and checked himself and his face relaxed and he said in a voice an octave and twenty decibels lower, "Nobody's got a vendetta against him, Danny."

"You could have fooled me. And he called me your secretary which kind of pissed me off."

"Don't let it get you down. You don't have the tits for that position anyway." Pavelko bent forward, scooped up the thumb drive and almost lost his balance getting to his feet. "Well Danny, fortunately you aren't the only iron in the fire. Have a nice night."

"You too. Drive carefully."

"I will."

"I thought Trace was driving."

"Sure."

He listened to Pavelko's heavy steps recede outside into the roaring night after struggling with the bolted door. He bent forward on the couch and put his face in his hands, released all the pent-up air in his lungs, then went upstairs.

He collected his pencil from under the bed, turned on the police scanner and fell into bed with his sketchpad and Gina on his mind. Even DMV Michelle would be a welcome miracle right now. Carrie Voelker was like attempting a moon shot with feathers and wax. Music from outside somewhere drifted through the French windows, what little melody there was warped by female police dispatchers' voices on his scanner and the hot wind carrying tales of an arsonist's empty rage.

He returned to his drawing of their house in Calendula. The second-floor bedroom windows didn't have screens so the kids would crawl out on the roof and watch the fireworks on the 4th of July. On a clear day they could see the ocean of a world young enough to still seem infinite. They hadn't seen the great *until*… looming in the darkening swirl of the future.

So Paul Kasho would die as Neil Weber and the others had died—as a footnote of fate, an arbitrary bit of horribleness almost immediately overrun by the next, and the next, until it was forgotten. There were always more victims.

CHAPTER 14

Danny's phone alerted him that Malibu Canyon was closed in both directions due to firefighting activity, so he wound his way up and down the consequently busier Topanga Canyon to PCH, along with everyone else in the state it seemed. He read his feeds as he drove past new billboards leering out from the hillsides—*Stop the drop! Use only what you need!*—while listening to Jimmy Cliff, which kept him from getting too frustrated at the traffic and too pissed at the long scratch running down the driver's side of his car.

Someone had keyed his car overnight and he deeply, passionately wanted that individual to grow at least one watermelon-sized tumor in their testicles and die alone under a freeway overpass covered in their own excretions as plague-infested rats chewed on their engorged beach balls. Seemed the devil winds brought out the arsonists *and* the assholes and right now he didn't know which one was worse.

Lucy emailed that the Justine London show, a current affairs program on cable TV wanted him to be tonight's guest for their Burning Question segment. A live video chat he could do from his computer. 7 PM Pacific. Delighted butterflies migrated up his belly. He confirmed back and blogged the update and tried not to wish that his father could have seen what he'd grown up to accomplish. He was a professional. A craftsman. A personality distinct from all the dysfunction that had formed it. He was on TV for Christ's sake. He was bona fide.

With the speed only social media could achieve Pepperdine students had organized a vigil this morning on the university's front lawn for the so-called Pepperdine Five—Katie Martyn, Lisa Higgins, Sondra Jaymes, Mario Sotillos, and Neil Weber. National news had picked up on it and now even the governor was attending, an announcement immediately matched by LA's mayor. Derek Cavanaugh was a coincidental tragedy.

With his fingers crossed—and the $50 bill ready in case—Danny handed over his media pass and CODA ID at the guardhouse by the tennis courts. The smell of smoke was strong while his window was down. The barrier arm lifted and the security guard waved him through, directing him to the public parking lot but expressing doubt he'd find a spot. Danny agreed, and instead drove straight up the hill past several black Suburbans for the dignitaries and parked illegally beneath the stained glass wall of barrel-roofed Stauffer Chapel. He nosed right up to the back of Ursula Ruda's red Nissan Versa electric with its Crime Time bumper sticker and green alien head antenna ball, arranged the recharging cable over the parking permit and got out, glaring anew at the long skinny gouge scraped out of the side of his Accord. Watermelon-sized testicular wishes. He wanted the bastard to be able to sit on his hideously swollen scrotum like a fucking beanbag chair.

Dirty gray smoke smudged the stark blue sky behind the Phillips Theme Tower, a slender 125-foot stucco obelisk with a cross elevated within it, erected obstinately in the park as if the school was permanently flipping Malibu the bird after its residents refused for the cross to be backlit nightly per its original 1973 design. Students in school blue and orange were already gathered on the manicured 30-acre front lawn overlooking the ocean—the cost of both the county- and state-imposed penalties for watering it had been absorbed by rising tuition fees—where just yesterday attacking Firehawk helicopters had set down to take on water from its two ponds. The American flag up at the president's house was at half-mast.

Danny took several pictures, a couple panoramas and a video, then started down the grassy slope and waded into the crowd.

According to its website the private Christian university had about 7000 students and all around him they were banded together in sympathy and loss with white remembrance ribbons pinned to their shirts. Many wore disposable masks against the fouled air. A group was singing a hymn but it could barely be heard over the flock of news helicopters hovering overhead—five choppers and two drones by his count. He stopped to get student reactions not quite at random—body language told him whether someone would want to talk, or be coherent doing so. The smoke plume, one young man with a mask resting on his forehead told him, was like the murderer sticking around to mock the mourners. You could point to it and say there it is—*that* killed them. Yet *it* was still here and their friends were gone.

To get a better view over the sea of heads Danny hopped up onto one of the large rocks behind a chubby blond girl who was sitting cross-legged on it, clutching wads of tissues and stammering to sympathetic friends gathered round her Birkenstocks. He slipped and grabbed her heaving shoulder for balance, earning dirty looks from her friends while she gaped at him, her eyeliner smeared down her cheeks like Alice Cooper's stage makeup, her pug nose issuing rivers of mucous, slack mouth strung like a harp with strings of saliva, bulging bloodshot eyes leaking saline rivulets of needy tears.

One of her male friends glared at the chalk body outline on his CODA hat. "Show some respect, jerk."

"Sorry," Danny offered, straightening his legs. Perched atop the rock he could see students were leaving flowers at a makeshift memorial and signing a large message board to the five cave victims, each symbolized by a white plastic cross three feet tall. Beneath each cross was an 18"x24" framed photograph of the student and their field of study, each of them ebullient with the sheer force of the life they wouldn't get to live:

Lisa Marie Higgins, 19, Economics—straight blond hair, crisp features, blue eyes that betrayed just a hint of mischief as if she would have found the fun in sneaking away to the cave. Her family had flown in from Denver to reclaim her body. Danny didn't know if they were here today but he doubted they'd want their own grief mirrored and amplified a thousand times over by complete strangers.

Sondra Catherine Jaymes, 21, Education—blond curly hair and brown eyes, a beautiful, classic-looking California girl with three brothers from an affluent family from La Cañada by Pasadena.

Katie Anne Martyn, 21, Psychology—Shirley Temple ringlets, glasses, a big smile that showed her gums. She was from Calabasas. The designated driver Thursday night, purposeful in her partying mission, a responsible, sober facilitator of good times.

Mario Alex Sotillos, 22, Business—swarthy and handsome, he hailed from Costa Mesa, sixty miles away in Orange County, and judging from the broad budding salesman's smile that dimpled his cheeks in his picture he looked up to being the life of any party anywhere.

Neil David Weber, 22, Business—his long neck alluded to a stature impossible to ascertain in the burned remains by the cave. The lone escapee in borrowed Uggs his feet wouldn't have fit into, but anything was better than bare feet when you were running for your life through a wall of fire. Had he panicked, tugged the boots from Lisa's feet and tried to save himself? Or did he have a larger plan of rescue in mind? Unrealistic salvation for he and his friends trapped in the cave if only he could make it?

Danny spied Carrie Voelker, resplendent within a group of reporters hovering around Governor Olsen and Deputy District Attorney Amy Childress. Ursula Ruda was there too, unmistakable if characteristically hard to spot in her safari vest. She had a folding tripod stand set up for her fancy camera. Amy Childress was an attractive woman of mixed black and Hispanic heritage, wearing a navy pant suit with a double-looped pearl necklace. Matching earrings peeked out from a cuddle of straightened brown hair. She portrayed herself as a tough-on-crime prosecutor—not an usual tactic for a budding district attorney—but had enough curb appeal to male voters who weren't looking to usher in a hen-pecking Mother Superior. In marked contrast was Governor Olsen, gaunt as an undertaker, with a small mouth, pronounced hawk nose, and aggressive snow-white eyebrows. The general election was in November and Olsen was stumping for Childress against her boss, longtime District Attorney Lyle Cunningham, who for his part was already accusing Childress's head-start campaign of financial impropriety.

Somebody elbowed Danny hard in the side and he toppled off the rock into the crying girl who sprawled onto the grass with a startled yelp that was cut off when he landed on top of her, knocking the sandals off her feet and the wind from her diaphragm. Angry hands pulled at him, grabbing at his camera as if trying to strip a football from a receiver. Danny kept his head down and crawled out of the scrum. The woman's enraged male friends loomed over him, feral as a pack of wild preppy dogs.

A tall guy who looked like a professional beach volleyball player planted a hand in Danny's chest. "Get the hell out of here before I kick your ass."

Danny murmured another apology to the sobbing girl and slipped away through the crowd, gingerly probing the sore spot by his kidney and thinking so much for Christian charity.

From a podium sporting the radiant school crest and a colorful crown of microphones set up between portable speakers the Reverend Randall Clarke, sweating through a somber dark suit, called the assembled to prayer. The Reverend was a rotund man gifted with a mellifluous voice and virtuous jowls and was often called upon to MC public memorials around town. LA County Sheriff Brandon Blauer stood nearby with a solemn entourage of bereaved relatives and fire and law enforcement officials. Handsome Mayor Alberto Reyes wore his shirt sleeves rolled up as if he'd come straight from the front lines of the battle to be here. He was talking animatedly with a queue of students as if they were clutching physical ballots instead of wads of tissues and commemorative speeches about their dead friends.

Danny wriggled over to Ursula Ruda and gave her a nudge. "Want me to lift you up on my shoulders so you can see?"

Her Tilley hat hung on her back with its strap across her neck. There was a delicate chain there too beneath her t shirt. At some point before the awards gala she'd told him she used to date a war correspondent and ended up incorporating many of his tips and tools, including investing in an expensive 21-megapixel digital camera with 70mm telephoto zoom lens. There was no arguing the quality of her shots but it was total overkill considering their material was destined for viewing on the low-res web. Danny figured that's probably when she started wearing the safari vest too.

"Does Dime Time pay double for open wounds?" He caught Carrie Voelker's eye and winked at her. Wondered if he'd been on her mind again this morning.

Ursula cradled her camera with both hands and glared at him through her red tinted clip-on lenses. "Is there a reason you're talking to me?"

"Why are you sneaking into hospitals to take pictures of car crash victims? You into nearly-necrophilia now?"

"What does your sewing circle say?"

"They say you got busted sneaking into a hospital to take pictures of a car crash victim."

"I don't sneak, I follow leads. Try it sometime."

"Oh *leads*—is *that* what you keep in all those pockets."

Reporters on either side shushed them. Moon-faced Carlos Esquivel offered a scrunched-up expression of his sternest reproach which Danny swatted away like a bothersome fly.

"You must be pleased with yourself," Ursula muttered.

"Daily. You not into the self-love?"

"I'm not into your blog even though it's the trendy thing right now."

"Majority rules, majority schools. Jump on the bandwagon baby, you might learn something."

"It won't take long for everyone to realize you're just an egotistical shithead. The only thing you care about is notoriety."

"Not true, I've been notorious for years. I'm used to it." Which was true, from a certain perspective.

Ursula said, "I know who your source is and I wouldn't be putting all your eggs in that basket if I were you."

"Where should I put them? In your vest pockets?"

Reporters shushed them again. This time Carlos was joined by Eric Garvey and two or three others so Danny clammed up for a few minutes.

Reverend Randall Clarke's devotion turned to sermon—themes of forgiveness, compassion, acceptance in the confused face of God's Inscrutable Will—the same empty explanation Danny had received as a child to replace the father who wasn't there anymore. There was a break in the wind long enough for the Reverend's words to become birds released into the wild to the simulated shutter snaps of digital cameras in lieu of wings.

The Reverend guided the first student to the podium, a young woman dabbing her eyes. The white ribbon on her little black mourning dress stood out like a nova glimpsed in deep space. In a shaky voice she introduced herself as Stacy Zybert, roommate of cave victim Sondra Jaymes. She'd known Sondra for years. They shared everything and did everything together, and the permanence of her best friend's absence was only just now—here, today, in front of everybody—beginning to sink in. She broke down quickly, sobbing "I love you Sondra, I miss you." The crowd cheered after a moment's pause while people put their phones away to clap.

Friends and fellow students followed, some in formal suits or dresses, others in collegiate clothes for the sense of community. Amy Childress gave each of them a protracted photogenic hug. Danny made a note to use the least favorable shot he took of her.

As Mayor Reyes began a few remarks he leaned over to Ursula and said, "So what were you going to do, congratulate Derek Cavanaugh on his driving skill?"

Ursula parted her lips to show her perfectly straight, perfectly white teeth which spoke not just to genetics and good dental hygiene but to some bizarre coffeeless lifestyle. "You don't know who he is, do you?"

Danny felt suddenly weightless, as if he'd flown through an air pocket.

"Maybe you should put some facts in *your* pockets," Ursula suggested, and repositioned her tripod a few feet away.

The electric bells within the tower began to chime and all the friends and relatives left the stage with the Reverend to make way so the politicians and officials could hold a press conference, which Danny thought displayed a degree of callousness only an election year could inspire. He wanted to leave to get on the Cavanaugh connection but everyone else was staying so he did too. If he'd missed something already he wasn't going to risk starting an avalanche of average reporting by missing anything else.

An LA County Fire Department public information officer began by listing the Backbone Fire stats on day three: 6500 acres burned. 15 structures lost. 2500 firefighters committed. 30% containment. While diminishing winds was good news for firefighters they hadn't yet turned the corner on the blaze. The date and time of the memorial for the two fallen firefighters had not yet been set but he would share that information as soon as he had it.

During Governor Olsen's turn at the podium he announced that he had declared Malibu a disaster area to free up access to emergency funding, while acknowledging that all the money in the world couldn't return the seven lives that had been lost. He offered his condolences to the families of the dead students and firefighters and urged the perpetrator to turn himself in.

"Do one decent thing with your life," Olsen said, holding a long forefinger aloft toward a smoke-shrouded heaven, *"stop."*

Amy Childress followed with a shortened version of her stump speech highlighting her tough-on-crime stance and high rate of felony prosecutions as the Assistant Head Deputy of the DA's Major Crimes Division. In addition to the governor's endorsement—for which she was "extremely humbled"—she noted that she had already received key endorsements from city council members, victims' rights advocates, various city attorneys, state senators and police chiefs.

"In the midst of a recession," Childress expounded, "donors—many of them struggling middle class citizens—have reached into their pockets and donated to my campaign because they share my belief that I am the most ardent chief prosecutor the people of Los Angeles could have, and the most vocal proponent of victims' rights the people of Los Angeles deserve."

Her aides applauded enthusiastically.

"Let there be no mistake—this massive wildfire was calculated, premeditated *murder*. This heinous crime has devastated a college campus, horrified a city, and galvanized an entire country. And I promise you here today—as your new district attorney there will be swift justice for the perpetrator, there will be swift justice for his victims, and there will be swift justice for the people of Los Angeles."

Her aides applauded again.

"Now I'll take some questions."

Ursula Ruda's hand shot up like a submarine-launched missile. "What's your response to the city Ethics Commission auditing your campaign for possible ethics violations of campaign funding?"

"Not only are audits mandatory, but it's a good sign for us that we're already being audited," Childress replied smoothly, obviously expecting the question. "It means we're raising a lot of money."

Her aides clapped. Danny grimaced—Ursula was playing softball.

A reporter from a local AM all-news radio station asked, "Can you respond to claims you hired an online marketing firm that paid people to view your YouTube campaign video?"

Childress said, "I wouldn't waste everyone's time responding to something so ridiculous. So childish, really."

Carrie Voelker asked, "Can you comment on the district attorney's allegations that your campaign is receiving illegal in-kind donations, including the office space for your election headquarters?"

That's more like it, Danny thought.

"I won't comment on every spurious allegation made by Lyle Cunningham, we'd be here all day and the people of Los Angeles don't pay me for that," Amy Childress smiled. "But I am serving notice—the cognac and cigars and private business clubs way of doing business downtown is on its way out, and Lyle Cunningham along with it."

As her aides started to applaud again Danny bullied a question over wee Carlos Esquivel. "After fourteen months and at least seventeen fires, given the scant physical evidence left at the scenes what besides the upcoming election makes you confident enough to promise swift justice now?"

Carlos looked around for other reporters to validate Danny's infraction but no one acknowledged the effrontery.

Amy Childress arched a pencil-thin eyebrow at Danny, a fine-tipped rebuke honed by years in the courtroom, as if she'd watched tape of her trial performances like athletes reviewed their games. "I must say I don't care either for your tone or for your categorizing the evidence we've collected as *scant.* I'm as confident as I am because we have the finest law enforcement and fire departments in the country investigating this heinous crime. We have a multi-agency task force—which *I* helped win budgetary approval for—working tirelessly alongside local, state, and federal resources. They're processing a staggering amount of information from witnesses, technical experts, forensic experts. We've put together a profile of the suspect, we know how, when and where he's starting the fires, we know what kind of boots he wears—"

Amy Childress stopped mid-sentence as if her playback had been suddenly paused, then smiled automatically and fumbled for a pick-up in a silence punctuated by cameras that still used the old-fashioned clicking sound and the silent vacuum of video recorders of various designs.

"I have the utmost confidence in our investigators, and the people of Los Angeles can have the utmost confidence in Amy Childress. Thank you!"

The politicians hastily retreated offstage. Danny blogged *Childress: task force has identified Backbone arsonist's boots.* Hesitated a second and added *Thorogood size 12* to keep Red Flag on point. It was out there now. Those boots were as good as gone.

Ursula deftly compiled her gear, looking unbothered and unhurried. She doesn't have the boots, he realized. He had missed something about Derek Cavanaugh, but she doesn't have the boots. She doesn't know what Amy Childress just gave up.

Carlos Esquivel popped up in front of him with his hands on his hips, spreading his crisp suit jacket open across his narrow chest. The high fused collar of his dress shirt was held tightly in place by a gold tie pin. "Screw you Kasho—don't do that again. Learn your place—TV comes first, *then* radio—FM *before* AM—*then* whatever the hell *you* are, you imposter."

Danny spotted the friends of the dead students on the service road between the ponds. "Imposter? Why don't you stand up and say that, Carlos? Oh, you *are* standing."

"You want to do it like that, huh? You're an asshole Kasho. Stay out of my way."

"I'd have to crawl to be in your way, chico."

"I won't forget this, tough guy."

"Don't forget your step-stool either, munchkin." Danny walked quickly in long strides to intercept the friends and said to an ashen-faced young man with a Marine Corps-style haircut and a dark suit who'd introduced himself at the vigil as John Renshaw glared at the politicians, "I'm sorry your vigil's been hijacked."

"This isn't what we had in mind." In his speech John said he and Neil Weber had known each other since childhood, growing up together in monied Montecito by Santa Barbara. They'd been like brothers, inseparable until now.

"My name's Danny Kasho. I'm a reporter for CODA.com."

"I know that site," Stacy Zybert sniffed.

"Who else knew Neil and the others were up at the cave?" he asked.

"Lots of people." John's shoulders sagged. "Everyone knew. We've all been up there before. That could've been any of us. *I* was supposed to go, you know that? I changed my mind at the last minute." He choked up. "Maybe I'd've been able to—I don't know. *Do* something."

"Does Derek Cavanaugh know what happened?" Danny asked.

"I don't know. But it sure won't be me telling him his girlfriend's dead."

"Who's that?"

"Sondra." Stacy's eyes welled up. "They'd been seeing each other all summer. I was the last person she texted. The police told me that. They have her *phone records.*" She made the investigation of death sound more intrusive than the death itself.

Other reporters were converging on them but Reverend Clarke got there first and grasped Stacy round her shoulders with his large hands. A signet ring glittered in the sunlight. "That there is enough."

"I swear to Almighty God," John Renshaw said, "there is no one here at this school capable of doing that to somebody. I told the police the same thing. I wish I knew who it was. I wish I knew why." He suddenly burst into shuddering tears.

"That there will *do!*" the Reverend bellowed, shielding the stricken students as other reporters pushed questions, microphones and cameras at them. "You may direct your questions to *me*. I'm Reverend Randall with two L's Clarke with an e."

Danny stopped recording as the Reverend Randall with two L's called for decency and reinforcements. Derek Cavanaugh was Sondra Jaymes's boyfriend—that's what Ursula had found out. That's why she was at the hospital. She probably didn't know he was in ICU—and already guarded by the cops.

"Where are you off to?" With ruby lips that drew attention to her mouth, canary yellow sleeveless split neck top and form-fitting white pants that drew attention to everything else, Carrie Voelker was a pastiche of different beauties.

"Doing an interview tonight," Danny managed. "Got to get my notes together."

"Who with?"

"Justine London."

Carrie's blue eyes widened in a way that made him feel like the momentary center of the entire fucking universe. He was pleased that he'd upped the thinking-about-Danny factor.

"Congratulations," she smiled.

And then they were hugging. She smelled like exotic flowers and secret oils and whispered pleasures under a Far Eastern sunset and released him too quickly for his liking, as if she could sense suction cups growing out of his arms.

"I'm impressed but *not* surprised," she gushed with an arch of her eyebrow. "When will *I* get to interview you?"

"Any time you want," he said to her mouth. "Any…time."

"Well I was going to see if you wanted to grab a quick bite right now, but you've gotta go—"

"I've got time," he said quickly.

"You have to get ready for your interview. This is the big time Danny—this is *cable*."

"I absolutely have time for a quickie."

"Ha. Okay. But it's on you if you biff your lines tonight. You know Drake's by the beach?"

"I do." He didn't, but Google would.

"Half an hour?"

"Perfect."

Without being too lecherous he watched her walk back toward her crew, then he started up the hill to his car, pausing by one of the palm trees to take pictures of the vigil as formality ceded to sad fellowship on the great green lawn.

CHAPTER 15

"It's so sad, isn't it?"

Danny watched with undisguised envy as a baby shrimp disappeared between Carrie's lips. She had a tiny mole on the side of her chin that bobbed up and down like a lure when she chewed or talked.

"Well? Isn't it?"

"It is." He chased a shrimp with some very cold Corona and thought this setting and this company were unsung perks of his job, worth any amount of strangers' blood and gore and infinite sadness.

They sat side by side in bar chairs facing the ocean at one of the salt-worn wooden ledges for two built onto the railing of Drake's deck. Their phones provided a quietly obnoxious soundtrack as they buzzed intermittently with incoming messages—his one long dash, hers two short dots. The sea breeze was constant but mild, offering no hint of the ferocious wind usurping firefighters in the canyon nearby. It was an immaculate afternoon, no part of it more lovely than the woman beside him, as if they were a couple instead of a couple of friends. As if she wasn't just the most curvaceous tip of the competition nipping at his heels.

Carrie said, "All those kids crying, it was so sad right? Everywhere I looked. Most of them couldn't talk or didn't want to. Did you get much?"

"Enough to illustrate the sentiment."

"Speaking of illustrating you should do a drawing of Amy Childress. What was up with her giving a stump speech in front of the pictures of the dead students? She's not big on tact is she?"

"I think I'm going to use the worst shot I took of her."

"You already made her look pretty bad so you're on the scoreboard."

"I just asked a simple question. She's the one who barfed all over herself."

"Right? Lyle Cunningham should use that—if you don't want a DA who barfs all over herself, re-elect me."

Carrie was an easy date because not only was she extensively beautiful but she kept the conversation rolling along as smoothly as if it were on ball bearings. Danny hoped her boyfriend, assuming she had one, wasn't some cheesy orange-faced anchorman or a pro beach volleyball player. She didn't wear a ring on that finger but she had a jade one on her left middle finger and an expensive-looking glittery silver one on the ring finger of her right hand—. She was drinking iced tea—her work day wasn't over yet either, she was going on TV later too. A seagull the size of a condor eyed them from the end of the ledge.

"How do you know Ursula Ruda?" Carrie asked. "Is she a night owl like you?"

The mention of the name took Danny by surprise. "We see each around town, that's all."

"Like we do?"

"Uh, no, not like that."

Carrie smiled coyly, her mouth working around a shrimp.

"Seriously," he said, "not like that. Either. What are we even talking about?"

"What are *you* talking about Danny?" she laughed.

He felt himself blush hotly and was even more annoyed at Ursula for her eggs and baskets and uninvited presence here at Drake's.

"I get it," Carrie said as she checked the newest messages on her phone's lockscreen.

"No you don't. It's not like that at all. I mean at *all.* It's about the Press Club awards in June. We were up against each other—" Danny paused, thinking he couldn't have chosen more appropriate words—"and I won for Red Flag. She's been pissed at me ever since."

"Really? Over that?"

"Yes."

"She doesn't seem the type to hold a grudge."

"Well she can, believe me. I bet the Rudas are notorious grudge-holders in whatever superstition-shrouded former Soviet bloc village they come from. How do you know her?"

"She contributes to our news sometimes. She's really nice, I like her."

Danny never would have guessed Ursula to be closet mainstream beneath her safari punk exterior. "I'm glad she's getting work."

Carrie laughed. "No love lost between you two right?"

He got the sudden sickening feeling Carrie and Ursula had talked about him, in some hideous level of quiet womanly emasculating detail. Ursula may have managed to seal Carrie Voelker's gate before he'd even begun to pry it open.

"Check this out." She wiped her hands with a paper napkin and thumbed her phone. "A viewer sent it in. He lives next door to the house on PCH that car almost crashed into. You hear about that? The owners found this in their tennis court. We're the only ones who have it."

She turned her phone and showed him a close-up picture of a California license plate bent within a blue and orange Pepperdine Waves frame laying on a synthetic tennis court.

"The viewer obviously has a crush on you," he said, staring at the pale dirt coating the plate like something unearthed from an archaeological dig.

"Probably, but it wasn't sent to me." She locked her phone and put it down. "Let me ask you something, before today did you hear anything about them finding boot prints up at the cave?"

So *this* is what she wanted, he thought. Being pumped for information took the romance out of things—even illusionary romance—but when it was Carrie Voelker doing the pumping you couldn't feel too turned-out about it. "I heard they might have been made by the suspect. Maybe."

"That's what I heard too! So why would Amy Childress tell that to everyone? It reminds me of somebody else who did that in the 70s, some serial murder case."

Danny relished Carrie's latent morbid streak. "It was 1985, the summer of the Night Stalker. Dianne Feinstein was the mayor of San Francisco at the time—this was before she was a senator—and at a press conference she gave away the kind of shoes Richard Ramirez was wearing at the crime scenes. The detectives had been holding that back. Ramirez threw the shoes off the Golden Gate bridge and came back to LA where he raped a woman and almost killed her fiancé. A week later he was recognized in

East LA and a mob of people there administered some street justice to him before the cops saved him. He died of natural causes in 2013 after being on death row for over twenty years, outliving some of the people who survived his attacks."

Carrie watched him with bright blue eyes. "You know a lot about that kind of stuff don't you." Another baby shrimp vanished between her succulent lips.

"It runs in the family."

"On which side?"

"My dad's, without a doubt. But maybe Amy Childress and the task force will get lucky and our Bug isn't following the news."

"Our *Bug?* Is that a new nickname I should be using instead of Angeles Arsonist? It's so hard to keep up!"

"Never change the brand. Alliteration works."

"Anyway I hear his type is obsessive. He's watching."

"He's probably watching you."

"Right? I can never have too many weirdoes in my life."

Like orange-faced anchormen or beach volleyball players, Danny thought. "So what made you want to become a reporter?"

"I made me. I wanted to be a journalist ever since I was a little girl. I'd interview my friends and make my little brother pretend he was the cameraman. I was so bossy."

Off the top of his head he couldn't think of a single time he and his sister had played together voluntarily, only when it was family night—back when they were a real family. He plucked a memory of one from the summer of '93—among the last family nights they had. Vanessa and Paul had brought an old board game down from the closet shelf and forced the kids to play while they drank and laughed about the tourists mispronouncing the city name. Danny remembered his father gesticulating at the Eton blue formica kitchen table with a juice glass full of cherry-colored Manhattans Vanessa had mixed up in a pitcher and declaring that Ca*len*dula, as some of the tourists were calling their city by the bay, sounded like a wood nymph bounding fairily through the forest. Calen*du*la sounded like a *city*. Sixteen year-old Victor thought *fairily* was hilarious and immediately put it into heavy rotation in his teenaged vocabulary of insults and teases, using it to describe everything and everyone, most especially his little brother.

Danny said, "Well you landed a good gig, so good job."

"Thank you. I worked hard to get it, like you did with CODA."

The name sounded like candy when she said it. His name did too.

"How long have you been writing Red Flag? Excuse me, I'm sorry—the award-winning Red Flag?"

"One year. To the weekend, actually—the Dillon Fire where I got onto the story was set on Labor Day weekend."

"So creepy. He's out there right now with his toady little mind thinking about burning things."

"Yes he is."

"And he finally screwed up and left footprints by the cave?" Carrie shook her head and her blond hair danced interpretive flourishes around her face. "Just incredible. You said they're Thorogoods?"

"I only did after Childress dumped them. I'd promised the investigators I wouldn't post anything about them."

"But you knew already?"

"Yeah, I knew about that and the 911 call." Danny was never comfortable with pride and felt like he was supposed to shovel dirt over the ember of it flickering in his chest.

"I heard the call was totally creepy."

"It was."

"You heard it?"

"I did. It was creepy. He was worked up. He has a strange high-pitched voice but he may have been trying to disguise it."

"Incredible, to hear his voice like that. What are Thorogoods?"

A question she no doubt had the answer for already; she was checking his answer against an internal Wikilist summary of the boots. He didn't mind being referenced like an expert—by now he *was* an expert. "They're specialized wildland firefighting boots. The guy's a gear junkie. According to my sources they're size 12."

"Are your sources Mark Pavelko?"

Danny bristled, annoyed at the echo of eggs and baskets. "Among others. Anyway the prints are a point of contention among the investigators. There's a camp that thinks they're genuine and a camp that thinks they're not."

"What does Mike Cruz think?"

Carrie was running all the bases. "I haven't gotten a chance to ask him about them yet. I tried to when I was at his house last night for a charity fundraiser slash luau drinkfest."

"Luau drinkfest! Where was my invitation? Did you wear a grass skirt?"

"No, but he did."

"Come on."

"And coconut boobs."

Carrie howled with laughter and dabbed at her lips with a napkin. "Wow. You are the man, Danny. You are the man. Whenever I try and talk to him he just blows me off."

"I bet that doesn't happen often."

"Never!" she scoffed.

He could easily imagine her in a very, very short grass skirt and coconut shell bra and knew if he got her number out of this he'd mention that to her when he inevitably drunk texted her. *Dexting*, that was the new euphemism of the day.

"So let me ask *you* something," he said. "You hear anything about a deal for Charlize Patron?"

"Not yet. Why, did you?"

"Nope. Just making sure."

"I mean, she's totally going to cut one."

"Absolutely. But I just hadn't heard."

"Well if I hear something I'll let you know. And vice versa. Deal?"

"Deal."

Carrie tucked her phone inside her big pearl-colored faux-leather tote, took out a smaller clutch and slid off her chair. "I'm going to the little girls' room. Be right back."

A male server held the door for her and watched after her longingly as she went inside. Danny caught his eye and nodded as if to say *Yeah buddy, she's with me.* If only for a little while. The condor-gull took a tentative step toward her empty setting, eyeing the shrimp cocktail even though it was just amputated tails sticking out of the melting ice.

Danny sipped his beer and scrolled through his messages. Michelle from the Holiest of Holies was asking if they were on for tonight. It took him a second to remember that she'd invited him for drinks—he didn't recall if he'd agreed to or not. He had a feeling he did. He didn't reply just yet. There were options and then there were options when you were out of options.

He scanned the comments section of Red Flag but still nothing stood out to him. No alarms, no surprises, just lots of commercially-viable people interacting with each other and—hopefully—some of the relevant or at least curiosity-arousing ads tucked along the sides. He was beginning to doubt Pavelko's plan of drawing the arsonist out through Red Flag was working, but according to CODA's site stats it was working out for him just fine.

He posted a link to video footage on another news site of the burned-over remains of the fatal LACoFD fire engine crash from yesterday. After having spent so many hours with firefighters—professionals and dedicated volunteers like Carl Tillson alike out in the heat and the dirt—it was impossible for him not to dwell on the unimaginable terror those two men must have felt in their final seconds. The worst fate was to have survived the crash and been alive when the advancing flames consumed them like a marauding army. Burning was such an acutely horrible way to die, like the testicular tumors were going to be for the eventually-homeless syphilitic piece of leper shit who keyed his car.

Victor once keyed the car of a guy growing up, a neighborhood bully who wouldn't let go of the Killer Kasho thing. Vic was drinking by then so his teenaged anger could already be measured in megatons. He was arrested that same night at the house in NoCal while Danny and Cynthia listened from behind their bedrooms doors Vanessa had ordered them to keep closed as if that prevented them from hearing anything. A cop had opened the door to Danny and Vic's bedroom. A female cop, taller than Danny was at the time. Her brown hair was tied back in a tight bun. She had cool gray eyes and was snapping gum like cherry bombs and the radio clipped to her leather duty belt was loud in the small room, as if she'd brought an argument in with her. She surveyed the boyish mess of the room, Danny's side somewhat tidier than Vic's. Maybe she had kids. Maybe boys their age. Maybe she was used to the chaos and disarray. Or maybe she just couldn't be surprised anymore; her expression never changed. She snapped her gum and wandered back to the living room to the other voices, other radios, leaving Danny's door open. He didn't close it, but sat on the edge of his bed wondering if he'd always be afraid of the police and the sound of their shoes on his floor. It wasn't Vic's first arrest and it wouldn't be his last, but at least the bully had deserved the damage to his car, even if it took Vic a year to pay reparations deducted from part-time jobs he attended instead of finishing high school.

He put his phone down and stared out at the water. Fifty yards offshore an elegant pelican rode the wave tips parallel to the beach and Danny thought about straight lines. Natural lines. Ley lines. He wondered where Derek Cavanaugh had been driving his BMW Thursday night prior to crashing it on PCH. He wondered how many BMWs had been on a dirt road ever in their whole anthropomorphic lives, from their inception in Bavaria to their compression in a car crusher in a junk yard in New Mexico or wherever.

Carrie's phone started buzzing anew in her purse. A different vibration pattern, repeated double buzzes. An incoming call. Danny wondered what her ringtone was when her phone wasn't muted. If it was one of the default melodic African percussive ones or something she went out and got herself, like a refrain from a pop song he probably wouldn't recognize.

Buzz buzz. Buzz buzz. Buzz buzz. Buzz buzz.

His beer glass left a ring on the tile as he took a thoughtful pull on it. Murderous wind in the canyons and lots of sailboats out on the water. Lucy Baskin was one of the sharpest people he knew, in or out of the business. The CODA writers were a self-motivated bunch, you had to be to survive—and get paid—and Lucy knew that a good way to provoke them was to insinuate there was news out there they didn't have but should.

Buzz buzz. Buzz buzz. Buzz buzz.

Information was a commodity. It was flirting, it was lying, it was cheating and stealing. It was hoarding when you got some. It was a race for secrets and a race to tell them and in the end it was no hard feelings. Information was a commodity and so were the people who traded in it.

Carrie's phone fell silent.

Behind the restaurant windows patrons ate and drank in profile to him at tables for two—Drake's was a good place for illicit affairs, illusionary or not. The other couples out on the deck were engaged with themselves. Nobody was looking at him.

A single long buzz signaled Carrie's caller had left a voicemail.

Danny looked at the seagull.

It winked an enormous red-rimmed eye at him.

He leaned over Carrie's purse and plucked out her phone. Three items were visible on the lockscreen, a missed call and two messages.

Liz Cooper now Voicemail & Missed Call

Liz Cooper 1m ago Also Myrna at KGO says they're running with it

Liz Cooper 5m ago SFPD source confirms MP violated restraining order and is MIA

Natural reporter curiosity would practically absolve him of swiping his thumb crosswise over the face of Carrie's phone, but on the remote chance it wasn't passcode-protected the swipe would empty the lockscreen notifications. Given how active her phone was if she returned from the bathroom to no notifications about all the messages and emails and calls that were sitting there it would surely tip her that he'd snooped her phone, or tried to.

He glanced over his shoulder as new patrons came through the door. What could he possibly say if she came out and saw him with her phone in his hand? *Sorry Carrie I spilled some beer, I was just making sure nothing got on your phone, tucked inside your purse as it was.* Maybe if he turned up his winning smile to the max that might be enough to excuse an errant finger swipe and the ensuing violation of her privacy. He tipped some beer out of his bottle onto his side of the ledge and wiped it around with a wad of napkins as he scrolled down Carrie's notifications in her lockscreen. There were other messages, disconnected snippets of text from at least five other people.

He flinched as the phone buzzed twice in his hand with a new message.

Liz Cooper now Find Kasho he'll know where he is.

Danny stared at his surname, buried like a booby trap in Carrie's phone. He put it back in her bag exactly as she had left it he hoped, leaned back in his chair and raised his beer to his lips as the door to the deck opened again and Carrie emerged. He wondered what she'd do when she saw his name in her notifications. Would she feign an excuse? Would he care? Would he tell her anything she wanted to know just because she could turn the name he'd always hated into sweet candy just by speaking it?

She touched his arm as she sat down and swept up her phone with a glance at the wadded-up napkins. "It's on every TV in there."

"What's that?"

"The boots. They're showing pictures of them."

"I bet Thorogood's going to hit their number this quarter."

He watched the muscles in her face momentarily tighten and her eyes look right through the ledge they sat at to the pounding foamy surf below like cold blue lasers. Her thumb swiped and scrolled as she backtracked through Liz Cooper's messages to put *Find Kasho he'll know where he is* in context. She looked up at him and their eyes met. He was watching her instead of looking at her and he was sure his expression gave his partial intrusion away like a banner ad towed by one of the planes that cruised lazy circles over the beaches.

She pretended to chuck the phone, the perpetual spoiler of good times, out into the sea. "I hate this thing sometimes," she pouted half-heartedly.

"Gotta get going?"

"Yeah." She snapped open her clutch, looking for a credit card. "Sorry, I wanted more time!"

She was going to try to find MP on her own first, before she asked him. Good for her. "This is on me," he said.

"Yeah? Thank you!" In a practically indistinct change of direction her fingers retasked to locating her valet stub.

"Absolutely. I hope we do it again soon. I like this place."

"Aww, me too."

They shared a quick, deeply symbolic hug over the bar chairs.

Carrie said, "Give me your number and I'll send you the picture of the plate."

Now she'd be able to Find Kasho if she needed to, if her DIY Plan A effort didn't pan out. He gave her his ten digits like each one of his fingers cupping her ass and pretended he was feeding her baby shrimp or chocolates or some numerical aphrodisiac, one succulent mouthful at a time for her tongue and teeth to work over. To taste and savor and knead. Like he was offering himself to her right then and there on Drake's deck, with his lack of gym tone and his tighty whities and dress socks and CODA hat.

"What time's your interview?" Carrie asked as she heaved her tote up onto her shoulder.

"Seven."

"Good luck! Be brilliant!" She squeezed his arm and headed for the door, held open by another attentive waiter.

Danny smiled after her, his nostrils flaring at the lingering scent of her perfume on the salty wind. He could still feel her in his arms as if he'd made a cast of her body.

Be brilliant.

He tried not to empower the guilty feeling that he'd seen her naked without her permission. It's not like he was a pervert or anything, and he hadn't seen anything but his own damned name. Still, he'd invaded her privacy. He'd sniffed her virtual underwear.

And he was a better man for it.

SFPD and *MP* were letter-shaped clusters of seaweed rolling out on the water and the toothy shadow of Liz Cooper moved under the waves, the link between what was visible and the cold, dark opportunistic worlds that were not. Liz Cooper knew who he was but he wasn't going to return the favor. He didn't need to know her. Liz Coopers were a type. They comprised a greater machine speedily sucking up and spitting out the same names and numbers and anecdotes. He wasn't worse than any of them and he was better than a lot.

He sympathized with Mark Pavelko because he knew all too well what it was like to have your life unraveled in public, upended like soiled clothes so all of your secrets and shames spilled out like spare change in front of judgmental strangers. Presumably Mark had more answers for his behavior than they ever had about Paul Kasho's, but Red Flag needed material. It was nothing personal.

He finished his beer and posted an update to Red Flag.

Forest Service Special Agent Mark Pavelko from Angeles Arsonist task force sought for alleged restraining order violation in San Francisco.

CHAPTER 16

Danny wiped a drop of sweat off his desk with his thumb and raised his eyes from his dirty leather wingtips on the floor up past the quartet of light bulbs beneath the fan to the place he usually went to find his thoughts, bumping against the textured plaster ceiling like untethered balloons. An artificial twilight tinted the walls a pretty shade of diluted blood as the smoke from the Backbone Fire drifted between the city and the setting sun.

Linda Fisher's tawdry restraining order violation that had San Francisco's Gold Coast tittering and Twittering happened last Tuesday—Mark Pavelko's birthday, when he'd supposedly been receiving handmade cards from his daughters Emma and Addison. Apparently Mark had showed up unannounced and drunk at his ex-wife's Pacific Heights home—not unlike his sudden appearance downstairs last night. He and Linda argued and he allegedly threatened her. A fight ensued between Mark and a male guest at the house and the scene spilled into the street. Neighbors recognized the male guest as a prominent aide to San Francisco's mayor named Ellis Rivera. Rivera's wife Susan was caught in the media glare like a rabbit in fast headlights. By Friday the scandal was all over the city and Mark had fled south to Malibu and the Backbone Fire. His involvement in the Angeles Arsonist task force wasn't even mentioned. He was a bit player in his own life. Danny wondered if he'd been reduced to acting out his frustration.

He'd called the Forest Service's Pacific Southwest Region headquarters in Vallejo but got no response, just different so-called supervisors' voicemails in between a lot of hold time on the phone listening to a woman's voice repeat fire safety and water conservation tips, as if there was any water left to conserve.

He wondered how soon Carrie would hit him up on how to reach Pavelko if Mark didn't respond to her—surely someone she knew had his cell number by now. He imagined Carrie calculating her approach right now. At least it practically guaranteed seeing her again soon. Maybe he'd say dinner. Maybe he'd say drinks. Maybe he'd touch that mole on her back with his tongue. And while he was bothered by how Ursula knew about Pavelko and Derek Cavanaugh it was like obsessing over how an opposing forward had made it past your defense to score. At the end of the day that was the game. Every day, every story. You had to play it tight and close all the time.

The Pepperdine social network was beginning to suspect Claire Coogan wasn't who she said she was, but in the time she had left she still enabled Danny to look around. Individual names became lights in a flesh and blood constellation of friends going to classes together, partying together and dying together, the lights going dark as suddenly as if the window looking into the night sky over Malibu had been slammed shut. They all knew each other.

All six of them.

Three couples had gone up to that cave Thursday night—Katie Martyn, Mario Sotillos, Lisa Higgins, Neil Weber, Sondra Jaymes—and Derek Cavanaugh, whose crushed BMW and ejected license plate bore the same pale dirt as Danny's scuffed court shoes. He'd liked those shoes. He'd put a lot of miles on those shoes. He didn't know why Cavanaugh left the cave but he was alive today because he did and he wondered if Derek knew anything at all about what happened, that his girlfriend Sondra Jaymes was dead with all of their friends up at the party cave that everyone knew about, that anyone could have been at, friends like John Renshaw or Stacy Zybert.

Danny imagined Cavanaugh weaving down Corral Canyon, narrowly avoiding the headlights of the man coming up to kill them all with his homemade weapon of choice, and wondered if the arsonist knew he left a witness. A potential witness anyway, depending on how banged up the kid was. Serious wasn't critical but it was bad enough. With a tube down his throat there was no tale to tell, yet.

The boot prints and a witness, all at the same fire. He'd probably picked up the pay phone to call 911 thinking he was infallible.

Danny scrolled through his vigil pictures and selected several to upload, including an especially unflattering one of Amy Childress, crow-like by the victims' portraits like a harbinger of doom in pearls. The scores of dazed and weeping students brought to mind the aftermath of a school shooting. All those white ribbons—which became the title of his post, pulling the starting balloon he needed down from the ceiling. He wanted his update online in time to drive people to the Justine London interview tonight—and back. The reminder to watch him on TV looked like a sentence written by somebody else and excitement fluttered in his belly.

He listened back to Amy Childress's vow of swift justice and wrote that the only thing swifter would be how fast voters forgot who she was after they *didn't* elect her in November. For all the people of Los Angeles deserved, they deserved better than Amy Childress. Drew the line right there. He hoped Lucy wouldn't be pissed—CODA generally abstained from political endorsements, but they were going to make an exception this time.

He uploaded the post and proofed it online. Satisfied, he emailed the link to Lucy, then texted DMV Michelle apologizing but saying he'd call her after the interview tonight. Maybe she'd feel like celebrating with him. Maybe even hot Gina the actress would. Meantime Claire Coogan's clock was ticking. He'd have to delete her account tonight, tomorrow latest. Online social vetting didn't take long these days.

He padded out to the living room and programmed the DVR. Fire coverage was on TV with the sound muted. The wildfire at night, with the smoke a wispy veil revealing the white hot centers of flames savaging the stricken hillsides, was one of those strangely beautiful disaster moments. With Garrett's downtempo electronica coming from upstairs as he got ready to go out the video could have been an art installation in a gallery. The nocturnal chaos of consumption set to relaxing rhythmic grooves.

He refreshed his iced tea and lemonade and returned to his desk. Drew two eyes, an arrow, and the words *LOOK HERE* on a Post-it Note and stuck it above the built-in camera on his monitor. Gave a meaningful look at the inspiring sign he made after visiting JPL: Dare Mighty Things.

His phone rang right on cue.

"Oh my God Danny, are you excited?" Lucy Baskin's mellow Hawaiian cadence belied her shark toothed editorial savvy.

"I totally am Luce, thanks for the opportunity."

"Hey, thank *you.* If one of my people is hot I say get them out there. Are you ready? Know what you're going to say?"

"I'm good. But I haven't heard anything about a deal for Patron, have you?"

"Not really."

When Lucy said *Not really* she meant *Yes really.* Everyone knew that.

"Well from who?" he asked impatiently.

"Nobody yet. That's why I asked you. Okay I'm going to put you on hold and then conference in the producer on the show. Good luck! Hold on."

The line went silent. Danny minimized everything on his screen, put his headphones on and positioned his legal pad of talking points. His leg bounced anxiously under his desk as he glared at his monitor, which showed a well-lit reflection of him glaring into the camera, resenting Nick Mendoza and Charlize Patron and all their misdeeds.

For interviews and video chats he used an Audio-Technica cardioid condenser microphone mounted on a boom stand—he was an habitual tapper and learned early on that the microphones dutifully picked up the noise. A pop-filter screen was mounted on a separate stand positioned a few inches in front of the mic. The setup was a gift from Garrett, as was most of the audio/video software and advice, and Danny had gotten it down to a fine art over time, adding a moveable background with a flat muted tone behind him to hide the bedroom interior, the sound-absorbing foam tiles and two special LED lights on tripod stands which ensured his sour expression tonight was professionally rendered. Fortunately he'd rarely been interrupted on air by a passing siren and his neighbors above and below and on the other side of his bedroom wall were all as quiet as church mice.

"Danny?" Lucy said.

"I'm here."

"I've got Denise from the show on the line."

"Mr. Kasho?" Denise said.

She mispronounced it *Kay*sho instead of *Kah*sho, a common side effect of his last name. He corrected her by rote and without judgment—it was rare when someone got it right the first time. Another reason Vanessa had wasted no time reverting to her maiden name McQueen which was as classic as it was unfuck-upable.

"I'll make sure that's noted for Justine," Denise said. "I'm going to give you our account login, okay?"

Lucy signed off. "Danny, I'll call you after. Have a good show guys."

Denise knew her stuff and soon Danny was looking at her in a full-screen chat window. Her wavy blond hair was past her shoulders and had dark roots where she parted it a little off-center. She had full cheeks and a nice mouth that was pulled into a polite smile as her narrow eyes moved around, judging his appearance on her monitor, and she ended the phone call now that they were connected.

He tweaked the gain of his input—a window on his computer presented the wavelength of his voice which was warmed by professional-level software from Garrett. As technology dismantled the holy trinity of TV studio, camera, and regularly-scheduled viewing audience, having a roommate who worked in the audio/visual industry proved to be a windfall. With the emergent fifth estate of bloggers information imprinted on individual receptors now had distribution limited only by signal strength.

Denise said, "Everything looks good so please don't touch anything, okay? Have you done this before?" There was the typical long-distance signal delay on the audio but way less than on national TV.

"Yes I have," he replied.

"Okay good. You'll appear at the top of the show during the preview so just look into your camera as Justine introduces you—not your computer monitor, eye contact is key, okay? Burning Question is the second segment, approximately six minutes in. It'll follow a 60-second commercial break, okay?"

"Okay."

"Please don't touch anything and try not to move. I'll be back in about five minutes, okay?"

"Okay."

Denise's chat window went blue but the connection remained live. Danny didn't know if she could still see or hear him, her and everybody else in the New York studio, so while he waited he kept quiet and acted natural, scrolling through his email on his phone below the view of the camera.

He was thinking that while psychologically the arsonist might still be able to prosper in a professional, accountable environment with a level of scrutiny, it wouldn't be long before he'd have to go out and set the next fire. Days at most. For all the control he might exercise in some areas of his life, ultimately his strings were pulled by the compulsion to burn. And the Angeles Arsonist had averaged a major blaze a week. It was unheard of. But then a ten-month hiatus was too.

Among his new emails was one sent by Anonymous from a weird-looking @nobody.an address. Given the militant efficiency of his spam filters Danny assumed it was a sketchy tip until its all-caps subject line made the hairs on his arms stand up.

HEY KILLER KASHO

Here it was at last. Nine years into his professional public life he'd been outed at last. He tapped the email to open it.

U WANT TO NO WHO?

I GOT PROOF

2100 COME ALONE

TELL NO 1 OR UL BURN 2

There were two links. The first pointed to CODA, the second to Google Maps.

He tapped the CODA link first and Red Flag loaded, auto-scrolled down into the user comments section and stopped at the latest post from member UCANBRN2. It said *NEXT UTUBE STAR?* and contained a YouTube link and an embedded photo of an apartment building.

Teetering with a sudden sensation of vertigo, it took him a second to realize it was *his* building. Taken from across the street on Franklin, in broad daylight. The U-Haul moving truck that had been here this morning was parked in front and he could see himself coming up the sidewalk with his head down and both hands on his phone, as oblivious as a lamb.

CHAPTER 17

Denise the producer's face reappeared in the chat window. "In ten, nine, eight..."

Danny cleared his throat and aimed a toothless smile at the camera under the *LOOK HERE* Post-it. His bedroom suddenly felt very close and very hot.

Replacing Denise in her window was the on-air shot of the Justine London show intro. Edgy tympanic music drummed up viewers' anticipation across the country. Danny's disembodied head floated with those of three other guests in the corners of the screen like a miniature Brady Bunch. Justine's was in the center, the star keeping all these interesting planets in a cohesive orbit for the next hour.

Justine London had titanium hair and skin the color of nicotine. Her mouth was a red and white painted snare, her eyes wide saucers of milk with a blueberry floating in each that caught the studio lights like sundials, as if she'd been genetically engineered for television cameras. Before she even spoke her expression guaranteed the viewing audience that she was here on their behalf to get to the very bottom of something serious.

"On tonight's show," Justine read from her teleprompter at what had to be the top of her voice, "reality TV star Pasha Penner! She calls herself a casualty of beauty and she's here to tell us why! Defrocked priest Charles Doughty—scourge or scapegoat? We'll be taking your calls! Our own Dr. Quick on the vanishing honeybees and why you should join an end of the world cult right now! And award-winning crime blogger Danny Kasho joins us from LA to answer tonight's Burning Question: who is setting Southern California on fire? Plus as always the latest news, views and reviews *tonight* on the Justine London show!"

Justine's permanently puckered bee-stung smile crinkled her cheek and the guests' floating heads dissolved to make way for the title sequence. Danny exhaled. He'd never seen her show before and thought she looked like a Wirehaired Fox Terrier.

Denise's voice came over the video: "Pasha Penner go in ten seconds. Danny Kasho stand by."

An on-set producer counted down and the show came back to Justine at her desk. She started a preamble about Pasha Penner, whose buxom figure in the picture looked like it contained more plastic than Danny's Honda.

"She's rich, she's got a hot young husband, she's on the cover of every magazine on the planet, so why is Pasha Penner claiming discrimination for her *beauty?*"

The image changed to the real Pasha sitting at the desk opposite Justine at an acutely bad angle for her collagen smile that betrayed her Gregorian age and manifest insecurity.

Danny checked the time and tuned out, working with his phone below the view of the camera.

UCANBRN2 had posted the YouTube comment at 12:41 PM today. People had replied with variations on WTF? and moved on, and the post had quickly sunk into the sediment of social commentary. Danny had received the anonymous email just six minutes ago but the plain English disclaimer among the gobbledygook in the expanded header unequivocally stated that the message did not originate from the sender address and had been automatically remailed after a random delay by free anonymizing remailer software.

He glanced at the on-air stream of the show. Pasha Penner was talking and flipping her dark hair over her shoulder as if it were an ermine stole that wouldn't keep still. With Justine London interjecting like a machine gun it was impossible to tell what question was being asked or answered, or by whom.

The Google Maps link opened to a remote location off Decker Canyon, another of the hairpin canyon roads snaking through the mountains from the Valley to the sea but farther west than Malibu or Topanga canyons.

The YouTube link led to a video posted by UCANBRN2. Today's date. Only eleven views. No comments. In the video a handheld camera spun the viewer in a quick circle, showing a rugged area split by a narrow rural road with a sliver of pale blue sky and smooth rock hills in the background. There was a crunch of dirt underfoot as the cameraman advanced up a dirt access road cut between dense shrubs. The camera was set down, propped on the ground and carefully angled. Sudden light saturation as a long stream of flame roared into the bushes, igniting them instantly. Three more blasts and the access road became a tunnel into the fire. The camera was picked up and the person gasped near the microphone and the 30-second video ended.

Knuckles rapped softly on the door and Danny jumped.

Garrett poked his head in, saw Danny at his computer with his headphones and lighting rig and gave him a thumb's-up, mouthed *Sorry* and quietly closed the door. A moment later the apartment door opened and closed and Danny was alone.

He grinned wolfishly, reeling with the lascivious image of a torrid threesome with Carrie Voelker and Ursula fucking Ruda. He was lord of his domain. He was sole proprietor. This was owned and operated by *him*. He didn't know if they could see him in the Justine London studio and he didn't care. This was epic hugeness.

Onscreen Pasha Penner was hawking a book she'd supposedly written all by herself and which Justine London was expertly holding to catch the maximum glare from the studio lights, rendering the title all but unreadable.

Wary of Denise's admonition not to touch anything Danny used his phone to navigate to CODA's signup page. Required fields were a valid email address, username/password, zip, age, and acceptance of legal terms. Only the email needed to be real, you had to click on a link in a message sent to it to enable the account. But often a lot could be gleaned once someone clicked Send.

He forwarded the anonymous email to Suge Litvinovs, leaving the expanded header but removing the message and the subject—which he replaced with *Fucking urgent need your help!* He clumsily copied and pasted UCANBRN2's links—a tedious process on his phone's tiny virtual buttons—and simply asked *Who/where/when?*

U WANT TO NO WHO?

I GOT PROOF

Danny stared at the picture of himself outside the building, a random moment frozen in time by a stranger. A stalker. Mark Pavelko knew where he lived. Mike Cruz could have followed him home. Maybe he had picked up a stalker tipster without even knowing it. It had happened before—he cringed at the memory of crazy Sabrina. Someone afraid they wouldn't be taken seriously without a sour cherry of coercion on top.

Pasha Penner's segment suddenly wrapped up and Justine returned full screen. "Burning Question after this!" she exclaimed, and the chat window turned blue as the show went to commercial.

Producer Denise's voice announced through his headphones, "Danny Kasho go in sixty seconds, Charles Doughty stand by." The defrocked priest with thick glasses and a lock of hair slicked across his forehead stared forlornly from a separate chat window.

Danny's heart rate started to pick up speed. He straightened his pad of talking points, grabbed his lucky pen so he wouldn't fidget and told himself to fucking focus. *This was national fucking TV, Daniel Edgar Kasho.* Like his mother used to call him when he was in trouble.

His email counter changed and he stabbed his phone.

Suge had the information supplied on the CODA registration: username UCANBRN2, password Fireman666, zip code 91362, age 40, confirmed email fireman666@fastmail.com. Member since September 4, 2018. Just three days after the Dillon Fire was set. Probably hours after Red Flag had been birthed. He'd been waiting this whole time to be recognized.

"Thirty seconds," said Denise.

Suge explained that the remailer was a dead end as no true IP address was passed on in the header, but assuming it wasn't sent from a mobile device there was a chance he could geolocate the computer the posts were made on and retrieve the registrant's physical address.

"Twenty seconds."

Danny dropped his lucky pen and grabbed his phone with both hands, his thumbs a flurry as he asked Suge to fucking go for it.

"Danny Kasho in ten."

He picked up his lucky pen and smiled like he was brushing his teeth.

The Burning Question logo—cleverly, an animated question mark *en flambé*—hovered tantalizingly over Justine London's shoulder.

"Tonight's Burning Question: who is setting Southern California on fire? Hundreds of thousands of acres of trees, homes of the innocent, and lives of those sworn to protect them have gone up in flames. Is there a serial arsonist on the loose in the bone-dry mountains around Los Angeles?"

Danny's disembodied head shared the screen with Justine's. He rolled his lucky pen in his fingers, unseen by the camera.

"Tonight my guest journalist Danny Kasho joins us to answer that question. His blog is called Red Flag and it wouldn't be unfair to call it the definitive source about the fires, is that right Danny?"

"I hope to be accurate at best, and entertaining at better." He'd thought of that line on the way home from Drake's and it went over well with Justine.

"Don't we all!" She jabbed painted fingers at the camera like a judo move. "So bring us up to date Danny, what's with all the wildfires in California?"

In his peripheral vision he saw his face go to full screen and he began his concise summary about the firesetting spree, how it began in July of last year and continued with growing destructive power into the murderous Backbone Fire in Malibu after a mysterious ten-month period in which they'd thought—they'd hoped—he'd simply stopped. Been incarcerated or died. Although investigators believed the Angeles Arsonist had set over fifty fires—some thought even more than that—Backbone was getting a lot of coverage due both to the deaths and the proximity to celebrities who live in the area.

"Celebrities are better than the rest of us," Justine deadpanned. "You will be too someday Danny Kasho, mark my words."

He fought the natural urge to look at himself in his monitor as he talked about how the arsonist was growing more confident, moving closer and closer to the city and its sprawling residential developments. Closer and closer to inhabited places.

"Is that going to bring property values down?" Justine quipped.

"It could—California's biggest disaster threat isn't earthquakes, it's fire."

"Last couple years you've gotten both! If it's not one thing it's another in California but everyone must be ready to dance a jig now that you won't fall into the ocean."

Danny was describing Dennis Abner's four types of arsonists when Justine jumped in again.

"Curious? What in the hell can they be *curious* about? How stuff *burns?* They should have paid better attention in *elementary* school. It's not exactly rocket science is it?"

"No, but building a flamethrower is pretty advanced. I've detailed in my blog Red Flag on CODA.com—" Danny made sure he looked right into the camera for that—"how he did it."

Justine's eyes narrowed into arrow slits. "He *built* his own *flamethrower?"*

"That's what he's using to start the fires. I know that for a fact."

"How exactly?"

Danny smiled and his eyes inadvertently dipped to the email on his phone. "Let's just say there's more to come on Red Flag."

Justine didn't smile back right away and he feared he'd just annoyed her by being coy.

She said, "It's a developing story, I get it. Now is it true people like him—deviant miscreant quote unquote *people—get off* pardon my French folks on watching the media coverage of themselves Danny?"

"Some of them do. It's empowering to them."

"Then you listen to *me* Mr. Fire*bug.*" Justine addressed the nearest camera and, by extension, the deviant miscreant arsonist pervert on the other side of the country, watching her on a small TV in a shoddy little cockroach-infested apartment somewhere. "There is nothing more beautiful than all of God's trees pointing up toward Heaven. There is nothing more sacred than a man's home, his castle, what he works for and strives to provide for his *family*. And there is nothing more precious than *family*—brothers and sisters, sons and daughters, mothers and fathers. You have ended people's *lives*. Please," her eyes softened into crescent moons, "*please* turn yourself in. It's the only way out. It's not amends until you say Amen."

The camera switched back to a two-shot that caught Danny looking bewildered at Justine in his monitor.

"This isn't the only case you're covering now is it Danny? You're also covering the Nick Mendoza trial?" She spat the name like rotten fruit, having bounced back from the edge of sympathy like a paper clip shot from a rubber band.

"That's right."

"No case is ever a slam dunk I know, but isn't it amazing whenever an impartial jury can be impaneled right in the city the crime took place in? The defense couldn't get it moved?"

"When the system works, it works, and it's flexible enough to allow for some give and take and negotiation."

Justine's eyes widened to where there was nothing but white surrounding her sparkling blue pupils. "And what have you heard about give and take, Danny?"

"We're waiting to see if Mendoza's girlfriend Charlize Patron makes a deal to testify against him in exchange for a lighter sentence."

"Doesn't everyone in that position take a deal?"

"Usually, but Charlize has been surprisingly uncooperative so far."

"Is her testimony critical to the success of the prosecution's case?"

"I think they can get a conviction without her but it would sure help them. I'm confident Charlize Patron will take a deal."

"*How* confident?"

He cleared his throat and fixed his eyes on his monitor's camera as if to stare the invisible everyones on the other side of it into believing him as he said in his best Handsome Actor voice, "I guarantee she will," and immediately thought *merde*. You generally wanted to avoid declaring absolutes on national television, lest ye be absolutely and publicly fucked, but there it was. Justine London had lit the coals and he'd just walked across them dumb as a drunk tourist. Patron had better play to type now.

"Charlize walks if Charlize talks." Justine London flared her nostrils. "We've heard that before, haven't we folks?"

Danny shifted in his chair. "I wouldn't exactly say *walks*—"

"Well she's not going to get the needle like jolly old Saint Nick is she?" Justine barked. "The lesser of two evils—the constant tug-of-war within the legal system folks we see it here all the time. Thank you Danny Kasho for answering tonight's Burning Question! Up next, Charles Doughty—priest or pederast? We're taking your calls, *next!*"

The show went to commercial and the live feed abruptly stopped. A moment later Denise's pretty face reappeared to amplify the interruption.

"Good job Danny! The show's replayed at ten Pacific, after which a copy of your segment will be available for download, okay? You'll get a separate email for that. Hope to have you back soon, bye."

The video chat connection closed.

Danny deflated into his chair, took off his headphones and placed them on his legal pad.

His phone buzzed with a text.

Then again, and again. Emails pinged joyously like a children's choir at Christmastime.

He turned off the LEDs and peered outside—Franklin Avenue was busy as usual with cars and pedestrians, only to get busier as late dusk turned into night in earnest. Nobody seemed to be paying any particular attention to his building.

He checked the time as he went back to his email. He had ninety minutes.

His phone buzzed again. Suge had replied.

UCANBRN2 had posted comments on Red Flag a total of twelve times—six times yesterday between 12:25 and 12:43 PM, five times between 5:32 and 5:45 PM, and once today at 12:40 PM with a picture embedded, which Suge pointedly noted CODA allowed registered users to do over his documented objections. Each of the posts was made from a computer at an address in Agoura Hills, which put it near the Hampton Inn where Pavelko was staying and the 91362 zip code for Thousand Oaks next door.

Danny started to enter the address into his phone to map it and it auto-filled for him.

It *was* the Hampton Inn where Pavelko was staying.

He sat back with a noose of confusion coiling in his stomach, thinking about task forces within task forces and the lengths someone would go to hide in plain sight.

He got up and went into the darkening living room and made double sure Garrett was gone. Waited there with his heart bumping around inside his chest like a bird trapped in a shoebox.

Each carpeted step upstairs became one of the unfinished plywood stairs that sloped away from the garage up to his father's workshop, to the broken railing and the drops of blood on the landing. Garrett's open bedroom door became the yawning door which silently screamed the end of the Kasho family to the whole interconnected world. Dread was still a tangible place accessed by ascending wooden stairs, the side of the garage with its peeling paint to the right, their back yard to the left, a visual and emotional leitmotif in the sad symphony of his life, as the orchestra plucked strings attached to his arms and legs like a marionette and led the little figure to a place of trespass he could never come back from.

Garrett's bedroom was not much bigger than his. The walls were the same distressed white, the paint artfully peeling in places. The ceiling was not as high as on the lower floor but it had its own master bathroom, walk-in closet, and adjoining office which Garrett used as his home studio and which was packed with computers, keyboards, a mixing console and monitoring speakers, and various outboard effects gear screwed into upright aluminum racks.

Danny opened the closet door and reached up for the pull-chain. A single bare incandescent bulb in the ceiling illuminated clothes hanging on one side and stacks of cardboard storage boxes on the other. A wooden ledge up by the ceiling supported shoeboxes, smaller containers and folded winter clothes from another climate. He tried to remember where it was Garrett had said he kept it. Then he remembered the acronym: All Day I Dream About Shooting Shit.

He rolled Garrett's studio chair into the center of the closet and climbed gingerly up onto it, the base swiveling left and right beneath his feet. He reached up and pulled down a blue and white Adidas box and removed the lid. Nestled into a crinkly bed of tissue paper inside was a stubby nickel-colored handgun about eight inches long. Only a pound and a half of cool steel, the contoured grip comfortable in his hand, his forefinger rested on the ergonomically-curved trigger as if the weapon had been custom made for him by Smith & Wesson.

But there was no magazine in the grip and none in the shoebox.

He took it anyway, and replaced the box and chair exactly where he found them. He glanced around Garrett's tidy bedroom hoping for divine inspiration to pinpoint a loaded magazine, but knew it was futile and went back downstairs.

He grabbed his wallet, CODA ID, phone and a bottle of water, glanced at the picture of himself outside the building and swore it wouldn't be the last one of him. He was not a victim. He was not a *possible* victim.

He pressed a fingertip to his sister's family picture and headed for the door.

CHAPTER 18

The hotel lobby was refrigerator-cold, almost more of a discomfort than a relief from the heat outside, and sported misleading earth-tone tile carpeting apparently designed to direct inattentive travelers straight into the corners. Luggage sets were arranged at a waist-high divider separating the lobby from a cocktail lounge noisily occupied by a group of men who would fit right in at a Mike Cruz luau. Part of the special agent convention, Danny assumed, as he stood rigidly in the center of the lobby with the ceiling pressing down on him.

He was greeted by a cheery boyish-looking clerk in azure-colored pants and matching shirt attending the marble-topped front desk. "Good evening sir."

The soothing instrumental background music buzzed in his ears like a dentist drill. "Can you tell me what room Mark Pavelko is in? He's a guest here."

"No sir, but I can call his room on your behalf if you like."

Surveillance cameras, discreet black plastic droplets, bulged from the ceiling tiles. "Sure. Please."

The clerk consulted his computer hidden beneath the counter and the seconds ticked by like axe whacks into a tree until he made a noise in the back of his throat. "I'm so sorry sir, but he's not a registered guest with us."

Danny spelled the last name for him.

"No luck I'm afraid," the clerk said with a tone of diminishing rainbows that made Danny want to hit him in the nose with something blunt and solid.

"When did he check out?" he asked.

The clerk's eyebrows rubbed up against each other like amorous sleeping bags on a camping trip. "I'm sorry sir, but he hasn't checked in."

"But he said he was staying here." The truth gaped at Danny like the toothy mouth of a leopard seal to a penguin. And he didn't like feeling like a penguin.

"I'm so sorry sir." The clerk shrugged helplessly as if at a distant relative's bereavement. "Perhaps he meant the Sheraton down the street?"

Danny's thumb hovered over Pavelko's name on his phone. Mark was a boat that had slipped its moorings in a storm and been propelled into his shipping lane. Collision was imminent and unavoidable. He tapped his phone and listened as it started to ring. He didn't know what he'd say. He wondered if his post about Linda in San Francisco had stoked Pavelko's anger, and at what degree it was burning tonight.

Voicemail.

He ended the call without leaving a message and looked at the clerk. The man's fingers were flapping over the keys like flags in a stiff wind and he might have been humming a merry tune to himself. He wondered how busy a hotel clerk was that he needed to be doing so much typing.

He asked him, "Do you have WiFi?"

"Of course sir, throughout the entire hotel. It's complimentary. For registered guests," the clerk added as if informing him that tiaras were only for princesses.

Danny hadn't thought to ask Suge if roaming laptops each got their own IP's or if UCANBRN2's would be under the hotel's umbrella, anonymous within the number of guests online at the time. Seemed like one of those things he ought to know by now, forensically-speaking.

"Perhaps your friend is waiting for you in our BusinessOn Center," the clerk suggested brightly.

"The what?"

"It's our internet lounge. Straight down the hall there, sir."

The BusinessOn Center was a standard-sized hotel room with low lighting and a pair of tan sofas set against the walls for laptop users. In the middle was a pinwheel of four small workstations with pull-out keyboard trays. A combination fax and printer stood in the corner. Only two people were using the room, a man on a sofa with a laptop, and a hip-hop grandma at one of the desktops wearing silver Bose headphones and bifocals that reflected the bluish illumination of the screen.

A surveillance bulb hung from the center of the ceiling.

Danny returned to the lobby and motioned discreetly to the clerk. The man came to the end of the desk where he hunched conspiratorially with the unused $50 from Pepperdine pinched between his fingers.

"Any luck sir?" The clerk's teeth were the size of a beaver's and looked like they were regularly wrapped in whitening strips.

Danny read his name tag. "Phil, I need your help with an unconventional request."

That seemed to pique the clerk's interest. "I'll try my best to help you sir."

"What I need—what I *really* need Phil, is to view the security tape for the BusinessOn Center for today, around 12:40 PM. I believe a person of interest in a major ongoing criminal investigation used a computer here today and I need to try and identify him for the police."

Phil's mouth went tight. His eyes turned blank as buttons and he suddenly resembled a giant sock puppet. "Of course I can't do that sir, but I can call our manager and perhaps she can help you."

Danny rubbed the $50 between his thumb and forefinger. "The thing is—Phil—I can't really wait. I need to see it *now*—before the police get here. 'Cause they'll be coming here for sure and I want to save them some time, see? Give them a head start in finding the guy before he hurts anyone else."

Phil blinked his button eyes and gave a brisk nod. "In that case you can *definitely* speak to my manager. The police can too. Sir."

Danny cleared his throat. "This will be completely confidential, I promise. Trust me Phil—I'm a journalist. No one will know."

Phil the clerk leaned across the marble counter, chuckling lightly as if at a gentle family-friendly joke and said quietly, "If you don't get that money out of my face they will fire me. And if they fire me I will come find you Mr. Journalist Man and I will kill you. I will cut up your body into little pieces and I will scatter those little pieces way out in the desert and no part of you will ever be found by anyone ever. I know how to do it. I've done it before and I never got caught, and I won't get caught because of you either. So if you don't want to speak to my manager, *sir*, leave right now.

Right this second. Or I will call security and you can watch *yourself* in a video—being *arrested."* Phil half-smiled as if at a fond memory of dismembered body parts and calmly returned to his place behind the desk, fingers a-flutter.

His mouth gone dry, Danny put the money away and looked around. Some of the men in the lounge were looking at him, having correctly surmised a failed transaction of some kind had just gone down. He figured most if not all of them had the actual power of arrest.

He stared at his reflection in the lobby's sliding doors, dressed all in black except for his glaring white New Balance cross trainers which had seen as much dirt as your average BMW, his forehead glistening with sweat despite the air conditioning.

Epic hugeness had its price.

It was going to be a blind date after all.

He made good time around the terra cotta affluence of Westlake Village, where each and every swimming pool remained obstinately filled, and turned south toward the hills still scorched from the Shiloh Ranch Fire last Halloween, cruising down a wide, empty boulevard between large homes set back from the road. He had a flashback to a story from years ago which had brought him out here when it was still bathed in what a cinematographer friend of Garrett's described as LA's signature "bastard amber glow" before the city's streetlights were switched to the cool bluish LEDs.

As the lights fell behind the narrow, curving canyon road began to unwind before his headlights. He had never driven Decker Canyon Road before tonight and he gripped the steering wheel with both hands and eased back substantially on the speed. Tiny tail lights far ahead of him appeared and disappeared as he rounded corner after corner, his headlights alternately flashing on guardrails, hillsides, and empty black air over sheer rocky drops. It felt like the weight of the gun was pulling his car into oncoming traffic, which already passed close enough to slap his Accord with colliding air of dissuasion. He stole glances at the animated map on his phone, suctioned-cupped in its cradle to the dashboard, as it ticked down the distance to UCANBRN2's chosen meeting place.

HEY KILLER KASHO

The putrid soup had been stirred so the not-quite-dead things bobbed to the surface, bumping against your spoon so you'd never want to use it again. How many spoons had he thought he'd thrown away only to find his hand in a white-knuckled grip around the same old handle. He'd Googled himself once and found the local Calendula *Crier's* 20th anniversary rehash of the "crime that rocked the central coast." It included interviews with people who were there, retired police officers, lawyers. It was so insulting he'd taken it as due punishment for looking in the first place. He just wished it hadn't shown up on the first page of search results. No one at CODA had ever brought it up and there'd been innumerable liquor-saturated social occasions for the topic to arise. It was his experience of it that kept the shame and resentment bumping along behind him like balloons knotted to a child.

He slowed but didn't stop at the lonely T-intersection with Mulholland. A few tight curves later his phone announced he'd arrived. He pulled over and stopped in someone's driveway rising into the hillside off an S-shaped section of Decker Canyon. It was steep and bordered with low unfinished granite stone retaining walls, ascending to a property he couldn't see from the road but which was given away by the paving and the ubiquitous tricolor garbage bins pinned by his headlights. The other side of the road looked out onto undeveloped land, the pure blackness you could only achieve with the complete absence of people and their stuff.

He turned off the engine and dimmed his phone's display to its lowest setting, then got out and quickly closed his door to extinguish the interior light. He listened. His ears hummed from neither wind nor traffic, which passed infrequently. He could hear nothing but the wind and the distant sound of a helicopter somewhere out there in the smoky moonlight which artfully highlighted the scratch down the length of his car.

He was twenty minutes early.

His pants sagged under the weight of the empty gun jammed in his waistband as he went quiet as a burglar up the driveway which split in a Y at the top with a metal gate swung shut across one arm. A fire road. He thought of Mike Cruz's maps, how the fire roads crisscrossing these mountains must feel as natural to him as the bones in his hands.

A house under construction materialized out of the darkness down the other arm of the Y, a large, angular two-story Tudor, its brick walls and steeply-pitched roof frames rising from the elevated plateau of a sheared hilltop. The whitewashed plaster between the timbers shone under the eye of the moon. Young trees were planted below it along a fence overlooking the canyon road. A wheelbarrow and a portable cement mixer stood on what would become the front lawn, currently just an expanse of dirt dominated by an industrial-sized wheeled Dumpster some seven feet high and twenty feet long, and a heavy-duty 4x4 pickup parked beside stacks of clay roofing tiles.

He stared at the vehicle, wishing his eyes had dilated more already. Or that he had night vision binoculars and some Navy SEALs too, which seemed like a reasonable request under the circumstances. The windows of the pickup were up and he thought that was a good sign there was no one inside, not in this heat, but he crept toward it in a crouch anyway, staying in the blind spot just in case. He peered carefully in through the dusty tinted windows. The back seats were empty. The front was empty. He didn't try the handle in case he set off a car alarm. It had probably been parked there at least a day when work paused for the long weekend.

He went back to the Y intersection and bypassed the gate by climbing up the hill around it. The gun was uncomfortable and seemed likely to invite whatever trouble it was supposed to defend against. Danny had always felt that way about guns. It was fitting that the one time he actually wanted one it didn't have any bullets.

The fire road curved around a stand of trees and he saw that it overlooked his car at the base of the driveway. Other than the empty truck there were no other cars around and nowhere to hide one.

He was alone.

CHAPTER 19

Danny squatted for as long as his legs could take it, then paced around, crouching whenever a car approached below on Decker Canyon—and invariably kept going. He was invisible, occupying a breath of space on a ghost's map. Eventually he sat down in the dirt with the empty gun on the ground beside him, sweating and uncomfortable and very thirsty, wondering if this was a journalistic high point or low and how long it would take to find out.

He tossed the empty plastic water bottle out into the darkness to assert himself somehow, with all apologies to Mother Nature. Heard it land in the bushes and something skitter out of its way. Robbed of his vision his ears went into overdrive, delineating such nuances as a change in wind in advance of a gust, the scuttle of animals aplenty through the bushes, some loud enough to jolt him upright and claw at his city-numbed senses. All around him the landscape moved and wouldn't let the night sit still.

But he was alone with the wind and the light pollution from the sprawl and the dull glow of the Backbone Fire rising behind the bumpy silhouettes of the mountains. He configured his phone to be ready to live-stream whatever it recorded directly to the cloud, then kept checking that it was, for something to do. The data was secure and everything else on his phone was already backed up anyway. Small but professional comfort should shit unexpectedly go south. Which seemed unlikely out here tonight, wearing validity like a pair of donkey ears for the ass.

The first time he'd driven into danger for a story was in 2014. He was just starting to make a name for himself, notably with his reporting of the notorious Connor Mack murders the year before for which he'd been a press club award nominee but wasn't selected. He didn't even get laid because of it. Unlike Ursula Ruda he didn't hold a grudge. That day five years ago a man had called his tip line—aka his cell phone—and told him he knew where a killer was hiding. Devon Johnson—DJ to his friends and LAPD detectives—was 35 and unemployed and wanted for the murder of a Hollywood publicist. The bloody ambush slaying of the woman—shot in her car while stopped at a red light in Beverly Hills on her way home from a movie screening—spawned tabloid conspiracy theories and an intensive manhunt once Johnson was ID'd on a surveillance camera leaving the scene on a bicycle, which turned out to be stolen. But weeks after the murder no one had found him, even though he wasn't thought to have enough resources to stay underground that long with LAPD shaking the palm trees so hard.

According to Danny's tipster he'd seen Devon Johnson with his own eyes at an apartment off Yucca in Hollywood, staying with a woman the caller knew as Carol Ann.

Some sad shit what happened to that lady, the caller said, *but all I know's my baby mama's livin' next door and he's got hisself a arsenal in there.*

What's your name? Danny asked.

Fuckin' Anonymous, the man said and hung up.

It was a five minute drive. Danny squeezed into a spot up the street and was sitting there watching the place, an ugly little pink stucco box divided into fourths with bars on the ground-floor windows, wondering where he was going to go when it came time to pee when Devon Johnson walked up out of nowhere and rapped on his window with hollow point knuckles.

The only other time he could recall such an utter suspension of breath, as if air itself could be bundled up with twine and literally pulled out of your lungs, was when he saw his father's distinctive necklace in the grasp of the dead man in the tall summer grass of Calendula.

DJ was standing sideways to his car, knocking on the window but looking back down the street behind him. He couldn't tell if DJ was holding a weapon down by his leg, all he could see was his stained white tank top wrapped like dirty gauze around his skinny torso, and patchy stubble on skin that looked more gray than black. There didn't need to be an arsenal when just one piece of it was only inches from your head. Danny tried waving him away as if he were an unwanted homeless window-washer.

DJ said *Yo man, open the door.*

There were few if any criminal geniuses, he already knew that by then, but Devon Johnson was a telling entry visa into how stupid most of them were.

Yo man, open the door.

Gosh man, sure thing, let me get that for you.

Surprising himself, considering the man was a murder suspect and the subject of a manhunt and was most likely armed, Danny replied with a cool, upwardly dismissive *Fuck off.* He saw the true feral face of the man appear then, with his bad teeth bared and uneducated indignation. DJ slammed his hand against the roof of the car and shouted *Fuck you too boy!* and continued down the sidewalk toward the pink apartment building, testing the door handles of every parked car along the way while Danny took pictures of him with his ass hanging over the waistband of his saggy jeans. DJ went around the side of the stucco box and Danny called an LAPD homicide detective he knew named Preston Dorff.

The first of many black and whites rolled quietly into place a few minutes later. A few minutes after that DJ was hauled out of the building in handcuffs, with his saggy pants down around his ankles, followed by a bony meth-faced white woman of indeterminate age Danny assumed was the less than fetching Carol Ann, similarly shackled but in a shabby blue track suit with cigarette burns in it.

Another pair of headlights coming from the direction of Malibu made a speedy approach to the turn on Decker.

CODA's scoop that day had started with a tip too, but a real one. Dorff even bought him drinks, and they'd stayed in touch over the years on a quid pro quo basis which had turned out well for each of them on occasion, so it had turned out to be a timely investment in the future too.

Yes. I'm calling to report a fire. Corral Canyon Road. There are possible victims.

An owl hooted and the hair on Danny's neck stood up. Then he smiled a little in the dark. He'd been here long enough for his eyes to adjust and his nerves to settle. He checked the time again. 9:48. So much for epic hugeness.

"This is bullshit." He stood up and stretched and swatted the dirt off his butt.

He started down the fire road to the driveway, looking forward to his car's air conditioning and an empty freeway to take him home. First to the nearest drive-thru, probably back in Westlake Village, for something cold to drink. Maybe there was still time to hook up with Holiest of Holies Michelle. Get his hotshot journalist groove back with somebody who didn't know any better, like Gina the actress who'd at least be able to fake it convincingly.

His phone buzzed with a new text. It was Mark Pavelko. *Where are you?*

He made a face as he crossed out of the dirt into the driveway. Where am I? I'm falling for everyone's bullshit today, that's where I am. Parachuting into great vats of warm fresh feces without rubber boots and a nose plug.

He stamped his shoes on the pavement, looked up and saw a minivan parked in the driveway with its engine idling. Behind the glare of misaligned headlights someone half-turned toward him at the open side door, rolling their shoulders as they shrugged something onto their back.

A breath of time no longer than the spaces between Devon Johnson's knuckle strikes on glass passed without movement. Then the person at the minivan straightened up and stepped through the jaundiced headlight pools toward him, distorting the silhouette, giving it long Edward Scissorhands limbs that stretched up the driveway to where Danny stood with his mind skipping like a scratched CD.

There's no face. There's no face. There's no face.

Their eyes were hidden behind bulky black goggles strapped around a dark helmet, their face covered by a black shield that hung to the chest of black coveralls. Braided black PVC hose connected the silver tanks on their back to a tube some three feet long with two grips like a Tommy gun, one grip in front of the other. The weight of the tanks made the person crouch as they started up the driveway.

Danny started streaming video on his phone and backed up with feet of cinderblocks. Fear was a paralytic toxin in the nervous system, snarling his legs like invasive vines. It was about to get him killed. Right here. Tonight, alone in this desolate place in the middle of nowhere as far as LA went. A few short seconds from now.

"Hey!" he shouted. *"Hey!* Stop for a second! Just *stop* for a second! Listen to me!"

The person leaned back to look up at him, elevated at the top of the Y intersection empty-handed except for his phone. The guy was big and his chest was heaving—the temperature was still in the 90s and he was carrying fifty pounds of flammable gas on his back. Danny was thinking about the range of Cruz's device—thirty yards for eight to ten seconds.

Thirty *yards.* He was *already* in range.

"You wanted me to come all the way out here, so I did." Danny's tongue had turned thick. "Here I am. Let's talk. Come on, talk to me. *Talk to me."*

The leading pause was filled only with the puttering of the minivan's motor. *The arsonist drove in from one direction, started the fire and kept right on going,* Mark Pavelko had said. As if he was intimately familiar with the M.O.

"I know what it's like to live with a secret." It felt like a rubber ball was caught in his throat that prevented him from swallowing. "You've always wanted to say something but nobody was listening. Well now's your chance." His voice cracked like a pubescent teenager's. *"Talk to me.* Tell the world what you want to say. You don't have to hide anymore."

With a dull metallic click the pilot light at the end of the tube ignited, impervious to the wind and bright as a tiny star trapped angrily on earth.

His movements slowed as if he was swimming through gelatin, Danny reached behind him and the empty gun rose at the end of his arm, a mean glint in the moonlight.

The arsonist flinched and a supernova-bright stream of fire sliced into the belly of the night.

Danny dropped Garrett's empty gun and sprinted half-blinded toward the darkened house shuddering in front of him with every pounding step. He ran past the pickup and skidded in the dirt behind the corrugated steel walls of the Dumpster. He stopped the video to dial 911, wiped the sweat out of his eyes and peeked around the corner.

Lit wanly by the headlights of the minivan, the arsonist stood in the middle of the Y intersection, looking straight up the road at the house.

A woman's professionally neutral voice spoke in his ear. "911, state your emergency."

"I'm calling from Malibu. I need to report a fire." As little information as possible to minimize the delay of being transferred from highway patrol, which picked up 911 calls from mobile phones, to a sheriff's department dispatcher who would actually send the cops.

"I'm sorry sir, I'm having trouble hearing you. Please repeat your emergency. Are you injured?"

The arsonist started to advance, searching, the tube swinging side to side as if trying to acquire Danny's scent.

"I'm calling from Malibu! Someone's starting a fire!"

The call was transferred.

"911." Male this time. "What's your emergency?"

The arsonist braced himself and Danny dropped to the ground and covered his head, tasting dirt as a searing jet of flame roared past the Dumpster. He thought of the two firefighters overrun by fire down in Malibu Canyon and wondered if the end had sounded like that to them, like Hell laughing at them.

"Hello? Is anyone there?" the 911 operator asked. "What's your emergency?"

Danny screamed into the phone, "Fire! Decker Canyon Road south of Mulholland! Fire! *Fire!*"

Eight to ten seconds' worth, Mike Cruz had said. May as well be eight to ten minutes.

Too much time.

"Are you witnessing a fire being set?" asked the dispatcher.

Another spray from the flamethrower left scores of hungry embers foraging in the side of the house.

Danny jumped to his feet and ran right into the portable cement mixer. His phone flew out of his hand as he sprawled to the ground. He stopped to look for it, his sole lifeline to anything on the other side of this moment, but two of the pickup's tires caught fire and exploded in a jarring double tap, sending him scrambling toward the house on his hands and knees with panic bubbling up his spine.

At the corner of the house bricks rose in a windowless bastion that would one day be the garage. The ground crumbled under his feet at the edge of the property and he slid part way down the side of the hill. He frantically clawed his way back up the loose dirt to a gaping window frame projecting a few inches out from the wall, swung his legs over and ducked inside. His shoes hit plywood. He could smell the sawdust in the exposed 2x10s in the ceiling. The unfinished walls were broken only by a blacker-than-black doorway. Without any source of light he moved forward carefully, mindful not to make any noise by kicking leftover tools or building materials. His legs felt raked by razor wire where he'd hit the cement mixer and he desperately hoped to live to feel even more pain, more wretchedness, more simple discomfort, and every joy there was to be had on the flipside of those sensations too.

Through the front door frame the fire from the pickup threw an eerie light down the plywood hallway, which was bent like a bonsai tree shaped to preference, angling past stunted branches of empty rooms. Danny moved away from the glow and slipped across the hall into another room with more holes of varying sizes cut out of the walls—plumbing and electrical outlets in the kitchen maybe. No cabinets or cupboards had been installed yet; like the rest of the house it was simply a collection of spaces shaped like plans.

He crept into a larger room at the back of the house with many window frames and a double-wide floor-to-ceiling door frame. A great stone fireplace occupied one side of the room, on the other a doorway leading to another room was blocked by a pair of sawhorses supporting 2x4's and a metal L-square ruler he briefly entertained using as a weapon.

A shadow crossed the firelight behind him.

Sweat stung his eyes and he held his breath, trying to hear something over his heart pounding away like a solo tom-tom.

Plywood creaked in the hallway and all the myriad night sounds fused into the singular rasp of the flamethrower.

With his hands shaking Danny backed away from the gaping mouth of the hall. He thought he could hear the arsonist's breathing over the hiss of gas, the heavy tread of his specialized boots on the bare floor. He'd found him. He'd found him and he'd come right to him and his impending death presented itself as an embarrassment. His smirking peers would all wonder what he'd been thinking. How he could have been so stupid. They would vow never to follow in footsteps so careless, never to feel pain of the severity he was about to feel. He was Neil Weber still with flesh hiding his muscles and organs and blood. He was something about to be destroyed, a miracle about to be mocked by pathologists and a general public that just hours ago had looked to him to be exceptional. He was ashamed at himself for being so easy to kill.

A burst of fire lit up the end of the hall by the front door. A second blast lit up a closer room on the other side of the hall.

He was going room by room.

Danny looked wildly around, willing something to appear—escape, rescue, *anything*. The room that was blocked by the sawhorses didn't lead anywhere. Crawling into the stone fireplace would be suicide.

He was trapped.

The glow in the hall intensified by the second. The arsonist could trap himself in the burning house too, but maybe that's what he intended to do tonight—to kill and to die.

Tentacles of fire stretched across the floor and up the walls like a cancer in the bones of the house. Smoke poured through the unfinished ceiling. The instinct for breathable air pushed him toward the door frame at the back of the room for a balcony. He stepped out and—

Free fall.

The ground slapped the wind right out of him and he tumbled downhill, crashing through a thicket of bushes into a wooden temporary fence at the tree line which arrested his fall.

Danny gasped and sucked air and tried to move. Separate sharp pains gouged him all over his body. He wiggled his fingers and toes, then bent his elbows and knees. Dragged himself up to his knees, tasting blood. But *tasting.*

The house was entering its death throes, succumbing to the flames. Smoke spewed from every empty window frame and billowed out of the massive chimney. Over the pejorative crackling came the oscillating wail of a distant siren.

Wincing in pain, he picked his way around the hillside below the burning house. He heard the squeal of a loose fan belt as the minivan sped away up Decker Canyon. He wished he had something to throw at it. Wished he could have hit it even if he did have something. To mark it somehow, like a dye pack in a thief's money.

Cringing from the heat of the fire, he found his phone in its glow a few feet away from the cement mixer. Other than the cracked display it was functional and he groaned with relief, then reared back and screamed himself hoarse in victorious, delicious survival, middle fingers upraised to the night sky smeared by an arsonist's rage.

CHAPTER 20

As he stared at the video on Danny's damaged phone the muscles in Travis Salk's jaw clenched and unclenched like brawler's fists before throwing a roundhouse. In the detective's meaty hands the little device looked as brittle as a graham cracker, something that could snap like his temper seemed about to. His face was red in the lights of emergency vehicles and Danny thought it would look just as red under one of the fire department's noisy generator-powered halogen spotlights illuminating the smoldering remains of the house, which had been reduced to two chimneys and brick walls exposed like separated ribs.

Due to the proximity of resources combating the Backbone Fire the response had been quick and overwhelming. It belatedly struck Danny as he sat on the stone wall on one side of the driveway to take the weight off his right ankle that he should have moved his car when he had the chance; now he was hemmed in by fire engines.

Igor Adjani was waving his vinyl notebook around the driveway as if he was swatting flies. "You didn't get a tag? A *partial* tag? *Nothing?*"

"It was a minivan, that's all I saw." He'd bitten his tongue when he fell out of the house and a chunk of it kept getting pinched by his teeth; articulation was boozy-sounding at best and there was barbed wire wrapped around his lungs whenever he inhaled.

"Color?" Adjani asked. "Make?"

"Dark and I don't know."

"How do you know it was a minivan? It wasn't a full-size van? Or one of those European-style vans like a Transit?"

"No. I don't think so." Danny wiped dust from his eyes. "I don't know."

The two detectives wore their ties loose and their shirt sleeves rolled up and were still sweating from the hike up from wherever they'd had to park. Decker Canyon was down to one lane and even this late at night traffic was piling up as each side took turns being escorted past the scene, there being no safe place to turn the cars around on the narrow canyon road.

Flashlights scoured the hills around them. Smaller midair lights indicated drones searching from a 50-foot altitude, and there seemed to be more radios than there were ears to listen to them all. Adjani and Salk were nearby at the Malibu/Lost Hills sheriff's station and had been about to finally head home when Danny called Adjani and everyone's night took a massive detour.

His thighs were knotting up as if he had charley horses. He'd struck the cement mixer on the upstroke of his right leg and then gouged a deep cut out of his left shin when he tripped over it. Blood had dribbled down his leg and thickened with the dirt in his sock. He wanted to untie his shoe but couldn't reach down to it without his back spasming as if electrodes had been placed along his spine. Skin all over his body twitched and pinched, some of it breached and bloody, other parts like his ankle swelling to grotesque Discovery Channel proportions. He'd be put on exhibit in med school like the freakishly-testicled asshole who keyed his car.

A fire department paramedic had looked him over before Salk and Adjani got here, dressed the abrasions on his hands, arms, knees, and shin, and wrapped his ankle. She recommended he go to a hospital to get x-rays on his ribs but Danny declined, cognizant of the looks he was getting from some of the first responders as if *he* was the one who'd started the fire.

Salk was at the part in the 58-second video where Danny was running for his life. The screen was black and all you could hear were the sound of his footfalls out of sync with his panicked breathing. Frightened whimpers escaped from the back of his throat, primal sounds which were embarrassing to listen to. Most of the video was grainy and dark and the audio was all one-sided. The arsonist hadn't said a word. Danny thought his clothing wasn't so much a disguise as a costume—he *became* Fireman666. He made a mental note to use that in his post, whenever he got home. *Home*, a near-mythical refuge he'd accidentally abandoned. All he wanted to do was celebrate continued life with some deep sleep and revisit this unholy mess on the other side of it. He sat up straight and his breath caught. He was going to be living with that for a few days.

But he'd be living.

"Are you sure he didn't say anything?" Adjani pressed. "No demands? No manifesto? No Hi My Name Is…?"

"I know where he posted from."

"What did he want, a romantic evening under the stars with you dressed like Johnny Cash in tennies?" Salk looked up from the phone at Danny and his black eyes were twin shotgun barrels. He tossed Danny's phone to Adjani who caught it one-handed. "I've been a homicide detective for a lot of years and I've smelled every variety of bullshit there is."

"My condolences to your nose."

"You knew this was going down tonight."

"I did not."

"You knew who your quote unquote tipster was."

"I did not."

"You knew and you didn't tell anybody."

"I did not know. I'm a reporter, I get tips all the time. They're my bread and butter. They pay the rent."

Adjani said, "So what was this—you were looking for a raise?"

"You do stuff like *this* all the time do you?" Salk asked.

"No, *this* is unusual," Danny said. "I don't usually get tips accompanied by pictures of me where I live. Unusual is why I'm here."

"Ego is why you're here and somebody's house *isn't* anymore."

"Didn't you take that as a threat?" Adjani asked Danny. "The email and the picture of you?"

"I didn't know if it was a threat or a warning. Maybe the person really did know something. Maybe they had information. Maybe I'd be in danger if I didn't follow their instructions to come alone and tell no one."

"Or you'll burn too. Sounds like a threat to me. With a picture of my house? I'd call the police. Why didn't you?"

"Because then he wouldn't have gotten all of this." Salk gestured furiously at the strobing rotors of the news helicopters hovering high above them. "In other words *publicity* is the name of his game. It's written all over your face, Danny. You wanted the story *that* bad. You set this up, didn't you? Didn't you?"

"I came here to meet someone who said they knew who the arsonist was!" Danny shouted back. "They said they had proof! It turned out to *be* the arsonist! I did everything I could to get him to talk before he tried to kill me! I didn't get the chance to ask him to give himself up, I was too busy running for my fucking life! But I know where he was today."

"So do I!" Salk shouted. "So does everyone! You know where he *isn't?* In the back of one of our cars. Because of you!"

"Whose gun is that?" Adjani pointed his pen at Garrett's gun, which was marked with a yellow evidence cone in the driveway where Danny had dropped it.

"Mine. Well, my roommate's. I took it."

"Is it registered?"

"I don't know. It's not loaded."

The detectives looked at him. If anything Salk's face seemed to turn even redder.

"What were you going to do," Adjani asked evenly, "throw it at him?"

Salk said, "Maybe it's not loaded because you knew it didn't need to be."

"I couldn't find the bullets," Danny replied. "Otherwise I wouldn't have just found him for you, I wouldn't have just drawn him out into the open for you, I'd have shot him for you too and mounted his head on your fucking wall. You should put me on the payroll."

"What does Killer Kasho mean?" Adjani asked.

"Nothing. He Googled me, that's all." Danny felt *he* was only an arm's length away, like the arc of a thumb drive tossed through the air to Mark Pavelko.

"You famous or something?"

"Everyone is if you drill down far enough."

"Everyone's a liar too." Salk's radio squawked. "Everyone keeps secrets. Why you? Huh Danny? Why you? Tonight? *Here?*"

"Obviously he's reading my blog."

"Stop hiding behind your so-called job, Danny."

"Me and my so-called job got more proof of him in five minutes than you've gotten in a year."

"Him? Him *who?*" Salk pointed at Danny's phone. "The video's like that movie of Bigfoot. You know the one I mean Danny?"

"Yeah. Except that was a hoax."

Salk took a couple steps closer to him. "You took the word right out of my mouth. This location doesn't fit with the others. This looks like someone else's choice. In other words I'm wondering how much your roommate looks like the person in your little video there."

Danny was feeling woozy. "Where's Mark Pavelko?"

"Why?" Adjani didn't look up from Danny's phone.

"It was his idea to use me to draw the arsonist out. I'd say it worked. Where is he?"

"How should we know?" Salk said.

"It doesn't say babysitter on our badge," Adjani added. "What'd you two break up or something?"

"Why don't you call him?" Salk said.

Danny was dizzy with frustration. He didn't think the detectives were in on Pavelko's task force within a task force. The sub-task force had a staff of one. One very determined, very sick individual. "I did call him, from the hotel he's supposed to be staying at. They said he's not. He didn't answer his phone. Have you seen him today?"

"Nope, had to cancel our tea party. Too many reporters."

Adjani asked, "What hotel?"

Danny couldn't keep the exasperation out of his voice. "The hotel where the arsonist posted to CODA from. That's what I'm telling you." He eased himself off the wall to indicate forward momentum, a gesture the detectives ought to understand, and a bolt of pain shot from his feet up his spine to his brain stem and almost buckled his knees. "I know the location the arsonist posted from," he gasped, "and they've got video cameras."

The man entered the hotel lobby Sunday at 12:36 PM. He was wearing a midnight blue t-shirt and trousers with a dark baseball cap pulled low over his eyes. He was big. If Mike Cruz's build was the supposed benchmark the man onscreen fit—but so did half the guys at the special agent convention at the hotel. So did Mark Pavelko.

The jerky frame-per-second surveillance footage reduced fluid movement to snapshots. The man appeared in three. He kept his hands in his pockets as he shouldered his way through a group of guests clustered between the front desk and the lounge, walking with his head down to hide his face from the 3/4 bird's-eye view of the overhead cameras. The camera in the hall picked him up—one frame—and then he appeared in the BusinessOn Center, slipping sideways along the wall to a workstation in the corner. He reached around the back of the desktop tower and his latex gloves glowed faintly. The light from the monitor flickered as he browsed. Only his shoulders and the top of his cap were visible to the camera in the center of the ceiling. Seven minutes later he reached around the computer again, stood up and left the room. He exited through the lobby into the parking lot and disappeared from view behind a blue news van parked in the foreground.

The Hampton Inn security office was a crowded, too-warm windowless room accessed through a door behind the front desk, humming with hard drives and smelling of burnt coffee. Laminated color-coded wall maps of the hotel's three floors hung beside the surveillance monitors. Blue ethernet cables climbed like vines up through the ceiling tiles, adding to the unfinished look of the cluttered space. Four widescreen monitors, each subdivided into as many as sixteen separate squares of closed-circuit surveillance, offered haunting scenes of the property—empty hallways, empty elevators, the empty loading dock, empty pool. With most of its guests tucked in for the night the hotel looked deserted. Only the parking lot was active with guests who'd come outside with their phones to watch—it was something besides pay-per-view, even if they didn't know what was going on.

The hotel's chief of security was a retired LAPD detective named Sackett, who'd been called in from home by the night security team—an older black man with curly white hair and a college-age Hispanic in matching suits, striped ties and gold name tags. Haynes and Sanchez. Cheryl the dowdy night manager hadn't dismissed them and no one had asked them to leave so Haynes and Sanchez opted to stick around and watch from a spot by the hotel safe and the fire alarm control panel with its rows of reassuring green lights.

Sackett wore the same kind of suit as the night team but no tie. Reading glasses were draped around his neck. He'd let Cheryl introduce him and otherwise said little beyond asking for a place to start in the footage after settling into the single high-backed chair at the desk. His long fingers operated the keypad and joystick like a maestro, his neck stooped like a vulture's toward the nearest monitor as if to better close the distance to the players on his stage. A hard candy clicked against his teeth.

"He plugged something into the computer didn't he?" Adjani said.

"Probably a flash drive with the photo of my building," said Danny.

The special agent convention was in full effect. Danny stood behind Sackett elbow to elbow with Salk on one side of him and Adjani on the other. Behind them was a second row of investigators that included Mark Pavelko and Tracy Orman. The rest he didn't recognize—and they overflowed the room out into the lobby in various states of dress, from shirts and ties like the homicide detectives to just-got-woken-up shorts and t-shirts.

"What time did you say you were here tonight?" Salk asked him.

"Around 8:15."

Sackett rewound and played from 8:05. There were three types of feeds available—fixed, motorized pan-tilt-zoom cameras, and 360-degree cams. The man walking with his chin glued to his chest had defeated them all. Danny had hoped for better quality video—in this day and age stop-motion Ray Harryhausen footage like this was inexcusable. They may as well use fucking claymation.

He had a weird out-of-body moment looking at himself onscreen as he entered the lobby at 8:14. Everyone squeezed into the room watched him linger and make a call.

"Is that when you called me?" Mark Pavelko wore a faded oversize t-shirt and shorts and his 49ers cap and looked like he'd come straight from bed—or wanted to look that way. "I texted you but you didn't answer."

"Neither did you." Danny didn't look at him. He didn't think Pavelko knew that he knew he'd lied about staying at the hotel. Pavelko wasn't part of the special agent convention, he wasn't officially sanctioned to be here at all. He didn't even have his own radio. He was off the reservation. MIA. He had lie balanced precariously on lie and his foundation was failing. Danny mentally compared his voice to the one on the 911 call and wondered what he sounded like when Mark was excited, when he was barely in control of himself. He wondered if his ex-wife had heard his different voices before she divorced him.

Onscreen Danny went into the BusinessOn Center. Without trying to avoid the camera his profile at least could always be seen, so the man in the cap had definitely been working at it. He came back out and made the failed offer to Psycho Phil, then left the lobby through the sliding doors.

"What was that?" Salk pointed at the screen. "What did you two talk about?"

Danny was acutely aware that Cheryl—murderously trustworthy Phil's boss—was in the room, watching hawkishly with her widely-spaced eyes and her arms folded across her blouse. She held her phone close, ready to update whoever she answered to—hotel chains had chains of command too. While Phil's astonishment at seeing Danny again—with the promised police swarming the hotel—brought a fleeting measure of satisfaction to an otherwise shit-soaked situation, Danny didn't want to see the guy get fired. Especially if Phil was serious about the whole dismemberment out in the desert thing.

He said, "I asked him if I could see the security camera footage. He said no."

"How much did you offer him?"

Danny cleared his throat. "Nothing."

Salk snickered. "Wonder if we'll get the same answer when we ask him."

"The guy's been here before, that's for sure," Adjani said. "He knew where the cameras were, brought everything with him, the flash drive, the gloves. He must have done at least one recon trip."

"And he wasn't wasting any time." Tracy Orman swiftly tied her hair up off her neck in a ponytail. "He was nervous. Or on the clock."

She wore an ATF t-shirt, jeans and blue and yellow Reebok running shoes with complicated soles and no socks. Danny wondered if she'd come straight from bed too. "He was here on Saturday," he said. "He posted at 12:25 PM and 5:32 PM." The round analog clock in the room read 1:05 AM. He was dead-on-his-feet tired.

Sackett had been looking sideways at the group as if awaiting his next cue, and now his hands moved. After a moment the man appeared onscreen wearing the same or similar clothing and cap, striding through the lobby Saturday night at 7:28 PM. The BusinessOn Center had three other users at the time. He left after eighteen minutes.

Sackett backtracked. Earlier in the day the man positively jogged into the place, bumping into someone on his way in at 12:22. At 12:45 he walked briskly out through the lobby, crowded with emergency personnel and hapless tourists. None of the footage from either session contained a better look at his face.

"Where were you at 12:40 today?" Salk asked Danny.

"In Malibu."

"Where in Malibu?"

"Drake's. I've got the receipt." Accountants and homicide detectives live by receipts. Danny had wanted to elaborate on the quote after hearing it from a detective years ago, but in the end had just left it at that in his post. What more needed to be said.

"We love Drake's," Salk said.

"Next time we can share a table," Adjani added.

Mark Pavelko was staring fixedly at the video on Danny's phone, the few frames that panned across the Angeles Arsonist when he leaned back to look up at him at the top of the driveway. His chest was heaving almost as much as the arsonist's was tonight as if they were holding something in their hands of his no one was supposed to touch.

"It looked like a snowtrooper face mask from *The Empire Strikes Back,*" Danny offered.

Pavelko looked up at him. His eyes were hard gray marbles in a puffy flesh-colored sock. Danny assumed he'd seen his personal life splashed across the news yet. Wondered if he'd seen it on CODA too. He had to have. Things were coming asunder.

"First thing I thought of," Danny shrugged.

"Sure." Pavelko cleared his throat and said in a big, confident voice, "Probably a wildland firefighting mask. Flame resistant, covers the neck. Goggles probably have ballistic lenses. The guy's a gear junkie."

Danny thought it sounded like he was trying too hard. "Any statements *you'd* like to make?"

Pavelko bared his teeth. "Not a single one, you frigging parasite. First Amy Childress fucks us like she owes us money and now you do. This is fucking unbelievable you did this to me."

"To you?"

"To us."

Salk said, "I don't want to say I told you so Marky Mark, but Mike was right about this. We all were."

Pavelko didn't take his eyes off Danny. "Thanks Travis, just what I need to hear right now."

"And I agree it *is* beginning to look a lot like sabotage," Salk said. "In other words why don't you tell us who really wrote this email Danny? Here's what I'm thinking—a creative writer with a taste for the limelight, and his roommate."

The hotel employees were tuned in like parabolic antennas arrayed in the desert, having finally picked up a signal of interest among the humdrum noise of space. Danny pictured Phil sharpening his carving knives and humming a merry tune. "And maybe we were both a hundred pounds heavier a few hours ago too. I should start my own diet craze."

"We're talking collusion, not craze," Salk said.

"Go ahead and chase your cottontails all you want running that down. Meantime I'll let my readers know to run for the hills—no wait, they'll be on fire because the taxpayer-funded federal task force is a shambles and is investigating each other. *I* have to find the arsonist for them. *I* have to draw him out. *Me.* The reporter none of *you* wanted to talk to. Now you're bitching about how I did it."

Adjani opened his notebook to a bookmarked page as if it was story time. "What was the registration info again?"

"Username UCANBRN2. Password Fireman666. Zip code 91362. Age 40. Email address fireman666@fastmail.com." Danny's modern e-memory had already embraced the alphanumeric outline of the person where it rubbed elbows with Carrie Voelker's. "His posts are all saved offline. The email came from an anonymous remailer so it's a dead end—"

"Says who?" Salk asked.

"CODA's content manager and IT guy. He's really good."

"I'm sure he's eminently qualified at changing toner cartridges but we'll go ahead and leave the forensics to *our* guys."

"They're really good too," Adjani agreed, making notes.

"What's the zip here?" Tracy Orman asked.

"91301," answered Cheryl the night manager. "91362 is Thousand Oaks. Is that individual a guest of this hotel?"

"I kind of think not," Danny said to Pavelko, who was staring at the image onscreen. Danny followed his gaze.

Sackett had quietly isolated and zoomed in on a single frame showing the man after he bumped into the guest by the front desk on Saturday at 12:22 PM. He'd lifted his head and turned reflexively toward the person and the camera had caught him in mid-stride, having momentarily dropped his technique to frustrate the surveillance cameras because of the unintentional jostling of another human being. One asteroid banging randomly into another and altering its orbit just long enough to see it, for the face on Mars to resolve into its true pareidolian mesa. The shadow cast from the brim of the baseball cap coated a soft chin. Darker shaded areas were maybe the shadow of a moustache or facial hair. But the prehistoric resolution had begun to pixelate the image into tea leaves.

"Without casino-quality software it ain't going to get any clearer," Sackett said.

Salk chided Danny, "Not exactly *exactly* is it?"

"No, but how's the bullshit smelling now?" Danny replied.

"I'd say it has a complex bouquet."

Adjani's phone rang.

"Can we get a printout of that?" Salk asked Sackett.

"Yup, but it's inkjet," the security chief lamented.

Salk addressed Danny in a voice not too low for every single cop in the room and then some to hear. "From now on Danny anything your number one fan does is on you, you understand? In other words this isn't going to pass lightly for you. If anybody else gets hurt or loses their life or loses their property or loses a night's sleep because of this—because of *you*—you are going to get way more publicity than you ever wanted, than you ever bargained for, than you ever imagined. You are going to drown in it and I will be pouring it on."

Adjani cupped his phone. "Abby's wondering if we're coming back there or staying here."

"We're here for the duration," Salk snapped, still staring at Danny, who was in turn staring at the image of the man on the video screen.

Adjani relayed the message then cupped his phone again. "He says that's fine, Mike just got there."

Danny blinked. For a second he and the cops all floated in space like out of control satellites. Pavelko's eyes had alchemized from marble into ice. He was giving no hint away of whatever demons he had burning inside him. He doled out dialogue at his discretion, at his chosen degree. Was he a good cop or a bad cop? A psychopath or a psychic? Was he framing Mike Cruz or the appropriate mugshot?

Danny started to say something but Salk got there first, squaring his shoulders to him and getting right in his personal space. "Alrighty then—Mr. Kasho, I very sincerely want to arrest you for something but I have to talk to some people first. We'll meet tomorrow and you'll give the next version of your formal statement then. Location and time TBD but plan on making yourself available. Do not make us come looking for you."

"I'm easy to find," Danny said to Pavelko, like a dare.

"That goes for your roommate too," Adjani added.

Danny winced inwardly at the thought of the hassle that was about to befall Garrett because of him. He said to Pavelko, "Well, like I told the detectives, your plan worked. Everybody's being drawn out of where they're hiding. There's just more of them than we thought."

Pavelko peered down his nose at him, his lopsided eyebrows slightly furrowed and chin upraised. He didn't blink, as if his ocular mechanism had been paused. He was still a formidable size, even with the softening of his build under excess pounds. In the crowded room he seemed to radiate his own heat.

Danny held his hand out. "Phone."

Pavelko licked his lips. "We're going to need to hold on to it." His voice sounded scratchy as if he'd swallowed too much of the sand blowing across the city on the Santa Anas.

"I'll send a copy of the video to Detective Adjani when I get home."

"We're going to need your phone—"

"You can have it when you show me a search warrant saying you can have it. You can have it when CODA's lawyers say it's okay for me to give it to you, and they're the first people I'm calling as soon as you give me my phone back."

That drew a round of muffled snickers from a room full of men and women who presumably knew search and seizure laws better than he did. For a moment Danny thought Pavelko's fist would close around the device and swallow it whole. The video and everything else was replicated in the cloud but still—principal mattered in these situations. He was nobody's tool and nobody's fool. Most of the time anyway.

Pavelko answered by slapping the phone into Danny's palm with a sound like a knuckle popping.

Danny rolled with his momentum and said to Salk, "Drive me back to my car and I won't bring a lawyer with me tomorrow."

"Oh you've got your own?" Salk said.

"CODA's owner makes more per year than your entire agency's budget. He's got lots of them. They're really good too."

The detective's eyes darkened. But his face wasn't red, so he wasn't that pissed.

Danny clarified, "I'm not taking the big blue bus back home."

"Public transportation's beneath you?"

"I don't have exact change."

Salk smirked. "You can have a complimentary black and white home. Enjoy the taxpayer's taxi. We will see you tomorrow Mr. Kasho."

A pair of deputies walked him out. The lobby was a kangaroo court crowded with cops convinced he was a suspect instead of a witness. Again. He had to shake that off fast, he didn't like the feel of it. Notoriety would come on its own in the morning like an unwanted uncle with a voice as loud as the internet.

The cops talked among themselves while Danny sat alone in the uncomfortable plastic back seat of the cruiser, wiping his eyes and quelling the shakes as they shot east across the Valley at a thrillingly high speed until they approached the interchange of the 101 and 405 freeways, announced by their sudden deceleration and the bright animated glow of the Delma tower.

Tonight the ever-radiant Delma's dedicated water conservation screens—another concession made by the vendor—urged motorists to *Do your part! Be water smart!* Elsewhere she advertised upcoming movie trailers, strobed aggressive political ads, pharmaceutical ads, smart drink ads, and solicited tax-deductible donations to the downtown microhomes project, a duplicate of the one which was working so well curbing the rampant homeless problem in Santa Monica. Danny glimpsed the familiar paternal bearded face of Zachary Abrams, a gazillionaire self-help guru who'd immediately embraced the towers, beaming his face and message warmly out at the defenseless audience of motorists as if they were a megaflock seeking his particular kind of megalomaniacal shepherding instead of frustrated citizens silently bemoaning the lack of functional public mass transit in LA.

The tower's signal didn't intrude into the police car, then they passed out of Delma's sphere of influence and the measurably darker freeway funneled them through the hills into Hollywood, its lights twinkling like exploded glass after a house fire.

CHAPTER 21

The 101 south to the 405 north to the 5 north to mom.

His mind churned like worms in freshly-turned soil as the minivan sped along in light late-night traffic. White headlights. Red taillights. Silver reflective safety barriers. All of it blanketed in blackness. He was being passed on both sides and they probably thought they were better than him because they could. They didn't know what he knew, what people like them never found out until it was them vaporizing in a white-hot blast at a church picnic.

People pushed back.

Like mom always said, the only luck he'd ever had was bad luck which was worse than no luck at all. He'd lived his whole life wanting to prove her wrong so bad and thought that's what he was finally doing. Mom and the rest of the universal peanut gallery. Until he witnessed the incomprehensible debacle with his own eyes. Until they said they were *closing in on him.* Until they said that they *knew* him. That they were *watching* him. Maybe they were. Maybe they really were listening to him. Following him with drones. Fucking things were all over the place now.

Like how the snoopy female cop who caught him one-handed with his pants down in Malibu Bowl downwind of the smoke on Friday had appeared out of nowhere. Like she'd parachuted onto the road where he was parked. She said she was too busy directing traffic to arrest him for indecent exposure and let him off with a warning and her condescending, pitying sneer, as if he was some kind of pervert. He specifically chose not to shoot her but he could have. He could have so easily. Her gun wouldn't have cleared her holster strapped to her wide child-rearing hips. But he chose not to end it yet there. With her. She wasn't worth it and he wasn't ready yet. He wasn't done yet. The mission wasn't finished.

They were saying on TV that people were being stopped and their cars searched. All their stuff taken out and thrown on the road in front of everybody. They had to put it all back themselves when they were let go. This was law and order. They hadn't tried that with him, not yet, and if they did, *that* he'd be ready for. He always carried at least one gun in the car and the only second thoughts would be theirs before they died: *If only I hadn't pulled him over.*

He had a small arsenal cached at Imelda's—a heavy-as-hell American army tactical vest he bought online from China, elbow, leg, and knee pads bought from same, semi-automatic SIG, Beretta, and Heckler & Koch handguns, and an AR-15 with about a thousand .223 Remington rounds. More boxes of ammo were packed tight around the toys he'd made at his place. Dozens more. Enough for the big party.

But for fuck's sake they said they knew what kind of *boots* he wore.

Air hissed out between his teeth, which were coffee-stained and not straight.

He was the type of person who thought about everything, every contingency, every last detail about everything, all the time. At work they said he was obsessive like it was a bad thing. That he over-thought things to the point of paralysis, whatever the fuck that meant. Like it was his fault he could always see what was wrong. They just didn't want to hear it and that wasn't his fault either. Imelda used to say that too—not in those words of course—but he'd straightened her out right quick about that. He wasn't about to take that shit from her too.

He half-thought they were making up the boot print thing. Finding *boot prints* at a *wildfire?* Any competent lawyer would say *Of course you did—they're* yours. They were sneaky liars, and there were a lot of them, and they were all working in concert together against him. Their great big gang. It was eight billion to one and it always had been. Mom was batshit crazy but she was right about some things.

That Him wanted to stay one step ahead of them and that confidence and a whole lot of beer was how This Him was going to do it.

He got rid of what he could in trash cans and Dumpsters all over the place. It didn't appear like much but it was the small stuff the pricks could pin on you. And to the people on TV these things were no big deal, these decisions, throwing away pieces of himself as if he'd cut out his own vital organs and stuffed them down the garbage disposal one after the other while he bled all over the floor. They thought they could catch him by cornering him but there were ways out of anything if your definition of *exit* was malleable enough. The end would be the end when he and he alone said it was. When it was time for the big party. When he'd make them understand what an *ending* was.

He'd sat in the minivan in the parking lot for a while, wiping away the sweat and staring at the men on the sidewalk. A black plastic garbage bag containing zip ties, rags he'd fashioned into gags, a flashlight, rope, gloves, and a hammer was tucked under his seat. He had some beer in an ice chest on the back seat; the person would be thirsty. He drank some of the beer as he waited and watched the anonymous Mexicans with his busy eyes, these nobodies served up like eggs on the long skillet of sidewalk. Cars and pickups came and went. Mexicans came and went too but mostly just loitered in place.

Getting the beer and the minivan turned out to be the biggest challenges of the day.

Imelda had both. The minivan would probably have gas in it, and she had a whole case of Heineken in her fridge, he'd seen it there the other day. But right off the bat she started up by saying no. No he couldn't take her car. No he couldn't take the beer. She said she bought the beer for herself but Imelda didn't drink beer, much less *Heineken,* which she'd never even heard of much less *drank,* which meant she was lying to him. Again. She'd bought it so a *friend* could drink it. A *male* friend, probably the one who lived next door, the guy with the dirty Santa Claus beard that was always over and never said shit to him. He returned the silence in kind. And in spades. Imelda was still his and everything she had was his too.

She just needed to be reminded about that because there she was stamping her bare feet on her kitchen's dirty linoleum floor and shouting that he couldn't do this and he couldn't do that and he hit her and she bounced right back up at him like she was made of rubber, clawing and shrieking and he came as close as he'd ever come to getting the Ruger from his car and coming back inside before she thought to lock the door and shooting her right in the center of her forehead, splattering her *pocos* brains all over her fucking kids. Traumatize the little shits like they'd traumatized him when he'd lived here. They'd have to be next—there was no getting around that. They were old enough to be witnesses and they knew his name, and besides he didn't need the little bastards coming back to haunt him. But he didn't have time and hadn't drank nearly enough for that. That was for later, during the big party.

He was about to hit her again when her fury suddenly turned off like a switch, so he took the goddamned keys and the goddamned beer and drove it back to his place to load up. Drank a few. Then drove here. Even with the windows down the smell of fuel and machine oil under the drop cloth in back filled the hot cabin of the minivan like he imagined a Thanksgiving meal smelled in a kitchen. He drew comfort from it and knew it would help—the minivan smelled like a garage. To whoever he picked the minivan would smell like that of a viable working man.

A note of caution there—he had to choose wisely. He'd been thinking a lot about that. The criteria wasn't easy. The Ruger .22 in the door pocket weighed less than a pound. It had been bought without a receipt, no sale recorded, so it was untraceable. But it was small, easily manipulated. He couldn't be fighting someone and trying to drive at the same time. That Him didn't drive, only This Him did. That Him only did one thing. This Him handled the rest all by himself. As usual. This Him always said something like this would happen.

And just like that the player walked onto his stage.

The Mexican stood in a patch of sunlight noticeably brighter than the rest. A big man with a baby face, in faded jeans and an old long-sleeved shirt and a baseball cap that looked newer than the rest of his clothing. He was clutching a brown paper lunch bag that was stained as if there was something moist inside it and smiling to himself as if he'd just seen something funny.

He didn't even realize he'd started the car until it was moving. Some of the other Mexicans rushed toward him but he pointed at the one he wanted and the baby-faced guy hustled over, smiling at his good fortune and whatever other ignorant superstitions kept him so happy.

The Mexican said *Got work?* Guy's teeth were worse than his own.

He said yeah he got work. He said something about quake damage and good pay, bullshit as bait, and suddenly the Mexican was sitting beside him in the car, smelling of sweat and manure, some olfactory hangover from his last job or maybe he just didn't bathe, and he thought that was poetic justice for Imelda making such a stink about him borrowing her car. He'd bring it back smelling like Mexican shit. So fucking there.

As he wheeled out of there he suddenly realized he hadn't thought of what to do with the Mexican until it got dark enough. There was still light for a good couple of hours, and he thought even the dumb Mexican would figure it out sooner or later when they drove and drove and drove but never got anywhere. The timing was critical or else one thing wouldn't connect to the other, and they had to. That was the whole point. He'd planned this out and thought it through and it would work. It would work. It had to work. He needed this.

He offered the Mexican a Heineken and the guy hesitated a second to make sure it was for real. *Go on,* he encouraged, as if the Mexican was a puppy or a kid. *Take it.* Of course the Mexican took it, they took anything you offered them. There was dirt packed under the fingernails of his rough and calloused hands and a gratitude in his ever-present smile that transcended mere joviality. Perhaps he was one of mom's china angels in a previous life. An entity so benign it bordered on the divine. A soul so pure and so simple you wondered how it had made it this far without some sort of divine intervention to keep it from being mowed down at the first opportunistic crossroads.

They dawdled in neighborhood after neighborhood around Malibu in a patient migration toward sundown. He and the Mexican drank beer after beer. *Bottomless well,* he said to the Mexican, knowing full well if the guy understood him at all he wouldn't be able to tell whether he was being offered drinks or about to have his dumb brown ass thrown down one. He liked having that inside information. That secret. That power. It was a turn-on almost as intense as the moment of release of flame from captivity.

He stopped now and then with the engine off to save gas—lots of things to do today—drinking with the Mexican, positive the Mexican was lost, and savoring the lingering smell of smoke in the air. He pretended to take calls informing him the project was delayed another half hour. Then another. He shrugged helplessly to the Mexican, like an equal. He assured him they'd get paid no matter what. They drank and he made up stories about the big house with the rich owner, a movie star, a mogul. Didn't know how much of it the Mexican could understand but it kept his simple imagination bubbling.

More toothy smiles and reassurances and beers all around.

When the sun finally began to sink into the sea like a projectile penetrating cold blue skin in slow-motion he found a spot on PCH across the street from the lagoon. The Mexican followed him to the path by the entrance. A park ranger was sitting in his truck, ready to lock the gate at sunset—trapping any car in the lot for the night that didn't get out in time—but the ranger was occupied with his phone and didn't notice them. He kept himself between the Mexican and the ranger as much as he could so if the ranger saw them he'd only remember seeing one person. The Mexican might as well be invisible.

The .22 was wrapped up in a red windbreaker he carried under his arm. Attached to it was a plastic 2-liter Coke bottle filled with steel wool with the bottom cut out of it. He'd opted for duct tape rather than a liquid rubber adhesive to affix it to the gun—the suppressor only had to last one shot and it had to come off easily as soon as he was done. He'd already wiped the weapon down, and he slipped on disposable gloves as soon as they got past the ranger—there were no shortcuts.

They followed the walkway into the reeds, him carrying his windbreaker and the Mexican carrying the boots in his arms. He'd wiped them down too. He didn't see anyone. They didn't pass anyone. When they were far enough he made the Mexican sit down and put on the boots. It was as easy as controlling a puppet. *Okay?* the Mexican said with his dumbass grin.

The Mexican tugged on both boots and looked up with that dumbass smile right into the open end of the Coke bottle and he shot the Mexican in the center of his dull brown forehead from a distance of less than eight inches.

Blood, bone and brains—the three B's of a head shot—coughed out the back of the Mexican's head in a fine pink spray almost invisible in the fading light. Before the castrated pop of the suppressed .22 receded—it sounded like a car door slamming—he caught the sagging body and squeezed the Mexican's fingers around the stubby grip of the Ruger, tore off the burned Coke bottle and pushed the body and the gun off the walkway into the water. He thought the splash was louder than the gunshot.

He didn't look back and he didn't run. That Him always vanished the second after something happened and This Him didn't like that, he was always left holding the bag. It happened all the time. When he got back to the parking lot the gate was locked and the ranger was gone. The parking lot was empty. It felt like an eternity waiting for the light to cross PCH. He dropped the Coke bottle in a garbage can at the gas station on the corner. His hands were shaking at the car door handle and he dropped Imelda's keychain with everything on it—the minivan, her house, two other keys he still hadn't found corresponding locks for. He didn't like that she kept secrets from him but he appreciated that he was thinking about Imelda instead of the Mexican back there in the water.

He turned around at the first available and legal opportunity and drove back up the coastal highway past canyon roads that squiggled through the mountains—Malibu, Puerco, Corral, Latigo, Kanan Dume, Trancas, Encinal, Decker. Decker's nondescript S-curve sloping up from PCH beckoned like an invitation to a secret party which he eagerly accepted with growing excitement. He literally felt jet engines under his arms, rockets blazing him up the road instead of Imelda's shitty little minivan which could barely make 30 on this road. He was already late and getting a little stressed about that. The timing was critical—the body was already in the water. One thing connected to the other. Kasho couldn't leave.

Decker wound on interminably and with every passing curve his stress increased. He became convinced Kasho wouldn't be there.

He can't leave.

He can't leave.

And he hadn't.

He spotted the silver Accord parked by the trash bins and probably smiled as dumbass a grin as the Mexican's. Kasho was paying attention. He felt compliance from Kasho at last as if he was down on bended knee in proposal. It was a delicious dough he could sink his teeth into, like the back of mom's neck.

He pulled in nose to nose with Kasho's car. The fuel tanks were already full so he only needed a couple of minutes to get everything on. He got the face shield in place and just when he got the tanks on he looked up and saw Kasho bathed in a blue-white moonlight glow like a doll illuminated by a TV.

They both stood there like idiots, looking at each other like hosts surprised to see their guests at their doorstep—they'd actually shown up instead of begging off under a last-minute excuse.

Kasho's mouth was moving and he realized he was talking to him.

Kasho was talking to him.

He wanted to touch him but he didn't want Kasho's skin under his fingernails or his sticky DNA anywhere near him. It had to be a clean, decisive, antiseptic connection made and broken within an instant.

The wind carried Kasho's words to him: *You have to hide.*

And That Him surfaced like a shark beneath a surfer. His fingers squeezed the triggers one after the other and the pilot light ignited and he thought *No hiding. There's no hiding from this. There's no hiding from* me.

Then he saw the gun and for that moment, that brown cardboard box full of secondhand time, he knew fear. He knew defenseless vulnerability worse than an upraised hand or a whipping belt or an adult's fist driven into a child's undeveloped stomach. He knew qualitatively something unfair and acidic—the purposeful, methodical stamping-out of hope like a cigarette under a boot heel.

Kasho was aiming a gun at him he thought *Do it. Pull the trigger. Kill me. I'm an abomination. I'm a deviant. I'm broken. I wasn't made right. I am wrong.* Dying might hurt but death wouldn't be worse than living was.

But Kasho didn't shoot him. Kasho didn't fire the gun. He'd anticipated the shot, the impact, the pain. Welcomed its coming and his release. Instead Kasho *ran.* He ran too—tried to, up the steep incline of the driveway. But running him down like a rat wasn't in the plan. Kasho wasn't supposed to get out of the dry grass and bushes. Kasho wasn't supposed to be *armed.* He was a reporter, not a cop. He wasn't supposed to have a gun. He'd planned it out and thought it through and in no scenario did Kasho ever have a *gun.*

When he got to the top of the driveway he didn't see him. That's it, That Him said, let's get out of here. Not so fast, This Him said, and made him look at the house. Saw it for what it was. The exposed wood was beckoning him, telling him to come, take it. Ravage it and all who were hiding inside like the drug house when he was eleven.

Do it! That Him screamed in his ears. *Kill him! Kill him now! Kill him right now!*

The next few minutes were a claustrophobic blur of right angles and blind corners and flames so close he almost caught fire too, the dog nearly turning on its master, a low growl emanating deep from its primal belly and vibrating into its sharp, canine teeth, making it dismiss instinct, dismiss loyalty and embrace the act of aggression itself, the freedom of movement uninhibited and unencumbered by any consideration of the next moment.

He felt the flames differently. Saw them for the first time with an unfriendly stance toward *him,* and he tried to hope Kasho died in the house. He put everything he had behind the wish but he knew Kasho was still alive. He just knew it. He could still feel him, closer than ever. Intimately, as if they'd each penetrated the other. That familiar vice grip squeezed his head and made him gnash his teeth in despair as he steered into the night. It wasn't just that he'd missed out on hearing the ecstatic music of Kasho screaming, it was that nothing ever worked out for him like it did for other people. For something to go right he had to make it happen, like having to pay a stripper just to get laid.

He heard mom's curse in every song on the radio: *The only luck he ever had was bad luck.*

He was amazed he could concentrate enough right now to drive. None of the materials stockpiled in his apartment suffered carelessness lightly. Focus was essential. The arrangement of jars and tubs individually wired to detonator cords had taken shape as naturally as if it had helped design itself, as if it had become self-aware. Now the triggers just needed setting, which he'd do when he got home. After that the big party would be like a fire—just start it. Then see what happens.

He made himself think again about where he'd go after. Alaska looked like a brochure state and people could really disappear up there. Mexico was closer and cheaper and warmer. He could disappear there too. He could indulge himself in all the things he'd never been able to do. Mexican girls were plentiful and cheap, pesos to penis. Sinaloa sounded like a verb.

This could work.

After Imelda. After Mendes. If there was anyone who needed killing on this planet it was Mendes, but it would be next to impossible to fit that into the mission. Kasho should count himself lucky, 'cause he sure never got to.

He pressed his foot hard against the accelerator which was already flat on the floor as they climbed another grade, the minivan barely able to pass an 18-wheeler trudging up the far lane. His headlights lit up the sign for Pyramid Lake out of sight on the left, a half-empty basin of water falsely created by a dam, a dwindling reservoir ringed by mountains he couldn't see.

He fervently wished the earth and rock would crack and split and the dam would fail and everything that had been held back all these years would, like him, finally cascade out into the unwitting world.

CHAPTER 22

Labor Day dawned undetected by Danny, who floated naked in inky darkness blacker than Johnny Cash's soul before he found God and June Carter. It was a void, but it wasn't soundless. It was like commercial radio. Noisy emptiness. Like the devil gargling.

And it hurt—a lot like commercial radio, mixed with the worst hangover ever, and a sudden redefinition of the word pain. Pain became a physical presence rather than a sensation. It made him feel like the little kid at the bottom of the dog pile, while being jabbed with forks by everyone on top of him. Big horror movie-style tridents jammed between his ribs—every time he did a little thing called breathe—and thousands of tiny shrimp forks twisted around everywhere else, between muscles and bones, bones and ligaments, right down into his cells.

His first cognizant thought was *I fucked up,* but it was in Vincent Price's voice, and then the gargling devil completed its metamorphosis into the grating buzz of his phone vibrating against his desk.

The plastered ceiling of his bedroom slowly swam into focus like a reef revealed by receding water. His bones felt as if they'd been replaced by hot wires and all at once he became convinced the pain was actually lingering echoes of previous sensations, ghost signals sent by nerve endings he didn't possess anymore, like remembrances from an amputated limb. His brain was listening to conversations with his fingers and toes that had already ended.

He was paralyzed from the waist down.

He closed his eyes but wasn't even able to muster a tear at his condition. He was going to have to pee through a catheter from now on and carry a biohazard bag around with him. *Scooch over Gina, I need room for my piss bag. Sorry, it's warm.* Eventually he'd have to move into a government-subsidized care home for semi-paralyzed assholes who couldn't piss like a normal person but were still deemed by people who had continence-control to be lucky. Lucky to be alive and in possession of a leak-proof bag of warm piss. Count your fucking blessings.

He dispatched desperate scouts down to his fingers and they moved. A little. He sent more scouts all the way down to his toes and they wiggled too. He thought they did anyway. He kept the scouts going until he was sure. They were moving. Definitely.

He pushed his head back on his pillow and groaned softly with relief. Pass the piss bag on the left hand side and send it on to someone else. It wouldn't be needed here after all.

He welcomed the pain. Pain was proof of life. He was alive and his dancing digits proved he was more or less intact. Someone had gone over and above in their effort to eradicate him, to try and take away what was rightfully his. They had failed. *He was alive.* He'd beaten the asshole hiding behind the mask who'd tried to inflict more pain and suffering on the Kasho family. Tried to shatter what had already been smashed.

After any trauma *mother* was usually the most instinctive place to turn, even his own, and while he waited for his body to complete its painful reboot he found himself reliving the last day the Kashos were together in the house on the steep corner of Grace Street in Calendula. A pair of old, thick oak trees shaded their sloping front lawn. From the upper windows you could see the ocean and the island—each of the kids had their own bedroom on the second floor and each one had a view. *The house I grew up in* would always be the house on Grace Street despite having abandoned the place when he was twelve.

That day Vanessa had gathered the children in the living room after she'd been gone for hours. Their dad had been in jail for two days already—two nights he didn't come home, didn't tuck his kids into bed and kiss them goodnight—and today was his court appearance. That's what Victor called it. Danny knew it was called an arraignment which sounded much more dire, as if there was nothing positive that could possibly come from having one. The kids had been watching for their mother's car from the upstairs windows and had bounded down the stairs to meet her when her gold-colored Volvo station wagon rattled into the driveway.

Danny had known immediately something was wrong when she got out of the car alone. Vic said to them, "He's just being processed." Danny didn't know what that meant but was pretty sure his brother was wrong.

The kids sat shoulder to shoulder on the sofa, looking up at Vanessa while she paced in front of them on the other side of the coffee table, eyeing each of them in turn with her lips pursed tightly as if trying to convey her message without actually saying it.

Finally she spread her hands—her ring finger was already bare—and said, "Children, I'm sorry but your father won't be coming home after all."

Her kids stared at her.

"Ever," she clarified. "Now run upstairs and pack your clothes. One suitcase each. Cynthia, use the big one. Just one toy Danny. Victor bring extra underwear."

"But where are we *going?*" Cynthia whined.

"We're leaving."

Danny had fumbled through his toys, action figures and cars, books and colored pens, unable to see through his tears. Victor cried too and threw things and shouted at him, calling him a baby and swearing at him and worse—saying that this was all his fault, which he already knew. He never imagined telling the truth could make something like this happen, dad not being here with them anymore as if he'd died. But he *wasn't* dead. This was the *opposite* of what was supposed to happen when you told the truth.

Vanessa had already found the foreclosure in North Calendula, the modest bungalow squatting on a treeless lot smaller than their back yard. Most of NoCal's dense grid of modest homes and service-oriented businesses was hemmed into a rough trapezoid by the four major streets that made up the business loop. Despite the development bulging its northern border NoCal was and always would be defined by its fast food restaurants, body shops, low-budget motels, discount stores, strip malls, and a growing number of available storefronts. The have-nots and gimme-mores, Vanessa and her friends used to call them, before she had to move there and the Kashos didn't have any friends anymore and Vanessa

McQueen—ex-housewife, then the least employable office temp in the city—had yet to make any new ones.

She had Danny stencil *McQueen* on the mailbox immediately after they moved in, which only added to the persistent unfamiliarity of the place. And then the Kashos went about trying to disappear in front of their former friends and neighbors.

At the time they moved to NoCal there was no end to the dislocation, there was only what *wasn't* anymore, and for each of them to adapt to it in their own way. All the while Vanessa insisted that they learn to think of their father as having run off on them or died in a car accident. The accident scenario always played out with Paul DUI, just to keep the blame properly assigned. It was not only better for everyone but absolutely necessary that they move on and never discuss him ever again, as if it were possible for the children to emulate their mother's complicated emotional response to the situation.

Thirteen year-old Cynthia got her own bedroom in the new house; Danny and Victor had to share one, which only fueled his brother's anger at him. But by the time Vic was seventeen he was spending more and more nights out of the house, often getting into trouble that would propel Vanessa out of bed to the police station in her house coat, and the solitude suited Danny just fine. He'd turned into a latchkey kid after Paul's arrest anyway, retreating into his own world from which he looked out with hostility and suspicion and resentment and curiosity. Parental supervision which before had been liberally spacious suddenly became nonexistent as Vanessa dealt with the fallout of her husband's unplanned and shameful exit from their lives. Danny had realized then that parents were greater than the sum of their parts—lax rules were better than no rules at all and with dad gone Vanessa drifted into a self-centered orbit not even her children could join.

Cynthia had been strong enough to stay in Calendula even when she had options to leave. Better options—good colleges out of state. Instead she chose to shuck the affliction of the Kasho family by starting one of her own. She got married at twenty-three and she and Will Smith, CPA moved into a house just three blocks away from the one on Grace Street, the place of magic from the life *before,* back when their unfettered dreams could fly like doves into a boundless sky. The house had since been repainted and cosmetically changed by consecutive owners who'd all be strangers in the place no matter how long they lived there.

Danny kept a framed picture by his desk of Cynthia posing with Will and daughter Celia when his now six year-old niece was only three, all smiles and baby teeth in front of Calendula's postcard-perfect marina, with the weathered edges of buildings abutting the rocky coastline, the blocky concrete aquarium and the old canning factories elevated on pilings, and the incongruous five-story Italian Renaissance hotel rising above the homes on the island in the background. Her young family was the very embodiment of hope and renewal, not just the lack of an anchor which had made it easier for Danny to set sail in 2001, soon after he turned twenty. He hopped a Greyhound south to LA with some cash and the name of a single contact in a bid to end the notoriety of being a murderer's son by vanishing in plain sight of an indifferent population. NoCal wasn't home to anyone but Vanessa and Victor, who split his bedtime between his old bedroom at Vanessa's and the apartments of successive girlfriends.

There was a thick, swampy taste in Danny's mouth. He could feel the Xanax hangover in the excessive grogginess—his eyelids had tiny barbells glued to them. He hadn't seen any LAPD patrol car assigned to his address when the deputies dropped him off last night and doubted there had ever been one. His fears didn't warrant official attention, only his faults. He'd limped alone through the red-lit lobby, jumping at every sound, listening to the old building groan in the wind with all the gratitude that had ever followed grace. The extant world was beautiful, even dirty old Hollywood which always slept like a well-dressed drunk passed out on the couch.

The last piece of business he did for the night was zip up the anonymous email and the video from his phone, upload them to CODA's server—he had faith in the cloud but not actual trust—and send a link to Igor Adjani for the detective to disseminate as he saw fit.

Using his arms alone he slowly turned onto his side, away from the bright windows, and was rewarded by high-res pain mapping his ribcage in 3D, which elicited a squeak from the back of his throat that sounded like the ceiling fan wobbling in its housing.

He rolled a bloodshot eyeball around and spotted his clothes from last night wadded up in a heap on the floor, destined for the trash. No amount of soap would ever banish the smell of fear stitched into them. They were like hand-me-down clothes from his father, a ghost's second skin that had been shed and left in a dusty corner of an abandoned house for someone who'd been close to the deceased to find. Put them on and become as the ghost was, faint energy dislocated between environments, one foot on the diving board of existence and the other in mid-air, leaping into the abyss in which you never touched down, never hit bottom, just flew lost as a loose feather on an unceasing breeze. He'd never wear those clothes again.

His skin smelled smoky, as if cannibals had started to prepare him and then went with something else. Thai, maybe.

Hi all. I ran into Gary Calder the other day and he said to tell everyone hi. Also someone called to tell him your father is ill. I thought you might like to know. Love, Mom.

For twenty-six years Vanessa Kasho had tried to wedge her maiden name McQueen between herself and the immutable facts of life linking her to a marriage and mating with a murderer. She'd left everything in Paul's workshop to student movers and storage boxes and moved the family to the new house and new schools on the other side of the city, which was as far as she could afford to run as she quickly transitioned from housewife to Calendula's most unpopular office temp. In the beginning sometimes people found out where she was working and called in threats against her and the children; she never worked in one place for long. Félix Robitaille's family and company both wanted to sue but were dissuaded—blood from a stone, it was argued, successfully. The children shouldn't be punished for their father's behavior. They would suffer enough.

And the Kasho kids did.

Vanessa's children were existential reminders of the biggest mistake she'd ever made and she quickly tired of being necessary, being the sole bread winner single-handedly raising and running the outcast family. She'd expressly forbidden them from having any contact with Paul, which wasn't difficult to enforce when they were all underage, but as soon as Victor was old enough for a learner's permit he insisted he was going to drive out to see dad on his own, and many screaming matches ensued. In the end he never went. None of them did. Even as they all got older and independent. Vanessa's rule had become unnatural law, a hex cast upon helpless babies.

Unbelievable, Danny thought as he groped for his phone on his nightstand. The cracked display distorted the pixels but there were red counters indicating texts, emails and voicemails aplenty.

It was 8:15.

Ever since achieving working adulthood he'd never once dropped the beat of his circadian rhythm that unfailingly awoke him at two minutes before six each morning, regardless of how late he was up the night before. Until today two minutes to six was something he could rely on. He had so many unread emails and messages and missed calls that the little red counters had to abbreviate the numbers exponentially. Receivers had already traced the shock waves of last night's big bang right back to its source. He wondered if there were news vans already parked downstairs waiting for him to emerge from the building like a fox flushed from its den.

"Well hi," Vanessa answered in his ear. "You're up early. How are you?"

The pitch of every sentence Vanessa ever spoke sank from high to low. Like her perpetually downturned mouth which sought to convey happiness some other way than smiling, joy to her sounded like a burdensome sigh. Vanessa could make *Hello* sound like *He died.*

Danny said, "I'm good. How are you?"

"I'm good too, thanks. What's wrong?" As if Vanessa's long-dormant motherly instincts could still detect the terror her youngest child had been in just hours ago.

But unlike Victor, Vanessa didn't get Danny's parking tickets in the mail—he kept his troubles to himself. "Nothing," he said stiffly. "I was just calling about your email."

"My email?"

"About dad."

"Oh. Well," Vanessa let her interest fall like a dead bird. "You know as much as the rest of us."

"Who's Gary Calder?"

"You don't remember him?"

"No."

"Gary is just a friend." As if he'd asked if they were dating. "He knows someone who works in the department of jails or some such thing. I don't know the details."

"Details?"

"I stopped being your father's secretary a long time ago, Daniel."

Right around the time she'd stopped being Vanessa Kasho, mother of three shell-shocked children, and embarked on her solo reinvention as Vanessa McQueen, single first, mom second. Danny didn't know the details of how that was going and he didn't want to. She'd noted many times that since he had amply demonstrated how much he didn't need her in his life, he couldn't be surprised by her alleged lack of interest in his. She called it *investment*, a phrase she'd picked up from her self-help program or whatever it was. But he didn't know how to tell her about last night, about how close she'd come to getting a phone call in the dead of last night. He could no more bring her to terms like that than she could bring herself to ask about them.

He rubbed his eyes, careful to avoid reopening the fresh scabs on his knuckles. "So what did he say exactly?"

"Who?"

"Gary. Calder."

"He said your father was ill. Didn't I mention that in my email? I thought I did."

Danny pressed a thumb into his temple. "I guess my question is how ill? Ill with what? What did he mean?"

"You'll have to ask him. Have you called your brother and sister yet?"

"No."

"Getting mom out of the way first huh?"

Danny's jaw tightened. That hurt too. "I just want some answers."

"Don't we all? I'm a lot closer to mine because I work at it. I learned to ask the right questions. Not to sweat the small stuff."

That almost made Danny bite. He silently rebuked himself. It was too easy to get into it with Vanessa, she was a quagmire of confrontation. He gingerly swung his legs off his bed and struggled to sit up as the room went all lenticular on him, alluding to depths that weren't there, shapes that redefined themselves as his eyes swept the room.

"Are you okay?" Vanessa asked. "What was that noise?"

"I just—threw out my back." His drawing pad was on the floor. Before he fell asleep or passed out depending on your definition of unconsciousness, he'd started a pencil sketch of the arsonist in his Fireman666 costume while it was still fresh in his mind's eye. The drawing didn't capture the hostility, merely described its shape, but even in the bright morning sunlight it was enough to give him a chill. He'd seen it with his own eyes. It was real. That crazy motherfucker was wearing it.

"Do you get any exercise?" Vanessa asked.

"No." He might have recovered faster from his *Man Who Skied Down Everest* uncontrolled cartwheeling tumble into the fence last night if he wasn't as graceful as a yak on roller skates.

"Writing is rather sedentary isn't it? You need to exercise. Otherwise you'll turn all to pudding."

Maybe Gary Calder worked with Vanessa in Calendula city hall where she was an administrative assistant to somebody. Maybe she assisted him. Maybe they'd had an inter-office romance. Maybe he exercised. Maybe he played tennis or pick-up basketball with the guys, or jogged around Calendula's pedestrian paths, vigorous and well-balanced, with muscular calves, monitoring his vitals on a sporty watch. "Where did you meet him?"

"Who?"

"Gary Calder. Did you meet him at work or in your group or what?"

"I can only assume what Victor has told you," Vanessa said archly, "and I assume you can tell the difference."

Danny groaned with his mouth away from the phone. Wished he could remove his head entirely for a few hours. Leave it in the sink or the fridge till he could bear to shoulder it again. "Between what?" he asked.

"Between truth and mistruth."

"You mean untruth."

"I mean what I say," she said louder, her voice acquiring a Ginsu edge.

"Okay, okay."

"Yes, okay."

"I didn't call to fight with you, Vanessa. I really don't care."

"Well that's a relief Daniel. Such a nice thing to hear from a child."

"It's not why I called."

"You know any mistakes I may have made, I made for you."

Danny frowned and making that expression hurt too, up around his eyes like the mother of all sinus infections. "What's that supposed to mean?"

"I'm sure you have a laundry list of things I didn't do right after your father left."

"Left?"

"You're the writer, say it however you want. Isn't it about time you give *me* some credit for making my own decisions? For living my *own* life? When do I not have to have anything to do with him again?"

"Dad's alive! He's real!" Raising his voice felt like someone was scouring the inside of his skull with an SOS pad. The pain almost literally brought tears to his eyes as if a doctor had begun a procedure before the Novocain had set in.

"He's your problem if you choose him to be, not mine," Vanessa said. "Are you sure you're okay? Did you drink too much last night?"

"How do I get in touch with him?"

"Call the department of jails—"

"Does Gary Calder know how to get in touch with him?"

"I don't know. Maybe, I suppose. Your brother seems to be upset by this." Vanessa sounded as disconnected as if she was commenting on a character on TV. "He seems to think he's owed something and I don't know what it is. Or why."

Neither did Danny, and he'd put at least as much time into that question as his mother had put into hers.

"Well?" she asked.

"Well what?"

"What do you think it is?"

"I think Vic needs to know what's going on with dad. Look, I'll just take the number if you've got it." This was expensive bribery—he wished he could just offer her $50 and be done with it. "Please," he added.

"Hold on, I'll find it." Vanessa put her phone down.

Danny climbed awkwardly out of bed and retrieved the drawing pad and pencil and eased gently back onto his mattress. He fought off the *what if's* which were strong enough to make him feel nauseous at how close he'd come to sharing Neil Weber's unimaginably painful fate, how much dying would hurt, and dying like *that*—and how much it would hurt what was left of his family. He couldn't be that reckless again.

Vanessa came back on the line. "Ready? I haven't called it so I don't know if it's right."

"I'm sure it's fine."

She sighed "You always were Daniel," and read off Gary Calder's number.

He wrote it down in his pad. "Always were what?"

"Always sure everything would be fine. Are you fine now?"

He didn't answer.

"Daniel?"

"I'm fine. I wasn't drinking last night. I threw out my back."

"So what are you going to do?"

"Go see a doctor maybe, if I have to. Or a chiropractor or something."

"I mean about your father. Isn't that why you called? You're not going to *visit* him are you?" She made it sound as idiotic as booking a Carnival cruise to a leper colony.

"I don't know," he said. "I don't. But I'd like to not be the only one in charge of doing something."

"Well Daniel your sister is pregnant and Victor—well, if he goes to jail they might not let him out. They might decide to keep him. Anyway you're the one who always wanted him back." Then she apologized with her mouth away from the phone. "I just mean if something happens, somebody will have to do something."

"No kidding."

"Daniel don't make this any harder than it needs to be."

"For who? Who is it hard for? Is it hard on you at all?"

"It's hard when my son is being sarcastic with me."

"Well I guess I'll let you know then."

"Don't go out of your way. But please call your brother, I know he'd like to hear from you."

"He has my number too you know."

"I know."

"I'll talk to you later."

"Thanks for calling, Daniel. It's so nice to hear your voice."

CHAPTER 23

He redressed the cuts, scrapes and abrasions with liberal application of Neosporin and inexplicable Sesame Street Band-Aids he found in the medicine cabinet. His right ankle hurt more than his ribs and thigh and everything else, but thank God, he thought with utter gravitas—thank *God* the face was unscathed.

He drank four ibuprofen with some Sprite he'd found like holy water in the fridge and wondered how he was going to explain it all to Garrett—the intrusion, the theft and subsequent loss of his gun, the threat of impending interrogation by the task force. He wouldn't blame him at all if he told him to move out—he certainly would if somebody stole something of his. Not to mention *lost* it. Not to mention if it was a fucking *gun.* The disaster was epic in scale and absolutely inexcusable. Indefensible. And the thought of losing the only real home he'd ever had in LA, his best friend, along with Garrett's circle of friends, many of whom had become his friends too, squeezed his heart in a regretful vise.

But that had to wait.

Careful not to prick his fingers with tiny shards of glass from his phone's cracked display, he started in on his riot of emails and texts, prioritizing as he went.

Carrie Voelker had messaged him this morning. Top of the pile at ten after eight. That's what had awakened him. *Lunch today? Xo!* A little emoji scared face like *The Scream* that wasn't particularly cute this morning. He stared at the *Xo* as if it was evidence of an indiscretion. Someone else's underwear in the laundry pile. If only he could credit the morning glory to his wit and charm at Drake's. If only he could discount the feeling she was nudging him like a shark testing the viability of a meal. He didn't reply but he didn't delete it. Now that he knew her number he'd be enticed to contact her off hours, probably when he was drunk, when it most seemed like a really good idea.

He scrolled through friends congratulating him on his Justine London appearance last night, which felt distant as a dream today. Lucy Baskin was trying to track him down with increasing irritation in the reverse chronology of texts:

Where the hell are you?

Call me need to talk now.

Call me please.

CALL ME.

He'd become headline news without telling her and Hawaiian or not, Lucy was pissed.

Detective Igor Adjani pressured him: *Call me, we need your statement ASAP.* Martha Simmons from CBS led the media assault: *Congrats D, you're news. Let's meet. Where and when?* He didn't even know Martha had his number. He didn't reply. He recognized some of the other names of reporters requesting—some brazen ones openly *demanding*—that he contact them ASAP. Everyone wanted to be first in line at his buffet.

His inbox and message app were brimming with ASAPs sneering at him from his own phone. Dozens of ASAPs masking an army of Peeping Toms slithering through his firewall to his front door, between the cracks, around the hinges and into his bed with him. Examining, probing, looking for the fastest way in. Leaning close with huge magnified eyeballs as if he was a specimen in a petri dish. Demanding answers only to question them, gut them, cut the whole apart like butchers. Prefacing their headline with SO SAD. He knew the drill. He knew exactly what was coming.

He had no intention of addressing the eighteen voicemails yet.

The subject of another email read *Wu and Fong NOT strangers Huan market.* No message in the body.

His fingertips tingled. There were people whose internal maps of Los Angeles were based on where they'd seen celebrities, at which restaurant, which store, which traffic light. His was based on bodies—name, age, cause of death. Cathy Wu, 27, strangled to death and bludgeoned post-mortem inside a motel room in Chinatown a year ago. A few hours later and barely three blocks away Patty Fong, 21, was shot point-blank in the face outside her family's home. LAPD had treated them as individual tragedies, disconnected apart from their proximity to each other. So had the press. So had everyone except the tipster.

Danny replied back to the sender thanking him or her, blind-copying himself so he'd have the address. Normally it was something he'd get on right away.

But normal had to wait today too.

Cynthia had emailed this morning at 7:30. Celia wanted to Skype with Uncle Danny—she had the day off from kindergarten. Among the many promises he'd made last night to leverage his survival was to be a more meaningful presence in his family's lives, before it was too late and time filled in the fissures like the whitewashed plaster between the timbers of a Tudor house. He hadn't even seen his niece in person yet and she was already six. He was *thirty-eight* and an *uncle.* He'd lived at the center of his own universe for too long—the cosmic bones wouldn't roll as fortunately for him again as they did last night. More to the point, he couldn't afford to put himself in a position where they'd have to—he could not be relegated to dusty photographs on Cynthia's wall, another permanently empty chair at Vanessa's kitchen table.

It was a quarter to nine. He emailed back *How about now? Let's do it!* As if nothing out of the ordinary was happening. As if everything was just peachy. He opened his laptop and scanned the news with a baggie of ice he'd crushed with whacks from a lemon zester pressed against his swollen ankle.

CODA had its red breaking news banner up, a fancy scrolling ticker tape Suge had created that today read *DEVELOPING STORY—SIEGE IN PASADENA—BARRICADED SUSPECT—NEIGHBORS SHELTERING IN PLACE.* A photo had been posted showing a nice residential street with big houses. Looked like an unusual place for a siege.

The house fire on Decker Canyon had been covered by a contributor named Jonas Wilkinson. Jonas presented the incident in isolation, so far unconnected to the Angeles Arsonist but directly connected to Red Flag contributor Danny Kasho. Jonas had emailed him twice already today too, but Jonas was way, way down his list of ASAP RSVPs within the communication avalanche.

Decker Canyon and Pasadena were just two spots of trouble in a galaxy full of it—a spectacular car crash had shut down the 710 freeway in Long Beach. An inmate died yesterday in the Twin Towers jail downtown. There was a vicious sexual assault in a park in Santa Ana. A man's body was found in Malibu Lagoon. A former teacher was arrested for molesting an 8 year-old girl in Inglewood.

CODA's bread and butter reporting.

Stalling on Lucy and hoping Cynthia replied soon, Danny read about the car crash. Two vehicles had apparently been racing on the 710 freeway, a north-south upward thrust from Long Beach through LA's midsection. One had predictably lost control and subsequently demolished an SUV driven by a family named Greene on their way home from vacation. The entire family of four was killed as well as all three occupants of the car. The other racers led police on a high speed chase before crashing their Infiniti into a light pole on the grassy island in the middle of the Los Alamitos traffic circle. The juveniles suffered only minor injuries and, being minors, their names had not been released. A contributor named Chad Logan got a good shot of the tributes of flowers and candles amassed on the sidewalk outside the dead family's empty house in the boom town of Signal Hill, haunted by the ghosts of old oil derricks.

Danny adjusted the ice pack and read his friend Ellen Lee's piece on the body in the lagoon. Ellen was a nomadic microblogger who never seemed to sleep. He liked her stuff. The body was found lying in the reeds beneath the wooden walkway when the state beach opened this morning. Responding sheriff's deputies found the victim, an unidentified male Hispanic, dead with a single gunshot wound to the head. A handgun was recovered nearby. Ellen had posted a photo of uniformed deputies and a detective in shirt sleeves and a tie looking over the edge of the walkway at the body face-down in the marsh. All you could see were the hump of the victim's back like a curious stone in the water, the legs bent at the knees, pale jeans terminating in a pair of tall black boots.

With a merry jingle of bells a chat invitation popped up on his screen. He put the ice pack on his desk and answered it. The faces of Cynthia Smith née Kasho and her pigtailed six year-old daughter Celia appeared, a little pixelated but nonetheless personable in the glow of their computer.

Celia shrieked and went screaming out of view.

"Celia!" Danny laughed. "Celia! Come back! Let me see you!"

"Hi Danny." Cynthia's smile dimpled her cheeks. Her hair was pulled away from her face in a ponytail. She wore a peach tank top and her bare shoulders were just beginning to soften with baby weight. She shared enough features with Vanessa to make it impossible not to think of one while looking at the other. Cynthia knew it and it was one thing the siblings never brought up. Another was the summer of '93 if they could help it. Too many painful years in the aftermath had set the embarrassment and shame like misaligned bones. A bigger shame he thought was the darkness it brought to as bright a constellation as the Smiths of Lyric Lane, like a barren moon passing between them and the observing eye.

"How are you, Cynth?" he asked.

"Almost as excited to see you as Celia is, but I'm not up for running anywhere right now."

"How are you feeling? How's it going?"

"So far so good. They say the second one's easier but I'm not sure I believe that."

"Relatively speaking I gucss."

"I guess. We'll see." Cynthia's eyes flitted watchfully to her daughter's activity off-screen.

"Do you know if it's a boy or a girl?"

"We chose not to find out this time. Will says it's one of the last things you can be surprised about in life."

"And it's one of the nicest. You knew ahead of time for Celia didn't you?"

"It was our first, we had to know—pink or blue? But Celia's in the second bedroom and we painted the baby bedroom mint green and white while it was the office."

"So either flavor of baby will compliment it like Baskin Robbins."

"Right! Celia, come here. It's uncle Danny! Come say hi!"

"Speaking of sweet," he lowered his voice a notch, "I just got off the phone with Vanessa."

Cynthia made an exaggerated O with her mouth. "How'd that go?"

"Sometimes her degree of apathy still amazes me."

"You get used to it."

"Do you?"

"It's not like it's a phase, you just live far away from it. We're here. These days she spends most of her time with her group friends anyway."

"Who's that?"

"Mom joined this—*group*, remember?"

"Her self-help thing?"

"Vic calls it a cult but mom gets mad when he does. She bought some books from this guy and then got really into it a couple years ago and started a local chapter of his…organization. Will thinks she's just lonely. When you come visit she'll tell you all about it, trust me. Celia, come over here. She even donated her car to them."

Danny snickered. "She managed to avoid mentioning that."

"She didn't tell us either. Vic found out the hard way—when she started having him drive her around. I can't because of the baby, so it's like he's living at home again."

"I didn't know he moved out." As if they were a family he was sponsoring on the far side of the planet.

"He moved in with Charlene last year."

"Charlene?"

"His girlfriend. She's kind of…young."

Danny winced. "Well as long as he's happy. Vanessa said he was upset about something but she didn't know what that could possibly be."

They both laughed lightly.

His niece crept into view in a rainbow tankini top and holding a furry stuffed animal, a dog or a bear sporting a bright yellow bow tie.

"I see you Celia!" Danny said.

She screamed and dashed off again.

Cynthia said, "Vic didn't get promoted to assistant manager at the store so he was all mad about that. I told him the way he gets mad about everything is probably why he didn't get promoted, but he doesn't listen."

"Is that at Pesto Pizza?"

"Gridiron Sports on the Loop."

In 1993 sixteen year-old Victor Kasho was a rising star at both football and baseball, but whatever college or professional sports career he'd dreamed of after graduating high school was derailed by the events of that summer, an offensive play he hadn't been taught how to counter and couldn't recover from. Vic didn't get what Danny did for a living either, the how or especially the why of it. He'd just turned forty-two but time had stopped for him too, working in a retail sports store and delivering for Pesto Pizza—*Pesto's the Besto!*—on the side. He still wore his faded emerald green Crickets hoodie most of the time—much of his clothing was merchandise of his high school football team. When the Calendula Crickets met the Smokies from San Sebastian for their great cross-bay rivalry every November he would watch it at Vanessa's with his girlfriend instead of out at a bar and spend the duration of the game telling them what the Crickets were doing wrong, because the last time they beat the Smokies was when he played for them. He'd added the resentment of Danny's unannounced exit from Calendula in 2001 to the pre-existing eight years of animosity between them, but on some level Danny knew Vic envied him for being able to leave their history behind, as much as anyone could, a feat Vic was incapable of duplicating.

"She said she didn't have anything to add to her email," he said.

"Did you expect her to?"

"I guess I hoped so."

"You *are* rusty."

"Who's Gary Calder?"

"We're pretty sure he's in her group. Vic knows him, he's a bartender I guess."

"How does he know dad? Vanessa has no idea how he came by the information, apparently."

"It's not on her radar. And it won't be, so don't waste your time. It's like a door mom's locked from the outside and thrown away the key."

"That's the part I can't get my head around yet. I mean, dad's *alive.* He's still here."

"Where is here?" she asked.

"Solano, near San Francisco."

"I've never heard of it."

"It's not as famous as San Quentin. She gave me Gary Calder's number, guess it's up to me to call him and find out what's going on."

"Is that your plan?"

"I don't know yet. Visits for sick inmates have to be approved by the prison warden and attending physician, if there is one. Maybe Gary Calder will know who that is too."

"Sounds like you've already looked into it."

"Just that far. Seeing what it entails. If…you know."

"Would you visit us here if you went to see him?"

"Of course. I need to see you guys anyway. Regardless, I mean."

Celia shouted something in the background.

"He can't see you Celia, come over here." Cynthia's expression changed. She narrowed her eyes and fixed them pointedly on her computer's camera, looking right at Danny as only a disapproving big sister can. "A little bird told me you made the news today."

A pit hardened in his stomach. "Pregnant women shouldn't watch the news. Too inflammatory."

"Did you get hurt Danny?"

He cleared his throat. "I didn't even come close." He held up his lesser-injured hand to the camera lens by the *LOOK HERE* Post-it. "See? Only a flesh wound."

Cynthia leaned toward her screen. "I think we have the same Band-Aids. Will reads your blog you know. He watched you on Justine London last night, said you were great. Celia come here, you said you wanted to talk to Uncle Danny, well he's here. Come talk to him. No dice," Cynthia sighed, "she's being shy."

"Well it's awesome Will reads me. Thank him for me."

While Victor insisted on disparagingly calling Cynthia's CPA husband *BillSmith*, deriding it as perhaps the plainest name in the world, he was Will to friends and family. Danny believed anyone who could make a Kasho consistently happy was some kind of saint or shaman so he was grateful for Will's presence in his sister's life.

"It was awesome until we heard how close you came to getting yourself killed," Cynthia said. "Will wanted me to ask if you still want to be a reporter."

"Tell him yes, because I don't trust the press. Where is he?"

"Working."

"How is he?"

"Busy but good. The economic downturn's been a boon because people suddenly have to start managing their finances, or what's left of them. He's thinking about getting into real estate but I don't know. It's so unpredictable these days."

"Unpredictable is the new normal."

Celia's feet appeared in a brief cartwheel behind Cynthia's chair and something went *crash* in the background.

"The economy sounds like a four year-old," Cynthia frowned. "Celia, *come here.*"

Celia suddenly popped up in the screen holding a different stuffed animal, perhaps a squirrel or a plush rat. "See Uncle Danny?"

"That's great Celia! How are you? What is that?"

"Mr. Fluffy!" Then she was gone again.

"I think you gave it to her for Christmas," Cynthia said.

"Oh, right." He must have ordered it online and had it sent to their house. Zero effort equaled zero recognition.

His sister pushed herself up to her feet. "Hold on, I'll try and redirect her. Celia, come here. Uncle Danny wants to talk to you, Celia. Celia? He can't see you over there Celia, come here please. Celia. *Celia!*"

Danny was left with the view of the empty chair and Cynthia's growing exasperation in the background as she tried to corral Celia—*He can't see you Celia, go sit in the chair, sit in the chair please Celia. I need you to sit in the chair. Do as I say!* There were so many *what if's* about last night, any of which could have killed him—or worse, left him alive but maimed, disfigured, something Celia should never have to see. A story she should never have to hear.

Off-camera his niece suddenly started to cry, then to wail. Cynthia questioned, scolded, then cooed. It was the cooing part, the soothing of her children's pain, that their mother had long ago given up on providing.

Cynthia leaned into view and the expression on her face said everything. "Danny I gotta go."

"That's okay Cynth."

"Let's try again soon okay? I love you, I'm glad you're okay. I'm proud of you. Let us know what you decide to do about dad, okay?"

Cynthia signed off.

CHAPTER 24

Danny stared at his sad clown smile displayed in the empty chat window for a second or two, then closed the app with a quiet sigh. Paul Kasho was a stubborn passenger they'd never be able to drop off. He was as persistent as radioactivity.

While little Celia Smith had a child's immutable power to definitively reprioritize a jumbled mess of an adult life Danny had no time to humor any PTSD about last night. A simple cosmic Whiskey Tango Foxtrot would have to suffice, and now he had to move on. And only become a ghost to his niece when it was finally really time to, just before he had to start wearing diapers again. He wasn't there yet.

He fished around in his desk for an old phone case with a display cover. You had to open the cover to access the touchscreen but at least it would keep the cracked glass contained. He hoped the asshole who keyed his car had problems that dwarfed even the Kashos', for instance a disease-swollen scrotum the size of a Volkswagen.

His phone kept buzzing with incoming emails and messages. He thought about texting Carrie Voelker but didn't feel strong enough. If he so much as cracked open that door she'd kick it down and barge in like a one-woman SWAT team in a spandex bodysuit that left nothing to the imagination, even one as vivid as his. Her interrogation of him would be embarrassingly quick and qualitatively all-encompassing. So no Carrie yet, despite how sexy a nurse she'd make.

He logged directly into CODA's server, bypassing the home page, and reviewed the pictures and video from last night. He hated the sound of his panicked breathing over the terrifying roar of the flamethrower, a disturbing auditory take-away from the video. He wanted to tear the guy's mask off and beat the shit out of him with a baseball bat like De Niro at the dinner table in *The Untouchables*. At some point he'd gone from pretending and playing dress-up and calling himself Fireman666 and decided to empower his demons and start killing people because the costume empowered him. But it *was* just a costume.

Mindful that the enemy was in the audience Danny began to type with his phone muted so he could concentrate. The keys chattered almost as fast as the words came to him, his hands aching as he physically wrestled each syllable onto the screen.

Yes the Decker Canyon house fire was set by the Angeles Arsonist.

Yes the Angeles Arsonist contacted him under the guise of an anonymous tip about the case.

Yes he had been wrong about it and had narrowly escaped with his life.

With careful choice of words he presented the path from anonymous email which he published intact and unabridged to near-death experience as demonic serendipity, a rogue wave that had nearly swept him into extinction. He wanted transparency—he'd neither invited nor invented the situation. Credibility counted. He got in front of it a bit by admitting he'd obviously been overzealous in his trust—which hopefully put his heart in the right place. He declared that the task force was a shambles, with infighting surmounting investigating, and stated at this point the integrity of the entire investigation was at stake.

Bigfoot or no Bigfoot he uploaded the 58-second video clip in its entirety but didn't publish it yet. He'd already downloaded the YouTube video via a third party app for safekeeping before it was taken down by authorities; it was all about evidence preservation now.

After he proofed the entry he emailed Lucy Baskin the link, then he emailed Suge, thanking him again for his help and requesting he be notified immediately if UCANBRN2 posted again or if the IP address was active under a different username.

While he waited on Lucy he found an old Ace bandage in the bathroom and wrapped it tightly around his ankle. There was nothing new from anybody about the Mendoza trial. He had keyword triggers in his news feeds but Gibson the Reuters stringer remained the only source about a possible deal for the repentant Charlize Patron. It bothered him like a rock in his shoe. Gibson had splayed his cards on the internet's table too soon. You generally wanted to avoid declaring absolutes on the internet, lest ye be absolutely and cyberspatially fucked. It was only the whole world.

He downloaded a copy of Claire Coogan's Facebook info and deleted the account, consigning her brief existence to a virtual dust bin in a remote server farm somewhere. Then he scrolled through the comments section of Red Flag, looking to see if someone had posted anything about the attack under a different username. The tone ought to be the same—he could disguise his voice but he couldn't change it. Nothing stood out.

He opened the email from the Justine London show and followed the link to his segment. Fast-forwarded through it while he worked the melting ice pack around on his ankle. He thought he looked as nervous as he'd felt. He was inside the story now. Sticky strands of complicity subverted his observer status and connected him organically to the crime, actions he'd inevitably have to examine and explain and most of all defend. He added the interview link to Red Flag without enthusiasm. Notoriety ought to feel good for a change.

He kept flashing back to his panicked run up the driveway to the house. He could still feel the palpable heat from the flamethrower at his back, still hear the sound of the arsonist's shoes on the unfinished floor.

The sound of his shoes.

Danny navigated to the master folder of CODA contributors and entered the admin password—a grandfathered-in permission Suge had been kind enough not to rescind—and scrolled down to Ellen Lee's. She had saved half a dozen more pictures apart from the one she posted with her piece on the Malibu Lagoon suicide. Some contributors only saved what they used. Others, like Ellen and himself, saved pretty much all their accumulated data, including excess or excessively graphic photos. One of her extra pictures was taken as firefighters and coroner's techs were removing the body from the water. The victim's wet black hair was matted around a small black entry wound clearly visible on the left temple like a clinging bug. The boots practically reached the guy's knees and seemed over-engineered compared to the rest of his clothing.

His phone buzzed. Suge reported that there had been no new posts by UCANBRN2 or from any other user at the same IP address. Danny didn't know whether to be relieved or dismayed. Travis Salk had cursed him with the fallout from someone else's free will—if UCANBRN2 vanished like the smoke from his fires it would be on him too.

He searched for more reports on the Malibu suicide and grimaced at Crime Time which had the very next hit. He rarely looked at the site, partly out of principal, partly because of the writing, and partly because there were too many intrusive ads. CODA's presentation was comparatively clean and uncluttered, the necessary ads not so much popping up in the viewer's face. CODA management—and more importantly, moneybags owner/publisher William Craig—seemed inclined to keep it that way at least for now, considering how well they did at this year's press club awards. The wins had earned them some leverage.

Highlighted on Crime Time's hectic home page were the two top stories of the day—the ongoing siege in Pasadena and the Decker Canyon house fire suspected of being set by the Angeles Arsonist. A click-through to Ursula Ruda's ongoing series on Amy Childress's campaign occupied a prominent place on the home page. He assumed it was from the woman-fights-male-establishment angle, not because Amy Childress herself was such an exceptional individual. It was a total conflict of interest for Ursula to gently lob fluffy questions at her subject during a press conference. Trying to make Childress look good instead of true.

Ursula had also found time to post a short piece on the body in the lagoon. Danny didn't know if that spoke to her prolificness or to serious staffing issues at Dime Time, which looked like a one-woman show. She'd posted one photo of the dead man, who was wearing a gray hoodie and had a child's-size red backpack still strapped to his back like a deflated balloon. The boots couldn't be seen. She referred to the victim as a "day laborer" but didn't give a source for the claim.

Her updates on the Angeles Arsonist case—he was delighted she had to use his sobriquet too—were reposts of the same details everyone else had. Nobody had Fireman666 but him.

His email chimed. Lucy had replied. *Everything but the video ok—checking w/ legal. Calling now PICK THE HELL UP.*

He flirted with the idea of posting a .jpg of the word *REDACTED* in lieu of the video, then simply published his Red Flag update without it, setting the facts free in the world with all the fanfare of a single click. The Decker Canyon fire *was* set by the Angeles Arsonist in an attempt to murder him. He was more curious than ever about how his work would be received, and by whom. If it would provoke another cryptic communiqué from UCANBRN2 or another visit from Fireman666. He longed for the latter—revenge was in humanity's DNA and could overflow the moral levees with less prodding than he'd suffered.

His phone buzzed again. He cleared his throat and carefully switched it to speaker. "Hey Luce."

Lucy Baskin blurted, "Danny oh my God."

"I'm sorry I haven't been in touch."

"Are you okay?"

"I'm fine."

"Oh my *God,* Danny."

"I'm fine, Luce, really."

"Actually you're an asshole is what you are."

Lucy had been managing editor for five of his nine years at CODA and he couldn't recall a time he'd ever given her such justifiable reason to be so mad at him. There'd been times, sure, but this was over and above.

"You don't go into radio blackout without turning in your badge first. I thought you knew that. I took it for granted you knew that."

"I'm sorry I didn't tell you about it ahead of time, Luce. It came together pretty fast."

"I don't have a problem with something coming together fast. I have a great *big* problem when I'm not told about it. I have an even bigger problem when one of my people goes out of their way to *not* tell me about it. This is incredible Danny, but this is not the way for me to find out about it."

"You're totally right, I'm sorry."

"You woke up alive today, I should have been your first call. After your mom."

"You—almost were."

"You're an asshole."

"Sorry I'm an asshole, Luce."

"You're okay?"

"Yeah, I'm okay."

Lucy loosed a long sigh. "This is incredible. I've never seen anything like this. We've never *had* anything like this."

"Will Legal let me post the video? What did Ron say?"

Ronald Schiff managed CODA, overseeing its day to day operations and reporting directly to publisher William Craig. He was a graying father of four in his mid-40s and distinguished, Danny thought, as if he'd come to City of Angels/Dead on Arrival from television production or the near-legendary realm of the *glossy magazine* instead of as a mid-tier content editor at a Seattle startup. In a different era Ron would have worn wide ties and been able to smoke at his desk. He'd been more or less at the helm of CODA for the last seven years and they were the better for it.

But still, there was a time and a place for management, and this wasn't it.

"I don't know Danny," Lucy said. "I don't know what the lawyers get paid for other than acting like baby chickens, you know? What did the detectives say?"

"I didn't ask them."

"Well I sent it over but wow, they're going to want to talk to you. Ron sure does."

"Off the grid includes lawyers. And Ron."

"You're not off any grid—I'm looking at you right now on TV. Channel 4."

Danny frowned.

"You look like you're in handcuffs."

"What?"

"Don't what me, it was your big night—you tell me what. I just sent you a screenshot."

He clicked Get Mail incessantly, with excessive force, until the new message appeared in his inbox. Attached was a .jpg from TV coverage of the Decker Canyon fire. The glow of the burning house cast across the driveway where Danny sat with his hands behind his back, surrounded by cops in an airship's quivering searchlight.

He thought, *fuck*. "I wasn't handcuffed."

"You look like you are."

"I don't care what it looks like. I wasn't handcuffed. I wasn't under arrest for anything. I'm not going to be either."

He knew Ursula Ruda must have been tickled at the sight of him apparently handcuffed, in serious trouble for something at last. He sensed more than saw Travis Salk's moustache and teeth in the water below his thrashing legs, ready to clamp on and not let go until the homicide detective had made some kind of evolutionary point of order in the frothing, bloody sea split with shrill screaming and splashing. And just what the fuck was it with all the shark analogies these days? he wondered irritably. Something for the unseen but inevitable shrink he could feel tapping him on the shoulder with bony PVC plastic fingers like one of those fake skeletons hung up for anatomy classes.

"Mike Cruz, isn't that the guy?" Lucy was saying. "The fireman? The guy you interviewed?"

"What about him?"

"Didn't you go to a fundraiser at his house?"

"Saturday night, why?"

"What was the address?"

He glanced at CODA's red breaking news banner about the Pasadena siege. It was more of a challenge with his phone getting into his map app and retrieving the address but he got it and read it to Lucy.

"That's the address," she said. "Something's going on there. Patrick's there already but nobody knows what's going on."

"Who?"

"Patrick Dearing, he writes our financial blog."

"We have one?"

"Danny."

He scowled, rubbing his forehead. Perfect, he thought. Just perfect. He was being usurped by the finance goon.

"I couldn't reach you and wanted to make sure we were on it."

"I was just heading out the door."

"That's what I thought. Don't go off the grid again."

"Okay."

"Danny?"

"Yeah Luce?"

"Don't go off the grid again."

"I won't. Sorry."

"It's unprofessional and I expect more from you. It's kind of insulting."

"I'm sorry. I am. I'll apologize more later. I gotta go." He hung up and looked up at the ceiling as if it were transparent Plexiglas into a sky as free of clouds as he wished he was of self-doubt and muttered, "This is bullshit."

CHAPTER 25

The police perimeter at the north end of Solita Road was marked by two Pasadena black and whites parked sideways at the intersection with Zanja Street, aiming the stylized rose in their mint-green *POLICE* lettering at the media scrum gathered at the end of Mike Cruz's street, which was caught today like a geriatric jaywalking across a freeway.

On all four corners of the intersection sandbagged tripod stands supported cameras and sun shades for TV reporters in temperature-defying suits and dresses. Cameramen lounged in cargo pants, t-shirts and floppy hats, always prepared for a long wait. Neighbors stood in threes and fours, watching from driveways and in the shade of tall old-growth trees evidently impervious to drought. Others stopped walking their dogs to observe, leaving the animals smiling magnanimously as they panted in the heat. There were probably two hundred people across two blocks—police, residents, media, looky-loos passing through hoping for a show. Two six-rotor drones cruised overhead but Danny didn't know if they belonged to police or media or brazen private citizens.

News vans with their antenna masts raised like lightning rods ready to attract the city's attention were parked along the curbs on both sides of Zanja, which was Spanish for ditch and alluded to water-capture techniques of early Pueblo de los Angeles, and north of the intersection up Solita, which was Spanish for usual, into a neighborhood of smaller tract-style houses, leaving a narrow channel through the intersection one car-wide. Nobody seemed to be doing traffic control. The intersection was normally so slow it didn't even warrant four-way stop signs.

Inside the perimeter half a dozen marked and unmarked police cars were parked in the street in front of Cruz's house halfway up the block. Nobody official or otherwise was speculating about what was going on. Where you stood on that was the eternal seesaw of journalism—either it meant nothing or it was huge. Danny was naturally pessimistic but he never looked a gift horse of a story in the mouth.

The intersection wasn't a proper perpendicular junction—Solita was refracted eastward about twenty feet by Zanja, where Garrett's Prius was parked facing the wrong way on Solita north of the intersection, glinting like a spent shell casing in the sun. Danny's pocket binoculars did him no good, they just brought the peoples' sweating backs and overheated dogs into greater focus. He had his phone plugged into the Prius's 12-volt power outlet and was checking into the TV stations' live streams being shot by their helicopters hovering high over the street. There was no police airship in sight; one of the drones might be theirs. He could see Cruz's backyard, the pool and the deck and the shiny barbecue grill and wondered if Cruz had his big widescreen TV on in the family room, his house and those of his neighbors full of his name and face as the story exploded around them.

Danny had said *fuck* so many times since Lucy called that he sounded like a foul-mouthed duck. His lower lip had divots pressed into it from his two front teeth, his maxillary central incisors which were white and straight and commended by dentists and more than a couple girlfriends' moms over the years—one went so far as to say they made his smile look almost unaffected, which in hindsight was sort of a shitty thing to say, but he understood why she said it. Any mother with any competence at all ought to say something dissuading to a daughter who brought him home. But he did have good teeth.

According to various unnamed sources—CODA finance goon Patrick Dearing not among them—Pasadena police were in a standoff with a barricaded suspect believed to be Mike Cruz, a veteran LA County Fire Department Captain and investigator on the Angeles Arsonist task force. The same unnamed sources said that a threat had been phoned in which resulted in the police response, but like everything else besides the homeowner's name the nature of the threat remained elusive, unconfirmed and unsubstantiated by anybody. Shoddy and inflammatory. No wonder Cruz didn't like reporters.

Mike fucking Cruz.

Was it really him last night? Was the minivan parked around here today or did he have it stashed somewhere? Was the decorated fire captain's alter ego really Fireman666?

There were so many unmarked cars and rentals on the street that Danny thought the entire task force had scrambled here. Maybe Cruz had threatened them. Maybe he had decided it was finally time to speak to Pavelko directly and things had gotten out of hand. Tempers had flared. Accusations had been made, threats. The story seemed to be coming from uncorroborated anonymous sources, which likely meant it was a media-driven story, which likely meant it was complete bullshit. He'd backtracked through his feeds but hadn't found the first mention of it yet, it seemed to come on all at once and he'd been too busy playing catch-up and absorbing the evolving situation to isolate the source.

The news cycle is like surfing the Pipeline at Oahu, Lucy always said—you ride it as long as you can before you fall off. The lead changed all the time. A petulant bitterness burned inside, unfounded and embarrassing to acknowledge—*I was just getting started.*

From what he could see police were coming and going in and out of Cruz's house. There was no standoff. No barricaded suspect. He marveled how Patrick Dearing couldn't have Cruz's name yet given all the TV reporters around him who did. He'd texted him that he was here but all Patrick replied with was *Great news!* and kept right on posting lame updates to CODA's general news page. Danny wanted to order him to stand down, not only was he here now but Dearing was out of his depth. A finance goon had no business covering any aspect of his story whatsoever apart from counting the revenue it brought in. Lucy had just suffered a momentary lapse of reason, that's all. Or she was using the finance goon as a paddle on his ass which pissed him off even more. Dearing's blog was called Balancing Act or something, some kind of stupid pun that accountants might find funny.

Fortunately Garrett had been home this morning. He was still asleep when Danny cringingly climbed those stairs again. Intruded again. Maybe Garrett wouldn't be alone. Maybe Danny was about to cement his standing as the biggest douche of all time. In a way it'd be fine if Garrett was busy or wanted to sleep—he was hoping to just get his keys and split without a proper explanation. But Garrett woke up surprisingly quickly and said he didn't have any plans for the day, so instead of loaning Danny his car he decided to take part in breaking news—long waits and fast food.

They'd gotten out of the apartment speedily enough, taking the back door to the building which led through the dusty industrial-looking basement furnace room to a common access shared with an adjoining property, a narrow overgrown chute with unlocked chain-link fences on each end. Danny had seen only one news van double-parked on Franklin—a situation the ever-roving bands of meter maids wouldn't tolerate once they came upon it—but they'd been buzzed from the lobby by more than one persons unknown asking for Danny Kasho, and mispronouncing his name.

He brought his messenger bag and J-kit, and wore jeans and his cross trainers with a light long-sleeve collared shirt—invariably you were taken more seriously by people you were proposing to interview than if you wore a t-shirt. Garrett stumbled out of the building in a sleeveless *2112* Starman t-shirt, shark-patterned surf shorts and flip flops, as if he was just running up the street to the grocery store.

Leaving their building Danny saw streets full of dark-colored minivans, heard the muted clicks of a myriad stranger shutters, walked sideways through crowded sidewalks teeming with suspicious characters, which in Hollywood was most of the population. Over the course of his career at CODA he had interviewed lots of people who for one reason or another felt they were being followed. Today he finally knew first-hand what they felt like. What it really felt like to be hunted, hounded, plagued, and not just imagining it like most of them were. Was it a blue van he saw double-parked with a shadowy figure at the wheel? Was it a bulky stranger looking at him too long on the sidewalk on their way to Garrett's car? As soon as you started looking over your shoulder you were a victim. Fear built its quick shell like a prefab emergency structure and the choice came immediately—break out of it or cower inside until whatever you were hiding from cracked the shell open and came for you.

They'd pulled off the freeway for a rolling breakfast. Impatient as he was Danny couldn't fault the logic—better a long wait on a full stomach than an empty one.

Garrett pushed his sunglasses up on his head and rubbed his eyes as they waited at the drive-thru window. "I didn't get to see you on TV last night, I was pulling an all-nighter at Sound Bay trying to fix what they broke."

"Sorry to wake you up like this."

"That's okay man, it's an adventure. It will be later anyway, in hindsight."

"So did you fix it?"

"I am pleased to report the doctor was in the house and now Paco's Tasty Signature Sizzlin' Fajitas are *sizzlin'* instead of *hissin'* which doesn't sound tasty at all, believe me." Garrett yawned like an animal in a National Geographic special and rubbed his chin. "How'd your thing go?"

"Okay." Danny handed him his debit card to give to the worker looming in the window. "I think I was a bit stiff."

"Well Justine London is pretty hot. She's a cougar, or whatever comes after that. Ocelot? It surprises me you don't do more of that stuff. You're a natural born ocelot-taming talking head. All you need is a coat with tails and a whip and an ocelot or two, which might be expensive."

Garrett pulled the bags of greasy food into the car and they got back on the freeway. LA was at its best with a third of its population out of town—Labor Day traffic was light, the freeways mostly a wide-open inviting green on the map on Danny's phone, which vibrated regularly with ever more incoming emails, texts and voicemails. Fame was the gift that kept on giving, like electronic herpes.

Garrett noticed. "You must have had quite the night losing your car."

"I didn't lose it, I know exactly where it is. I didn't lose it." He didn't mention that someone had keyed it too. So much bad shit happening to him at once was almost enough to make him believe he'd brought it on himself. Some karmic thing, something he would be helpless to navigate except by Doing Good Deeds. And Garrett would say exactly something to that effect and he didn't want to hear it right now.

"So what were you doing way the hell out on Decker Canyon? I haven't been there since high school. We used to take it down to the beach all the time." Being the considerate type Garrett had saved his questions for when Danny couldn't avoid answering them.

Having known since the age of twelve that inevitability comes long before you're ready for it, Danny told his friend everything that happened last night, from receiving the anonymous email right before he was about to go live on Justine London, to getting Suge's info, snooping around for, finding and taking Garrett's gun and going to the hotel, to the Decker Canyon ambush and narrow escape—thus finally explaining the Sesame Street Band-Aids and profound soreness and hostile half-daze he was in today like a homeless person. He admitted the police had confiscated the unloaded gun and would probably want to talk to him about it, and that he felt like the ultimate douchebag of all time. He was a bad roommate, a bad friend, and he was sorry for it all. He could take nothing back. He could fix nothing. Undo nothing. He felt like he'd kicked over somebody's sand castle without provocation or complaint. Danny was That Guy, and he was profoundly sorry and ashamed.

He held his breath while they sped through Eagle Rock's deceptively undeveloped stretch of freeway in silence. He checked his news feeds and thought about the tedium of apartment hunting, and how anywhere was going to be an existential step down from the Villa Carlotta.

Finally Garrett asked, "Why didn't you call the police?"

Danny knew he was going to be defending himself on that point for a while. Faith alone was a fragile fortification. And there was something deeper there too—even though he interacted with the police on almost every story, beneath the surface lay Victor's bitter indoctrination to his younger brother, how he'd painted the cops with such an adversarial hue that he still had to make a conscious effort not to see them that shade.

"I thought it was a tip," he said. "A good tip. An epic tip. They said they had proof. I saw a flamethrower. I saw my house. I said okay, I'll come. I believed it."

"You wanted to believe it."

"Yeah, I did."

"It's like you want to believe there's a pot of gold at the end of every rainbow."

Danny raised his eyebrows.

"Sorry man, it's still early," Garrett said. "It's that you don't think there's any rainbows at all."

"Rainbows, Gare?"

"Your job has made you overly cynical."

"I don't know if it *made* me, but I realize it doesn't help exactly. But that's not the point."

"It *is* the point Danny—with you there's no greater explanation *than* the explanation. Every bit of badness has to have its own road map so you can drive it. There's no rainbow, it's just physics."

"Are you saying I've lost my wonderment and awe at the human condition?"

"I'm saying you've lost your ability to be surprised by it."

"A pot of bones is at the end of all our rainbows. That's physics too." How about that for a Hallmark moment.

"You'll never be able to offer the insight you could as a reporter if you lose the ability to empathize with people. Admit it—people can still surprise you."

"Sure they do, all the time. Just usually not pleasantly."

"A pleasant life sounds like an ancient Chinese curse to me. Just say no to pleasant lives. You meet strangers who say they know something about something all the time and you don't bring a gun. Which means you thought last night was something else. It was different. There was an unwelcome element of surprise to it. But you didn't call the police."

Danny had been preparing this part. "I didn't call them for two reasons. First because I thought it was a genuine tip about a breaking story.

Second because the tipster made a point of making sure I knew he knew where I lived. He wanted to be taken seriously. He wanted to make sure I came one way or another."

His audiophile friend listened intently as if trying to spot an errant wavelength in his voice. "Sounds like two perfect reasons to call the police. Which brings us back to your decision that you felt you needed to be armed. Have you ever fired a gun before?"

"No."

"Ever held one?"

"Not really, no."

"And yet you report violent crime for a living."

"I cover, I don't commit. I was exercising an abundance of caution. Orange Grove Boulevard—this is us."

Garrett took the exit. "Sounds like an abundance of caution would have been to not go at all and call the police, not necessarily in that order. Maybe then he wouldn't have set that guy's house on fire and you wouldn't be so banged-up today, mentally, physically, and karmically."

Danny picked at the Band-Aids on his knuckles, ashamed at being unable to meet Garrett's eyes, a tell of dishonesty as transparent as clearing his throat when he was being purposely ambiguous. He welcomed the distraction of trying to find a place to park near Cruz's street and Garrett didn't raise the issue again, but it lingered like an unwanted guest. Danny sat low in the passenger seat, wearing sunglasses and a non-CODA baseball cap, silently resenting having to hope that no one spotted him. There'd been more than enough of that feeling growing up and this was just hitting too close to home.

Carrie Voelker texted again. No *Xo* this time, just the belated picture of Derek Cavanaugh's mangled plate laying supine in the Malibu tennis court like an otherworldly asteroid embedded in a farmer's field. *Here it is! How are you? Worried about you! Call me!* A straight-up emoji happy face with fucking hearts for eyes. Like a *kunoichi*, a female ninja would distract you with while dissolving poison in your tea, Carrie's tone was enticingly between concern and curiosity, a careful contrivance that made you want to talk to her, made you want to feed her facts like baby shrimp just to watch her mouth take them. He wondered if she was here somewhere and if she still needed him to get to Pavelko. If he was lucky she was getting desperate—insofar as Carrie Voelker could get desperate about anything—but he couldn't ignore her. Even though the thrill was gone the thought of never having another Drake's date with her mocked the effort he'd put into this story.

Thanks! he texted back. *Slammed today but let's get together soon!!!* He added the touchy-feely exclamation points because it was Carrie Voelker. He almost added *Please!* but refrained to retain some amount of dignity.

Denise from the Justine London show wanted him back. She'd cc'd Lucy for protocol and luckily Lucy hadn't replied yet either way on his behalf—but he knew of course she wanted him to, even though she was pissed at him. She couldn't send the finance goon this time. And he'd do it, of course he would. Although the baby chicken part of him wanted to skip the fight and go straight to flight and wait it out somewhere well-stocked with self-medications, those sticky strands of complicity weren't about to let go.

Case in point: the newest text from Pavelko. *STATEMENT TODAY ASAP* in abrasive all caps.

He replied: *I'm at Cruz's house.* Where *you* should be, he thought, living up to *your* pretense.

Garrett had run out of diversions on his phone and was beginning to get antsy. "So where is the gun now?"

"The detectives took it. They asked if it was registered."

"Sure it is, but not to me. It was my stepdad's and he was a bona fide Texas Ranger so they can take that as far as they want. My mom gave it to me after he died. She thought I'd want it but she just didn't. It's been in that box almost twenty years. Surprised you even remembered where it was. I don't even remember telling you about it, I'd forgotten about it myself."

"It was a long time ago, right after I moved in."

"Well I'm glad it didn't have any bullets, it probably would have blown up in your hand."

"I'm really sorry, Gare. I really am. Especially then turning around and asking for your help to drive me here today—I'm really, really sorry."

"Well you didn't ask me to drive, I did sort of volunteer, but I get your point. This will be exciting, sort of. If anything happens. But I gotta tell you Danny, I've got a thing about funerals and no offense, I love you man, but I don't want to go to yours, you know? Like my stepdad once told me, a puppet doesn't dance when someone pulls its strings, it just jerks around. Don't be a jerk Danny—next time grab the strings and *pull.* Or cut them, or whatever. You get the idea."

"When did he say that to you?"

"I was a kid, screwing around with the wrong crowd." Garrett stretched and yawned. "One night he had to come get me out of jail. He didn't tell my mom, he was cool about it. I appreciated that."

"How old were you?"

"Oh I don't know, fourteen, fifteen. Something like that. The age of irrelevant rebellion."

"Landing in jail by fourteen is pretty rebellious."

"Hey, like I told him, it wasn't my fault. It was guilt by association."

Pavelko texted: *WHERE EXACTLY?*

So he *was* here. Danny peered through the windows with a creeping anxiety, but didn't see him lurking in the crowd of reporters, spectators and police.

Mark Pavelko had wiggled him around like a fence post in wet earth. He'd made every imaginable trifle Danny had yet to live through suddenly gleam like a football field of crown jewels, like achingly beautiful women posed just out of his reach. Pavelko had infused the life Danny took for granted with a desperation he didn't need, and he didn't know whether to thank him or swing a shovel into his head.

But fear hadn't filled in the post hole in time and now anger was, like a predatory animal momentarily spooked, but only once. There was nothing to fear from Mark Pavelko in broad daylight in front of a crowd of potential witnesses. The Angeles Arsonist was a remote creature, he wasn't into confrontations unless the odds were stacked in his favor. Lies couldn't hide in their shadows when the sun was this bright. Mark Pavelko was a liar and he was on the run. Maybe his own desperation lay behind today's so-called siege. Maybe his personal crown fire was burning down once and for all. All Danny had to do was keep thinking. Write it. Tell it. Make it real.

Pull some fucking strings.

He replied: *Silver Prius. Solita north of Zanja.* Thought that sentence was pretty to type, and then decided that was exactly the kind of fanciful bullshit distraction he couldn't afford right now.

"Did *anything* good come out of last night?" Garrett asked. "Did you get anything besides the Bigfoot video and the continued use of your skin?"

"We know he's posted comments on Red Flag."

"Are you serious?"

"He calls himself either UCANBRN2 or Fireman666. And there's that little issue of him knowing where we live."

Garrett snorted, then made a show of yawning again. "Yeah well, he wants to bring the noise he is more than welcome to try. I've got nine newer millimeters that are begging to differ with him."

"You have another gun?"

"Sure I do—you know how much money I've got plugged in upstairs? Remember how not worried I was when all that lootin' and thievin' was going on after Inglewood? But if it's all the same to you I'm not going to tell you where it is."

"That's more than fine with me." That didn't sound like an eviction notice but Danny didn't want to get his hopes up.

"I'd like to say this came as a total surprise," Garrett said, "but after that other guy—what was his name?"

"Devon Johnson. I was thinking about that too. When Good Tips Go Bad."

"I figured it was only a matter of time before something like that happened again. You're the most cynical guy I know but anything that smells like a tip turns you into a hooker eager to jump into the next car that stops."

"Thanks."

"Hey, you should hear it from somebody, may as well be me. *Cojones* aren't worth a damn unless you've got a woman like Gina to tickle them for you."

Danny laughed.

"If you choose to live for nothing else, live for that."

"Your stepdad taught you that too?"

"In a nutshell. It was a long night of straightening out wayward youthful priorities. Who's that?"

Danny looked up from his phone and saw Pavelko striding toward them in a shirt and tie and jeans and his 49ers cap. Both of his hands were balled in fists and his eyebrows were bunched like feral animals behind his sunglasses. All at once Danny's bravado fled and a knot tightened around his throat like a noose. "That is my source."

"Does he always look that mad?"

"Lately he does."

The ugly dance of his thoughts held Danny's inner gaze like the movements of a prima ballerina. Did Mark Pavelko really try and kill him last night? Pavelko *knew* him. He knew he was *real.* He knew he had friends, a job, a family, even an occasional girlfriend. Was he really consumed by an anger so extreme it had turned outright purposeful? Objective-driven? Fanatical as religious zealotry in its lust for inflicting violence and pain in the guise of Fireman666?

Pavelko crouched beside the Prius and crossed his arms on Garrett's open window. He was sweating profusely and squinted meanly at Garrett through his Ray-Ban aviators. "Who's driving Miss Danny today?"

"A friend," Danny said.

"A roommate friend?"

Danny's skin crawled again with the feeling Pavelko had been following him for some time. Days. Maybe weeks. Maybe he'd been the man's obsession this whole time and had never known he had a psycho as a source. Fucking perfect.

Garrett was never one to shy away from anything—today proved it in spades—and he extended a hand to Pavelko. "Garrett Scott."

Pavelko didn't take it. "Danny tell you what happened last night, Garrett Scott?"

"He sure did." Garrett clapped Danny on the leg. "I'm proud of my boy."

"At least somebody is. We're going to need to talk to you about the weapon recovered at the scene so plan on making yourself available."

"Whatever you need officer."

"That'll be Special Agent, fella. And we need to get *your* statement today too," he said to Danny. "As in now."

"Now has to wait, I'm working."

"You call this working? Sitting around with your thumbs up each other's asses hoping something's going to happen?"

Garrett said, "I can attest to that, except for the thumbs up the asses part."

"There's no standoff," Danny said. "Cruz hasn't been arrested—what's going on?"

Pavelko showed his teeth. "It kills you not to know doesn't it?"

"It's my job, remember?"

"Your curiosity killed your chances of getting out of this. You dealt yourself in last night."

"You dealt me in on Saturday with your task force within a task force bullshit."

"Now it's time to pay for both our sins. I presume since Garrett Scott is driving your car is still at Decker Canyon, right? That'll work out nicely, everyone's waiting there for you."

"Everyone who?"

"Everyone who isn't a fan of yours today." Pavelko stood up and dropped his hand flat on the roof of the car with a bang that vibrated through the car. "Let's go get your wheels, Danny."

He checked the time on the dashboard. 11:20. Looked at Garrett.

"It's okay," Garrett said. "My buddy's got a home studio in South Pas I've been meaning to check out. This gives me the perfect excuse." They clasped hands. "Watch your six."

"Oh for fuck's sake." Pavelko came around the front of the Prius. "Move it."

Danny easily imagined him hurrying through the lobby of the Hampton Inn with his brain boiling and a flash drive in his hand. He retrieved his messenger bag from the back seat with exaggerated slowness, noting the twitching anxiety that gripped Pavelko like a fever. This was broad daylight, Mark looked to be unarmed and there were witnesses all around them. He couldn't try anything. Danny wasn't afraid—he *refused* to be. Curiosity had killed his chances of getting out of this without knowing the truth.

Pull some fucking strings.

Pavelko said, "Right this way Danny." He glanced around and hurried them away from the commotion along a verdant block-long tunnel of shady oaks with a view of the scrubby hills behind the golf course in the arroyo seco below.

Danny's ankle was stiff and his thigh was sore and he made no effort to keep up with Pavelko. He made sure he saw him texting. Exponential potential witnesses. Small but professional comfort.

"Who's waiting for us?" he asked.

"What?"

"At Decker Canyon. Who knows we're coming?"

"Why? Afraid I'm gonna do something to you?"

"Pavelko!"

They both stopped and turned around. Tracy Orman was beckoning at them from the intersection.

Pavelko grabbed him by the elbow. "Come on."

Danny tugged out of his grip and they stood face to face in the middle of the street. Pavelko's lips were drawn tight. Dark bags hung beneath his eyes and his stubble had grown from unkempt to uncaring. There was a buzzing anger flickering behind his eyes like a faulty fuse.

He spat, "So this is how you repay me Danny? By ambushing me? The credibility of the entire investigation is at stake Danny? Is it? Is that what you think?"

"Mark!" Tracy called again, walking up the street toward them. She had her gun on her hip.

Danny stared back at him. "Tracy wants you, Mark."

Pavelko licked his lips and seemed on the verge of either saying something or punching him. He wasn't armed with anything that Danny could see but he might have a weapon in his car. Otherwise he was a bully—and as easily disarmed when the odds tipped against him.

"You going back to Decker?" Tracy asked as she caught up to them.

Pavelko hesitated without looking away from Danny. "Yeah."

"I'll catch a ride. Where's your car?"

A skeleton key of relief loosened the band of fear around Danny's chest.

Pavelko stirred. Moved one foot in front of the other robotically. Gestured down the street like a tour guide. "Right this way."

CHAPTER 26

Tracy Orman rode upfront which suited Danny just fine. With the cramped back seat of Pavelko's rented victory red Impala to himself he sat sideways and stretched his legs, elevating his right foot with the sprained ankle. It had to be just a sprain. Nothing as fleeting as a story—even a big one—deserved to leave a permanent mark. He dry-swallowed some more ibuprofen from his J-kit and wished he had something stronger, like past the border of legal and straight on to potent kind of stronger.

Pavelko's suit jacket was impaled on the hook over the driver's side passenger door. The interior of the car reeked of evergreen air freshener and previous drivers' cigarettes and Pavelko's jacket would too. And all three of them. It was disgusting.

Pavelko loosened the knot of his tie with two fingers and drove aggressively, swearing at other drivers on the freeway and shaking his head at them as he passed.

Tracy Orman pretended not to notice and for the most part stayed preoccupied with her phone. "Did you get the thing with your card cleared up?" she asked him.

"I put it on mine," Pavelko snapped too loudly in the confines of the car. "That's why we've got the rolling ashtray." He forced his way into the carpool lane and gunned it, fuel efficiency be damned. *"Assholes."*

Tracy glanced up from her phone, hearing the same bitter note in his tone Danny did. Danny sat up straight and buckled up. Apart from the whine of the feeble air conditioning the car fell awkwardly silent for a few miles. Danny wanted to look in the Impala's trunk. He wanted to know where Pavelko rented this car and when exactly. He wanted to know what he was driving last night since he wasn't staying at the hotel he said he was, where all the bona fide investigators were staying. And why, if there was anything like a siege involving Mike Cruz, were two of the top people involved leaving the scene?

It would take an hour to get to Decker Canyon if traffic stayed this light the whole way; a bit less with how Pavelko was driving. Danny had spent much of the last three days crisscrossing the Valley but today he was doing it with a firebug—a *potential* firebug, *potential* murderer, *potential* destroyer of people and things, *confirmed* liar, *confirmed* asshole—behind the wheel of a car doing ninety with two potential victims trapped inside with him. If Pavelko's world was coming apart in long strips like old wallpaper who could say whether he wouldn't suddenly yank the wheel and crash through the median into oncoming traffic, ending his life and theirs in blaring horns and squealing tires and exploding glass and metal and blood. Once a person proved themselves capable of committing one kind of horror it was an easy descent into the others.

Billboards blinked: *Preserve and conserve! Every drop counts!*

Garrett texted: *Vive la résistance! Tell the swine nothing!*

There were no new updates about Cruz from the underwhelming finance goon Patrick Dearing.

Danny thought this was bullshit. "It doesn't look like Mike Cruz is barricaded after all."

"Sure he is. Behind a lawyer. That's what he was waiting for. What the reporters all think they're doing I can't say." Pavelko spoke with a strangely syrupy cadence, tugging on his ear lobe with his left hand, his elbow propped against the window.

"Why was he in Malibu last night? Did he say?"

"He said talk to my frigging lawyer, Danny, that is what he said."

"Then why'd you move on him?"

"*We* didn't move on anybody—*you* served up some slander for breakfast and Mike called *us.*"

"Me?"

"At least me and Mike agree on something—you were a bad frigging idea. A bad frigging idea."

As far as Danny could see the first mention of a Code 3 to Cruz's address was posted by someone listening to a police scanner, of which there were many such hobbyists in and around LA. But that was response to the initial dispatch, which meant Cruz had already called them on his own initiative. Forced the task force within a task force's hand. "I didn't say anything about him."

"Not by name maybe. Guess he's more deserving of discretion than other people, eh Danny? Anyway I wouldn't worry about Mike if I were you. I'd worry about you."

Warming to Pavelko's angry current Tracy Orman half-turned in her seat to face Danny. "Peter Buckstein. Remember the name—that was his retirement house he was building on Decker Canyon. Now thanks to you there's nothing left of his dream a bulldozer won't fix."

"Yeah it's the *thanks to you* part I have a problem with," he replied, glaring at the back of Pavelko's head. "Who says the arsonist wouldn't have torched the place anyway if I didn't show? Then who would you be blaming? All apologies to Mr. Buckstein but my ass is worth more than the market value of his dreams. Who gets to retire anymore anyway?"

"I hope you get the chance to ask him that." Tracy turned back around.

A fine gold chain crossed the back of her neck and Danny wondered what pendant hung from it, snug against her chest beneath her t-shirt. Bravado's momentum propelled him forward. "Know what else I'll tell him? I'll tell him not to worry, if a reporter can find the Angeles Arsonist, the person who *actually* burned his house down, surely a federal task force will have no problem doing it too. Surely I ought to be standing on the shoulders of such giant expert managers of information dissemination."

Tracy shook her head. "You really are something. You're not going to take any responsibility for this at all are you? All you had to do was set your ego aside long enough to do the right thing but you didn't. You chose to try to get your fifteen minutes of fame instead and it cost that man his *home.* You're not talking your way out of this—you made last night happen and you will be held accountable."

"Um—the guy with the *flamethrower* made it happen. You might recall that I was the one running *away* from him?"

"You were the enabler."

"Only in the off-season."

Pavelko grinned at him in the mirror. "See Danny? We're just getting started on this thing."

Tracy inclined her head toward him.

Danny stared at the back of their heads. "So what about the task force within the task force? Care to answer a few questions about *that,* Trace?"

The ATF agent said, "Go fuck yourself, Danny Kasho."

"Get that advice a lot, don't you Danny?" Pavelko smirked. "How's that for the integrity of the investigation?"

The Impala's air conditioning barely made it over the front seats and there were no vents in back. Danny was getting testy. "And why aren't *you* back at Cruz's? Wasn't his guilt your foregone conclusion in the first place? Instinct is one thing but too much of it starts to look like something else quote unquote, isn't that what you said Mark? Wasn't there anything of interest in the stuff I gave you last night? Why aren't you back there taking the credit?"

Pavelko licked his lips. The inadequate air conditioning seemed to be getting to him too. "Because I am needed back at headquarters."

"In Vallejo?"

"That's right Danny. In Vallejo."

"Because whatever you're needed for in San Francisco dwarfs the supposed major break in the Angeles Arsonist case, is that it? Can I quote you on that? Gee I wonder what it could be."

"You do what you're told in the Service, Danny. You should try it sometime."

"You see your case through to conviction Mark. Unless it isn't your case anymore."

"You rent cases, you don't own them. You don't own cases and you don't own people. You don't even own yourself."

Danny was going to say something about Hallmark but concentrated on searching his news feeds while they all listened to the sounds of the speeding car and their own inner monologues.

"Agents get assigned and reassigned all the time," Pavelko said carefully. "That is the job. Nothing lasts forever. But first I have a few things to wrap up."

Danny looked up at the rearview mirror and caught Pavelko looking at him before he returned his eyes to the road.

They bullied their way onto the 101. Six miles later the Sepulveda Dam slid by on the right, a spindly centipedal comb of concrete with seven sawhorse ribs fronting an arid wildlife preserve. The dam was built in 1941 by the US Army Corps of Engineers to stave off floods, a disaster which in this new era of perma-drought, so dry the air itself crinkled like tin foil, seemed as menacing as an attack from Mars—which admittedly looked to be underway with the Delma media tower assaulting the intersection, practically transparent in daylight apart from her screens, her many thousands of photovoltaic cells soaking up and storing the bright, endless, brutal, desiccating sunshine that powered her endless informing. Before they sped out of her range the audio of the nearest screens blared through a movie trailer and two different pill commercials, before handing them off to the last screen spouting Zachary Abrams's mellifluous voice urging them to do better, live better, be better, with his help.

Danny's phone buzzed with a hit from Mendoza-related keywords. Gibson the Reuters stringer now claimed court was reconvening tomorrow morning at ten. Apparently Charlize Patron hadn't needed much time to think. Gibson posting it twice was good enough for him so Danny added it to his Mendoza blog Investment In Murder, slowed down if not outright hampered by his phone's cracked display. On this of all days.

Patrick Dearing the finance goon finally posted an update: the house belonged to LA County Fire Department Captain Mike Cruz. Bravo, Danny thought. *Police dispersing. Show's over folks.* He winced at Dearing's prose but it confirmed what he already knew—there was no standoff. There never had been.

Pavelko was furious because neither the flamethrower nor Mike Cruz were home today.

* * * * *

The blackened ruins of Peter Buckstein's dream house could have risen as a dilapidated headstone within a garland of bare trees in a wintertime cemetery devoted to his botched retirement.

Traffic on Decker Canyon remained cinched to one lane and was backed up for mile after twisty mile in both directions. Groups of cars took turns driving past what had grown into a major crime scene overnight. Fire trucks, police cars, and a pair of brightly-colored local news vans took up an extra length of the southbound lane. Ursula Ruda's red Nissan Versa with its green alien head antenna ball was squeezed in like a strange bead on a necklace.

Danny scoped out his Accord as they passed. To his relief it looked unscathed—and unticketed. You could never be sure, even at a crime scene. And CODA manager Ronald Schiff frowned at expensing parking tickets.

Pavelko had to park a couple hundred feet down the road, which he noisily protested to an overheated uniformed deputy directing traffic long enough to make Tracy Orman intervene out of embarrassment. Pavelko slammed his door when he got out. So did she. They trudged single-file up the shoulder with Danny lagging behind, buffeted by gusts of hot, dry air pushed at them by impatient motorists accelerating away from the scene.

He wondered why Ursula wasn't staking out Cruz's house. Maybe she'd been forced to choose and picked the Decker Canyon house fire—allegedly set by the Angeles Arsonist—a story which was picking up traction in the media. *His* story. When you were freelancing or between assignments you sometimes had to roll the dice like that on stories and hope you picked a good one. But if Dime Time was any indication Ursula was never between assignments, she seemed to have a quota of stories she needed to hit every day.

Two TV reporters were doing stand-ups a few feet away from each other at the foot of the driveway. It was 12:30 PM, still enough time to make the midday news broadcasts. Danny recognized one of the reporters, Stephanie something from Channel 5. Dark-haired and pretty in a thin cream-colored peasant top blouse and fitted slacks, the kind of generic beauty acceptable to the widest possible viewing demographic. She could have been wearing a bikini and a sash and a tiara and biffing heady questions like *If you were a strawberry smoothie, what fruit would you be made of?* She wasn't in Carrie Voelker's league, and once again Danny found himself grateful for not having to try to make a living on TV.

In the dirt turnout between the road and the trash bins he spotted Ursula Ruda wearing dark cargo pants and a white cotton t-shirt under her safari vest, which blended in with the earth-toned rocks of the retaining walls bordering the driveway. She was talking to a diminutive man with wild bushy Beethoven hair who looked to be in his 60s and stood nearly eye to eye with her. When he wasn't waving his arms around like an interpretive dancer he was hugging himself. Danny assumed he must be Peter Buckstein, the owner of the deceased house, wearing the same t-shirt and shorts and sandals he'd tugged on when he was roused from bed sometime overnight to the news his dream had burned down. Ursula was nodding under the wide brim of her hat with her fancy camera slung over her shoulder and her arms folded across her chest. She wasn't holding her digital recorder so she must have already gotten what she'd needed from him. Since Stephanie Something and the other reporter were doing stand-ups they had to be finished with him too. Now Peter Buckstein was talking because he needed to talk to somebody and she was indulging him. She'd turned as soft as a Care Bear.

A wave of bilious guilt made Danny look away. Defensiveness was misplaced in the face of such an obviously distraught man, but shame on Peter Buckstein for still believing in dreams.

Ursula spotted him. She brought her camera up and shot probably twenty pictures that fast, then hung it over her shoulder and returned her attention to Buckstein. Stephanie Something and the other reporter didn't take note of him. He wondered if his anonymity would outlast the time it took for him to give his statement. He delicately brought up the anonymous email on his phone in preparation as they ducked under the barrier tape and started up the driveway. He and Pavelko were both breathing hard; Tracy Orman not so much.

Detective Travis Salk waited at the top of the driveway with Dennis Abner, Candrea Rooney, and four other detectives Danny didn't recognize, all mirrored Oakleys and incredulity. Pavelko hadn't made or taken any calls during the entire drive from Pasadena so Tracy Orman, who had seldom looked up from her phone, must have alerted them they were en route.

"Appreciate you coming Danny." Dennis Abner was freshly-shaven and wore a polo shirt and a green LASD baseball cap. Wraparound Nike sunglasses had replaced his wire-framed glasses. Nothing wrinkled, everything squared away. Same disapproving jut of his chin like a battering ram poised to dash mislaid hopes.

Danny tried subtly to keep his weight on his left foot. "I was working."

"So were we." Travis Salk's perfunctory smile bent the graying ends of his moustache. "We were all here scratching our heads and trying to figure out how you could cause such a colossal fucking mess unless you were really trying to. Really, really trying hard."

Candrea Rooney's badge was clipped to the waistband of her slacks and her half-smile looked as smooth as sandpaper. "Mr. Kasho. We meet again. You look like you got hit by a train." She looked him up and down. "Almost." She left her disappointment at the near-miss in her tone like a poisoned consolation—*better luck next time.*

None of the other detectives introduced themselves but there was a collection of badges hanging from lanyards and clipped to gun belts. Danny assumed a mix of local detectives and state and federal special agents, of which there was never a shortage.

Dennis Abner pushed out his chin. "Walk us through it if you will please Danny. Start at the top."

"Last night I received an anonymous email from someone alleging to know the identity of the Angeles Arsonist. I brought a copy of the email on my phone." He handed the damaged device to Abner.

He told them about discovering the source of UCANBRN2's posts was the Hampton Inn's computer lounge, and how he decided to bring Garrett's empty gun with him, just in case. Tipster or no tipster he was concerned with being out there alone in such a remote area, but the fact that the gun was unloaded showed the most he ever intended to use it for was as a warning if necessary, not a weapon—he didn't expect a fight. Of course he didn't. He was a reporter, not a fighter.

He led them up the fire road to the spot where he'd waited. In daylight it offered a sweeping vista of the incongruously green Malibu Country Club golf course nestled in the bosom of the dry dirt-brown canyon.

"Have you ever received an email like that before?" Candrea Rooney shaded her eyes with her hand and her wedding ring twinkled in the sun.

"I get tips but they're always from active addresses. The ones I follow up on are anyway. Anything that looks like spam goes to my junk folder."

"Is that where you found this email? In your junk folder?"

"No, it was in my inbox, it hadn't been filtered out. I get a lot of spam because my email's in every post."

"Lucky thing you read it," Salk said. "In other words how would he know you would? In time to meet him, I mean."

"Why wouldn't I? It's my public address, that's what it's there for." He glanced at Tracy Orman, who happened to be in his line of sight, and immediately felt like he'd given something incriminating away with the gesture.

"So anyone can contact you?" Candrea Rooney asked.

"Anyone. I read everything and respond to what interests me."

"Do you ever meet them face to face?" Salk asked.

"Sometimes."

Dennis Abner asked, "Like how often?"

"I don't know."

"Half the time?"

"Sure."

"But I'm still troubled," Salk said. "You said something earlier about how you didn't think the arsonist would go all the way up to the cave on the *chance* he'd find someone there to kill. There's nothing accidental about the arsonist is what you said. In other words why would he leave something as important as scheduling a meeting with you to *chance?* What if you didn't read his email in time? See, we're just trying to drill down on that email—we've got someone who leaves nothing to chance sending his favorite *blogger* an anonymous email to meet in only a couple of hours. But in fact since remailers are delayed as you were quick to point out, there's no telling *when* you might receive it, isn't that right?"

Danny said, "First, *I* didn't say there's nothing accidental about him, Mike Cruz did. Second, I can't speculate on his frame of mind or comment on a bunch of hypotheticals. He sent it, I read it, I came."

"Just as you were getting ready to leave?" Dennis Abner asked.

"I felt like I'd waited long enough. I thought it was turning out to be bullshit. When I got to the driveway he was already out of the minivan. The sliding door was open and he was putting on the flamethrower."

"Sure it wasn't a full size van?" one of the detectives Danny didn't know asked.

"It wasn't an Econoline, it was a minivan."

Another detective asked the expected next question, "What color was it?"

"It was dark."

"That's it?"

"Do you see any street lights here? It was dark-colored. It wasn't white, it was dark-colored. It had four wheels and a sliding door and a loose fan belt."

"Well that's something," one of the other two detectives said unenthusiastically.

Many notes and photographs were taken. They trooped back down to the driveway. The pavement radiated heat like a frying pan and all Danny wanted was a fresh bag of ice for his ankle and fistfuls of pain meds. The driveway was actually a private road which continued past the burned house and curved steeply down into the canyon to ranch-style estates and a burgeoning vineyard hidden at the bottom. Last night the distance to the house had seemed like a mile away but in daylight he saw it was only about a hundred feet. The house looked smaller too, but who could judge the cut of meat by the gristle left on the plate.

"Tell us how the conversation went again," Dennis Abner said to him. "You were standing where? Here? About where I am?"

"Right where I'm standing."

"Perfect. Hold still."

Everyone took a picture. Candrea Rooney made a noise in her throat that made him feel as if he was standing there with his fly open. Ursula and the two other reporters gathered at the foot of the driveway photographed him too and it took an effort not to flip them all off Johnny Cash-style.

"What did you say to him?" Abner asked.

"I was just trying to get him to talk, trying to coax him into saying something. It wasn't a conversation, as I'm sure you've all seen on my video by now."

Salk said, "You said you know what it's like to live with a secret. What does that mean? What secret?"

No doubt about it, Danny grimaced, it sucked being on this side of the questioning. "I was trying to be sympathetic. I was trying to sound like I was on his side. I told him he could talk to me, that he didn't have to hide anymore."

"You said that to him?" Rooney asked. "That you thought he was hiding?"

"And then he shot the flamethrower."

"Guess he didn't like your advice," Salk smirked.

"Then what happened?" Abner asked.

"I ran as fast as I could toward the house."

He retraced his route with the investigators trailing behind him like a glum wedding party. An octocopter drone came into view above and he assumed it was videoing him, not the smoking ruins of the house, sending video somewhere to be analyzed, his body language interpreted for signs of guilt.

The pickup was burned yellowish-white and sat low on its rims. The glass had exploded out of warped empty window frames. Inside the cab the upholstery and dashboard had burned or melted away. The Dumpster was unscathed but the portable cement mixer he ran into was tipped over with its legs in the air like a dead dog. Everything was still saturated from the fire department's assault. Firefighters paid no attention to the group as they continued mopping up what was left of Peter Buckstein's dream.

Danny looked through the front door frame into the blackened hallway soaked with dirty ashen water. A charred staircase rose aimlessly to the nonexistent second floor. They rounded the garage and he showed them the window frame he'd crawled through.

"Why'd you go inside?" Dennis Abner asked.

Danny gestured at the bramble of bushes and shrubs below. "Where else was I supposed to go? I couldn't see anything. I just wanted to hide."

"Didn't you think he might come in after you?" Candrea Rooney asked.

"I wasn't thinking anything past my next step. I wanted to get away from him, that's all. Running was survival. Running and time. I'd already called 911."

"Still, it sure looks like you put your back to the wall," she said.

"Well I'm alive so I guess it worked. You want to critique my special weapons and tactics you go right ahead. I'm alive, that's all I care about."

Travis Salk held up a finger. "Ah, but that's *not* all you care about is it Danny? You care about having a story to sell."

"Look," Danny snapped, "we can do this with CODA's lawyers present if you want. I don't mind. Want to know what I think? I think you guys are lost. I think the task force—however many of them there are left—is fumbling around in the dark hoping someone turns on the lights for them. That person is me and the taxpayers will be informed of it. You guys are like Area 51 now. You're blown." He blinked rapidly and swallowed. It was a lot easier to be a bad ass when there weren't nine cops glaring back at you.

"Let's continue," Abner calmly suggested, as if the outburst had all been in Danny's imagination.

They snaked their way back to the front door, Danny simmering like the pot of an amateur cook, and carefully went inside. Abner and Rooney and a fire captain led the way. The smoky air immediately hit Danny's lungs but he wasn't the only one coughing. He wished he'd worn rubber boots instead of his cross trainers. Always the wrong footwear these days. Abner and Rooney stopped to examine points along the strange scaly texture of the charred walls and floor, as if they had entered the belly of some enormous lizard. The investigators each looked around, making notes and taking photos and video, conferring, pointing.

Danny found himself alone in a large room in the back. The fireplace was still intact, its stone chimney pointing straight up to the clear blue sky. With the warm wind and the smoke blowing around him he knew the crown fire metaphor was accurate—Fireman666 wasn't going to stop until he was stopped by force. Until he physically had no fire left in him.

CHAPTER 27

In spite of the circumstances a vivid memory blew in on the breeze like a wounded bird and the familiar simulacrum of Paul Kasho's face appeared in the swirling smoke.

It was early in the summer of '93, the only summer it ever was in his memories. School had just gotten out and Danny hadn't been offered the job at the hotel yet. Most of his friends were at a two-week camp popular with parents who could afford to stave off having their kids at home with time on their hands for nearly three months. Victor and Cynthia had both gone when they were his age—and he knew his mom was all for him going too—but he had been granted an eleventh-hour reprieve by his dad who saved the summer for his youngest son's exploration and growth.

One day he and his dad walked to the scene of a house fire which had occurred some days before in an unoccupied old house near the Calendula veteran's cemetery. Paul made him change into jeans and sneakers instead of his customary summer uniform of tank top, cutoff shorts and flip flops, and brought along an army surplus duffel bag and two pairs of heavy-duty gardening gloves, the kind with leather palms. Danny's hands practically disappeared inside them. They reminded him of those big foam hands people waved at Vic's football games.

The firemen, investigators and insurance people were long gone, as was anything of value. Every window had been blown out. The roof had partially collapsed, leaving the dormer windows reclining like precarious skylights. Exposed wires dangled around them. Naked springs corkscrewed out of cushionless furniture frames. Jagged edges of unrecognizable things lurked in the shadows like wild animals, watching the intruders warily. Through an open door Danny saw the metal frame of a bed warped like a bowl, as if a hippo had sat on it.

Anyone else would have known it was dangerous, certainly no place for a child, but that was his dad. As long as he was with him he knew he'd be safe. He didn't know what they were doing there and it didn't matter—he was simply enjoying being on an adventure with his dad. *Especially* since they were doing something sneaky. He knew his dad hadn't told his mom where they were going. He couldn't wait to tell his friends about this place when they got back from camp.

Paul moved cautiously inside the ruin. He scanned the remains of the living room, then led them carefully down a hallway tight as a swollen artery. Broken glass crunched underfoot. Danny's sneakers were darkened with soot and he wondered if he was going to get in trouble when they got home. He had to be careful not to fall through one of the holes in the floor or cut himself on something. Then he *would* be in trouble.

"Looters steal," his dad told him in a voice as serious as when Vic got in trouble for taking the Citroën without permission—without even a license. "Looting and stealing are the same thing." He balanced carefully on a portion of collapsed wall and edged a piece of blackened timber with his shoe. "But when an accident like this happens and there's no owners, no one to claim anything, whatever's left becomes public domain. With a critical eye and a good heart the treasures are there for the taking."

With the allegations of robbery leveled permanently against his father the phrase *the treasures are there for the taking* would haunt Danny for the rest of his life. As would his father's supposed good heart.

"A-ha! Here we are."

A wooden bookshelf lay on its back across a gaping hole in the raised foundation of the house. A strip of sodden insulation had fallen over it. Paul moved it aside as Danny peered up through what used to be the ceiling and the roof above that to the branches of a tree looming high overhead, the ends of which had been licked clean by the flames. Paul crouched over the rows of bumpy leather-bound spines in the bookshelf. Some had slips of brittle yellowed paper tucked between the pages, forgotten bookmarks of their forgotten owners.

"Each one of these was hand-made by somebody a long, long time ago. They survived a lot of years, close calls like this, to be able to come home with us." He stood up with an armful of selected books and bent forward so Danny could reach. "Top one's yours."

It was a slender volume bound in blackened leather without title or any other illumination as to its purpose or content. Delicate brass clips held it closed. Danny opened them with his fingernail; an inscription on the inside cover was too faded to read. Its pages were rough-edged and stiff—and blank. He looked up at his dad.

"You're always writing in that little black book of yours." Paul quickly placed his own selections into the duffel bag. "That's good for when you're on the go, you should always have something portable on you—and a pen or pencil too. But when you want to write something longer, something you really care about, you can write it in this."

They walked home down the middle of the streets except when a car came, carrying their smoke-scented treasures in shafts of light filtered through an almost unbroken canopy of trees, Danny skipping ahead of his dad with a wondrous buoyancy in his stomach, gleefully waving his new book through hovering clouds of gnats and feeling so happy that his feet might leave the ground too.

Paul had seemed indestructible back then. Danny didn't know what he'd do if the next look he had at him was an autopsy photo, since every prisoner who dies in jail is automatically autopsied. He wondered what happened to the leather book with the little brass clips.

The floor creaked behind him as Mark Pavelko stepped into the burned-out room, dissipating Danny's reverie like candle smoke in a Santa Ana. The investigators' movements throughout the house were marked by their voices and radio chatter over the white noise of the fire department fans.

"This where you jumped?" Soot smeared the center of Pavelko's forehead like a penitent on Ash Wednesday.

"Where I fell, right." It was a good fifteen foot drop from the balcony and he was surprised he didn't break anything. He didn't think he had anyway, though his ankle felt like it. Only the fence had stopped him from dropping down onto Decker Canyon where Fireman666 could have run him over in lieu of burning him alive.

"Last night make you think of anything you hold dear, Danny? Anything you care about?"

"Besides my life?"

"Yeah. Besides yourself for a change." Pavelko spoke with that same creepy syrupy slowness. "Like your family in Calendula. You thinking about your family at all today Danny?"

A chill rode the burnished edge of the wind.

"'Cause you should be." Pavelko took off his cap to scratch his head, revealing the ugly bruise on his forehead. "I've seen it a thousand times you know, people who wish they hadn't done something, or wish they could take something back, whatever it is that just ruined their life or someone else's, which is practically the same thing consequentially. Life all alone isn't worth much is it?"

"Unless you're a conjoined twin you live your life alone. You're either alone with somebody or alone by yourself, but you're alone."

Pavelko snorted. "Not even you are cynical enough for that islands in the stream shit."

"What are you cynical enough for Mark? Or mad enough to do? Which is it?"

Pavelko blinked. "What the hell are you talking about?"

"Bullshit, that's what. All your bullshit and lies."

"You sound like a chick, Danny."

"Do I? Do I sound like Linda Fisher?"

"You sound like someone who desperately wants to get his ass kicked."

"Kicking my ass isn't as easy as you think is it Mark?"

Pavelko stepped to within inches of him. "What is your fucking problem Danny? I thought I was doing you a solid and this is how you repay me for the access *I* gave you? For the trust *I* gave you? In the end our so-called friendship didn't even slow you down, did it? You took your shot the second you had the chance even after you agreed not to say anything."

"I didn't say anything about Cruz. It didn't come from me."

"And where did my personal life come from Danny? You didn't even ask me for my side of the story. So much for journalism 101."

"News is news, I don't know what you think you're owed." He realized he must sound like Vanessa speaking to Victor. "So let's talk about your side of the story Mark. You had some birthday Tuesday didn't you? Hand-made cards from your kids and a restraining order violation from your *ex*-wife. Are you even supposed to *be* here?"

Pavelko was about to reply when Salk came into the room carrying his notebook in one hand and his phone in the other.

"Alrighty then," said the detective. "Danny we're going to have to continue our discussion later today. Think you can find your way to the Malibu/Lost Hills sheriff's station?"

"I think I can." He hadn't decided yet if he'd come armed with a lawyer. That would involve not only Lucy and Ronald Schiff, but possibly William Craig himself, the great leviathan who stirred whenever his legal hounds started barking. He needed to know where Lucy and Ron stood before he asked for help.

"Danny it goes without saying but people like you make us say it anyway—*do not* post anything else about this on the internet. In other words keep your trap shut for us. Think you can do that?"

"Until I give my statement."

"And then what changes?"

"Everything. Everyone else is on it already."

"Publicity is your problem, the integrity of this investigation is mine." Salk handed Danny his card. "Six o'clock. We'll probably be late but you be right…on…time. You coming, Mark?"

Pavelko started. "Sure." He passed close by Danny and murmured, "See you soon Danny."

Danny followed them out, keeping one of the other detectives between him and Pavelko. Fresh air was the kiss of life and once again he embraced it hungrily. He got a couple good shots of the burned house from the road and wondered what was happening to get the detectives going like that. Maybe Derek Cavanaugh was conscious. And talking.

Peter Buckstein was on his phone, waving one hand around at the smoking ruins as if to help illustrate the scale of the disaster to whoever he was talking to. A younger Asian woman had arrived and was stroking his back with abject concern. Danny thought of approaching him, knew he should but didn't know how, and definitely didn't want to do it in front of the two TV reporters who were converging on him like homeless people to a discarded sandwich as he limped down the driveway. There was no sign of Ursula Ruda.

"Danny is it true you met the Angeles Arsonist last night?" Stephanie Something shouted. "Is it true you didn't contact the police?"

"How do you respond to accusations your publicity stunt has endangered lives?" The other reporter was a slender man with very white teeth and sculpted wind-proof blond hair to whom Danny took an immediate dislike.

"No comment everybody. Sorry," he added emptily. Parasites was right. He looked beseechingly at the deputy and the cop got into gear.

"Okay folks, make room."

The gouge from the key was down the driver's side so every time he got in or out of his car it was right there. He'd already moved on from anger to embarrassment—it was obvious someone keyed his car, obvious someone hated him. Someone who'd recently joined the league of extraordinary assholes.

He made sure the media parking permit was safe in the glovebox and waited with the AC blowing on high as traffic was stopped while a fire truck was repositioned. With the Klieg light of public interest swinging his way all he could think about was where the flamethrower was. Did Mike Cruz really stop short at just designing—but never actually *building*—the device? Or was Mark Pavelko hiding his Fireman666 costume and the Thorogood boots somewhere?

Stephanie Something came over—no microphone in hand, no cameraman in tow, still about as safe as a snake in a handbag. Nonetheless Danny felt obliged to roll down his window if only for the way the hot wind flattened her blouse against her chest.

"Come on Danny. No comment at all?" She leaned in his window and he got a good look at the top of her breasts. "Amy Childress says you could face charges."

They'd talked once or twice before but he was sure the only reason she knew his name today was because her assignment editor had told her. Her perfume mingled with the smell of the smoke into something pagan. "Sorry." He dry-swallowed some more ibuprofen. Figured the holes he was burning through his stomach lining would hurt less than everything else did now.

"Saving it for CODA? C'mon, give me something." She smiled with her lips closed. Carrie Voelker showed her teeth when she smiled.

He pried his eyes away from her chest—the deputy had stopped traffic and was beckoning at him. "Sorry Stephanie, got to go."

"It's Sheri."

"Sorry. I'll see you."

"Sooner than you think I bet."

Danny checked the time as he backed out onto Decker Canyon. He had to decide where he was going right now—the deputy was motioning for him to hurry up. He drummed his fingers on the steering wheel and said *fuck* a half dozen times, then turned the wheel, setting up a southbound departure. If it had been a breeze getting here from Pasadena, he reasoned, it would be a traffic jam going back. Some massive multi-lane Sigalert traffic jam to rewrite the rest of his day.

Show's over folks.

It was 1:40. He needed gas. He needed a new phone. He could use a little time by the sea.

There were worse places to kill an afternoon than Malibu.

CHAPTER 28

The surface of the sea sparkled beneath stringy taffeta clouds and was interrupted only by a distant pair of cargo ships on the horizon between the coast and Catalina Island. Decker Canyon wound its way down to its terminus at the ornate gates and wealthy landscaping lining the ocean side of PCH and Danny relaxed into the easy coastal highway, a relief after the unrelenting tight curves and concentration demanded by the canyon road, even at relatively low speed.

He opened his windows and the warm salty air siphoned out some of his anger, as he'd hoped. He could ride PCH down to Santa Monica and take Wilshire over to UCLA Medical Center, a section of which had only recently reopened after repairs for damage from the Inglewood quake, and see if his hunch about Derek Cavanaugh was right. Maybe he'd see Ursula there. Come to think of it she was probably there already, hiding under his bed with her fancy camera.

He sped past the long white sliver of Zuma beach with his sunglasses on and the glistening ocean gently pushing white swells up onto the sand. *Save water*, the nearest billboard stated, *save Earth!* The thirstiest state in the union stared at all that water, unable to take even a sip. The beach parking lot was packed, the pale blue lifeguard towers almost the same color as the sky all open and staffed. It was a beautiful day and the holiday beachgoers could be forgiven for ignoring the diminishing plume from the Backbone Fire drifting silently out over the ocean behind them.

Law enforcement was driving its giant pushpin into the cumulative event of last night, examining split decisions under a microscope the choices themselves couldn't withstand, like admitting to the police the necklace in the dead man's hand twenty-six years ago belonged to his father. It was easy for someone to say he'd done wrong, easier still to gang up on him about it. He alone was out here at the edge of the continent and the edge of events, living them as they unfolded. Legacy media's predictable perspective had been irrevocably overrun by people like him, equipped with little more than a cell phone and a critical view and the unwillingness to be spoon-fed.

The emails, voicemails and texts were piling up. Lucy wanted to know which interviews she should confirm—there were numerous offers across all four mediums. She naturally wanted to say yes to everything but he was nowhere near being able to. She didn't revisit Legal's opinion about whether to publish the Decker Canyon video. High-priced baby chickens driving high-priced baby chicken cars made of gold-plated feathers. Chickens who preened themselves to try to look like eagles without doing anything at all.

There were no further updates from finance goon Patrick Dearing and nothing new from anyone else. The story was already in re-run. Cruz and Pavelko had some fathomlessly deep dislike for each other the way only males who consider themselves alphas can have, as a transcendental threat to their forceful outer shell and flimsy inner symbolism.

PCH angled away from the ocean and carved out the thickest section of Malibu north of Point Dume. Danny passed a sign for Heathercliff Road, slowed suddenly and turned, and cruised around the gas station where the 911 call had been made. The post office across the street was closed and the only people on the sidewalk were day laborers waiting for work, which was a seven days a week job. The police had come and gone and local routine had returned. Some of the laborers gestured at him—*Pick me, pick me*, prostitutes for work instead of sex dressed in jeans, work shirts or t-shirts, high-top shoes or work boots, carrying backpacks or plastic bags with lunch and water. Durable clothing for any job they might be lucky enough to land.

Danny turned around and continued east on PCH. He managed to put his phone on speaker and called Ellen Lee.

"Danny, what's up?"

"What's going on, Ellen?"

"Down in PV baby. Brain matter of the rich and famous."

Danny didn't know what she meant—he felt like he'd been living in a silo.

"What's new with the Backbone Fire?" she asked. "Great name by the way. I saw you on TV. Good job. You look so grown up! I was like, look at Danny!"

"Thanks Ellen. I wanted to ask you about the body in Malibu Lagoon this morning. The suicide."

"Sure, what's up?"

"Did the victim look like a day laborer to you?"

"Suppose he could have been. Why? Got an ID?"

"No. But did the boots he was wearing strike you as strange?"

"Boots?"

"He was wearing big black boots. Unusual footwear for a day laborer."

"Maybe he wasn't one. I picked it up on the scanner on my way down here."

"Well I'm just killing time between things and want to look into it a little if you don't mind."

"Run with it. Keep me posted okay? Gotta go. Congrats again!"

Traffic slowed as he approached the intersection with Corral Canyon. A dozen fire engines were parked on the shoulder. There was a gas station on the corner here too, with a closer public phone than the one Fireman666 used. After starting the fire and killing the students he must have driven until his nerves settled enough to stop and pick up the phone to make his special call, sweating and nervous, speaking quickly in a high-pitched voice strained by excitement.

Where was Pavelko staying if not at the hotel? He should have thought to ask Phil the clerk if Tracy Orman was a guest there. Maybe Pavelko was staying with her. Maybe she didn't know about his problem in San Francisco. Maybe he'd pieced together a collage of half-truths she accepted because she wanted to, so she wouldn't feel guilty about what they were doing. Maybe she was lonely. Maybe she was in love.

A pair of serpentine skid marks veered off PCH to where a white Metropolitan Transportation Authority truck was parked while its crew replaced the broken callbox. A sheriff's patrol car and two yellow

Department of Water & Power trucks were parked nearby—Derek Cavanaugh had hit something more substantial than trees.

He rolled up his windows as traffic approached the plume, passing through it in a few seconds. Definitely a different fire today. And that itch beginning to burn out there somewhere in the bright sunshine like an insect under a magnifying glass, unsatisfied by the utterly non-fatal Decker Canyon fire last night. He'd *planned* to kill Danny, there was no doubt about that. He'd thought about him, obsessed on him until he could conjure the rage. And not only had Danny not died, he'd *seen* him. *Drawn* him. Told the whole wide world about him like the most epic show and tell. Against the bully's will. Against his plans, against his intent. He'd sent him running scared in his shitty little beat-up minivan and for an encore he was going to point the way for the torch-wielding mob to find him. Time to help administer some street justice.

The gate of the marshy Malibu Lagoon estuary was open on the exit side with a black and white parked prohibitively across the entrance. The deputy inside was on the phone with his elbow sticking out of the open window. Before the light changed Danny noticed a pair of Hispanic men standing on the corner on a patch of grass under the gas station sign. They were talking and gesturing toward something across the street at the lagoon entrance.

He pulled a brazen U-turn at the tile-covered Adamson House and doubled back to the gas station. His phone started ringing as he pulled up to a pump. It was a video chat invitation from Carrie Voelker. Accept or Decline. A dirty trick, he thought with his thumb hovering over the softly-glowing green button, about to make a connection as inevitable as DNA itself. If Carrie Voelker hovered in the air off the edge of a precipitous cliff there would be no shortage of men stepping, leaping, plummeting into thin air with a howl like a Stuka to try and somehow catch her even at their own peril, just because.

"You rang?" He said when her lustrous face appeared on his phone like a cracked apparition at a séance.

Her smile instantly doubled its luminance. "Danny! I'm so glad I got you!" She was in her car—she was driving, she wasn't a passenger in one of her station's news vans. The phone was at eye level and steady in a dashboard mount.

"What a day huh?"

"Um for some of us more than others Danny—oh my God are you okay?"

"Yeah I'm okay, thanks."

"This is incredible! And you are out of your mind!"

"I know, I get that a lot."

"I bet you're getting it a lot," she purred.

Naughty Carrie.

"Did you get anything the police can use?" she asked.

"They're going over everything now. I don't know what they'll get out of it."

"But you're okay."

"I'm okay. A bum ankle, some cuts and bruises. I've got Grover on my left hand and Animal on my right so I'm ready for a rematch. But so much for hot tips," he added, reinforcing the rationale.

"The video is incredible Danny! I mean I can't believe you're okay! I mean I'm glad you are—oh my God!—but you know what I mean right?"

"Right. And thanks."

"So it's all true!"

"What is?"

"He uses a flamethrower?"

That was old news. They were getting down to the wire on *who*. And Ursula under Derek Cavanaugh's hospital bed, eavesdropping like a bug. "Yeah that's true."

The two Hispanic men on the corner stood and stood. Looked around at everything and nothing. Talked and squinted.

"And what's up with Mike Cruz?" Carrie asked. "Were you there today?"

"For a little bit."

"Did anybody even see him? Did you?"

"I didn't."

"Maybe it was someone else at his house. I mean is it really him? Everyone's saying it is. My Fire Captain, My Fire Bug. Good huh?"

"Now look at who's into the classics."

"You must be thrilled."

"At what?"

"This has been your story from the beginning! Way to go Danny!"

Carrie was laying it on a little thick and he was beginning to feel smothered. "Well, it's developing isn't it."

"Do you wonder where the flamethrower is? They didn't bring in any forensic team by the time we left. The drawing you made of his costume is so awesome by the way. So freaky and so awesome."

"The stuff is probably in a Dumpster somewhere with the boots."

"Do you think Mark Pavelko knows?"

Question of the day. "I don't know. He might."

"I must have an old number for him, nobody's picking up. What number have you got?"

Not her smoothest segue but it got her there, like an old dress that still fit her in all the right ways. Pavelko's blood had been drawn and the feeding frenzy was on and Carrie was late to the game. Maybe she'd repay the favor someday by wanting him for hot sex out of the blue. Facts were chum at this point with all manner of people ripping bloody chunks out of Pavelko's life. Danny gave her the number without having to consult his phone.

She said, "Thanks! You're the best!"

"Tell him I say hi."

"I will. What are you doing now?"

"I'm actually chilling in Malibu."

"At Drake's? Who with? I'm so jealous," she teased, but her heart wasn't in the line. She was distracted, probably texting someone at her station as they talked. Her eyes kept flitting to a second device she held out of view in her lap.

"I'm between statements," he said. "Thought I'd catch a wave or two."

"Do you surf?"

She definitely wasn't paying attention. The real Greek tragedy in all this was how fast he'd been dismissed. "Well anyway, I gotta run."

"Me too. Talk to you soon!"

Carrie hung up before he could say bye or hope so or what color underwear are you wearing?

He took the pocket binoculars from his messenger bag and looked from the two men across the street to the lagoon entrance. A couple of votive candles, a small white cross, and a tricolor Mexican flag were set up in a shrine under the Wrong Way sign on the median.

The day laborer community mourning one of its own.

As he gassed up he gingerly tapped and swiped around his phone's cracked display and found the Malibu Labor Partnership was located just up the street. Malibu residents generally disliked day laborers gathering around unsupervised, and the non-profit MLP was the solution. It organized and centralized the labor force, and its bilingual staff gave the workers that registered with it the feeling that should an employer not pay—which wasn't uncommon—there might actually be some sort of recourse.

Danny drove past the local shopping center's collection of fashionable boutiques, Starbucks, restaurants, and movie theater. The MLP was located at the end of the road in a trailer painted in a colorful mural of laboring Mexicans in what he supposed would be called historical-stereotypical dress. The white HLR Laboratories buildings, where Boeing and General Motors conducted R&D for high-tech defense contracting, perched like a medieval castle on its hilltop, an unremarkable building which looked like it belonged in an industrial park.

Several men stood together in the parking lot in work boots, jeans, long-sleeve shirts, ball caps, gloves tucked into back pockets, holding paper cups and talking. No traditional ponchos here. No big black boots either. They surveyed Danny and their expressions turned dismissive in an instant, seasoned professionals at distinguishing a potential employer from a nobody since their survival depended on it.

Up the steps to the trailer door where notices were taped in Spanish with excessive exclamation points. One prominent sign handpainted in English proclaimed *No human being is illegal.* Each letter was a different color including many hues that human beings didn't come in out of the box.

The office smelled of dirt and body odor and looked like an add-on to a real structure; there was a noticeable slope to the floor. Fake wood paneling on the walls and harsh fluorescent lights. A dozen molded plastic chairs with metal legs placed along the walls met at a five-foot folding table set up at one end of the room. A coffee machine in the corner belched the acidic reek of burnt cheap beans. The round 15" analog wall clock read 2:25. Ten minutes slow. Every other chair was occupied by an Hispanic man of indeterminate age, sitting quietly with hands patiently folded across his belly. Danny checked out their footwear—running shoes or the common ankle-high wheat-colored work boot. They looked at him as if he'd stepped into the wrong bar.

A skinny white male volunteer in his 40s wearing a *London Calling* t-shirt sat at the folding table. Danny bet the guy liked music snobbily. Defensively. He and his opinion would take all the fun out of anything. His straight brown hair was kept mostly out of his face by a limp ponytail that reached halfway down his back. A thick loose leaf binder lay open in front of him and he was talking on an old-fashioned beige landline with a curly cord and buttons glowing and blinking across different lines below the number pad. The window-mounted air conditioner forced him to raise his voice. English sounded like a foreign language here.

After a minute the volunteer hung up, and with his finger poised over the next blinking button peered up at Danny behind wire frame glasses barely the size of his eyes, taking in his cartoon-bandaged hands and the smoke smell he'd brought in with him like a special needs child. "Can I help you?"

"My name's Danny Kasho, CODA.com." He held up his media pass and ID. "Wonder if I could ask you a few questions." He had to raise his voice too.

"What about?"

"Did you know the man whose body was found in the lagoon this morning?"

"I can't help you." The man's tone wilted in mid-air. He waggled the clunky telephone receiver like a sap. "We've already spoken to the police, and *you're* not the police, so you'll have to excuse me, thank you."

"You knew the victim?"

"I did not."

"I heard he was a day laborer."

"If he was he wasn't registered with us. And don't try asking the questions I told you I can't answer."

"Given the number of people who come and go through here how can you be so sure?"

The volunteer gave him his best withering stare. "Because they don't all look the same to us. Suicide isn't a story, it's a tragedy. If we had better social services in this country there'd be less of that and more work getting done and then even the One Percent would be happier. What *you* are mister is an ambulance-chaser."

Danny thought it beat being a parasite. "Don't you want justice? The police aren't going to investigate it."

"They already are investigating it."

"They're just filling out forms because they're obligated to. They've already cleared it as a suicide. If you want a real investigation you need the media. And we're free."

"What I want is to get back to work. Like I said, I can't help you." But he still hadn't picked up any of the waiting lines.

"Who knew him? Where can I find them?"

"Since I didn't, I can't say."

"Look, what I publish is going to bring the police here. I want to put the best face on this—the human face. Otherwise your business is going to dwindle to nothing for a few days while the cops are here."

"We're a non-profit and we've nothing to fear from the police. No one here should."

"Think your clientele can afford a few days off? Every good deed deserves to be investigated and you wouldn't hear any objections from your rich white neighbors. They'll welcome your removal with big shiny smiles."

The volunteer scoffed. "You'd have better luck scaring me with tales of the zombie apocalypse. Why don't you ask them about the suicide?" He waggled the receiver at the men in the chairs, who appeared to be paying no attention to the conversation, and pressed the blinking button. "MLP, how may I help you?"

Danny wished he was able to unpleasantly surprise the volunteer with some snappy bilingualism, something colloquial and profane that would make the coarse men laugh. Instead he calmly reached over and pushed down on the solid glowing button and disconnected the volunteer dickhead's call.

"Oh my God," the man gaped, "you did *not* just do that."

Danny raised his voice more than he needed to in the small room. "Someone in this community—*your* community—is dead. People who truly do not care about that are dismissing it as a suicide. What if it's not? *Prove* you care. *Prove* you actually mean something to this community beyond money."

"We prove it every day, not just when somebody dies." The volunteer pushed his glasses up on his nose with his middle finger and pointed at the door. "You need to leave. You've been asked to, now you *have* to. I don't want to call the police but it's not because I don't genuinely think I should mister."

The laborers shifted uncomfortably in their seats. One guy got up and left.

Danny said, "If not you, who? If not here, where? Tell me and I'm out of here."

"It says a lot about you that people have to barter with you just to get you to leave."

Danny spread his hands. "I'm only trying to help."

"Aren't we all." The man's phone blinked and blinked. "Try the hardware store."

"Which one?"

"The Best Value on Heathercliff." The volunteer depressed a blinking button. "MLP, so sorry to keep you waiting—how may I help you?"

As Danny left he wondered why the dickhead didn't just say that to begin with. He could be making it up, but how would he know Danny wasn't *loco* enough to come back?

Another man had joined the group in the parking lot, just returned from a job, smiling with cash in pocket. Poor and marginalized, unable to immigrate or get steady work, maybe an employee withheld payment one too many times, and one of them somehow gets hold of a gun, walks into Malibu Lagoon at night, and shoots himself in the head. If he had a gun why not sell it for quick cash? How would he get a gun in the first place? Why wouldn't he just return to Mexico, defeated but alive? Couldn't he? Did the shame of failure in America overpower the want of the next breath?

Danny drove away thinking about resilience in the face of public shame, and who among us was qualified to judge another person's point of surrender.

CHAPTER 29

There were two entrances to the Best Value Hardware parking lot, each dressed by a pair of thick date palms bending in the wind. Ready and willing workers were ranged along the sidewalk in front all the way up to the gas station on the corner. They stood in loose groups—not close enough to dissuade anyone needing only to hire an individual—and wore old denim and cargo pants, faded sweatshirts, souvenir shop hoodies, baseball caps. One old *hombre* wore a cowboy hat. Ubiquitously dressed and socially invisible unless it was your corner of paradise they were standing on.

Danny parked in a spot that nosed up against the grassy median between the parking lot and the sidewalk and rolled his window down. Immediately men approached.

"Work?"

"Information." Danny pointed at himself. *"Reportero."*

That dispersed them like tear gas.

One man lingered. He had wide Mayan features, like an Indian teleported into the present day in a black Air Jordan cap and paint-spattered blue Yale sweatshirt. "Information?"

"I'm looking for anyone who knew the man who died in the lagoon this morning. Did you know him?"

The man took his hands out of his pockets and crossed his arms. "Seen him around."

Ultimately, Danny thought with satisfaction, the MLP dickhead couldn't help but do the right thing. He couldn't even call the cops on someone who'd barged in and hung up his phone on him. Danny would have. Garrett probably would have shot him. "Did he wait here like you?"

"Si."

"Have you told that to anyone? The police?"

The man smiled. He was missing his front teeth.

Danny took that as a *no*. "Did he know anyone else here?"

The man shrugged, smiled. *"No sé."*

Danny hoped he had something smaller than the $50. Fortunately he had a $5 which he palmed over. The man's fingers were short and rough and he looked at the crumpled bill as if he'd never seen a denomination that small.

"Sorry," Danny said.

"Shit, man." He nodded at a group of men standing halfway up the block by a telephone company terminal box plastered with remnants of stickers.

Danny grabbed his messenger bag and got out. The men watched him approach with marked disinterest after seeing the others walk away. Nothing about him said *money* as he limped over to them. They shifted their weight from foot to foot, the timeless gesture of people with nothing but time.

Danny held up his media pass. "*Por favor*, I'm looking for anyone who knew the man who died in Malibu Lagoon this morning. *Reportero.* I just have a couple questions."

The old man in the cowboy hat went right back to his copy of *La Opinión,* his indifference quickly mimicked by others who turned their backs and returned their patient hopeful attention up the road.

"Reporter?" asked one of two men who remained.

He was young and carried a black LA Kings hoodie and a plastic bottle of water that was half-full. Facially he reminded Danny of the actor Timothy Hutton, but Mexican and with thicker eyebrows. The other man was older, with lighter skin and a blue backpack slung over his shoulder.

"I'm looking for information on the man who died in the lagoon this morning. I'd like to talk to anyone who knew him. Just a couple questions."

"About what?" the Mexican Timothy Hutton asked.

Danny tried the same approach he'd used at the MLP. "I want to see that his death is properly investigated. I want justice for him."

"Police been here already."

"They don't care. But I do."

"Oh I see *señor*, *you* do. You *care*." Both men grinned. About five pesos worth of dentistry between the two of them.

"If I make enough noise the police will *have* to be thorough. I'm a popular reporter."

"You on TV?"

"Online."

Timothy Hutton grunted and made a face. The other man didn't react at all, as if online had something to do with laundry.

"They're already calling it suicide and nobody's questioning it," Danny said. "Nobody but me. Tell me who he was. Help me bring him back to life. He deserves better than what he's going to get."

A pickup honked and men hurried over. Only one got in; the others returned to their places on the sidewalk.

"His name was Jorge," Timothy Hutton finally said.

"Jorge what?"

"Ochoa. He didn't kill himself."

"What makes you so sure?"

"He's my cousin."

Bingo. "I'm sorry. What's your name?"

"Luis. This is Julio."

They shook hands. "I'm Danny. When did you last see Jorge?"

"Yesterday."

"About what time?"

"I don't know. Late."

"Late," Julio agreed.

"If you're not back when Manuel leaves, you take the bus," Luis explained.

"Did Jorge take the bus last night?" Danny asked.

"Don't know, he didn't come home."

"Where does he live?"

"El Segundo. We all live there. Manuel drives, unless he has work or his truck is broke."

"When Jorge didn't come home did you think something had happened?"

"We thought he didn't get paid and didn't have money for the bus. We'd see him here this morning. I brought him a sandwich."

"Not first time," Julio said.

"Did Jorge have a gun? Or any way to get one?" Danny asked.

"Gun? No, no, no gun. Nobody has gun," Luis said.

Julio said, "We all been robbed. Sometimes a gun in their hand, sometimes a knife."

"They know we carry cash at the end of the day," Luis sighed.

"Was Jorge upset about anything?" Danny asked.

"Jorge no get upset." Julio tapped the side of his head.

Danny didn't understand.

"Estúpido," Julio clarified.

Luis clucked his tongue and rebuked Julio in rapid Spanish. Julio shrugged and went and stood at the edge of the sidewalk with his hands in his pockets.

"Can I show you a picture?" Danny brought up Ellen's bookmarked article on his phone and zoomed in as far as was possible with the cracked display.

Luis crossed himself and looked sadly at the image of his cousin's waterlogged corpse on the tiny screen. His brown eyes turned wet and he wiped them with a dirty thumb.

"I'm sorry," Danny said, tempering his impatience.

"I don't know what happened," Luis sniffed and wiped his nose on his sleeve.

"That's what I'm trying to find out. Are those his boots?"

"No. His were like mine, we got them together in Venice." Luis lifted a foot to display the standard ankle-high wheat-colored work boot. Not the militarized Doc Martens, the over-engineered size 12 Thorogoods. Luis fished a thin canvas wallet out of his pocket and took out a photo. "Me and Jorge in Rosarito."

The photo showed Luis and Jorge smiling at the camera, arms around each other's shoulders, the statue of Christ of the Sacred Heart looming in the background, stuck onto a hillside like a gigantic dashboard overlooking the ocean. Jorge Ochoa was a big guy with close-set eyes and a round child's face. He wouldn't look intelligent in any culture. And in the end even the simple had to fend for themselves so he'd stood out here day after day with his cousin and their friends, putting his simple trust in the safety of the process itself—that demand wouldn't devour its supply.

Until yesterday, when something took a bite.

Danny took a picture of the photo. "Tell me about the last time you saw him."

"I was here, Julio, Cesar, some others. There's work 'cause of the fire, cleaning and hauling. Sometimes earthquake repair."

"Did somebody hire him?"

"I just saw him get in. Usually he tells me, but he was already getting in."

"What kind of car was it?"

"A van I think."

"A van or a minivan?"

"Could be a minivan, yeah."

Danny's fingertips tingled—the specialized firefighting boots the Angeles Arsonist was no longer free to wear were already in police custody. "Did you see the driver?"

Luis shook his head.

"When did you leave?"

"Six o'clock maybe?"

"How long had Jorge been gone?"

"Oh, I don't know."

"Did you get any work during that time?"

"No."

"So after Jorge left you were here, what—an hour? Two hours?"

"Maybe an hour." Luis shrugged. "I don't know. We had to go, Manuel was leaving."

Another truck came trolling down Heathercliff. Workers went to greet it. Even the old man in the cowboy hat, who had a limp worse than Danny's. The driver took two men—Julio was one.

Luis clucked his tongue again.

"Is there anyone else who might have seen something?" Danny asked.

"Maybe Cesar. But he's inside the store." Luis patted his belly. "Tummy trouble. They don't like it when we use the bathroom."

"What does Cesar look like? What's he wearing?"

"Red poncho. Sad face," Luis called over his shoulder as he went to rejoin the others.

Danny watched him walk up the sidewalk toward the gas station, passing fellow hopefuls without acknowledgment. Every day was hand to mouth competition, even among amigos.

The arsonist had made his 911 call from the same place he chose his stand-in to kill. He knew this place. His comfort zone was right where Danny was standing. His vanity in emailing Danny and posting on Red Flag had sealed his own fate; his viciousness had sealed Jorge Ochoa's. That was why he was late to their meeting last night, Danny realized—he had to wait until dark to dump Jorge's body in the lagoon wearing his boots. He'd driven around with the laborer captive inside the minivan for hours, dead or alive. For hours.

There are possible victims.

He'd been so dispassionate about them, so detached, but he'd gotten right up close to kill Jorge Ochoa. Then he came to Decker Canyon to kill Danny. Desperate and decompensating and as dangerous as anyone he'd ever known. He knew where he lived. He could find him anytime he wanted to if he wasn't stopped. And unless someone compared the boots Jorge was wearing to the Backbone prints they'd wind up in a Goodwill or a landfill, and Jorge's body among the unclaimed and indigent ashes the county buried in mass graves each year in Boyle Heights east of downtown.

CHAPTER 30

He slipped between the Best Value's extra-wide sliding doors and immediately dodged a cart loaded with lengthy 2x4's aggressively pushed by an outgoing customer.

He took a moment to bask in the refreshing industrial-strength air conditioning, favoring his sore ankle, and checked the time on his phone. 3:15 PM. He didn't know how the day laborers stood outside all day. If one of them collapsed from heat exhaustion who would call 911? Who would pay?

He suddenly realized he was thinking like the MLP dickhead. Empathy was a communicable disease.

The lumber department was at the closer end of the main aisle. In the opposite direction, past lawn care supplies and a barbecue display, was the garden center. End caps of different sections stood inbetween—paint, plumbing, tools. A half-staffed row of cashiers and self check-out stands stood like sentries in front of the two exits. There was no sign for the restrooms but Cesar would ultimately have to head for an exit so Danny went that way, watching for a red poncho and a sad face.

He weaved through the asteroid field of customers and carts, moving targets all around each in their stubborn trajectory, and took up position by the plumbing section. From here he could almost see both exits at once; he had to walk past a couple of aisles to fully see one or the other but it was the best he could do. Excitement fluttered in his belly like moths in a mason jar—he had the man's boots. In some Old West kind of way that had to mean something.

He recalled what Mike Cruz said: *The device can be assembled with parts from any decent hardware store. All over the counter stuff.* Best Value was a giant candy store to a diabolical creativity bent on assembling an instrument of mayhem from individually harmless gaskets, tubes, valves, and hoses. Someone so angry that destruction had become his only form of expression.

Danny's eyes drifted into the garden center where a beeping forklift was moving around, and the big natural gas grills sitting stately as culinary

Rolls-Royces with smaller propane grills displayed around them like shiny economical imports. The increase in humidity from the garden center was slight but noticeable as he wandered over after another look around for Cesar. He didn't see a red poncho or pullover or anything remotely like it—given the heat most of the customers were in tank tops and shorts.

The natural gas grills stood as tall as his chest, burly stainless steel and chrome-plated aluminum, backlit control knobs like his laptop's keyboard. Their disconnected hoses were neatly coiled, alluding to a future connection to a fuel tank such as the empty ones conveniently located beside each. A flamethrower by any other name, if only for luaus.

The forklift driver was repositioning the vehicle to raise a palette of grass seed bags up onto one of the display racks. He looked over his shoulder in the mandated check to see that nobody was behind him and momentarily locked eyes with Danny. Black olive pits hung from a prominent ridge. The nostrils of his flat nose flared and he opened his mouth, then snapped it shut, jiggling his double chin.

Danny looked away, embarrassed at his own infamy. Instead of warmth from flickers of recognition he felt like a cheap celebrity just trying to blend in and conduct his business unobserved. He pretended to consult the signs over the aisles as if he was looking for something and went back the way he came, realizing he'd seen the forklift driver before. Email addresses and faces were two strengths his memory had, two kinds of recollection he could rely on. He knew he'd seen the guy before, probably here in Malibu. Sometimes working local stories made you a local, if only for a little while.

His ankle was smarting and he figured he had as much chance of finding a red poncho as he did a ship-killing iceberg. Six o'clock felt like an eternity from now. Maybe Cesar with the sad face had rejoined his amigos out on the sidewalk. He limped out the nearest exit into the parking lot, out of sync with the movement of cars and customers and wondered where Cruz was if he wasn't at his house. And what Derek Cavanaugh was telling Detective Salk, and how he could find out while steering a wide berth around Mark Pavelko.

He didn't see anyone with a red poncho on the sidewalk. He didn't see Luis either. He got in his car and started the engine to get the air going, backtracking through Red Flag media with abbreviated swipes in one section of the cracked display, wondering what the hell he should do now. He'd already accumulated so much material. He pricked his finger with a tiny glass shard and kept scrolling incrementally through history. He was near the beginning—driving up Corral Canyon with rogue investigator Mark Pavelko on Friday.

He wiped the sweat from his forehead and looked around again. Cesar wasn't wearing a poncho. He probably walked right by him in the Best Value. He was probably gone before he got there. He scrolled again and stopped at the image.

It was the first frame of a video. The hair was different. He'd shaved it down to his scalp since then like a landscape messily burned of its vegetation.

Danny tapped to play.

Mind if I ask you a few questions?

You a reporter?

Danny Kasho, CODA.com. What's your name?

Tillson.

He glanced up at the rearview mirror.

The forklift driver was coming out of the store, walking quickly in black running shoes, jeans, and the Best Value uniform blue shirt, oblivious to the cars moving around him. A dark SUV swerved to miss him and honked but got no reaction from the frowning man staring fixedly in front of him.

I'm a volunteer firefighter. They need all the help they can get up there.

Danny turned in his seat and stared at the man hurrying across the parking lot. Tillson's physical bulk belied the boyish voice in the video clip, which was higher-pitched than you'd expect from a big guy, as if the strain of containment was pulling his vocal cords taut.

You been up there yet?

'Course I have. What TV show do you work for?

It's online, CODA.com. What's your first name? For your permission to quote you.

Carl.

A store manager in a short-sleeve shirt and tie stood in the entrance beside an employee in a matching shirt to Tillson's and an apron, searching the parking lot with their hands on their hips.

What do you do when you're not volunteer firefighting, Carl?

Wait for the next season like everyone else.

Got any thoughts on how it started?

A white pickup with a lightbar and a red stripe down the side bumped past out of the parking lot. Carl Tillson was hunched over the wheel.

Looks deliberate to me. Know why?

Danny backed his Accord out and jammed it into gear. He tried to follow at a discreet distance but he was no pro at spontaneous mobile surveillance. The white pickup turned right on PCH, cutting dangerously into traffic. Danny had to wait at the corner by the gas station for some cars to pass before he spotted the pickup in the long left turn lane for Kanan. Unless he had business in one of the secluded neighborhoods tucked away up in the mountains, Carl Tillson was headed to the Valley. Danny was too now and he still couldn't say exactly why. Malibu was twenty miles long and skinny as a strung-out starlet. It wasn't inconceivable that someone who worked in the area volunteered as a firefighter in the area too.

He barely made it through the light and accelerated past gated mansion driveways before the canyon road's curves began in earnest. Kanan was two lanes in both directions for a while and drivers jockeyed for position before the single lanes started at the tunnels, slowing traffic to the speed of whatever car was at the head of the line. He glimpsed Tillson's pickup pointlessly tailgating the car in front of it through the curves.

The clip replayed as he drove but his phone was in its death throes, dropping frames in the video and pausing playback every couple seconds.

Active perimeter of thirty miles. Fifteen hundred firefighters. Zero percent containment. It's bad alright.

What TV show do you work for?

It's online, CODA.com.

They passed through the X-shaped intersection with Mulholland and the turn for the Seminole Overlook where Pavelko confided his suspicion of Mike Cruz. A few minutes later an elevated Jack In The Box sign announced the return to civilization. Danny watched to see if Tillson turned left on Agoura Road, a paved demarcation line between the city and the undeveloped land, which would take him to the Hampton Inn. But he didn't see the pickup and so he rolled through the light as it was turning red and an oncoming driver was flashing his headlights at him.

Coming up on the 101 freeway now—signs pointed right for Los Angeles, left for Ventura with a bright billboard exploding in digital droplets—*When you save water it saves you back!* Cars were busy maneuvering and he didn't know which way he should go.

Then he spotted the pickup over the bridge in the left turn lane and swerved into it with only one car between them. The light turned yellow and he was once again the third jerk through the intersection, receiving admonishing honks as he sped down the onramp. The freeway was wide open. Tillson was doing 70 and he changed lanes repeatedly and without signaling. Danny changed lanes only when necessary to keep him in sight, anxious about speeding in a stretch of freeway popular with CHP.

Three miles later the pickup veered across four lanes of traffic from the number one lane nearest the median to the white-walled offramp for Hampshire Road. Danny braked and got over quickly, narrowly avoiding a speeding black Range Rover. Tillson was turning right. Danny was too close and waited a moment longer before he made the turn. A concrete monument on a tree-lined median welcomed him to the city of Thousand Oaks. Hampshire dead-ended at a shopping center and most of the traffic was going left on Thousand Oaks Boulevard.

The light was already green and Tillson was several cars ahead. Danny got antsy, crept up on the car ahead of him.

"Move," he urged the driver, and the driver ahead of that one, *"move."*

The light abruptly changed, severing the two lanes of vehicles in mid-stream.

Danny cursed extravagantly. He was two cars out of the intersection and trapped in the median-side turn lane.

Thanks for your time Carl. Good luck, he heard himself say on the video, which ended again, barely cycling back to the first jittery frame showing Tillson's black eyes staring out at him from the shade inside his pickup.

CHAPTER 31

Blood, bone and brains popped out of the top of mom's head and spattered across the low ceiling clouded by years of cigarette smoke and the yellowing wallpaper of bare fall branches climbing like varicose veins across the walls from out behind the cabinetry and appliances and the large coppery sun burst wall clock which read one minute past three.

There were lighter chunks in her soup that looked like bits of cheese but overall mom's blood looked almost black, darker than he imagined it would be even in the dim nighttime lighting inside her hot box of a house. As if the fluid had thickened like tar from the hundreds of thousands of Kools responsible for the oppressive, sickly-sweet mentholated reek choking the mobile shotgun shack on its deflated cobwebbed wheels.

Her upholstered chenille recliner finally came to rest with a muted squeak. The chair sported cigarette burns and food stains and real wood trim on the arms, and was covered in a shawl imprinted after many years with the sweat-darkened horseshoe shape of her copious backside and thighs. Its footrest didn't go all the way up or down anymore, the hinges were broken and jammed halfway. It was aimed at the TV barely three feet away which she kept on, always. It was the captain's chair, where she lorded over her empire of clocks, buying and selling them online, cruelly, exactingly dissecting other sellers' praise or criticism in order to leverage the best position for herself in each transaction. Like she'd always done with everything. Taking her pound of flesh from everyone she could. She stored all her victories here, packed tightly into this shitty little cave she lived in.

His chest was heaving and his right arm burned from shoulder to wrist from swinging the 3½ pound blue Estwing steel hammer a hundred or so times. He was out of breath and sweating.

Mom's mouth was open wide, frozen in the elongated yawn shape she'd made as she shrieked *You!* before he pinned a hand over the gaping orifice. He knocked some of her china angels off a shelf when he reached back with the hammer, and swung it from behind his head right down through the top of hers, visualizing the steel sparking on her old-fashioned silver fillings that filled her horrid mouth. She'd have pried them out and sold them by now if they'd been worth anything. He'd hoped she wouldn't have a chance to say anything. He didn't want to hear what she had to say about what he was doing. He thought at this hour she'd be asleep, that she'd go down silently for once. Leave it to mom to spoil that for him too.

You.

Her head had always been a mess and he studied the chunks of it on the chair and the wall as he pushed one of her fringed sofa pillows into her blood-covered face. She wasn't struggling, not with her head all caved in like that, but she was making a weird whining noise like a failing motor. He stayed like that with all his weight on top of the pillow for long minutes until his arms were sore and he was certain she was finally gone. The trailer park was a familiar place. It got awfully quiet here at night. Her idiot neighbor was old but he wasn't deaf.

Mom was slumped over in the armchair with her head on her chest as if she had drank herself to sleep with her Kools and ceramic ashtray and vodka. He could practically hear her snoring and grumbling to herself; even in her dreams she'd hassled him. Her favorite portrait of Jesus—only Jesus was allowed to share wall space with her clocks—looked on sympathetically, Him too spattered with her dark stuff.

Him.

He'd fantasized about killing her for years. More than once she'd caught him in his bedroom with his pants around his ankles having an energetic go at one of those fantasies—but the reality wasn't living up to expectation. He hadn't planned on being scared when the time finally came. He'd *never* been scared when he started a fire and he'd had some close calls. Real close calls. He'd been nearly spotted before. Two or three times he'd been nearly *stopped.* That was part of the thrill, the part he couldn't control, the eerie calm amidst swirling needles of anticipation and excitement. Even he found it eerie, the way no other thoughts intruded. When he was truly consumed by That Him, when he was untouchable, unstoppable, unquestionable. And that's what he'd expected to feel tonight with this—this act of mercy. Sparing mom so she wouldn't have to yell about him at the TV. It was This Him's idea.

There was still a buzzing sound in his ears, a shrill metallic screaming of judges and bosses and presidents and mothers and wives and he almost started bashing the hammer into his own head, but after a minute the noise subsided enough for him to hear the fluids and junk dripping out of mom's head and down the walls onto the floor, and the ticking of her many decorative clocks. Antique clocks. Cuckoo clocks. Rolling ball clocks. Torsion pendulum clocks. Striking clocks. Cartel clocks. Cat clocks. Dog clocks. Not one of them in sync with another. It drove him mad when he was here, the random mish-mash of alarms and chimes over the constant oscillating fuzz of hundreds of little machines—movements, mom insisted on calling them—ticking and buzzing, all slowly unscrewing on the inside, like him.

A piece of her skull had plopped onto her TV tray which she had moved to the side and slightly behind the recliner, clearing the way to the hallway and the bathroom. Knife and fork and the same dinner plate she always used, remnants of the microwaved Cornish game hen she'd partially eaten tonight still stuck to them all. She'd consumed most of a tumbler of club soda, now flat, with bits of bird and rice floating in it. The tray rattled uncertainly when he dropped the hammer onto it.

He bent to stare at the piece of skull. Limp strands of mom's straight slate hair sprouted from the top, run through with white, which she cut herself at chin-length with her orange-handled kitchen shears. He stepped heavily over a section of carpet which was saturated with her oily black blood and picked up the fragment with his thumb and forefinger. It was about the size of a quarter and came off the countertop with an audible sucking sound. A single fat dollop of blood was centered in its slightly concave underside like an iris within a pale blind pupil. It was neither hot from the blood in the brain it had encased nor cold as the petrified bones mom's corpulent leathery skin wrapped around. He couldn't really sense it at all. Its temperature so perfectly matched his own it was as if it wasn't even there, like it was an extension of his hands, a nerveless, hairy deformity.

Like mom hadn't even been here.

Had she been? Had she *really* been here this whole time?

Or was she an inanimate figure brought to life by his fears, written on the scraps of paper she used for her clock receipts and stuffed into her mouth? That mouth which never closed, ever. Not in nightly sleep. Not even in eternal sleep. As if the organ always needed to be gulping like a fish so the sea of silence wouldn't drown it.

He brought the bone fragment up to his lips, held it an inch away from his mouth with his black eyes crossed to see it, then dropped his jaw and extended his tongue, wet and quivering, bringing the bone to it like a surrogate nipple to suckle. Mom's hair tickled his nose as he pressed his tongue onto it. It was slightly sticky. He slid the wet muscle slowly up as he brought the fragment gently downward, smearing the bloody iris onto his taste receptors. Then he put it in his mouth like a hairy communion wafer, his tongue working around it, pressing it against the roof of his mouth in a saliva bath.

Nothing.

No taste of mom. No hint of her at all. As if it was stage blood and horse hair glued onto a piece of a broken tea cup.

He bent over and expelled the bloody hunk of cranium and hair and fell to his hands and knees and vomited onto the tough Berber carpet. It might have been white when it was first laid but it was a sooty gray now and dirty with things, ash, scraps of old food, foil from cigarette packs, mom's phlegm when she missed her dinner plate or an empty glass. And now puke. Fitting. Mom would really hate that. To her this place was spic and span and *he* was a savage. Maybe in the end she'd been right about that too.

There was the acidic and all too familiar aftertaste of disappointment. Disappointment was real. His whole life had been a disappointment. His family, his wives, the handful of friends he'd ever had—mostly people he drank with at bars and didn't even know the names of. It was always the same, rejection and dismissal. But they couldn't dismiss him any longer.

That Him had fled the scene and wasn't coming back. There'd soon be nothing to come back to. It was just him now. Singular and divine.

Him.

He emptied the contents of the dusty bottles in the liquor cabinet and a bottle of vodka he found in the freezer onto mom and jammed three cigarettes between her fingers. When they burned down seven to eight minutes after he lit them with her Bic her alcohol-saturated chair and floral-print nightgown would ignite and her crappy old body she used to complain about all the time could finally be washed down a drain. It might almost look like a tragic accident, which is sort of what it was. *He* was her accident—she'd said as much many, many times over the years. Mom's Big Regret. The thing that kept her from having *any* adventure in her life, *any* excitement, *anything* to look forward to, as if her four previous kids had all been born completely independent of her after the gnarly umbilical cord was hacked apart. Her oldest son, the apple of her eye, the brother he didn't even know, was already in jail by the time he came into mom's bleak picture.

You.

Yes mom. Me.

I.

"Bye mom," he whispered, as he always did when he was leaving, even if she wasn't awake, like now. Old habits.

He locked the door behind him and checked to make sure there were no snoops around, watching from behind threadbare curtains hanging in darkened trailer windows. He was practically invisible in his black clothes but you never knew. He took a last look around as he got into the minivan which was filled with the tangy perfume of gasoline even with the windows down. Mom's trailer was two-tone washed-out yellow and white baked almost the color of sand. Dirt and empty flower pots in front, in a patch not cemented over for walkways or driveways. A stubby wing leaned on each side of it—the wing on the left shaded the front door, the wing on the right acted as a carport. She didn't own a car so that space sat empty except for the trash bins and a coiled-up garden hose shrouded in thick spider webs. She paid a mildly retarded man who lived in the trailer park a pittance to walk her pre-packaged clocks to the nearest shipping center, a mile and a half trek the man-boy made two or three times a week. He came by daily to check if she needed him. His name was Timmy or Tommy. But he could walk and he could pay and the shipping center never cheated him and mom stayed afloat in the secondhand clock business. Everything running just tickety-boom for the two of them.

He wondered what the retard would do when he found out what happened to his best customer, and why Kasho didn't shoot him when he had the chance at Decker Canyon and save stop this when he had the chance. Now things were happening. The mission had gotten underway without him even realizing it. There was no going back. Mom's clocks were still ticking, faster and faster and faster even after the flames ate away their shells, the tiny gears grinding bone and brain and blood.

He drove a couple blocks south down Q Street and pulled over. Turned in his seat to look through the rear windows and waited, counting down the minutes, anticipating brightness in the distance and all that he had to do next. Mission protocols hit him like sniper fire. When he could just make out a burgeoning glow from the trailer park he put the minivan in gear and drove away. The 204 to the 99 to the 119 to the mighty 5 south and the funereal radiance of Los Angeles waiting over the horizon. He'd be back before dawn and at work by nine, give or take. Funny to be concerned with being on time to work today of all days. Old habits, like old mothers, died hard.

You.

CHAPTER 32

Danny drove a mile and a half to the Moorpark Freeway, then turned around and came back up Thousand Oaks Boulevard's unbroken chain of retail, restaurants, and automotive stores. His head swiveled through tight degrees, searching, willing the white pickup with the red stripe to appear amidst the four lanes of traffic. It didn't. Of course it didn't.

In frustration he pulled over in front of a storefront foot spa which shared a wall with a karate studio. The bare hump of the Hillcrest Open Space Preserve rose behind a strip mall across the street like a humpback whale out of range of the harpoons.

He's a volunteer firefighter. He works at Best Value Hardware in Malibu. His name is Carl Tillson and he gives me the heebie-jeebies.

He could just imagine what Travis Salk would say to that.

He banged his fist on the hand brake. "This is bullshit." His father hadn't even *tried* to run—he'd stayed upstairs in their bedroom until the jarring knocks thundered at the front door and policemen prowled the back yard and peered in the windows with their guns drawn. Danny had led them straight there that day. Where was Carl Tillson leading him today?

With a squeak of undersized brakes a red Nissan Versa electric with a green alien head antenna ball pulled in behind him.

"Oh no," he groaned, "no, no, no, Jesus no."

His eyes flickered to the time and temp readings in his center dash. 4:10 PM. 104°. Ursula wasn't moving. She'd removed her hands from the steering wheel and was just sitting there. With the glare off her windshield he couldn't distinguish her head from the driver's seat headrest.

Three months ago he and Ursula fucking Ruda had arrived at the bar in the foyer of the downtown Biltmore's historical Crystal Ballroom at the same time during a break in the LA Press Club awards. They were both well on their way to sodden and even later after mining in detail the conversation they had while waiting for their drinks—vodka tonic for her, gin and tonic for him—he couldn't come up with a specific line or cue that had triggered them to walk together toward the bathrooms by the stairs. At the left/right split for the genders she'd taken his hand and he entered the sanctum of the women's bathroom. The bathroom wasn't empty. An elderly woman in a strapless salmon pink tulle and lace ball gown with a white bouffant was reapplying lipstick in the mirror over the sinks and gave Danny a wink as he and Ursula teetered into the handicap stall, slapping the door shut behind them and sliding the lock.

It was a crash course in Ursula's sexuality. It was the taste of her mouth, her lipstick, the vodka hot on her breath. It was the discreet sibilance of the zipper in the back of her fitted black sleeveless chiffon H&M dress, the elastic snap of her underwear waistband. It was the things she whispered, directing him, spurring him on. It was all of three minutes.

He'd exited the women's bathroom without incident and without shame, and with a newfound swagger that could only be described as Sergio Leoneish. Ursula lingered to recompose herself with the magic contents of her slender clutch. They each returned to their respective tables separately, flushed and thirsty and trying not to look at each other. He was certain his Gomer Pyle grin and her lingering perfume on his hands would give him away. He noticed her every move, the way she moved her hands, crossed and uncrossed her legs, how she tilted her head when she smiled so her hair brushed the top of her bare shoulders where his fingers had gripped her, how her smile widened ever so slightly when she saw him looking at her.

Then their category came up.

There were five finalists for the best online investigative award. Danny had read Ursula's piece on South LA's so-called 911 Killer and thought it was excellent, if a little dry, which is how he'd thought of Ursula Ruda until that night. Competent but uncharismatic. He hadn't even noticed she wore a hearing aid until he was nibbling on her neck. Pleased to have just been nominated, he wasn't expecting anything except to get hammered on William Craig's dime with his friends at the CODA table. He didn't expect to win. He certainly didn't expect to get laid in the process. Nothing that serendipitously inappropriate had ever happened to him. Not at the height of the roaring twenties' blur of hook-ups and detachments, not thus far during the twilight of the dirty thirties' slog of "relationships". Then all of a sudden, out of the blue—and in a public place during a work function—Ursula Ruda's hot doppelganger bestows herself upon him like a pornographic lady of the lake. As if she was a secret she'd only ever told him.

Lucy Baskin elbowed him in the side after he didn't react to his name being called. He blinked and saw his stock avatar exploded to 4'x6' onscreen above his CODA credentials. Then the screen split to a live shot of him at the table looking infinitely less professional, all blushing cheeks and goofy Billy Bob teeth, nervously blinking at the shiny faces and things aimed at him, the light stands erected on alternating balconies on the second floor beaming accusing supernovas at him. He knew the old lady in the pink dress was somewhere in the gilt ballroom, nudging the person beside her and saying *That's him. That's the one.*

He threaded his way around the tables and chairs in a daze, accepting congratulations as he went, handshakes, high-fives and fist bumps—fireworks and octopus—all the way up to the stage. He crossed the suddenly expansive dance floor without slipping or weaving excessively. Careful on the steps, he mounted the stage in front of the three looming decorative archways lit dramatically from below and received the award to cheers led by his standing CODA colleagues. He read the speech he'd composed and printed on a folded piece of paper, which had gotten crumpled when he was stepping on his pants in the bathroom with Ursula. The paper quivered in his hand like an exposed nerve ending and seemed luminescent under the lights, highlighting each crevasse and ridge like her naked skin which kept flashing before his eyes as he thanked everyone in the whole wide world.

He returned to the CODA table clutching his plaque like an accidental war trophy, as if a feared enemy had tripped and fallen on his bayonet. Fresh corks popped, champagne foamed, and during the next break in the ceremony Ursula appeared at his elbow, her face as bright as her little red Versa was today. He choked on an ice cube from someone's glass who wasn't drinking their water—he was so goddamn thirsty. It was a moment absolutely tumescent with awkwardness, her standing there rigidly, her lips which had been so industrious earlier now drawn tight as a crossbow, Danny coughing and apologizing for coughing and then coughing some more, struck dumb by some kind of nervous consumption.

Ursula's terse congratulations was three words aimed like misplaced acupuncture needles in his face:

"Good one, shithead."

Four if you counted *shit* and *head* separately.

Then she turned and walked away, straight as a torpedo through the milling crowd that made way for her like startled fish, the sound of her heels on the dance floor like live rounds being chambered one by one in a long gun.

Danny came away from that long braggadocio-filled night with a deeper respect for his friends and coworkers who could tell something apart from professional courtesy was so obviously up between him and Ursula, but had the decency to let the topic lie like an animal struck by a car on a highway. It wasn't dead, but it was seriously fucked up and they all knew it. No need to draw undue attention to it. Lucy had kept track of his plaque for him because he'd been far too drunk to.

Since that night he'd seen Ursula working around town but had made no attempt to approach her. They hadn't said anything at all to each other until Friday at the Backbone Fire Incident Command Post. He knew and would always know that lurking beneath her utilitarian clothes, her hat and safari vest and clip-on sunglasses, was a woman who moved and touched and desired with the force of a cheetah. But she had withdrawn behind her battlements and raised her drawbridge and left Danny the advantageous dragon panting smoke futilely across her perilous moat. Three minutes, then three months. Was it worth it? At the time he'd confidently, even smugly thought *Fuck yes it was,* interpreting the impromptu liaison as an additional prize accompanying the plaque. An unexpected, unwritten, unspoken bonus. Something about spoils going to the victor. Rendering unto Caesar and all that. Which for once, that night, was him.

But here now her sitting in her car like that behind him, unmoving, waiting for him to break first because with no phone and intolerable music on the radio he *was* going to break first, was the knowing wink of the old lady in the gleaming Biltmore bathroom.

That's him. That's the one.

"This is bullshit," he muttered as he got out.

A sizeable dent depressed the Versa's front bumper like a red philtrum and he instantly thought of five good lines to say to her about women drivers.

Ursula Ruda rolled down her passenger window and took his picture with her fancy camera. "Wow, it's like a star sighting."

He bent to lean in her window. "Except this star will actually talk to you. Don't get psyched out by the fender bender, it happens to all girls, especially teenaged girls with crushes on stars like me. Practice makes better so buckle up and quit stalking me."

"Who are you following?" Ursula's auburn hair traced her cheek as smooth as an architectural design. She regarded him coolly from behind her rectangular clip-ons, the Sesame Street Band-Aids on his hands and the sweat on his face disproportionate to the temperature outside, unless he'd been driving with the air off for some fool reason.

"Who are *you* following?" he asked.

"I'm following you. And you're lost."

"I am not lost. You can't *get* lost in this day and age. Why are you following me?"

Ursula considered him for a moment. "No, you're not lost. But you lost whoever you're following. Are they connected to Jorge Ochoa?"

"Well done, you know his name."

"I knew his name before you did. You didn't even pick up the story, someone else did. I think her name is Ellen."

"So what?"

"So after your meet 'n greet with the cops at the house you burned down you went straight to Malibu and you've been all over that story ever since. Don't you have your hands full?"

"You may not recall but I have really big hands."

"Why you and not Ellen?"

"She's working in Palos Verdes. Dime Time doesn't have anyone there because *you're* here. Why are you following me?"

"I heard what happened in PV. Way more interesting than the lagoon suicide. You glommed onto that in the middle of your Red Flag press junket and I want to know why. And what they're going to charge you with."

"They're going to name a building after me and the suicide struck my curiosity. I'm a reporter, curiosity happens."

Ursula flipped up her clip-ons with a black middle fingernail. "You'd only be curious about it if it involves Mike Cruz."

Danny glanced at her charity bracelet with rising annoyance, irritated by the heat and the fact she made him feel like he had something to prove beyond a successful three minutes in a handicapped stall. He remembered her lipstick had been black too, and wound up smeared across her ivory cheek. Their carnal knowledge of each other was like dirt under their nails from a shallow grave they'd both dug but refused to acknowledge.

"Heard anything about what happened today?" he asked.

"I heard everyone showed up for a party but no one was home."

"Is that why you're not there?"

"Why aren't you? You and Mr. Wife Beater Mark Pavelko totally made this happen. Primo source by the way. Has he turned himself in yet?"

"Turned himself into what? A pumpkin at midnight?" Danny wiped sweat out of his eyes.

"Don't you read your own posts?"

"Sounds to me like the husband has more explaining to do than the *ex*-husband."

"Yet it's the ex-wife who's caught in the middle of it all as usual."

"Maybe she's the *cause* of it all, ever think of that? Or is this the time when you say leave it to a man to say that?"

"I say leave it to an uninformed shithead to say that. No woman has ever been the cause of man's inbred stupidity."

Danny wondered how that might apply to Nick Mendoza and Charlize Patron's defense. "The only uninformed party in the transaction last week was the *husband's* wife."

"Know her name?"

"I haven't looked for it yet. I haven't had time."

"You don't know where to."

"I haven't had time, Ursula."

She leaned her head on her hand and gazed at him. "Why are you so defensive of Mark Pavelko? What is it between you two? What did you agree to do in exchange for getting access like that? Are you Pavelko's snitch or his bitch? Or are they the same thing?"

"Like any good reporter I channel my inner Switzerland before going all factually fascist."

Ursula made a face. "Did you just make that up?"

"I'm a quote savant like Amy Childress, only not so full of shit."

"You're an opportunistic shit*head*, that's all."

"Is that one word or two?"

"Just like Mark Pavelko, you're somebody who doesn't step into trouble, you jump with both feet, hoping there'll be someone there to catch you before you get dirty. You should give him more credit on your blog, without him you wouldn't have a story, everybody knows that."

"By everybody you mean you and the other Dime Time writers slash janitorial staff? What do they call you guys, custodian contributors or contributing custodians? How long have you been following me?"

"Since Decker Canyon. It's one lane and you were ahead of me. Without running you off the road I had no choice."

"Looks like you already tried to run someone off the road. Or was it one of those pesky inanimate objects like a tree or a building?"

"Don't laugh, it saved your life."

"Decker Canyon doesn't lead here."

"All roads lead to *you* Danny, like you always wanted. Last night you put yourself front and center. So here you are, the master at work, lost on the side of the road."

"I'm not lost!"

"Cool your jets, turbo. It's not like whoever it is you lost is going to come back to give you another crack at it."

The sun burned the back of his neck. There were no trees other than the ones planted by the city; the store awnings were deep here for a reason. He gestured to Ursula's passenger seat. "You mind?"

"I do."

"You're the one following me."

"I'm just driving around. Or is this the time when I say something about this being a free country?"

"Then what are you here for? If you're not going to talk I'm leaving, and now that I know you're following me I'll drop you in sixty seconds."

"Think so, Mario?"

"You won't know what I'm doing until you read about it like everyone else."

"When you get arrested? Ooh—killed! I'd cover that like a blanket."

Danny tapped the frying pan roof of her car.

She made a show of mulling it over, then moved her bag and hat into the back seat and let him in. The corner of her door scraped the hot sidewalk as he pulled it closed.

"Good one, shithead."

Deliciously cool air blew from the paddle-shaped dashboard vents. The LAPD Citywide Dispatch and Hot Shots/Code 3 scanner feed was playing through the stereo instead of music—Danny often did the same thing. As if they both loved the same indie band. A GPS navigator was suction-cupped to the windshield and a six-pack of Arrowhead water bottles sat on the passenger floor under his feet; one was secured in a cup holder in front of the gear shift. The gray cloth interior of the car was spotless and it still had that new-car smell even though he didn't think it was—Ursula took care of her stuff. He didn't see her digital recorder which probably meant it was tucked into one of her myriad safari vest pockets, actively listening. She apparently didn't take off her vest even when she drove.

He said, "Is your insurance going to cover the ding on your bumper or are you going to try and fake it with a neck brace?"

"I never fake anything. Are you an over-achiever all of a sudden or is there a connection between Jorge Ochoa and the Angeles Arsonist?"

"I'm an over-achiever, all day long."

"No you're not, you're a barely-achiever. I read Ellen's piece and she didn't say anything about him being a day laborer. *I* did. You got that from *me.*"

"So thanks for saving me five seconds' worth of thinking."

"You'd have never worked that out on your own."

"That a Hispanic guy dressed like a day laborer *was* a day laborer? Okay—six seconds. Is that why you're following me? Isn't that like cheating? Who'd you follow to find Derek Cavanaugh?"

"Not Mark Pavelko."

"Obviously, none of your sources are that good."

"They were good enough to find Cavanaugh. Who *isn't* about to be declared a fugitive like Mark Pavelko is."

Danny stared at her, thinking back to the Backbone ICP, who was there, where the overlap was with the car accident on PCH. "The EMTs. Young crash victim being so close to the young students at the cave—"

"And you have to wonder if he crashed his car leaving the scene." Ursula snapped her fingers. "The detectives you've been palling around with."

"The detectives."

"City or county?"

"These were county. Big fans of yours. They wanted to know who it was that was trying to sneak into Derek Cavanaugh's ICU."

"And I bet you told them."

"Absolutely. I'm a concerned, upstanding citizen. I gave them your phone number and known aliases too. What were you thinking? That's crass even for Dime Time which speaking of over-achieving looks like your lame-ass solo album."

"Some of us don't have a script writer like Mark Pavelko telling us what to write. Remember when the free press was actually free?"

"I remember when it used to rain too. And as if Amy Childress doesn't approve of your messages. You're her PR department, you don't write about her, you write for her. Meanwhile I've been busting my ass out in the sun and the dirt and the smoke for fourteen months. *And* I won a fucking award for it."

"Is that what the award was for? No wonder it fit in your hand."

"You just want to find the next quick story so you glommed onto mine after I did all the work because Auntie Amy isn't going to deliver in November."

"I owe it to myself and my readers to document your decline and fall into self-absorbed self-destruction."

"I'm not self-absorbed—you're obsessed with me. This is transference. You need a shrink. You need to be the focus of a clinical trial or two."

"You need a babysitter."

"*This* is how you apply for the job?"

"Getting murdered by your story is stupid. If *he* knows you're following him, Danny, he *will* try to kill you again. You're just taunting fate. That's stupid too."

But he didn't believe in fate. He believed in free will and the unlimited capacity for people to make short-sighted decisions. Him, his father, anybody. "So why are you here Ursula? If PV is more interesting *and* safer."

"I'm seeing my Good Samaritan rendering aid to a stranded shithead act through."

"I'll add stranded shithead to my recap of the day." His phone chirped with a new email. "I have a better idea—go play house with Amy Childress and stop following me around."

"There's no separating *you* from *it* anymore. I read your post about last night. You didn't just report the story, you made it happen. You stopped covering it and went and caused it. And Peter Buckstein's house burned down and the Angeles Arsonist is free to kill even more people because of *you.* He could have been arrested and the whole thing could be over. Reporting isn't enabling—you crossed the line."

"There is no line! Not when the story says be here at this time or else."

"Or else *what*, Danny? What do you think was going to happen? You thought it through and you chose not to call your county detective pals. Now you're just an angle to this story. You're public domain. I hope allowing a mass murderer to come and go was worth it to you because you're going to be explaining yourself *forever.* And I hope they charge you with something."

"You want to race me to jail?" He jabbed another tiny glass shard from his display into his thumb and savored the pain. The email was from Suge. *UCANBRN2 new post at 1614. "Tell Mendes to kiss my ass." Diff IP, address below.*

He sucked air between his teeth. Tillson wasn't running. He was saying Here I am. Come and get me. But who was Mendes? Wasn't it supposed to be *Tell* Kasho *to kiss my ass?* He was tempted to ask Suge if he was sure but he knew he was sure. This was the sort of thing he would be sure about. Suge was always sure.

Hoping the address listed in the address was genuine, Danny tried to map it but his display wouldn't respond to any of his increasingly desperate taps or swipes. Despite all the expense and technology behind its touted aluminosilicate durability, his phone was bricked. The cell phone was, like the key to the car, one of the last few symbols of independence, and he'd just lost his. Now he needed help. He could no longer progress on his own. Last night had been a Pyrrhic victory and the cost was coming due already.

Tell Mendes. The ever-expanding umbrella of threat made Danny feel almost inconsequential. He fished the business card out of his pocket. Fortunately he hadn't yet entered it into his phone and tossed it like he always did with people who still used paper business cards. He cleared his throat. "I need to use your phone."

"No." Ursula didn't look up from using it.

"Mine's broken."

"Get better gear. I'm kicking you out anyway, I have things to do."

"You have other people to stalk today besides me?"

"My car, my rules."

Danny gritted his teeth, composing in his head his request to Suge to send him a map. Saw himself getting out and finding someone to ask for directions, if anyone even still did that anymore.

Dispensed with all the fantasies.

He was stuck.

He said, "I was following a person of interest in the Angeles Arsonist case."

"And?"

"And that's who I was following."

"Who is he?"

"A person of interest. An interesting person."

"How'd you get his address?"

"A tip."

"How convenient. What makes him so interesting?"

"Do the heebie-jeebies count?"

Ursula shrugged and went back to her phone.

Danny drummed his fingers on the plastic armrest. His leg bounced up and down, bumping into the low-slung glovebox. "I interviewed him on Friday before I got up to the Backbone ICP. He just saw me today and ran."

"Ran?"

"He left work."

"Where?"

"A hardware store in Malibu."

"You mean the Best Value? That's where you saw him? What's the connection?"

"Heebie-jeebies."

"Get out of my car."

"I'm serious!"

"So is my pepper spray. Get out of my car."

"It's the boots."

"What boots?"

"The boots your girlfriend Amy gave up at the Pepperdine vigil. Jorge Ochoa was wearing them when he was killed. I just got an address and want your fans at the county sheriff's to know about it. Come on."

"You think the boots belong to the person you were following? And lost?"

"A definite maybe. I don't know, that's as far as I am with it. Come on Ursula, I'm calling the cops. You can't say no to that."

She waited a beat, then gave him her phone. Hers was the same as his, just in a beefier case. He texted who he was and that he was about to call from a different number, and counted to twenty while Ursula took the phone back, switched it to speaker and clicked it into its dashboard mount. She extracted a palm-sized notepad and a stubby pen from vest pockets and waited.

"Mr. Kasho," Travis Salk's voice filled the cabin as if the detective was sitting in the back seat, "you better not be trying to postpone your statement." He spoke over noises in the background—PA announcements, various beeps and tones. As if he'd stepped out of a hospital room into a busy corridor of UCLA Medical Center.

Danny said, "I know where he lives."

"Who?"

Something banged on the roof and both Danny and Ursula looked out the driver's side window.

"Who?" said Salk again.

Danny whipped his head around and faced someone looking in through the passenger window at him with a dark cap pulled low over polarized sunglasses that distorted his surprise like miniature funhouse mirrors.

CHAPTER 33

Something banged against the passenger door three times. Maybe the butt end of a flashlight. Maybe the business end of a bad idea.

Mike Cruz made a downward motion with his other hand for Danny to lower the window. His flinty moustache hung like solemn drapery over a tight baseboard mouth while his big class ring glittered in the sunlight like a mace.

"What's he got in his hand?" Ursula asked.

"Who?" Salk's irritation was rising with the volume of his voice.

"Mr. Cash Oh," Cruz said through the safety glass, "a word if you please."

"Captain Mike Cruz," Danny said for the benefit of Salk. "What are you doing here?"

"Open the window." Three more metallic taps emphasized each of Cruz's words, something factory-molded and solid against the cheap aluminum siding or whatever it was Ursula's car was made of. Cruz was wearing a forest green polo shirt and kept checking the sidewalk like Devon Johnson had.

"What is he holding?" Ursula asked again, quieter, fear exaggerating the natural upward pitch at the end of her question.

Salk was silent.

Danny licked his lips, fantasizing about drinking all five water bottles at his feet one right after the other, and pressed the black plastic button on the shallow armrest. The window sank into the door. Hot wind howled like a chorus of tempers around Cruz's torso which blocked most of the small rounded space.

"Mike," Danny said nice and loudly, "I thought you were at your house."

Cruz squatted and crisscrossed his thick forearms on the passenger window frame, just inches from Danny. He cocked his head to look inside at Ursula who sat stiff as a mannequin in her cloth seat. She gave a hesitant little wave. He said, "You were saying something about knowing where someone lives? Who?"

"What are you doing here Mike?" Danny asked.

"Who are you following?"

"An Angeles Arsonist suspect."

Cruz looked thunderstruck. "Another one? Who is it this time?"

"His name is Carl Tillson," Danny said clearly for Salk's benefit.

Ursula's pen twitched on her notepad a second after Cruz's cheek jumped. It was as if Danny had buzzed an electric edge with the tweezers playing *Operation* and shocked them both at the same time.

Cruz asked slowly, "Who is he?"

"He's a volunteer firefighter. I interviewed him in Malibu Bowl on Friday on my way to the Backbone ICP to meet Mark and you and I just saw him at Best Value Hardware in Malibu."

"So what?"

"So as soon as he saw me he walked off the job. I followed him here—to Thousand Oaks," again for Salk, "but lost him."

"Great story," Ursula muttered.

"What happened today?" Danny asked Cruz. "What was the siege about? What started it?"

"I wouldn't know. I wasn't there."

"You're peddling for widows and orphans on one hand and wasting taxpayers' dollars with unwarranted call-outs to your house on the other? How severely is that going to hamper your fundraising efforts when the story gets out?"

Cruz said nothing.

"Mark said you called them."

"Them who?"

"The task force within the task force."

"The what?"

"What did you say to him?"

"We're old friends, he and I. I told him I was coming to see him."

"What were you going to do?"

"Discuss things like civilized people."

"As civilized as a hundred cops in siege mode at your house? I'm sure your neighbors are stoked with your definition of civility. What did you say to him?"

"What did Pavelko say to *you?"* Ursula asked Cruz.

"Almost as much slander as the libel you posted," Cruz said to Danny.

"I didn't say or write anything about you." He jerked a thumb at Ursula. "She may have."

"Don't trust him," she said. "You can talk to me."

"Did you two finally have it out?" Danny asked Cruz.

"What did Mark Pavelko say?" Ursula asked.

"Jesus!" Danny snapped at her. He said to Cruz, "So you're what—following me to have it out with me too?"

"Do it," Ursula said.

"Am I the only one working today? If I'd have known I was leading a parade I would have hired a marching band."

"I'm seeing that no one else suffers a similar fate," Cruz said. "Who is Carl Tillson?"

"Why are you following me?"

"Answer my question."

"You answer mine. Start with why you're following me. Follow that up with why a hundred cops are housesitting for you while you're following *me* around sunny Thousand Oaks." He almost added *Follow* that *up with who Marvin Akon is. Or Lemarr Armstrong. Or any of the other men in that secret black binder in your garage.*

Cruz seemed to sense Danny was on the verge of saying something and there was another chassis-level bang of metal on the side of the car. The air inside the Versa went very still, the air conditioning surrendering to the invading hot wind. That was the difference with Devon Johnson, Danny thought—DJ knocked with the knuckles of an empty hand as his other one was busy holding up his piss-stained pants. Mike Cruz used their own fear as a leash by leaving the nature of the threat to their imagination. To

Danny everyone was someone else right now except the woman sitting beside him.

"Why are you following Carl Tillson?" Cruz demanded.

"He walked off his job—"

"That's not the real reason."

"Tell him about the boots," Ursula said.

Danny glared at her. Back in the day if he'd been a Christian and Cruz a lion Ursula would have been prodding him toward the teeth and claws with a pointy stick.

Cruz's eyebrows hovered over his sunglasses. "Boots?"

"He thinks he knows how the arsonist got rid of his boots," Ursula said.

Danny balled his fists and seriously considered socking her in the jaw. One clean left jab to knock her unconscious like in the movies, or at least daze her enough to shut the fuck up.

"Pray tell," Cruz said with the false encouragement of a game show host guiding a contestant to predetermined failure.

"I can prove the arsonist killed a man named Jorge Ochoa after putting his boots on him—the ones that made the prints *you* found at the cave," Danny said.

Ursula's face developed a deeply skeptical crease down it. "Prove?"

"The person I met last night who said he knew who the Angeles Arsonist *is* the Angeles Arsonist. He just posted to Red Flag again a few minutes ago and I got the physical address of the computer he used. I know where he is." Danny paused. The only one here who had UCANBRN2 was him. On his phone, in his right hand, and seared into his brain already as if by a glowing hot alphanumeric brand. No noise came from Ursula's phone; Salk had seemingly muted his and was hopefully listening to everything.

"You know the address of this Carl Tillson?" Cruz asked.

Danny shook his head, feeling like he was taunting the lion with himself as a chew toy.

"Did you see Carl Tillson go into a residence at that address?"

"I lost him in traffic."

"Weak," said Ursula.

"Then what does Carl Tillson have to do with that address?" Cruz asked.

Danny swallowed and it was like the water had been turned off on a Slip 'n Slide. "Maybe it's just coincidence."

"Great story," Ursula said.

"I didn't invite either one of you here to find out."

Cruz said, "Give me the address and I'll pass it along the proper channels this time. Make sure no one else gets hurt or suffers any needless damage."

Danny glanced at Ursula's phone in its dash-mounted cradle. He had nowhere left to go. He recited the address Suge had given him minus one digit in the street number and hoped Ursula wouldn't fuck that up too since the contradiction was staring her in her face from her phone's display.

Cruz stood up straight. Backlit by the glare of the sunshine he was an inscrutable mountaintop ringed by an eclipse. "There, that wasn't so hard now was it? Travis did you get all that?"

After a pause the disembodied voice of Travis Salk came out of Ursula's car speakers. "I did Mike."

"This young man's done his community a service," Cruz said. "He should be rewarded with safe passage home."

"He's going to the Malibu sheriff station first," Salk said.

Cruz smiled emptily at Danny. "Sounds like your dance card is full. Good day Mr. Cash Oh." He turned and walked away up the sidewalk behind them.

Danny ducked and bobbed as he rolled up the window, trying to track Cruz in the side mirror and see what he was holding. "Travis, here's the full address." Danny read it back to Salk with all the numbers, twice. "Someone there just posted to Red Flag again as UCANBRN2. It's the same zip code he used for his CODA registration, 91362. He's here in Thousand Oaks right now—and so is Mike Cruz."

"I heard."

"Is that supposed to be coincidence?"

Ursula was jotting down bullets: *UCANBRN2*, probably spelled out phonetically. *Volunteer firefighter. Carl Tillson. Hotel video.* She was concentrating, memorizing. And she was wearing perfume, or maybe it was her shampoo or skin lotion, but her scent was distracting as hell under the circumstances.

"What did the new post say exactly?" Salk asked.

"It said *Tell Mendes to kiss my ass.*" Mendes, an anonymous pushpin on someone's mental map.

Ursula's pen quivered across her notepad.

"Mendes who?" Salk asked.

"Why don't you ask Mike Cruz that? Are you getting in on this or what?"

"We'll check it out. Now do everyone a favor and walk away."

"Okay."

"Okay." The detective grunted. "Should I speak to whoever's phone you're using? I got their number now too."

Ursula's nostrils flared.

"Okay," Danny said again.

"Very well Mr. Kasho, like Mike said you've done your civic duty. Go get a Happy Meal. Now you've been told twice. Don't be late for our appointment this afternoon." Salk hung up.

Danny fidgeted with frustration at the worthless hunk of unrecyclable plastic and microcircuitry that was his phone. If ever he wanted to be blogging it was right now, right this very second, and he'd been slapped with a technological gag order.

Unlike Ursula, whose GPS had already recalculated a new highlighted route on its color map. Left at the next light and up two blocks. Left again, then right into a cul-de-sac. 0.2 miles. Estimated travel time two minutes at the maximum legal speed limit of 35. Danny was pretty sure he had the route—not a hundred percent sure—but one wrong turn and it wouldn't matter. He'd be lost in the baking suburban wilderness while everything went down.

Ursula dimmed the display and looked at him. "Can't say it was a pleasure. Get out of my car."

"Ursula—"

"You can't be part of the cavalry if you don't have a horse."

Danny pulled on the door handle, which looked like a belt buckle and was one of the few pieces of metal in the Versa's cabin, and the plastic-sounding door popped open. Ursula checked over her shoulder and dropped her hand to the gear shift. He paused halfway out of the car with the blast furnace outside bearing down on him, looking at her.

"Close the door!" she shouted.

Instead he jammed it on the sidewalk so she wouldn't be able to close it from the inside and went and got his messenger bag from his car. He scraped her door across the cement as he got back in.

"You're so paying for that, shithead." As the electric car pulled silently away from the curb Ursula noticed the scratch down his car. "Oh look, your shithead fan club's growing by the day."

"Geronimo."

They zipped neatly through a break in traffic into the intersection. According to the GPS it was 4:20 PM. Mike Cruz was gone and Fireman666 was a thousand feet away and closing.

CHAPTER 34

They drove past the entrance to the cul-de-sac. Ursula stopped, then reversed neatly into a space on a meager shoulder sunbaked down to the dirt which had sprouted dusty cars with For Sale signs instead of grass. Small drab houses hunkered like succulents into an arid landscape, hemmed in behind faded wooden fences across from an expansive and mostly empty RV-rental lot.

"Can you see anything?" she asked.

Danny checked her GPS, then twisted around the molded headrest to look. His ribs jabbed him like so many aggressive tribal spears. The address was tucked away out of sight up the cul-de-sac. "No."

Ursula rolled down the windows and turned off the engine. Extremely hot, dry air blasted into the cabin.

"Hey!" Danny balked. "If you're that hot take off your Animal Kingdom souvenir vest."

"I don't have the gas for a stakeout," she snapped, *"or* the blood sugar level. *Or* the shithead tolerance."

"Perfect. I could have just driven myself, at least I'd be cool."

"You were so cool lost on the side of the road. If your shoes work any better than your phone, hit the road."

"And let you steal my story?"

"Your story? Have you read Tony Tama's piece on the task force yet?"

"I've never even heard of Tammy Toto."

"Sure you haven't."

"Seriously Ursula, I haven't."

"Well you should, he's good. He's got a source or two inside too."

"Which is still two more than you have."

"Two's a crowd when it comes to *your* sources."

"Sometimes they don't come in droves. Like boys don't with you."

"All dick and no balls. Story of your life."

Danny turned and looked again but still couldn't make the building attached to the address appear. He didn't see Mike Cruz's white Ford 4x4 anywhere. He glared out the window at the nearest dumpy little house. Who was Tony Tama? Was that some kind of cheesy pseudonym, a made-up name for their virtual stage? All it took for any asshole's opinion to masquerade as fact was an internet connection, Danny would be the first to admit that. But did Tony Tama know about Pavelko and Cruz? Who did he write for? Had Ursula had adventurous sex with him too?

"Man are you ever going to get over the awards?" he grumbled.

"What?"

"You've been a c-word to me ever since."

"A c-*what?*"

"A c-*word.* Get over it. Maybe you'll get lucky next year."

Ursula squared her jaw. "The only reason you won that stupid award is because your story was flashy and current and mine was cold and about fringe dwellers—black women, prostitutes no one cares about in a poor part of town no one cares about."

"So make better story choices."

Her cheeks dimpled. "You don't have to go out of your way to be a jerk just because we slept together."

"We were standing up. In a handicapped stall. For three minutes."

"More like half that, but don't beat yourself up. I'm sure you tried your best."

"Not really."

"Well Danny on behalf of the taxpayers who are going to foot the bill for this thing, if you have any objections speak now or forever be held liable. If you're wrong about this your goose is going to be monumentally cooked. The lawsuits will bury you and your little website too."

He struggled against the sudden urge to recant—especially in front of her. He wasn't chickening out. In Suge We Trust. He pushed open the door and got out, ignoring the angry protests from his ankle and ribs and thigh and shin and everything down to his pancreas. At least his back wasn't sweating against the car seat anymore. He left his messenger bag with his useless phone on the seat but took his camera. "Stay here."

"Like I was offering to go anywhere. You should be thankful your hat still works."

Danny closed the lightweight door more forcefully than he needed to and cut off her cry of *Shithead!*

The sidewalk spilled out of a storm drain clogged with dirt and dead leaves and Danny followed it around the mulch lawn of a ranch-style house on the corner. There were three houses on each side of the cul-de-sac, which gently inclined toward two houses angled together at the back on a slight elevation. According to Suge's juju and Ursula's GPS, UCANBRN2's latest post had been sent from a computer in the house angled on the left. It was the color of sand and small, maybe a thousand square feet, with no trees to shield it from the unrelenting sun. A kitchen greenhouse window stuck out between the front door and a square bathroom window. A blue recycling bin held a peeling wooden gate closed in the driveway; space for a car to park in front was empty.

A bulge of bare hills was visible through the trees behind them—the Hillcrest Open Space Preserve where the Angeles Arsonist set his first known fire.

The cul-de-sac was shuttered like a town before a gunfight. Heat waves shimmered in the torpid sunlight, buzzing with the sound of air conditioners. A couple of cars parked on the street. A couple more in driveways. No white pickup. The only screen he had was a pair of skinny Mediterranean Cypress halfway up the street, if instead of using the sidewalk he picked his way across front lawns while keeping the trees between him and the house—and hope no one was watching out the greenhouse window. No sound of incoming sirens—so much for the cavalry.

Nagging doubts flared up like spot fires. He knew he should stop, turn around and return to Ursula's stupid car and belittling sarcasm. Right or wrong he'd called in the air strike, now he should just sit back and wait like he promised.

He almost glanced back at her car but he wouldn't give her the satisfaction of appearing stymied by second thoughts. His fingers touched the steel pole holding the yellow-on-brown street sign as if to ground himself and dispel the rising fear. This was safe. This was broad daylight. There was no ambush. Just take a look, take some pictures, and walk away. The cops would be here any second. This was his only chance. He wasn't taunting fate or anything else. He was doing his job.

He stepped over a low brick retaining wall onto the shredded woodchip mulch with his heart pounding in his ears, ignoring the pain in his ankle and the warning in his gut. He was less likely to be arrested for prowling than shot by some overzealous homeowner. He skirted empty plastic chairs arranged beside the corner house's garage and darted as much as he was able to across the next house's grass yard. He swung his legs over a waist-high picket fence and stepped onto a pile of hard-packed dirt. Someone was in the midst of some light landscaping—an aluminum ladder lay on its side pinning a blue tarp over some wooden planks and a pile of oblong brick pavers.

He crouched behind a big black Dodge Durango hybrid with tinted windows that was nosed up to an iron gate in the driveway and zoomed in on the sand-colored house over its contoured hood. He thought he smelled smoke.

A dog barked right behind him and his shoes cleared the ground.

He spun around, instinctively raising his hands to defend against a canine assault, and saw Ursula Ruda had jumped off the sidewalk all the way into the street, her surprise flash-frozen on her face. An enraged brown and white mutt with a spiked collar and three legs was hopping back and forth behind the iron gate in the driveway, apoplectic at its inability to address their trespass. It was the kind of dog that barked at anything and everything at all hours of the day, that never saw the inside of its master's house, the kind that could be relied on to announce anyone's arrival like a megaphone.

He took Ursula's picture and smirked long enough for her to see him doing it. After all the lecturing and moralizing she was just like him—she needed to be there when it went down too. She marched up the sidewalk in quick steps, offering her middle finger to the dog, which only barked harder as if it understood the insult. Danny hoped it barked so often that residents of the cul-de-sac had grown to ignore it and its noise wouldn't draw anyone to the window.

"I thought you were going to stay in your car." He had to raise his voice over the noise of the animal.

"You're the story now shithead." Ursula's cheeks were flushed. "Which one is it?"

"Last one on the left."

She rolled her zoom lens between her fingers and thumb and shot a rapid-fire series past the bulbous back end of the Durango.

"You stay here," he said. "I'll be right back."

"Geronimo." Ursula strode up the sidewalk without using anything as a screen between herself and the sand-colored house.

Danny didn't like it—cul-de-sacs were isolated communities by design and she didn't look like she had any reason at all to be here. His way was harder, slower, and visually way more suspicious, but better tactically. Ursula finally only crouched when she reached the empty driveway of the house next door to the sand-colored one. The properties were separated by a common unpainted fence that leaned to one side.

The dog was still barking furiously.

Ursula looked through the cracks of the fence. "What are we looking for?"

The driveway felt hot enough to melt the carbon rubber soles of Danny's shoes. He wanted to say he'd know when he saw it but he didn't. He was looking to not get shot, that's what he was looking for. He wasn't looking for another award, he was looking for answers and an exit, not an exit wound. Normally that wasn't too much to ask. He moved to the other side of Ursula and peeked between the boards into the back yard.

In the space between the gate and a one-car garage that was the same dried-out color as the house was wedged a green minivan.

A fist-sized pit formed high in his stomach, sucking all the moisture from his mouth to form its solid core squeezed into shape by nervous pressure. He knew the minivan's engine would start with a banshee howl from a loose fan belt. He knew inside it would smell like the gasoline and diesel that had leaked from the flamethrower. He knew Jorge Ochoa's blood or terrified sweat had stained its worn-out upholstery. He knew that supreme cruelty was measured in the simplest of terms—*want,* and the utter lack of inhibition about satisfying it at any cost. For the Angeles Arsonist going without was harder than simply taking, and he wasn't going to stop taking until the day he was stopped by force.

He took two photos of the minivan between the fence slats and grabbed Ursula by the arm. "Come on."

She jerked free. "Let go of me. Do you smell smoke?"

"Exactly, let's get out of here."

"It's not from Backbone?"

"It's too far away and we're upwind. Let's get out of here. *Now* Ursula."

Leading by example he went limping up the sidewalk, telling himself to act natural despite feeling crosshairs on his back and fighting the urge to run, or try to—his ankle wasn't tolerating weight on it.

Ursula easily caught up with him. "What's going on? What did you see?"

She didn't sense the danger, just the urgency. That was good enough for now. "Nothing. Come on."

She had to shout as they passed the three-legged dog. "What did you see Danny? Tell me!"

"I'll tell you in the car."

"Tell me now!"

"With the air on."

"Baby! All dick and no balls."

With his ankle throbbing he couldn't maintain much of a pace and Ursula stalked ahead of him. Her waning blood sugar amplified the seriously high threat level. She was already halfway to the street where they had parked. Maybe she intended to drive off with his bag and his dead phone and leave him here by himself. Maybe he deserved it. Maybe he deserved some more quality time with the thing he helped not destroy last night.

He stepped out into the street, unable to deny the growing smell any longer, and looked back at the house at the end of the cul-de-sac. Black legs of smoke were climbing out from under its flat tarpaper roof.

The unmistakable roar of propelled fire behind him cut off Ursula's shrill scream.

CHAPTER 35

Danny turned around so fast his ankle gave out and he fell onto the prickly brown grass of someone's dead lawn.

Oily black smoke billowing from where Ursula's car was parked registered a fraction of a second before he saw Fireman666 coming around the corner carrying the tanks and the rifle-like flamethrower, shielded from humanity like a soldier in apocalyptic black fatigues, gloves, goggles and helmet, the face mask like a grotesque breathing appendage after the entire atmosphere had turned to poison. He was a manmade monster come to kill. He was thirty yards away at most and Ursula was between them, rooted in place on the sidewalk, her mind short-circuited by terror.

A stream of fire spat from the rifle-like gun of the flamethrower and the mulch yard on the corner began to smoke.

Danny snatched up his camera, sprang to his feet and screamed *"Ursula run!"*

She snapped out of her stupor and bolted toward him in a flat-out sprint crying *Oh God oh God oh God oh God,* her eyes wide behind her clip-on sunglasses as flight took over from fright and her body focused its adrenalized energy on escape. Escape and survival, fleeing back into the cul-de-sac. Back into the dead end.

Behind them the flamethrower hissed and its unnatural heat licked their backs.

Danny grabbed her by her safari vest and they stumbled behind the Durango. The three-legged dog barked and snarled, gnawing furiously at the bars of the iron gate.

"Danny I don't want to die because of you!" Ursula cried.

"We'll be okay!"

"I don't want to die!"

Despite the SUV's bulk he knew they'd made a terrible mistake coming here. The Durango couldn't protect them—nothing could. The flames were too thirsty for flesh and they'd been trapped like dumbfounded amateurs in the dead-end street. All he could think of was telling Vanessa he was sorry. Something bad was about to happen, something permanent, and he'd never ever wanted to cause the kind of pain she was about to suffer, and Cynthia and Victor and Celia and her little brother or sister that he wouldn't get to meet. No self-help shtick or time-weathered papacy would anchor the soul set adrift by the loss of a second child.

I'm sorry. Mom—I'm so sorry. I screwed up and I'm so sorry.

A police helicopter snarled overhead low and fast, capturing the attention of all three of them for a second.

The Angeles Arsonist dropped his chin to his chest for a moment, making the industrial material in his black mask buckle.

Danny hoped he was listening to the voice of common sense that was urging him to give it up. Shuck off the flamethrower, let it drop to the pavement and raise his gloved hands, then lay down for the felony arrest—face down, arms and legs spread wide. The cavalry *was* coming—there was no way out. He had to know that now. He had to.

Give up.

Stop.

But after a few seconds, just as Danny aimed his camera the arsonist raised his head and resumed his determined death march into the cul-de-sac, straight toward the Durango. Forty yards or so that were shrinking with every step he took. There was nowhere for them to go.

He hadn't survived last night because of luck and it certainly wasn't fate, but by not staying still. Time equaled distance. "We've got to keep moving—if he corners us we're dead."

Ursula was breathing rapidly as she took pictures. "If I die because of you I'll kill you, do you hear me? I'll kill you."

He saw the arsonist's posture change and shouted, *"Get down!"*

A spray of fire hissed past the back of the Durango, loosing embers in the cypress and lighting them up like Christmas trees.

"Go go go!" Danny led Ursula away from the car, through the wall of acrid smoke and up the sidewalk curving around the end of the cul-de-sac. He didn't care if he broke his ankle or anything else—he was running.

Gunshots crackled through the air.

They dropped to the hot pavement and covered their heads as round after round poured into the cul-de-sac. The cavalry was finally here—but the two of them were in the line of fire. Anything that the arsonist's body didn't stop would keep tumbling supersonically through the air toward them.

Danny raised his head to peek. Ursula was beside him, an arm's length away, propped up on her elbows and fumbling with her camera. She'd lost her glasses and her hat and her eyes were wide with the earthy terror of the hunted.

There were no police here. Both of the arsonist's hands were on the modified gun grips of his flamethrower, just like Mike Cruz had described it. Just like he'd designed it like a skeptic reverse-engineering a magic trick. And now he was only twenty yards away, close enough that Danny could see the pilot light glowing eagerly at the end of the tube, no less diminished by the daylight.

The gunshots weren't coming from behind them, where the arsonist was, at the entrance to the cul-de-sac—they were coming from one of the houses in front of them. They sounded like they were coming from the house that was on fire.

Panic flooded Danny's nervous system, clouding his analysis of the situation beyond an insightful *This is very bad.* They were trapped out here in the open between Fireman666 with his flamethrower—a thirty-yard range, Cruz said—and an unseen gunman. Was it an over-defensive homeowner? Was there an accomplice acting as sniper?

But the gunshots started cracking at a rate impossible for one gun—impossible even for a machine gun. They were clustered and grouped like a fireworks accident.

They had to get out of here.

A line Lucy Baskin once said to him came to mind: *Only first responders and first reporters head for a burning building.* She'd been using it as a metaphor for something but it was appropriate today. Their only chance was to get into the yard of the house beside the burning one and hope there was a way out of it—and no dog. Not a big one anyway. He'd throw Ursula over the fence if he had to.

He clamped a hand around her arm and heaved her to her feet, and they ran together toward the driveway to the left of the burning house where they'd looked through the fence, Ursula shooting with her fancy camera like make-believe covering fire. Maybe the keys were inside the minivan. Maybe he could back out and run over the firebug psycho.

He said, "Head for—"

They were thrown to the ground as abruptly as if invisible pranksters had table-topped them, one prankster pushing them over a second prankster waiting on hands and knees behind them for a jolly fucking laugh, then started indiscriminately hurling hot, sharp fragments of metal, glass and plastic at hundreds of feet per second all around the cul-de-sac.

Dust and pebbles and sand raked their skin as the small loose stuff on the street around them was sucked into the trailing rarefied vacuum that billowed under a black and orange umbrella of a fireball rising under a widening smoke ring into the clear blue sky.

For a moment there was no other sound in the world.

Danny found himself on his back, clutching his camera to his chest, blinking and gaping up at the smoke-smeared sky, as sucker punch-stunned as when he found himself on the losing end of his first fight at the far end of the yard on his first day at the new school in North Calendula. Victor wasn't there to come to his rescue, he was fighting his own battles at a new school too. It wasn't Danny's last fistfight and he never got any better at it, he just healed faster and minded the pain less while his threshold for it toughened like scar tissue.

He turned his head and saw the fence between the houses had been flattened. The minivan was burning, doorless, windowless, billowing pungent black smoke. He could discern a dull, indistinct roar, as if his head was being held underwater. He watched the three-legged dog scuttle away around the back of its owner's house with its wire-thin tail tucked behind its single back leg, then a warped green car door fell smoking onto the roof of the Durango with an expulsion of safety glass from the SUV's windows and Danny's hearing rebooted.

In came the harsh sonic mess of bleating car alarms honking and beeping through the tinnitus and the sirens and the choppy fuzz of the helicopters—flat on his back he could see that the orbiting police airship, painted black and white like an LAPD patrol car, had already been joined by a news helicopter, colorful as an exotic bird high on a camera-steady perch.

As if from the helicopter's point of view he saw the triangle of himself and Ursula, who had rolled onto her side and was getting shakily to her feet with her fancy camera in her hands, the smoldering Durango with the minivan's burned and battered door upside down on its roof, and Fireman666, who had drifted over to the far side of the street as he approached them as if he was dizzy or drunk and unable to walk a straight line. Danny instinctively calculated the distances like the Pythagorean theorem. The attacker's legs were moving—theirs were not.

He rolled over and grabbed Ursula. Her black fingernails dug into his arm as a blast of fire came up short and he led them staggering back across the open street toward the Durango. There was no safe place—they were just stalling for time now, hoping the smoke screened them, hoping precious seconds of fuel dwindled to none and going where there was the least fire in this kill zone of a cul-de-sac.

The front door of the burning house burst open and a dark-haired woman wearing only a white bra and shorts ran barefoot outside into the street, screaming and swatting at angry flames attacking her bare legs and arms like a swarm of glowing ants. Ursula saw her and screamed and she and Danny tripped into the driveway glittering with chunks of safety glass, scraping their palms and arms and slamming sideways into the shiny chrome wheels of the Durango.

The woman collapsed in the street, screaming for help, ablaze and alone, fully conscious while suffering the devastation to her soft tissue as the heat and the flame burned it inside and out. Like Neil Weber in the borrowed Uggs, caught in the kindling below the Malibu cave, shrieking and helpless, writhing and squirming as nerve endings blackened to charred crisps. Death with as much pain as possible.

A Ventura County Sheriff's Department black and white Ford Explorer interceptor utility vehicle screeched to a stop at the entrance to the cul-de-sac. Two uniformed deputies bailed out and took cover behind their open doors. Ursula crouched at the corner of the Durango and Danny dropped to his belly, videoing in the space between the ground and the bottom of the SUV as the arsonist turned and shot a long fire stream at the cops. It blew out the windows of the cruiser and sent the deputies scrambling as two more cars arrived, a marked Dodge Charger and an unmarked older Crown Victoria.

At once the police opened fire.

The snapping of their handguns echoed off the houses. Tufts of fabric and smoke tore from Tillson's black jacket and combat pants. Bullets clanged eerily off the two metal tanks strapped to his back and ricochets bit into the Durango with violent *thunks* that made the big vehicle tremble. Danny dragged Ursula behind the engine block and hoped nothing skipped under the car into them as the arsonist staggered under the barrage and dropped to one knee, wearing black running shoes in lieu of the boots he'd tied onto Jorge Ochoa's feet before he dropped him in Malibu Lagoon.

The gunfire stopped.

There were the sounds of arriving sirens of the police and fire department and the crackling of things burning. So many sirens, as if the entire Ventura County Sheriff's Department was responding—Travis Salk had rung some major bells and Danny hadn't been wrong.

Ursula shrugged off his hand. "Get off me!"

The burning woman was rolling over and over on the pavement in a futile attempt to douse the flames on her skin. It was maddening to witness her torture and not be able to help her, to somehow stop the excruciating pain. Danny couldn't close his eyes and un-see it. Whoever the poor woman was, she in her agony would be with him forever. He peeked around the left front tire of the Durango. Ursula edged around the other side and was crouched at the right rear tire.

Fireman666 was down on one knee. The cops were edging out from behind the cover of their cars, yelling over the noise of the circling police chopper for the suspect to drop the weapon and get down on the ground. They took short, cautious steps toward him, closer and closer.

Suddenly the arsonist pushed himself up and limped directly at the gathering police force, leaving fat dollops of blood behind him in the street. His flamethrower hissed and spat—the tanks were emptying for the last time but the stream was still strong enough to scatter the closer deputies like leaves while the rest of them concentrated their gunfire on him again.

Two loud, sharp cracks from their side of the street sparked something on the side of the arsonist's fuel tanks and he briefly vanished inside a balloon of fire hot enough to make Danny and Ursula duck behind the Durango. The rapidly escaping gas knocked him forward toward the police, increasing the accuracy of their shots until shouts brought the gunfire to a stop again.

The house at the end of the cul-de-sac was completely engulfed in flames—the gunfire had stopped from there too. The burning woman was fully overcome by the flames; she wasn't screaming anymore. You almost wished she was dead already, free from the pain, but she wasn't.

A team of firefighters in full bunker gear screened by a police SUV jogged extinguishers and medical packs over to the burning woman as deputies armed with shotguns warily approached the arsonist's smoking body, barking commands.

Danny and Ursula bumped into each other as they switched places around the Durango.

"Are you okay?" he asked.

"Get out of the way!" she screamed.

The fire extinguishers' dry chemical clouds quickly smothered the flames on the woman. Silver duct tape was singed into her skin; strips dangled from her wrists and ankles. A uniformed deputy with a shotgun held inches from the arsonist's head kicked the tube away from his limp hands. Other cops with handguns aimed at his head and chest stood on his legs and arms as a firefighter neutralized the flamethrower by shutting off the valve to the tanks which were too hot to touch. His smoking limbs were bent like a downed pugilist until they rolled him onto his stomach to handcuff him.

Danny zoomed in as they tugged off his hardhat and mask.

Carl Tillson's shaved head had been blackened. One of the lenses of his goggles was shattered. Blood covered his bared teeth and his face was contorted in pain. The collar of his blue Best Value Hardware shirt was visible beneath his black jacket. The helpless and hurt bully squealed in his boyish voice over the cops and the radios. "I need an ambulance! I need help! Help me! Get me an ambulance! I need help!" As if the woman he'd set on fire wasn't even there. He spotted Danny and lifted his head off the pavement. He'd been half-blinded by a gory wound to an eye socket which was already swelling grotesquely. "Killer Kasho! Look what you did! Killer Kasho! Look at me!"

Some of the deputies looked and saw Danny and he made sure they all saw he and Ursula were only holding cameras. Nervous cops were almost as dangerous as nervous criminals.

"I need an ambulance!" Tillson dropped his head to the ground. "I need help!"

Shocked neighbors were just beginning to emerge from their homes when a second thunderclap explosion cracked through the air.

CHAPTER 36

Danny imagined this was what Carl Tillson's mind was like, the internal monologue where other people humored private thoughts, worries, fantasies, their own personal encouragement or criticism, insults and applause. Tillson's was swirling metallic chaos in preternatural heat and confusion, a 360-degree environment of boiling anger or revenge or insignificance or whatever it was that fueled his violence, that turned the noise behind his eyes into skin-flaying shrapnel and fire and terror.

Firefighters attending the burned woman shielded her ruined body with theirs. Cops ducked, their reaction time far slower than the speed of anything that might be bearing down on them, but Danny saw no plummeting debris this time.

He processed the second explosion within the gruesomely analytical strategy familiar to a generation raised on religious hyper-violence—the first bomb to kill and attract first responders, the second bomb to kill them too. Religious extremists had mentored everyone from drug lords to lone psychopaths.

Once again keening sirens and squawking car alarms and the jackhammer of thumping helicopters filled his ears with the comforting din of life.

Ursula was up on one knee with her camera to her eye like a sniper's scope.

A cop had his hand in Tillson's back to keep him down but some of the other cops had backed off—you could tell they were thinking *suicide vest.* There was no safe place here and Danny and Ursula were well within the radius of destruction Carl Tillson had devised.

He continued videoing as firefighters carefully moved the flamethrower off the street, tender as bomb techs. The wounded so-called volunteer firefighter had his single functioning eye fixed on Danny while everyone else was watching a plume of gray-white smoke rising from the street behind the house. Tillson was down but on *his* terms—and above all he wanted Danny to know that.

A fire department ambulance drove cautiously with two wheels on the sidewalk past Tillson to the woman, surrounded by a cordon of uniformed deputies, off-duty cops and detectives in plain clothes. If the woman even survived the next few hours the severity of her injuries would define the rest of her life, tormented years dedicated to pain management and the psychological trauma of being disfigured. Life as she knew it had already ended because Carl Tillson had wanted it to. Danny wanted to know who she was and what she meant to him to warrant such a horrific assault.

Embers were already falling onto neighboring roofs, spreading flames like a plague. Firefighters needed more engines and more hoses which meant they had to get Tillson out of the way. Satisfied he had no weapons or explosives hidden beneath his clothes, four deputies, one on each limb, carried him to the side of the street nearest Danny and Ursula. His perforated body was leaking from a dozen holes and he left a splotchy, smeared blood trail like an oil slick across the debris-strewn pavement. When they dropped him on the sidewalk he didn't raise his head again but their guns didn't waver off him; they weren't taking any chances.

Immediately two fire engines rolled into the street and their crews clambered out to start running hoses.

"Hey!" One of the cops on the edge of those guarding Tillson pointed at Danny and Ursula and shouted, "You two—get inside!"

They lowered their cameras and looked at each other.

The cop realized they *couldn't* go inside—they didn't live here. Which meant they had no business here. Which meant they had to go. He marched over and forcibly escorted them out of the cul-de-sac and handed them off to another cop who led them around the corner to a spot by the RV-rental lot's chain-link fence, where they were told to stay put along with shocked neighbors and a growing number of curious passersby.

Danny and Ursula stood on the narrow strip of grass with a dusty path cut through it. He took pictures of the damaged police car and what was left of her Versa being doused by firefighters, smearing blood on his camera from his cut palms. She did exactly the same. He realized if he hadn't gone to look at the house—and if she hadn't followed him—they'd have both been inside the car when Tillson torched it, accomplishing twofold what he couldn't do last night, when he couldn't kill anything but Peter Buckstein's retirement dreams.

Ursula wiped her eyes and didn't look up from her phone. Her hands were cut too. A deep scratch on her right cheek was angry and red and hadn't clotted yet. Blood had smeared on her arms and shirt from dabbing at it. Danny's hands were shaking and he couldn't stop thinking about how he and Ursula fit into the life and torture killing of the burned woman. Their first date had consisted of spontaneous sex which turned a clear-cut professional victory bittersweet. Their second was their own attempted murders. Whatever had come between them because of the awards night had surely been dispensed with today.

He put his arm around her and she jumped as if he'd Tasered her.

"This is your fault!" she screamed. "This is all because of you! You shithead!"

"What?"

"Shithead! Shithead!"

"You're the one who wanted to tag along!"

"You're irresponsible!"

Danny clenched his teeth. "You want to know what it takes to write award-winning stuff—now you know! Stick to the Amy Childress fluff! You're a powder-puff pastry chef, that's all!"

"You're an asshole!"

"You're an amateur! Take your fancy camera and go be a wedding photographer!"

"Shithead!" Ursula stomped off.

"At least you don't have to fix your fucking bumper anymore!" he yelled after her.

She flipped him off over her shoulder and would have kept walking if a female deputy didn't notice her and stop her further down the path.

The ambulance emerged from the cul-de-sac and turned on its siren to clear a path through the perimeter of police, spectators, and gathering boots on the ground of local media. Danny didn't know where the nearest hospital with a burn unit was and didn't want to think about how close he'd come to finding out—twice. He fought the rising nausea and cleared his throat to keep tears from flooding his eyes as his stomach twisted and turned and threatened to empty itself. He didn't see the three-legged dog anywhere and didn't care about it. Fuck the SPCA too.

He leaned against the chain-link fence and scrolled through the pictures on his camera with the edge of his hand to keep from getting blood on it, communicationally impotent without a phone or a carrier pigeon, unable to do anything but wait. He savored the picture of Ursula right after she'd been scared by the dog, her face jolted into an exclamation point like a cartoon character. He was going to do something with it. Didn't know what yet, but something. Maybe Photoshop a moustache on it and send it to Amy fucking Childress from an anonymous remailer.

A motley group of cul-de-sac residents was being bustled out to the street by police in full tactical mode—lacking absolutes they were absolutely prepared for anything. The residents were a mix of ethnicities and ages, dressed lightly and sharing looks of disbelief and shock. Some of their homes were burning now too.

Danny glanced at Ursula—she was pressing a napkin to her cheek and being talked to by the female cop and hadn't seen them. Neither had the local news crews who were setting up. He wasn't being guarded so he hurried over to them, honing in on an older white guy with a full white beard stained the color of nicotine around his mouth and a beer belly barely contained by a tight Harley-Davidson tank top who he sensed had lived here a while.

"I'm Danny Kasho," he said. "I'm a reporter for CODA.com. Can I ask you a few questions? Do you live here?" His voice sounded high-pitched and strained and with his ears ringing he couldn't tell if he was shouting.

The man was wide-eyed with incomprehension. "I don't know. I hope I still do."

"What's your name?"

"Jesse Lynne Jr."

Without his phone, Dictaphone, or even a pen and paper he had to commit whatever he saw and heard to memory, the least reliable source for information retrieval there was. "Jesse I'm Danny. I'm a reporter but I can't prove that because my wallet and ID burned up in that car over there."

Jesse looked at it and shook his head robotically. "Did he do that too?"

"Who?"

"Carl motherfucking Tillson."

A satisfying flush of validation coursed through him but Danny kept his face neutral. "Did you know him?"

"Let's just say we've exchanged pleasantries. Most of the time he'd pretend not to see me if I was outside when he was over."

"How long have you lived here?"

"Going on fourteen years." Jesse Lynne Jr. couldn't stop shaking his head, marveling as time had turned tangible and then to ash before his eyes. "Not for much longer though, even if it don't burn down. I'm a long-haul trucker but I've been out on disability. Ain't enough money to keep a roof over my head. Had to sell my rig and without that I got nothing anyway. Just odd jobs and eating shit. Me and Imelda would talk all the time, she was out of work too. We'd sit in her kitchen and drink and talk and I can't believe this." Jesse slapped his forehead with meaty fingers so hard it was as if he was trying to smack the old reality—the one that was gone forever—back into existence.

"Is that the woman's name? Imelda?"

"Imelda Vasquez. She lives next door to me in the bowl with her two boys." The man's eyes filled with tears. "What happened to them? Are they okay?"

"I don't know, I haven't seen them come out, if they were in there. I hope they weren't."

"What about Imelda?"

Danny cleared his throat. "It looks pretty bad. What's the bowl?"

"The end of the street, the round part, you know, the bowl versus the stem. He's a bloodsucker, that guy. That's what I told her. Imelda was exhausted, just drained by him."

"Do you know where he lived?"

"He moved into an apartment a mile from here after she kicked him out."

"When was that?"

"A year, year and a half ago maybe."

Danny blinked, thinking about epicenters shifting like tectonic plates. His mouth was very dry. "Where is it?"

"Corner of Hillcrest and Erbes. I've had to take Imelda there before. Not far enough away if you ask me. He was always over, arguing with her, trying to discipline her kids like he had any right to. Borrowing stuff he never gave back. Even borrowing her car, and she's got kids."

"What kind of car was it?"

"A '96 Plymouth Grand Voyager minivan."

"Is it green?"

"Most of it is. There was always something wrong with his truck, his piece of shit Toyota."

"What did it look like?"

Jesse snickered and wiped his nose on his tank top. "Couldn't miss it with the red stripe and the lights on top. His homemade official vehicle. I think he slept in it. He always had one reason or another why he had to take hers. Imelda couldn't say no to him. My opinion, he was just a cheap asshole who didn't want to spend his own money on gas. He'd leave his parked in her driveway when he took her car. He'd take the key with him so she couldn't move it. I damn near tried to hotwire it once but honest to God I was afraid to touch it. He'd bring hers back empty. He was just draining her."

"Where would he go?"

"Who knows, but he drove the shit out of it. And it needed work done."

"Like a fan belt?"

"Like everything. Imelda couldn't afford it. I tried not to get involved but sometimes she'd have to ask me to drive them someplace 'cause he wasn't back and she had to take the kids to school or whatnot. Just yesterday I had to take them to the grocery store because he wasn't back and wouldn't answer his phone. They were out of food! He didn't care. I don't even have car seats."

"He borrowed her minivan yesterday?"

"Yeah."

"Like what time?"

"Around lunchtime I think. Never came back with it, at least not that I saw."

"It was parked there today behind her gate."

"He usually just leaves it in the driveway, blocking the sidewalk."

"It blew up."

Jesse stared at him as if he had just told him the minivan had turned into a stegosaurus. But the surprise faded fast. "Is he dead?"

"I don't know."

"Well I hope he's fairly fucked up if he's not. I didn't even know he was here, I was watching TV when I heard all the noise outside. Then all of a sudden *boom.*" Jesse shook his head. "I swear he set off a pipe bomb behind Imelda's house a few months ago. I told her to get a restraining order on him but she knows them things ain't worth the paper they're written on. I told her to get a gun too. I said Imelda, he's going to kill you if you don't. I truly believed it would come to that. But not…*this.*"

"Did Imelda get a gun?"

"I don't think so, but I know *he* had guns there."

Danny thought of the shots popping off inside the house. "Carl had guns in there?"

"Imelda never showed them to me and I never asked. She didn't like it 'cause of the kids. He'd come over with something in a box and leave it there, tell her not to look inside. And she wouldn't. *I* would have, you can bet your ass on that. I don't know how such a deadbeat got to be a firefighter."

"Is that what he told you?"

"That's what Imelda said. I never asked. I don't know where or with what department but he'd wear the boots and the pants with the suspenders and all that, like we were supposed to be impressed. He'd just sit there, drinking her beer and watching her TV. I told her she should call the cops."

"Did she?"

"Once. They came around another time too, I don't think she even called them that time. I thought maybe something would happen you know?"

"What happened?"

"They talked to her and that was that. They didn't do nothing."

"Did she tell you what it was about?"

Jesse shook his head. "Nope. Soon as they left he came back like it never happened. He was already killing her without killing her. But I never—" His voice cracked and he wiped his nose with a forearm covered in old tattoos. "I never thought he could do...*this.*"

A gaggle of TV reporters crowded against the startled residents with mics and lights and cameras.

"Hillcrest and Erbes, is that right?" Danny asked him.

Jesse nodded and wiped his eyes. "Goddamned unbelievable."

Danny thanked him and wished him luck and made a beeline through the crowd over to where Ursula stood on the grass strip leaning against the fence, cradling her phone in her bloodied hands and staring bleakly at the ruins of her car, now a smoldering piece of evidence with a melted alien head attended by firefighters and cops. Everything she had with her had been incinerated inside it too. The female cop was elsewhere.

"Get away from me Danny," she sniffed as he limped over to her. She wiped her eyes with a part of her hand not covered with blood and was pressing a wad of blood-darkened napkins to her cheek. She kept opening her mouth as if she was yawning to make her ears pop.

He took a picture through the legs of cops and firefighters of Carl Tillson's body lying in the street. An ambulance hadn't come for him yet.

There was an unwritten pecking order to medical treatment at a crime scene that superseded severity of injury—civilians and law enforcement first, *then* suspects. He wondered if the cops would be called out on it later. His mouth was as dry as the golden state of California. He was dizzy and dehydrated, his body tightening up to perform an internal, automated self-check that wouldn't deliver happy results apart from a pulse and a newfound sense of direction.

He said, "This isn't where he lived."

"Who?"

They were both shouting.

"The guy with the flamethrower? The guy who just tried to kill us? I got his name *and* his address. He lives a mile from here."

"So tell the police. Get away from me."

Danny looked around to make sure no one was too close to them and tried to lower his voice. "I propose we go see his place before it's sealed off."

"Have fun. I'd give you a ride but my car won't start. *Ever.*"

"You've got a phone—call somebody. I'm asking you to go with me Ursula. Come on, I don't have a horse, remember? I need your help."

"I don't want to go anywhere with you. Get away from me."

"This is our last chance to own this. We were first here, we can be first there."

"Walk back to your car and drive yourself."

"And I would except my keys were in your car. Along with everything else." None of that loss had registered yet, but it would. The Louis Vuitton and his J-kit and everything in it was gone. At some point in the future he'd look back on this as a clean slate, a fresh start, but not yet. "Is somebody coming to get you?" he tried.

"Of course you don't have any friends you can call."

"Nobody that's telepathic—I need a phone. I just thought you'd want in on this."

"In on *what?*"

"It's a mile away, Ursula. We're not doing anything here. We'll drive over there, take some pictures and come right back. We'll be gone fifteen minutes. Nobody here will even notice. We're not a priority here. What happened here is half the story—let's go see how the other half lived."

"He burned that poor woman to death!" she screamed, and a fresh rivulet of blood trickled down from beneath the napkins.

"Her name is Imelda. He took it out on her before he took it out on the world. Don't you want to know why? See while you've been sitting here feeling sorry for yourself I've been working."

"Get away from me."

"Come with me Ursula. Come on, come with me. We've come this far."

"Just get away from me."

"Well how long will your friend take?" he asked in exasperation.

"None of your business, shithead."

His mind teemed with non-existent alternatives. It was a short teeming. "Corner of Hillcrest and Erbes. Karl Chillson. Karl with a K, Chillson. Now can I borrow your phone?"

"No." Ursula wiped her eyes and started walking down the path by the chain-link fence. "But you can tag along."

CHAPTER 37

Dazed as a crash test dummy and with his ears droning manic white noise, Danny shuffled along in a stupor as if the zombie apocalypse was upon them and he was a card-carrying member of it. He followed Ursula away from the smoking cul-de-sac along the dirt path which ran the length of the RV rental lot fence. His brain switched into self-defensive neutral and distracted him with a childhood memory of following another girl down a dirt path, but racing headlong fast on their bikes along the narrow, winding, bumpy sliver of accessibility tramped through the overgrown forest of old cars.

The path wasn't easy with the branches and twigs clawing at you and the exposed roots knobby enough to stop a front tire and then *hello* end-o—and Danny and his friends eschewed helmets when they were out of sight of their parents. He remembered the pure elation of furiously pedaling his Dyno Compe cro-moly with its laid back seat post and anodized blue pedals—the twisting, bumpy path was more dangerous and way more fun that way—keeping his eyes squinted and his mouth closed against the clouds of gnats swarming in the air. The girl's speed on her bike had surprised and overjoyed him and he'd pursued her essence as much as her back tire.

Her name was Lola Kendricks and he had loved her the way only a twelve year-old boy could—incompletely, yet with all of his emergent heart. Even sometimes in his dreams. They went to the same school but their paths had only finally intersected for the air tour. On the last day of school he had asked—*reserved*—Lola to watch the arrival of the planes with him, panicked by the thought that unless he did he wouldn't see her for *two months* unless he accidentally bumped into her, which even in a town the size of Calendula was unlikely. People tended to disappear over the summer only to magically reappear for school in September.

He found her in the parking lot of a local strip mall popular with kids from Aurora Middle School, where they went, trying to meet older Balfour West High School kids. Panting from pedaling so hard and with her friends watching and sneering he gasped for air and screwed up his courage and as if he was asking her for a dance many songs in the future blurted *Lola will you please watch the planes with me please?*

On cue her friends started laughing at him. He knew all of them and didn't like any of them. They probably hadn't known his name. He wasn't big, he wasn't popular, at best he was Balfour West's sports hero Victor Kasho's little brother. He had his own friends but they weren't big or popular either, they were a tribe of runts with elaborate nicknames for each other who rode around Calendula's social and geographic peripheries on BMX bikes.

His face had turned hot with embarrassment and he was about to hop back on his bike and ride away *fast* when Lola took a step forward, looked at him thoughtfully through her pink star-shaped sunglasses and said as clear as the sky that day in a voice loud enough for her bitchy little friends to hear, "Okay."

Okay!

Danny had sped home doing wheelies and jumps off the sloped corners of paved driveway aprons, a lighter-than-air feeling that would be rivaled only by the experience of getting the books out of the remains of the house fire with his dad a couple weeks later. It was going to be the best summer ever.

And two months later, the day after they watched the biplanes arrive together from out on the wide rocks of the breakwater, Lola was riding in front of him, leading the way into the forest of old cars, showing him she wasn't afraid to go where no girls *ever* went. She was so fast with her long brown legs—Danny's were gangly and very white—pumping her expensive bike's pedals as hard as any of his friends could. He wasn't going to tell them about this. Lola Kendricks and this exhilarating moment was his secret to enjoy unsullied by his friends' mocking.

They stopped in the tall grass behind one of the deteriorating machines littered with crushed beer cans. They got off their bikes and she came to him slowly, until they were nose to nose, then their mouths touched and she became his first, second, and third kisses, the last rays of delirious sunlight before darkness fell for good. She made him pinkie-swear that they'd be friends forever. That day there'd been no one else in the world but them, and as much as he could desire any one thing in the universe it was that this day and this time with her would never end.

But after that day he never saw her again, after he'd turned around, noticing the concentrated hum of fat summer flies a second before the carrion smell hit him like a primal fear, something terrifying yet irresistible. He took hesitant steps into the undergrowth, the grass tips tickling his bare knees, thinking an animal had died. A big one, to attract all those flies. Something he could tell his friends about. Maybe even impress Victor.

Lola whispered his name from close behind him. He tried to say *Don't look* but a moment after he saw it she screamed, a short, shrill noise that was the very sound of his regret. A man's body lay imprinted in the grass a few feet off the path, inanimate as a felled tree with his head cocked unnaturally over the collar of a peach and white C2C golf shirt, his half-closed eyes fixed accusingly on them as if he'd caught them doing something wrong.

In a shaky voice Danny told Lola to stay with her bike and he ran for his. Fast as she was she wasn't as fast as him and he couldn't be slowed by anything. He left her there and pedaled as hard as he'd ever ridden to the closest place he knew with adults—the restaurant at the nearby marina where many of the flyers from the air tour were mingling with tourists and out-of-town reporters. He tearfully convinced two cars of them to follow him and they barely kept up as he raced back to Lola with a sense of urgency that surpassed even his summer-long yearning to find a good place on the breakwater to watch the planes coming in with her.

She was still there, sitting on the ground near her bike which lay on its side across the path as if it was wounded, rocking back and forth with her knees drawn up to her chest, her arms around her legs and her head down and the thing in the grass just a few feet away from her, stinking and drawing flies. Danny sat down beside her, sweating and out of breath, and put his skinny arm around her and held her without being self-conscious while the adults exclaimed and swore and made calls until a lone siren became a mournful counterpoint to her whimpering. The last day of magic that summer had collapsed into devastating illusion.

A proper sidewalk emerged under he and Ursula's feet as they reached a block of neat townhouses. They didn't look back. They didn't look at the police cars and fire engines still streaming up the street toward the billowing smoke as a post-traumatic sun followed the pair's guilty flight like a searchlight. Neither of them would be here today if not for that fateful bike ride with Lola Kendricks. Every moment was affixed to every other one like knots on a vast net.

He blinked the sweat out of his eyes and saw the doughy face of Calendula Police Department Detective Alistair Gretsch hovering like a sweating beetle inches away from his own, his sagging jowls, the pits in the bulbous, rosacea-flushed nose glistening with nervous perspiration like potholes after a rainstorm, his hot breath sickly-sweetened by beer. Danny had smelled it before on his dad's breath sometimes when he came to kiss him goodnight, but it wasn't until many years later when beery breath on his cheek provoked a Pavlovian stomach-churning response with a girl he'd been trying very hard to liberate from her clothing did he finally gain the proper insight into the detective's behavior that day. Gretsch had arrived at the scene in the forest of old cars skeptical and underdressed in a t-shirt, Bermuda shorts and sandals, having been caught passing the festive day at his backyard barbecue grill instead of searching for the foreign national—the multi-*millionaire*—who had vanished in his town. Alistair Gretsch had been embarrassed that day, and to some people shame was a prime motive for bullying.

The detective spoke to the child and his voice never rose above a murmur, as if he was confiding a dangerous secret, like the presence of a bone lurking in a bite of fish, the boy crying but the questions persisting, the demands rising with the child's fear, the man's tone growing edgier like a self-sharpening knife serrated with impatience. Gretsch swatted away flies like regrets, self-conscious in front of the small crowd of cops, civilians, and tour personnel who had gathered around the gruesome tableau at the center of which was the dead man, the detective and the boy, who was staring at the little metal writing nib on the leather strap stained brown by years of contact with flesh dangling from the end of a ballpoint pen the detective held unsteadily in front of his wide, wet eyes.

He'd been looking at it since his first cognizant moments supine in the crib, the necklace his dad always wore, the one his mom gave him before he was even born, and through blinding hot tears that's what Danny told Detective Alistair Gretsch.

Twenty-six years later he was still haunted by the man, linked to him like a curse, half-expecting to see him appear with every piece of bad news he received, every tragedy great and small. Maybe Gretsch was the anonymous *someone* who'd called Gary Calder about Paul's illness. If maybe announcing that he was *ill* brought the detective—long retired by now—full circle on the biggest case of his career.

After Vanessa moved them to a different part of the city and Danny, Vic and Cynthia summarily switched schools Lola's parents, of a much loftier income and known locally as The Kendricks, installed her in a private school, uniform and all. At the time she'd been rebelling as much as she could against them, wearing bright colors and mismatched items whenever she could, and Danny could easily imagine private school coming upon her like corporal punishment. He'd dared her to go into the forest of old cars that day. She wouldn't have been there if not for him, her parents wouldn't have reacted that way because nothing would have happened to her, nothing would have changed, and her life today and every day since would have been what it was supposed to be.

She would be his age now. A grown woman, probably with a family, stable and mature. Twenty-six years ago, with his arm around her bare shoulders, Danny already sensed the chasm that had opened, an undefined spread of forcible change coming down like a bad rain, backing up out of the psychological storm drains, washing the ground away and leaving only the fading scream of familiarity.

CHAPTER 38

A group of people was gathered on the sidewalk outside a plain two-story white box of a building nestled into the armpit of an intersection. Two of the intersection's four corners were residential, upper middle-class houses of a couple thousand square feet on one side and boxy mid-century two-story apartments on the other. A tidy K-12 school was on the third corner and the fourth was an undeveloped hillside like a bald spot rising to million-dollar houses peeking over a dense screen of oaks at the top.

Four blocks away from the cul-de-sac, almost a quarter of a mile, practically infinity to Danny's throbbing ankle, Ursula led them to a jasmine green Subaru Forester hybrid idling quietly at the curb. She slid into the passenger seat and he eased into the back, sweating from the pain as much as the heat. The interior of the car was pristine and reeked of perfumy air freshener. Ursula's very gay friend Rick who happened to live in Thousand Oaks was at the wheel, gaping dramatically at the cut on her cheek and the plumes of smoke from the cul-de-sac being whipped up by the wind. She didn't introduce Danny and Rick didn't ask. She gave him the address Danny had gotten from Jesse Lynne Jr., Rick tapped it into his phone, and they were off.

Danny spent the short drive clutching his ankle, which had swelled to the size of a bowling ball, dabbing at the dirty cuts on his hands with brown Starbucks napkins he found in the back while Ursula did the same, and muttering curses under his breath at the absence of painkillers and the young-sounding female pop singer Rick was playing whose voice had been forced into tune by software and not skill. Rick had a motormouth and talked nonstop, animatedly and sarcastically, providing a much-needed respite for Danny and Ursula who didn't say anything, as if they'd each retired to their corners between rounds.

They approached the intersection from the east, between the school and the bare hill. Rick made a left and Danny looked at the white apartment building and the people in front of it. Air conditioners bubbled like warts out of its cheap hide. Small square windows were punched into the sides like air holes in a pet carrier. Just past the driveway to the parking lot Rick pulled to the side with his hazard lights on and Danny bailed out, leaving the dirty Grover and Animal Band-Aids behind as a token of his appreciation. He took a few quick establishing shots and limped across the street during a break in traffic. Obnoxiously loud techno music pummeled the air like a piston.

The people on the sidewalk wore shorts and sunglasses, tank tops and flip flops, and held cell phones and drinks in bottles and plastic cups. They all looked agitated and angry. Danny guessed the volume—and origin—of the music had something to do with all the gesticulating and head shaking they were doing. Nobody was outside exposed in the sun voluntarily today unless you were at the beach or a pool.

He caught the eye of a woman in the group, Hispanic, 20s, big lips and penciled-on eyebrows, spilling out of a black tank top with a silver sequin flower and the word *Hyna* stenciled on it and short shorts smaller than the frown creasing her pimply forehead. He shoulder-checked Ursula—she still hadn't gotten out of Rick's car. She was over-thinking things which you couldn't do in the mild state of shock like they were both in. You had to fight through it or else it would envelop you like seaweed, drown you with weighty inactivity.

"I'm Danny Kasho, I'm a reporter." He made a conscious effort to speak at a lower volume than he thought he was. He tapped his chest. *"Reportero."*

The woman shaded her eyes with her hand and puckered her face at him. "Seriously?"

"Do you live here?" He had to stand close to her to be heard over the music.

"Yeah?" she half-shouted back.

"Does Carl Tillson live here?"

"Yeah he lives here." Her fingernails had tiny flowers painted on them and her pillowy arm aimed one of them at a window on the top left side of the building. Venetian blinds were drawn tight behind a sliding glass pane like a teller window, which looked to be open. "Second floor, unit twenty-seven. Assholeland, where the rave is. We couldn't get the twins down to nap with the noise. We couldn't turn *our* TV up loud enough."

"What's your name?"

"Rosario?" There was an audible question mark at the end of her answer as if she was guessing.

"How long have you lived here Rosario?"

"Like six or seven months?"

"Has Carl lived here the whole time?"

"Yeah he was here when me and my boyfriend moved in. Do you know him or something?"

Ursula had come over and was trying to interview a shirtless skinny black guy who seemed more intent on conveying his displeasure by displaying his overly-defined abs than providing any meaningful information. She was rattled, off her game. And not even able to hear well without her hearing aid.

Danny asked, "Does Carl normally play his music that loud?"

"He watches TV kinda loud sometimes but nothing like this. We live right below him. We have the twins so I guess I can't complain about noise? But I never knew he was into techno. What's fatty gonna do, get his moobs painted and dance around with glow sticks? What's his problem?"

Where would you start? Danny thought. "When did the music start?"

"Like an hour ago? We knocked but he won't answer. My boyfriend was kicking the door so hard I thought he was gonna break it. I don't think he's in there. We called 911 but like the cops care about noise complaints? We told Arthur but like he can't do nothing."

"Who's Arthur?"

Rosario rolled her eyes. "The apartment manager, according to him. There's all kinds of things busted in our place and he never fixes nothing. And we got the twins."

"Is his last name Mendes?"

"No."

"Do you know anyone named Mendes?"

Rosario frowned and a good portion of her face caved in on itself. "Not personally. Why?"

"I'm surprised the cops got here this fast."

"'Cause of the fires, right? You can see the smoke from upstairs, it looks like after the earthquake remember? We heard booms too, like something blew up? Two booms. Did you hear them? My boyfriend was in Iraq and he said they sounded like car bombs. What'd you do to your hands? I think we have the same Band-Aids."

"Have you seen Carl today?" Danny asked.

"No."

"Have you seen him recently?"

"We're like not on the same schedule? Sometimes in the laundry room but like he never says nothing. Who are you a reporter for?"

"City of Angels/Dead on Arrival."

Rosario pursed her lips and gave her head a skeptical shake.

"CODA.com?" he tried.

"No. I never heard of that."

He aimed a finger toward the second floor of the building and turned on his winning smile. "Mind if I go take a look?"

"Why? He ain't answering. I don't think he's in there."

"You're probably right. Who could stand that music?"

"Seriously."

"Can I take a look anyway?"

Rosario waited a few seconds, thinking it over, then shrugged her meaty shoulders—one sported a dark tattoo but Danny couldn't distinguish the design, maybe a rose like the sequined one on her tank top—and led him over to the front gate.

Slender multi-tiered lamps hung like stalactites over the entrance, which was braced by severely-landscaped hedges and shaded by the slate columns of the façade. In curly metal lettering mostly obscured by *Podocarpus* conifers trimmed to match the height of the building, the structure's fanciful name adorned a section of the building like the nose of a World

War II bomber sporting the likeness of a buxom pin-up girl: *The Shangri-La.* Earthly paradise indeed.

Rosario jabbed the three-digit passcode into the security box with the flat of her ringed index finger and the gate unlocked with a cranky buzz. Danny ducked inside and the immediate dose of shade hit him like a narcotic. Past the bank of mailboxes was a small rectangular courtyard with a pitch of dead grass and a round metal table encircled by a mixture of plastic chairs. A kidney-shaped pool in need of a skimming was dug out of the other end, fenced-in with a bold red and white sign warning *No Lifeguard On Duty* and another pleading *Hey man don't be a fool! Please don't whiz in our clean pool!* screwed to the gate.

"Upstairs to the right." Rosario glanced at Ursula, who had materialized at Danny's elbow. "Number 27. But I'm telling you he ain't in there."

Danny struggled up the concrete stairs two at a time with Ursula right behind him. They came out at the second floor walkway, which ringed the interior of the property above the courtyard. He switched his camera to video and started recording. The railing was just wide enough to support an ashtray, of which several were balanced around its circumference in front of every second or third door. The units were all studios with four one-bedroom apartments, one at each corner of the building's upper level, whose occupants probably got first dibs on the covered parking spaces, the rest being assigned on a first-come, first-served basis. Either scenario was better than at his building, which had no parking of its own and made every return trip home an exercise in gladiatorial combat for an empty ten-foot stretch of legal curb within a mile of the place.

He followed the escalating unit numbers, glancing furtively through doors left open by their owners to help ventilate the pressure cooker heat building inside them, apartments that were dark caves compared to the glare outside. He glimpsed eyes blinking out at him from some; others were empty apart from the cheap furnishings, futons, old chairs, TVs on but silenced under the techno onslaught, the smell of cigarette smoke and pot lingering in the air.

He stopped short of unit 27. The techno was banging away loud enough to make him pray for death. The window was screened by dusty Venetian blinds. There was space between the bent plastic slats to peer out if someone was in there, but he knew the apartment was empty. And he knew he had good reason to be afraid of Carl Tillson's empty apartment.

Some doors around the complex were decorated with dried flowers or beads or sports logos, small and symbolic items to the occupants. The door of unit 27 bore no such ornamentation. It was painted the same workaday brown as the others and featured only the small brass unit numbers screwed into the wood above a thumbnail-sized peephole, a sturdy deadbolt, and the doorknob. Like the building as a whole the door frame had been built on the cheap and had warped and bowed from decades in the sun, leaving a sixteenth of an inch of space on the side with the lock in which Danny could see that the deadbolt wasn't engaged. He didn't smell any gasoline or oil or grease like he did in Mike Cruz's workshop. There was no hint of what lay on the other side of unit 27's door.

He wiped sweat from his eyes and looked back at Ursula. She waved him on with her hand that wasn't pressing the napkins to her cheek. Mouthed *Geronimo!* Prodding him once again toward potential danger. That woman, he thought sourly as he turned back to the door, holds a serious grudge.

He shaded his eyes with one hand, pressed his face to the dusty window and peeked between the blinds. The napkins stuck to his palms had bled through with dark spots. The window vibrated from the sonic pulses, so loud his teeth ached as if his fillings were being pulled out of his mouth. The darkness inside was magnified by the glare from outside but stubborn slivers of light fell onto unidentifiable objects close to the window and reflected off metal a few feet further in. Not any one kind of thing but an assemblage of them. The studio apartment looked cramped, its meager floor space choked with Carl Tillson's choice of décor.

Danny reached a tentative hand and his fingers closed around the oddly cool stainless steel knob. He tightened his grip and slowly twisted his wrist.

The knob began to turn.

He stopped.

Licked his lips.

Glanced back at Ursula again who stood a few steps away but with her fancy camera up now. Like they were kids on a dare.

Carl Tillson may have left his apartment unlocked on purpose. He may have had a very particular reason for not stopping anyone from coming inside.

"Who are you?"

An older man who looked like Gandhi, or Ben Kingsley playing Gandhi, had come upstairs with a pair of uniformed sheriff's deputies, two big white guys in tan and green uniforms and matching crew cuts. Over the blaring techno Danny and Ursula hadn't heard them coming. Gandhi wore an unbuttoned loose white cotton shirt, sandals and knee-length shorts, and had selected a key from a large key ring when he saw them at unit 27's door.

Gandhi lifted his stubbly chin and squinted at them through his glasses. "You're not residents here. What are you doing here?" Shouting over the din the man didn't sound like Gandhi. Or Ben Kingsley playing Gandhi.

Before either of them could answer one of the deputies got in front of him and simply bellowed, "Get downstairs!" Danny and Ursula slipped past them before Gandhi could draw any more attention to the obvious fact they didn't belong here.

They followed the ground floor path around the pool and went out through a gate at the back of the building. There were two stories of apartments on the side facing the street; on this side with the parking lot there were only second-floor units. Sixteen parking slots with padlocked storage cabinets were tucked beneath them. Most of the covered spaces were empty. Most of the uncovered spaces were full. No white pickup with a red stripe.

Danny wondered if Tillson had managed to snag one of the storage cabinets. How much of a treasure trove this place would turn out to be. Then he realized the second explosion at the cul-de-sac might have been the white pickup, and thought about car bombs in America and shock waves like tsunamis pushing unwanted memories of the moment in front of them, forcing their foreverness on the unfortunates caught in their path.

"What did you see in there?" Ursula worked the Starbucks napkins around her hands with Girl Scout skill as they walked around the side of the building to the driveway out to the street.

"I saw another press club award for me."

"So nothing?"

"The blinds are down and the rave is on and when they go through the door we'll see what happens."

Someone listening to them might have wondered why they were shouting at each other since here the building blocked the music enough to make shouting over it unnecessary.

"What do you think's going to happen when they go through that door?" Ursula asked.

Danny thought of the cool door knob under his fingers. How it wiggled invitingly with bombs for breasts. "I wouldn't want to guess."

"What did you say his name is again?"

"Chillson."

"Chillson?"

"Right."

"Karl with a K?"

Danny cleared his throat. "That's right."

They got to the sidewalk. The residents were still waiting out front by the black and white Thousand Oaks PD patrol car. A crowd and a cop car was enough spectacle to entice passing motorists to slow so they could gawk. The music was giving Danny mental trauma on top of everything else. Tillson could have put a single song on repeat but techno all sounded the same anyway. It was cruel and unusual punishment.

Suddenly there was shouting.

The cops were coming out of the entrance of the building. Fast. They looked more scared than authoritative as they hustled down the sidewalk with Arthur the Gandhi-lookalike apartment manager jogging behind them, looking over his shoulder as if something was chasing him.

One cop was talking breathlessly into the radio clipped to his shirt. The other made sweeping movements with his arms and shouted over the noise, "Everybody get back! Evacuate the area! Evacuate the area!"

The residents scattered into the street, some oblivious to traffic which honked and squealed and somehow managed not to hit anyone.

Arthur was hurrying past so fast Danny practically clothes-lined him. "What's going on?"

The man's eyes were bugging out, he was obviously terrified. Danny thought there was a body in there. Maybe Tillson had gone completely off the reservation and there were body *parts*.

"It looks like spaghetti in there!" the little apartment manager cried. "There's wires everywhere!"

At once Danny grasped the deviousness in the hollow center of Tillson's depravity. He entrapped people. He was smart enough to be cunning and broken enough to be callous and egotistical enough to be content with his epitaph being a bomb crater. Tillson was more than okay with that—he *wanted* it.

Danny found Rosario in the remnants of the crowd of residents the moment her eyes popped open. She shouted *Oh my God! Oh my God! The twins!* before she bolted screaming toward the front gate. One of the cops shouted and gave chase but with the gate propped open he couldn't catch fleet-footed Rosario in time before she was through and inside, screaming wildly at the top of her lungs.

Fear propelled Danny with the rest of the tenants down the street away from the building. He took pictures automatically and wondered how far was far enough when you were talking about an apartment-size bomb. The pain in his ankle and everywhere else was forgotten. He'd nearly been burned, shot, and killed by a car bomb and Carl Tillson still wasn't done.

Rick's Subaru rolled past with the passenger window down. Ursula leaned out of it with her middle finger raised.

"Hey Danny! Karl with a K says have a nice walk, shithead!"

Rick managed to squeal the little hybrid's tires as they peeled away.

Danny took a picture of the car for the hell of it. Getting back to Imelda Vasquez's house wasn't a problem, just a matter of time. Standing out here in the sun without water or his hat, which he'd lost at some point in the cul-de-sac, *was*.

Sirens converged on Shangri-La. A block away from the building Danny asked the residents if he could borrow a phone. No one obliged. He sighed to himself and stared up the road, holding his camera ready so if the unimaginable happened he'd be able to prove how it did.

CHAPTER 39

The chassis of Detective Travis Salk's maroon-colored legacy Crown Victoria creaked as Mark Pavelko leaned on the open passenger door. His tie was two-finger loose, his shirt damp with sweat and his sleeves rolled up, and he looked as if he'd just had to put his dog down. They were at the edge of the wide perimeter cast around Imelda's cul-de-sac but well within the reach of the lingering smoke.

"Hi there, Danny."

"Mark."

Danny sat sullenly in the passenger seat with his camera in his lap and one leg out the door, tapping an empty water bottle on the seat, dying for information as much as a drink and trying not to dwell on the image of Imelda Vasquez engulfed in flames, a visual which would surely sap some of the frivolity from the rest of his life. Spectators had noticed him and taken his picture, assumed his involvement, his degree of culpability. He wondered if CODA regulars like CrmnlyMandy would defend him from the anonymous onslaught. The sticky strands of complicity were delivering him to them like the arms of an octopus ushering dinner into its horrid beak—he knew he was about to get chewed up. He knew Carrie Voelker was somewhere close, the beautiful, graceful shark circling with her mouth open now that he was her story like he was Ursula's and Martha's and everyone else's. Little Carlos Esquivel was going to jump at the chance to stick a mic in his face, and jump is what wee Carlos would literally have to do too. Danny would stand on his tiptoes if need be. The best defense was a good offense—he needed to get to work and he couldn't. He couldn't do anything but sit here and think about all the things he couldn't do.

He'd convinced a cop directing traffic away from Tillson's apartment building to radio in about him being a witness to the related scene at the cul-de-sac. He dropped Salk's and Adjani's and Cruz's names from cop to cop and somebody relayed the message to somebody because only twenty-five minutes after fleeing Tillson's building—and two hours after calling him from the cul-de-sac—Travis Salk came to get him. His unmarked

Crown Vic was among the last of its era, discontinued in favor of smaller cars with better mileage but without the brute force, and would only keep rolling pending the availability of parts. Someday detectives would be rolling up to scenes in Smart cars. The cop car that smiles. The accumulated stress of Salk's endless hours crisscrossing the county in the department-issue sedan permeated the worn vinyl interior. Danny figured his Accord felt that way to strangers but couldn't remember the last time he had a passenger.

Salk had been tense and irritable, half-listening to the radio he held as he drove and half to Danny as he told him what happened since he called. Salk asked few questions and answered fewer—it wasn't a long drive, especially with the wig-wagging headlights and red and blue flashers in the grille. He'd been on his way to Imelda's when he reluctantly detoured to pick up Danny. Igor Adjani remained elsewhere—with Derek Cavanaugh at the hospital, Danny assumed. Salk wouldn't say.

Danny had barely finished telling his side of the story by the time they squeezed into a space at the perimeter. Salk got out and told Danny gruffly to stay put. Years of breaking down suspects in interrogation rooms to get the confession and close his case had made the homicide detective a master at applying guilt, which was a conditioned reflex to Danny anyway. He felt for Salk's kids. Terse as Salk was Danny missed even that much company after he was abandoned in the measly shade of the car, waiting interminably, thirsty and angry, hot and hurting with the nerves and the shakes and the epic dwelling on things, wondering if his hearing would return to normal or if he'd be staring at people's lips for the rest of his life and asking himself over and over again if it was worth it. Of course by then it wouldn't be.

After what felt like an eternally damned length of idle time Salk returned with a Ventura County detective named De la Rocha, who made Danny move into the back seat. Danny made sure the back door didn't close and lock him in. They took his preliminary statement and he repeated his story again and then again. Fortunately his phone call to Salk—before everything happened—was like a get out of jail free card. The detective couldn't threaten to arrest him for anything this time.

Finally the detectives relented and Salk allowed him to borrow his phone. It was 7:45. Danny crossed his fingers and called Garrett. Salk didn't even pretend not to be listening from the driver's seat while De la Rocha checked his voicemail and wrote in his notebook. Fortunately Garrett was reachable and willing to bail him out with another big drive for the second time today. He said he'd hurry but the reality was it was going to take a couple of hours to get here from there and navigate through all the diverted traffic. Unlike Ursula he didn't know anybody who just happened to live in Thousand Oaks. Before today he'd never even stopped here.

Salk took his phone back and he and De la Rocha left. After a minute Danny moved back into the passenger seat. By now the sun had set and he was grateful for the shadows. He wondered how to celebrate his survival, what to do, and with whom. There were short-term solutions like fleshy Band-Aids—Gina with the belly button ring, even Holiest of Holies Michelle—but close to dying was close to his father and only his family would understand that.

Mark Pavelko loosed a long sigh. "Well If this isn't the mother of all clusterfucks I don't want to know what is. You know at first I thought you were just unlucky."

"You'll have to speak up." Danny pointed to his ears. "I can't hear shit."

"Now I realize you're just like this," Pavelko said, louder. "And here you are, in a police car."

"At least I'm in the front seat."

"This time, but you of all people should appreciate the irony. Props to your IT guy's kung fu anyway. Maybe he should get a real job. Geeks are the new G-Men."

"The geeks shall inherit the earth."

They watched another ambulance carefully maneuver through the fire engines into the street.

"Days like this," Pavelko breathed, "they can have it."

Imelda's street had evolved from crisis zone to crime scene to encampment. There were temporary structures and chains of command, floodlights and fire damage, news vans and helicopters and drones and spectators with their phones. Danny remembered seeing their house on TV that summer of '93 with the lone cop guarding it, the bright yellow crime scene tape cordoning it off as if it was a piece of debris that had gotten caught around them, as random as a jet engine crashing through the roof. They'd already been displaced to a neighbor's where they saw how the end of their family would be televised for everyone to see. Then the neighbor had a quiet word with Vanessa in the kitchen and they were on the move again.

Another scene was unfolding around the secondary explosion on the street behind the house. Rosario's boyfriend was right—two vehicles had exploded. The second was a white pickup with a red stripe. The lightbar landed mostly intact on a nearby roof. Violence being an unpredictable and imperfect science, whereas Imelda's minivan blew up about as well as one could expect a car to, in the parlance of the bomb squad Tillson's pickup had low-ordered, or failed to completely detonate. A passing fire engine en route to the cul-de-sac had stopped and quickly extinguished the fire. Evidence would surely be recovered but it was all just a post-mortem now.

"I hear they're still trying to get into the apartment." Danny had kept checking in that direction, expecting the plume and delayed loud crack of high brisance explosives, but so far there'd been nothing.

"They got a robot and cameras. There's a lot of stuff in there. Hear it's all wired together like a spider's web. Gonna take some time."

Danny fidgeted with the empty water bottle. *Water is the most precious element in the world*, one billboard he'd seen between here and Tillson's building had read, and it bugged him no end that taxpayer-funded initiatives like the omnipresent conservation billboards could be factually incorrect—water was a compound, not an element. Everybody knew that.

He cleared his throat and said, "I almost opened the door."

Pavelko inclined his head. "You almost opened the door to someone's apartment?"

"It was unlocked."

"You tried it?"

"I was just looking."

"You just said you went from *looking* to *trying*. That's a common trait with you isn't it? I think they call that trespassing. I think they can arrest you for that. Penal code 459 if I'm not mistaken."

"Even if the place is unlocked?"

"A private residence? Convince the DA, you two are buddies."

"She's only a deputy DA."

"Not for long. The DA's office is the multi-headed Hydra come to make or break your case. You never know who your next boss will be. You should know that by now."

"Amy Childress can take a number. Salk has dibs on me anyway."

Pavelko smiled more honestly than Danny had seen in days. "Yeah he wants your notch in his bedpost something bad over last night. I don't blame him either."

"Yeah well, let him try. The only reason you guys are here is because of me."

"And your IT guy."

"I told him what to look for, he told me where, I called Salk."

"Sounds like you've been rehearsing that."

"I've been sitting here a long time, Mark."

"Don't you *Mark* me, you're miles out of my jurisdiction so make yourself comfortable. Count yourself lucky, I'd have already paraded you around in cuffs in front of the cameras like they do in Mexico. See what that does for your *blog*. Oh I know all about you Danny. Don't think everything you've done for the last 24 hours won't be scrutinized."

"Be my guest." He rubbed his eyes. "What time is it?"

Pavelko casually checked the watch on the inside of his wrist. "I've got 8:15."

Danny imagined Garrett hurtling down an empty freeway, like post-apocalypse empty, as devoid of traffic as California was of potable water or the radio of good music. But he knew he was really only doing about five miles per hour, wherever he was, puttering up one of the clogged concrete arteries with a million other unhappy motorists.

"Anyway," Pavelko said, "it's probably a good thing for you and everybody else there that you *didn't* open that door, which, it ought to be emphasized for your edification, you had no right to open in the first place. You likely would have blown yourself and everyone else in a five hundred-yard radius to kingdom come. While nobody might miss *you* you can't say that about the rest of them, so it's nice to see you can exercise a little restraint now and then, when you really put your mind to it."

Ursula was finally released from the back of another unmarked car and walked briskly past the Crown Vic without looking at them.

Pavelko squinted at her. "Swell place for a date. Who is she?"

"Ursula Ruda from Crime Time. That was her car over there."

"Why do I know her name?"

"She tried to get into Derek Cavanaugh's hospital room on Saturday. The exotic one."

"That's right." Pavelko scowled as the eye candy deteriorated into a cavity. "Frigging parasites."

Ursula crab-walked under the police tape and vanished into the crowd. Danny didn't see big gay Rick but knew he had to be parked somewhere nearby after bringing her back here and briefly stranding Danny at Tillson's apartment. Rick was the kind of friend that would wait all night if necessary, on call. Danny chastised himself for caring. He had a friend coming too. "How is Derek Cavanaugh?" he asked.

"Just swell. What isn't broken is bruised. Kid's got no front teeth, he looks like a hockey player. Doesn't look anything like his school photo anymore. He'll look different forever, like that actor who played Luke Skywalker did after the car accident. But Derek is alive, and that's the important thing, isn't it Danny? He is alive, his friends are dead and he's thinking maybe, just maybe he could have done something about that if he hadn't been such an asshole and left them. And the parents of the dead kids are all thinking the same thing. Maybe he was their kid's best chance and he blew it. Who's to say?"

"Then there'd have been six bodies at the cave instead of five."

"But right now Danny, right now that's all Derek Cavanaugh wants. To be as dead as his friends. And you know what? I believe him. It'll pass, but right now that golden boy with every opportunity in the world is laying in an ICU craving his own death. Who says life isn't an ambivalent cunt?"

"You should use that line on your Hallmark application."

"Think so? I could do a Stern But Honest line of greeting cards for people who won't figure it out any other way."

"What did Derek Cavanaugh say happened Thursday night?"

"He confirmed what we already suspected." Pavelko put his hands in the small of his back and arched backwards with audible pops like someone hitting a pillow with a stick.

"No offense but what you suspected turned out to be bullshit. I'd like to hear it from him."

"Hey, if your exotic little gymnast friend can't get in to see him your ugly ass sure as hell can't. I mean look at you. I thought *I* looked like roadkill."

"I feel like roadkill served up at a luau full of dudes in Hawaiian shirts. It's ugly."

"It sounds ugly. It bugs you not to know, doesn't it?"

"Isn't that why you're here? To tell me?"

Pavelko made a sad-clown face. He shook his head as his eyes became distant, focused somewhere far past the smoke. "I had some questions for him, you know? I wanted the chance to ask them. Face to face. I was really looking forward to it."

Danny realized Mark was talking about Carl Tillson. "You're disappointed about that?"

"I am greatly disappointed about that. Suicide by cop is offensive as hell to me. Suicide by anything is, but when you put it on somebody else to do it for you…" Pavelko shook his head again. "I wanted to knock on his door just to see the look on his face—I love that look they get. It's more than surprise. It's like you caught them naked *in flagrante delicto* with the dog."

"Sick, man."

"There's an embarrassment there is what I'm saying. That's what I live for. Finding whatever's there that can still feel embarrassment and dancing on it."

"You a good dancer?"

"I'm like Fred frigging Astaire with the right suspect. Yeah some want to gloat, yeah some want to brag, yeah some just want their mommy, but in the end they all get this defeated look like I walked in on them doing something shameful, something they know is terrible, something mommy would disown them for. And they've been caught—by me. And at that moment it's either fight or flight and most of them just curl up and suck their thumbs. They lash out but they don't fight."

"I'm not sure anyone would understand your definition of fight if today doesn't count."

"I guess it's dialogue. I wanted to introduce myself and sit down with him, listen to all of his bullshit and all of his excuses and put it together so the DA or *deputy* DA couldn't screw it up and they could plant his dumb ass on death row. I didn't even care about that so much. Let him live out his days looking over his shoulder in a Level Four playground for all I care. I'd prefer that actually. It's like dying a little every day." Then he blinked and glanced at Danny, then looked away, having remembered Paul Kasho.

Danny didn't begrudge him. You couldn't force people to be attuned to your issues, conscious and delicate with them. Kid gloves didn't even work with kids. "You never thought he'd get away?"

"No. Never."

"Because you're naturally confident?"

"Because he was too fancy. He went too big too many times in a row. Week after week after week. I knew he was going to be expensive to clean up after and I didn't know how many people he was going to hurt or kill before we got him, but his rampage was unsustainable. I knew we'd get him."

"Too fancy."

"Too fancy. You gotta pace your indulgences. Moderation is the key. For mass-murdering arsonists too."

In hindsight Cruz's maps hadn't been commemorating the fires, he was tracking them just like Danny was on the maps in his bedroom. Mike Cruz was here too, at the cul-de-sac. Danny glimpsed him standing with other fire officials, motioning, directing, instructing, as close to the flamethrower as he could get. "But isn't that precisely why you thought Cruz was the Angeles Arsonist? Because of the fanciness of the device?"

"And other reasons. The stuff we talked about."

"I bet he's looking forward to being Stern But Honest with you."

"Mike? Me and Mike are old pals. I think he was overly proud and put himself in a bad position, that's all."

"What happened today that sparked the turnout? He wouldn't tell me."

Pavelko shrugged.

"What'd he say? Did he make a threat? An accusation?"

"Things got a little heated. Some things were said that you shouldn't say, not in public, not in that situation. Not over the phone. Some people reacted. Maybe some people overreacted. Anyway it wasn't my call. That's what I told Mike. Out of my jurisdiction. But he shouldn't have left when things started to escalate."

"Did you tell him you weren't considering any other suspect but him?"

"No, because that isn't true."

"I didn't see any indication you were looking at anyone else."

"You didn't need to. I wanted your help with one aspect of the case and I got it. You were a pain in the ass and a heap of trouble but I got it. You think task forces are informational sieves? Look at that—I guess we can keep secrets after all. Anyway, me and Mike are good."

"You're good?"

"Sure."

"Bullshit."

"It's true. He blames you."

"Perfect. Do you at least have a bottle of water I can have?"

"I'm fresh out of humanitarian aid. Travis told me you met him."

"Who?"

"Carl…Wayne…Tillson."

"I met him on Friday in Malibu Bowl on my way to meet you. He was there, watching. Enjoying it. *Into* it."

"Like a child molester watching a playground."

"Who's Mendes?"

"What, you haven't figured that out yet?"

"I'm fresh out of phones so I can't do any more of your work for you."

"Whoever it is it doesn't sound like Tillson thought he'd have time to get to him. *Tell Mendes to kiss my ass* implies Mendes would still be alive after Tillson wasn't. And he knew it."

"Coworker maybe."

"Maybe. We'll find him. Maybe Mr. Mendes will be able to shed some light on who Tillson really was."

"He was a complicated mess like anyone else."

"Sure. Haven't we all wanted to build a frigging flamethrower at one time or another?"

"Did Cruz? Or did he just design one?"

Pavelko looked genuinely pleased. "It bugs you not to know doesn't it?"

"Hell yes it does. I've been chasing this guy for a year too. Why did he choose that hotel? For the proximity to investigators?"

"You want to know who—Tillson knew you couldn't resist that. You don't believe anything unless you see it for yourself, that's what your problem is. And he knew it. It's your problem and your weak spot."

"I only have one? Not bad."

"I know why you do it too."

"So I won't have to live in a cardboard condo on Skid Row?"

"You want to know what happened when your dad killed that guy."

Danny blinked.

"You want to know what really happened and why it happened so you dig into other peoples' crimes to get closer and closer to the moment of truth."

"Oh Jesus."

"You're a classic head case. The truth is it's never going to happen Danny. You're never gonna know. Give up on it already and move on with your life. It's a gift."

"You definitely have to bring your gift to Hallmark."

"You've got trust issues and you don't *want* to stay out of trouble. And they're connected somehow, but I'm not a frigging psychiatrist so go figure it out on your own card before you get yourself killed. Or worse—someone else. Like all the people at the apartment building today while you were thinking about opening the frigging door just to satisfy your frigging curiosity. They're all more deserving of the gift than you."

"What gift? What is this gift?"

"*Life*, Danny—are you paying attention here?"

"Maybe you're not Hallmark material after all."

"Maybe you should talk to Killer Kasho."

Danny took a deep breath and said nothing.

"Where is he?" Pavelko asked.

"Solano."

"I know Solano. It's in Vacaville, up by San Fran. Medium security. But that's not where he is."

"Did they move him again? It's what the website said."

"Oh it's what the website said. I guess the ten commandments would be posted on blog these days."

"So where is he?"

"California Medical Facility, right *next* to Solano. It's a prison, but a hospital too."

"Who gets moved there?"

"Sick prisoners, Danny."

"I mean how sick?"

"Well they don't put you there for the sniffles."

Your father is ill.

Really, really ill.

"You have any contact with him?"

"We haven't seen or heard from him since the day he was arrested." Danny just blurted it out, left it there, and wasn't surprised at all by the lengthy silence that followed.

"Do you think he did it?" Pavelko finally asked.

"Of course he did it. It was never a question of if he did it. It was always a question of why."

"Why do you think?"

"I don't know. Honestly, I don't. But it wasn't over money. Money wasn't his thing. Murdering a stranger for what he had in his wallet—it doesn't make sense."

"Who says things always make sense?" Pavelko said. "Who says they have to?"

"Have you ever closed a case on a lie? Or a half-truth?"

"You asking if I was a good cop?"

"I asked the question I asked."

"I was a hundred percent certain a hundred percent of the time."

"I would think that's unlikely."

"I was a good cop."

"And a good Forest Service special agent?"

"I got the Angeles Arsonist didn't I? Almost anyway."

"Yeah you're welcome for that by the way."

"Who lied in your dad's case? Who could have? It was his word against a ghost wasn't it? Dead men don't tell tales, much less tall ones. Félix Robitaille was rich too, wasn't he?"

"Beyond rich."

"And were the Kashos of Calendula?"

"Not so much." But Danny still didn't believe they'd fought over money, as if theft was a more shameful excuse for murder. He'd never believe that. Their family had been comfortable, at least from a child's perspective. He didn't remember them lacking for anything, he didn't remember undue friction between his parents. They didn't have to go without in a way that made any kind of impression on the boy. They'd been comfortable. They'd been normal, their innocence there for the taking.

"So what do you think happened?" Pavelko asked.

Danny sighed. "According to the autopsy Félix Robitaille was struck in the head by a blunt object, then toppled from the landing outside Paul's workshop and fell head-first onto our back yard, breaking his neck. The spinal cord itself wasn't damaged and the official cause of death was asphyxia from the crushed vertebrae."

"Not bludgeoning? I thought it was bludgeoning."

"Part of the legend of Killer Kasho. Lizzie Borden didn't give her mother forty whacks either."

"So what happened?"

"I think it was an accident. I don't know why they got into a fight, but it was an accident. Just a bad one."

"Some accidents are so bad it's like somebody did it to you on purpose. Sometimes they don't have much of an explanation either."

"There's an explanation. There always is. It may be complicated or it may be chimp-simple, but there's always an explanation. Might not be what everyone things it is either."

"You just hate not knowing."

Danny looked at his hands. "More than anything. More than I'd like some water right now, and that's saying something."

Pavelko smiled again but this one was stained with sympathy. "Sounds like you've tried to put a lot of distance between you and this thing. Sounds like you failed frigging miserably too."

"Some things follow you no matter how far you walk."

"You *walked* all the way from Calendula? I'd say you *ran.* At top speed. Been thinking about him a lot lately haven't you? There's no such thing as compartmentalizing, Danny. Let me tell you from my own harsh experience, life has a funny way of popping out of those neat little compartments when you least expect it. Like whack-a-mole. Like the song says, you don't know what you've got till it's gone."

"Did anyone from the Forest Service know you were here? Were you even supposed to be?"

Pavelko's tongue worked around the inside of his lip as if he had a wad of chewing tobacco wedged in there. "I've been on this case since day one, since the Fort Tejon Fire."

"Saturday July 28th."

"I'm supposed to be impressed you can remember a date?"

"It means I'm vested too, Mark."

"You're a frigging *reporter.* Stop pretending what you do is anything close to what we do—it's not. It's not the same frigging thing at all. Jesus, Danny."

"Stop saying *frigging* and just swear, would you?"

"It's about discipline, Danny. It's about making the effort."

"For who?"

"My family. Myself."

"Okay Mark. Make an effort and tell the truth. The whole truth. Speaking of the wisdom of leaving when things escalate—what's the real reason you're going back to San Francisco? Now?"

Pavelko looked away. Put his hands in the small of his back and let a long breath out as he stretched. Nodded in fake recognition to someone among the emergency personnel. "Like I said, you get assigned and reassigned all the time. This is routine."

"How much trouble are you in for threatening Linda at her house?"

Pavelko rapped his knuckles on the roof of the car. "I didn't threaten her! I've never threatened her! And I don't owe the world an explanation! It's between us, not the viewing audience at home with your feet up, treating other peoples' crises like sitcoms. Bite-size traumas to help you ignore your own." He snorted angrily. "It's getting harder and harder to be personal, you know that? To make something personal and keep it that way. What are you smiling at?"

"I wish I had my phone so I could record you and post it online for everybody to hear."

"You're all voyeurs and perverts."

"It's a matter of public record."

"Your personal life isn't supposed to be."

"Having a restraining order against you is. Why can't you let it go?"

"Because it's not a *case*, it's my *wife!* It's my *girls!* It's my life, I can't just file it away in a cardboard box and forget it. You sure can't and you've tried a hell of a lot harder than I have."

"Somebody popped your binder in a high wind and you're running around trying to save each piece of paper."

"That's illuminating Danny. That's frigging helpful."

"Why did you get divorced?"

"It's nothing dramatic. Nobody cheated or anything like that."

"Really."

"Really, Danny. We just grew apart. People do that. People change and society pretends you'll both change in the same way at the same rate, and appreciate each other's changes and all the rest of it. But you don't. You never do. Some marriages are elastic and can take it, others aren't and can't."

"You grew into the Forest Service and she grew into what?"

"A bullshit scene with bullshit friends. Rich and phony."

"Sounds like you were the odd man out."

"And I want my girls out too. That shit is rubbing off on them and I don't like it."

"Did you and Linda try counseling?"

"We went a couple of times. It only served to illustrate how much we don't have in common anymore and aren't going to bother trying to find anything. It made perfectly clear that we haven't been friends for a long time. Just roommates."

"She has a big house."

"And I slept on all the sofas, believe me. I'm the father of her children and I ended up being a tenant waiting to be evicted."

"Is that what happened last Tuesday?"

Pavelko winced. "That was a misunderstanding in the making. And I lost my temper. A little."

"Why? Because there was a guy there?"

"You say that pretty casually, Danny. Casually enough for me to know you've never been in love, not seriously, and have never come close to a situation like that."

"But a guy was there."

"Yeah a guy was there."

"Was it the first time?"

"No."

"So why'd you lose your temper?"

Pavelko shrugged but it was more like he was simply rolling his shoulders after throwing a long pass that missed. "Bad timing I guess."

"Doesn't sound like a misunderstanding."

"A guy sitting on your sofa? His feet up on your coffee table? Drinking your wine? About to go fuck your wife in your bed?"

"You lost your temper."

"Fuck yeah I did. Fucking guy deserved it."

"Sounds like you've failed miserably to put some distance between things too."

"This wasn't twenty-six years ago Danny, this is still breaking news. You're the one that's fucked up."

"But now you are where you are, Mark. You're kind of fucked up too, aren't you?"

Pavelko looked away and sighed. Nodded lightly. "I guess I am. Wouldn't be the first time."

"So what are you going to do? Move back to Chicago and see your kids once a year?"

"Or stay in San Fran and see them about that often? I don't know. Linda and I have some things to work out. My girls are priorities one and one-A. Just because me and Linda can't keep it together doesn't mean they have to have a surrogate father who's a self-absorbed, self-centered asshole."

"Did you land some punches?"

"Apparently I broke his nose."

"Damn."

Pavelko raised his 49ers cap and the bruise on his forehead appeared like a storm on another planet. "I may have headbutted him."

"Damn!"

"So I gotta contend with that when I tell a judge I'm more fit to be my girls' father than the rich punk I made cry in front of them."

"That's going to be a tough sell."

"Yeah I'm not looking forward to it. But I can't be far from my girls, so I gotta figure it out. We'll work something out, me and Linda."

"Think so?"

"Yeah. Sometimes you try so hard to keep things from changing you forget what they actually look like. You start chasing an ideal. An invention."

"Everybody does—it's called hope. But no matter how much effort you put in, life is the universal letdown."

"Man you really are the life of the party. You get that a lot, sunshine? We'll work at Hallmark together."

"Did Carl Tillson ever cross your path?"

"Mine personally? No. Never met him. Never will."

"I mean the task force. Not the task force *within* the task force but the real, actual, authorized, honest-to-God bona fide federally-mandated and taxpayer-funded task force."

"I don't know. Maybe."

"Maybe? When? What happened?"

"The investigation took over a year didn't it? A lot of people crossed our path for one reason or another."

"Obviously Tillson wasn't investigated thoroughly."

"You mean obviously we weren't wearing our swami hats and reading tarot cards that day? What kind of a thing is that to say Danny?"

"How'd he come to your attention in the first place?"

"As if I'm at liberty to say."

"*Somebody's* going to say. Somebody's going to be doing a lot of saying if you guys had Tillson and didn't pick him up."

"Only idiots would say that. Investigators come and go, so do suspects. It shouldn't surprise a so-called veteran crime blogger that law enforcement can't act on everything we *think*. It's not what you *think*, it's what somebody else can *prove* beyond a reasonable doubt in a courtroom two or three years later. Due process ring any bells with you fella?"

"Carl Tillson didn't ring any bells with you? With the task force?"

"I can't say what he did or didn't do until we—until someone—reviews the paper we got on him."

"You have some?"

"Sure. We got some on you too."

"How Hooverish of you."

"Don't flatter yourself, it ain't much and it's a boring read. Your love life is crap."

"Well I'm sorry for you anyway."

Pavelko rolled his eyes.

"I mean it," Danny said. "I'm sorry you put yourself in a bad position."

"Me too. More than that I'm sorry you even know about it." Pavelko drummed his fingers on the roof of the car like a hail of hot resentment. "It's like you got no space left anymore, the scrutiny is overwhelming. You can't even breathe anymore. Everything's a boomerang, you know? It all comes back to you."

"So what did Derek Cavanaugh say happened Thursday night?"

Pavelko rubbed his cheeks, drawing the stubbly skin downward into the sleep or peace of mind he so obviously craved. "He said they were going up to party at the cave. He said he got started early on his own. By the time they bought party favors at a local grocery store he was already fighting with Sondra Jaymes, who died with a blood alcohol content of exactly zero. Nothing's as unfunny as a drunk when you're sober. He says he's pretty sure they met him when they were getting gas at the station across from Malibu Lagoon."

Danny realized he'd been walking in Carl Tillson's footsteps all day. He'd talked to Carrie Voelker at that same gas station before going to the

Malibu Labor Partnership. Looked at the votive candles and the small white cross and the tricolor Mexican flag on the median. In memory of Jorge Ochoa, anonymous and forgotten. Almost.

Pavelko said, "And I hear you have some theories about the body they found *in* the lagoon."

"We're past theories—somebody needs to get those boots. I told Salk about it. Three or four times."

"We got them."

"Aww, you're welcome again. So what happened at the gas station?"

"Derek said while they were getting gas he and Mario Sotillos talked to a guy on the other side of the pump who was dressed like a firefighter—blue t-shirt, the pants with the suspenders, whole nine yards. He was filling up fuel cans with gas and diesel. They start asking him all kinds of questions, what he's doing, if he's helping fight the fire or start one of his own. And in his own words, just not stopping."

Danny imagined the college kids unwittingly stoking a fire whose reach they couldn't comprehend, egging on the big man with the little voice who in the short span of their exchange had decided to kill them all, his way.

"Derek's not sure who left first, him or them, or if somebody said something about the cave. Maybe he just followed them. When they got up to the cave Derek kept drinking, he and Sondra kept fighting, and after a few minutes he left and drove away. He's not feeling too good about that decision today, let me tell you."

The ironic thing was that despite being drunk Cavanaugh had made it all the way down Corral Canyon in the dark, which was hard enough to do sober in the daylight, only to total his BMW on Pacific Coast Highway's relative straightaway.

"Speaking of decisions," Danny said, "I have a question for you."

"Of course you do," Pavelko sighed.

"Were you interfacing with Tracy Orman last night between 8:15 and 11:30?"

Pavelko opened his mouth to say something, then snapped it shut.

"Decisions, decisions, Mark."

"Your true voice yet again Danny. CODA's no better than a tabloid."

"Your non-denial is duly noted. I should have asked what room she was staying in when I was at the hotel."

"You gonna hook up with that reporter? What's her name? Carrie Voelker."

"You *federales* spy too much."

"Your tax dollars at work. It's not what you think. Me and Trace."

"Holed up together in a hotel in the Valley? Seducing her with that I've Come To Save The Bunnies speech?"

"*Lepus californicus*, the Golden State's black-tailed jackrabbit." Pavelko hitched up his jeans. "You watch your tail too, Killer."

"And you keep your mind on yours instead of Tracy's, Marky Mark."

Pavelko fake-laughed as he walked away. "I frigging hate it when he calls me that."

CHAPTER 40

When Carl Wayne Tillson had his first and last out-of-body experience he saw his body from above laying on a flat stone plateau surrounded by a swirling pool of molten fire like a lava flow in the shape of Imelda's cul-de-sac, eating away the uplift below the plateau, which would soon crumble and dissolve under its own angry mass. It felt like his arms and legs were spread wide, as far as he could stretch them, but he could see from here that they were actually trussed up behind his ruined body in white hot handcuffs, his gloved fingers bent like broken twigs.

He could still feel his body through tenuous transparent connections that were snapping one by one like power lines from the heat. The asphalt was a hot skillet against the pitted skin of his cheek, and the taste of the pavement and his own blood gave him an unquenchable thirst. Coarse gravel stuck to his cracked lips like polyps. He felt a terrible weight pressing on him and his head was pounding something fierce as if his nervous system was compensating by hyper-activating what was left of his body that still functioned. It felt like a doctor was drilling through his scalp and through his skull and was scratching the jellied surface of his brain a thousand times a second. Awful pain had a grappling hook in his eye socket and dragged him to the edge of consciousness—and stopped there, right at the edge of the abyss. He didn't pass out. He didn't fall limply into death's gnashing jaws to be quickly and mercifully consumed. This was a slow, prolonged ingestion, inch by inch of the parts of his body he couldn't even feel anymore. He smelled Kools and fuel and his own cindered flesh. He heard mom's voice shouting over the void of silent, dead clocks.

You!

Kill me! Carl screamed. *Shoot me in the head!*

He knew they could hear him but the cops couldn't kill him even when they tried to. Now they were ignoring him, letting him bleed out with the sun baking his burned skin. He wanted to hurry up and die like everyone he'd ever known who was drowning in the flames below him—mom was there, and her favorite convict son who Carl never knew was there, all three of his ex-wives, Imelda and sad Sue and Bonnie the bitch with Mendes the motherfucker right beside her of course, people from his childhood—some he thought he'd long forgotten about, others he still genuinely hated. All of them melting away in a glowing sea of flailing limbs.

Kasho wasn't among them.

Kill me! he coughed. *Kill me!*

In the end it didn't matter that the cops got here as fast as they did and that Kasho was still alive. He'd accomplished as much of the mission as he could. He wouldn't be able to get to Mendes and he wouldn't be able to get back to the store but they'd remember him now. They'd remember him forever because Kasho's survival meant Kasho would be talking about *him* forever. He was immortal now.

It was his own personal counterpoint to mom's so-called thunderclap of silence that happened when souls ascended, except those of the wicked. There would be no silence after this. The soundtrack to his death would be the voices of the news anchors and blabbermouth talking heads and the snoops like Kasho filling the coming days with *him.* Mom couldn't criticize or belittle it and he wouldn't be around to have to listen to it even if she was.

You!

Me.

Carl.

I did this, mom. I did all of this.

This.

Is.

Mine.

The oozing lava dried up and became barren and hard and gray and the plateau abruptly crumbled into dust.

His out-of-body ascension ceased.

Uncertainty sheared his blackened skin and he wavered in mid-air like a glider in a downdraft. He began to disintegrate. The only silence amidst all the noise was his own airless scream, an empty exhalation into an unsparing wind.

CHAPTER 41

The staccato timpani soundtrack martialed viewers' attention to the screen where Justine London's sharp-as-daggers indignation was framed. Danny and three other guests, two men and a woman, formed the familiar quadrangle around Justine's red, white and blue terrier snout.

"*Tonight!* A special edition of The Justine London Show! City of Angels/Dead on Arrival and so is the Angeles Arsonist who's been terrorizing Los Angeles for over a *year!* Crime blogger Danny Kasho was there at the beginning, he was there at the end, and he is here with us *tonight!* Texas Governor Gary Weinrib and lawyer Seth Pratt from the Innocence Mission face off over no less a topic than the *death penalty*—what constitutes cruel and unusual punishment when you're talking about a *child rapist and killer?* The case of monster-in-residence Alexi Packer *the third* sparks tonight's Burning Question! We'll be taking your calls! Betsy MacFarlane aka Betsy McBuff, former adult film star and author of *Betsy MacFarlane Why Are You?* talks about being reborn after porn in our increasingly hedonistic world! Plus as always the latest news, views and reviews *tonight* on the Justine London Show!"

Denise the producer's voice came over the video of the title sequence: "Danny Kasho go in ten seconds, Betsy MacFarlane stand by."

The artist formerly known as Betsy McBuff smiled benignly in plain bangs and a turtleneck with a little gold cross hanging on a delicate chain. The turtleneck looked as alien as a bronze atmospheric diving suit at a luau to viewers in late summer LA.

Danny cleared his throat, took a deep breath and ritualistically touched his legal pad and his headphones and the boom stand holding the pop-filter screen in front of the microphone, picked up his lucky pen and looked steadily at the camera and let the breath out slowly. His lips bent in a tepid smile aimed at the thumbnail-sized camera in his monitor, below the *LOOK HERE* Post-it Note he'd since adorned with brightly-colored doodles of fireworks. LED lighting was good, sound was good.

Another deep breath, and…go.

Onscreen the show's set was replaced by a dark exterior video taken from an airborne platform, a helicopter or drone. It was close so probably a drone. No one had confirmed the assets used in the operation yet. A police officer was standing on the roof of a boxy black SWAT truck, barely visible in the limited lights outside an apartment building, holding a camera on a long pole up to a darkened window.

Justine London commenced her voice-over. There was never any warning when your face would appear so Danny kept smiling.

"Throughout the day we have been riveted by the images coming out of Thousand Oaks, California," Justine intoned. "Police officers responding to a *noise complaint* at an apartment building looked through the window and saw *wires.* There are believed to be *explosive devices* in the apartment wired and ready to blow. Police have turned off electricity in the area, the building and those around it remain evacuated at this hour, the residents displaced with nothing more than the clothes on their back and the fear in their hearts. Danny Kasho, good to have you back."

The scene resolved to a two-shot of Justine in her New York studio and Danny's disembodied face widened by his headphones and his smile in his bedroom, not that Justine London's sizeable viewing audience knew that's where he was with the background in place behind him.

"Thank you," he smiled, "good to be here again. I actually spoke to a woman who lives directly beneath that apartment who had twin babies at home."

"*Twin babies!* Are they safe?"

"I would assume so, Justine."

"And this man, this homicide suspect, arson suspect, *deceased* suspect, Carl Wayne Tillson, 41, of Thousand Oaks, California—he turned his apartment into a *bomb* Danny?"

"His stereo was set on a timer to play music at full volume, it was turned all the way up."

"Let me guess—rap."

"Actually it was techno."

Justine's nose crinkled as if she'd stepped in dog shit in her Manolo Blahniks.

"It looks like his plan was for the police to enter the apartment—"

"Danny excuse me but is it true there was a *tripwire* inside the front door?"

"Yes. That's why it took so long getting in, they had to figure out how to disrupt the first tripwire."

"And what would have happened if that wire *was* tripped Danny?"

"An explosion that would have surely killed the responding officers and possibly everyone else in and around that building."

"It would have killed the *twins!*"

"Without a doubt, Justine." He knew after they showed his third video clip later Justine was going to circle back to tighten this first screw.

Video played of the dominant footage from today—the white and yellow Ventura County Fire Department aerial truck up on stabilizers with its ladder extended sideways over the lawn to the second-floor window of Carl Tillson's apartment during the break and rake—breaking the windows and raking out the blinds and glass shards. Two helmeted bomb squad techs in the basket looked through the empty window frame, assessing the environment inside darkened unit 27. Danny had wondered if Dennis Abner and Candrea Rooney would have wanted to be up there in the basket instead.

"They say there are dozens of explosives in there—*dozens*, Danny?"

"Tillson had a long time to fixate and to fantasize. His engineering skill is what made his obsessive violence so dangerous. It enabled him to turn his fantasy into reality. It enabled him to *become* Fireman666—the Angeles Arsonist."

Justine's jaw dropped. "Fireman666?"

"That's what he called himself. Among other things."

"Yes Danny, there is a book deal in this. So Carl Tillson dressed up in a costume and used a flamethrower to set hundreds of thousands of acres of *public* forest on fire. This land is our land because we *pay* for it! And he burned it to a crisp with his homemade military-grade *flamethrower?* This isn't something you'd use at the back yard barbecue is it Danny?"

"Not unless you wanted your back yard to look like Vietnam. Or Malibu right now."

"Vietnam and Malibu—have they ever been used in the same sentence before tonight folks? Danny they say there are guns in that apartment, ammunition, *chemicals?* Gasoline, unknown machine parts—*machine parts?* What exactly do *chemicals* and *machine parts* constitute Danny?"

"He was a builder, a welder, so the machine parts could be anything metallic, ball bearings, screws, nails—"

"In other words *shrapnel.* You know what I say about the untimely passing of Carl Wayne Tillson? I say *good riddance!* Adios amigo! But the real problem Danny correct me if I'm wrong is determining exactly what *kinds* of explosives are in that apartment. Especially if they're *chemical weapons.* I would think you have to be pretty sure about something like that, after all they are *bombs* not brownies. Doesn't look like we had to go all the way to the Middle East to find WMD's after all did we Danny?"

"You absolutely have to be sure of what you're dealing with, a known explosive device versus an unknown or incendiary device. From what I understand among other things Tillson set up canisters of thermite, which burns too hot for water to put out. He poured ammonium chloride, which is an ingredient in fireworks, in zigzag strips across the floor. Different devices and methods require different approaches."

Justine puckered her lips. "Danny who in their right mind wants to join the bomb squad? Mommy and daddy, when I grow up I want to disarm *bombs* left by *psychopaths* intent on *mass murder!* Sound good? Okay with you mom and dad?"

"They're interesting people. They enjoy puzzles."

"Only *their* puzzles can literally blow up in their *face!* Unsung heroes most of the time, we've seen their skills put to the test all day today. Danny one of the most exciting aspects to this story is that you reportedly met the psycho arsonist bomber himself is that right?"

"We actually met three separate times and he tried to kill me on two of them."

"Sounds like a dysfunctional relationship Danny. Walk us through it."

He began his concise thirty-second sound bite-friendly synopsis of the events of the long weekend starting with meeting Carl Wayne Tillson the self-described volunteer firefighter in Malibu Bowl Friday afternoon. He talked about how Tillson had stalked him—being active and argumentative in the comments section of his blog, lurking in the street outside his home, no doubt keying his car—and finally made contact through the 911 call and the anonymous email.

"He emailed you directly?" Justine London asked.

"Through my blog Red Flag on CODA.com, where I've been covering the fires."

"You actually christened him the Angeles Arsonist, didn't you Danny?"

"Yes I did."

"They're all called something aren't they?"

"So are wildfires. At the end of the day it simply helps delineate them. There's nothing romantic or glamorous about them, they're just tags, that's all."

"What did the email say Danny?"

"For legal reasons I can't quote it exactly—"

"Of course you can't! We don't expect you to. But *in general* what did it say Danny?"

"The gist was that the tipster knew who the Angeles Arsonist was and would tell me if I met with him. It was compelling enough to get me out there to meet him, find out what he had or thought he had. *If* he even showed up." He was careful not to mention the gun.

"You thought you were literally about to meet someone who'd just murdered five people and you didn't call the *police* Danny?"

Justine's second screw beginning to tighten.

"I thought I was going to meet a bona fide tipster at best and a time-consuming crank at worst. I didn't know which it would turn out to be but they'd gone through a lot to convince me to meet them. I get a lot of tips and I give the benefit of the doubt to the good ones. It's my job." Danny knew in his gut that *Wu and Fong NOT strangers Huan market* was a good tip too. Just sitting there, waiting for someone else to get to it first.

"And that's all this was to you?" Justine clarified. "A garden-variety *tip?*"

"Not at all, that's why I went." Danny cleared his throat. "I did not expect to come face to face with Carl Tillson."

"Because people are saying that *you* Danny had the chance to stop this monster right then and there. Sunday night, before he *burned* Imelda Vasquez to death and *murdered* her two children. Before he turned Thousand Oaks into a thousand circles of *hell!* They say *you* didn't call the police because *you* wanted the exclusive *interview.* They say that *you* enabled that man as much as his alleged mechanical prowess. How do you respond to such scathing criticism?"

Justine London was fun when you were holding the Hot Topic sign but she was the first to pry up your pinkie when your grip started to slip.

"I would remind *they* that reporting *is* enabling," Danny said. "It enables the truth to be wrested from the grip of people who'd prefer to keep it all to themselves. Journalists are the Robin Hoods of information." Justine started to say something but he rolled right over her. "The public only knows what it's told—they can either put their trust in the people who spin the news or the people who've gone out and seen the news for themselves, which sometimes carries risk. Ask anyone reporting from a war zone or hot zone. It doesn't serve the public interest to play it safe when you're looking for the truth, for facts, verifiable, incontrovertible facts. Because of what happened Sunday night Tillson posted to my blog again on Monday and we were able to find him. Otherwise he might have had even more time to prepare and who knows what scale of tragedy we'd be talking about tonight."

Justine winked at him. "Isn't trusting a reporter on par with trusting a politician Danny?"

"People have every right to be suspicious of us. I am. That's why I am one."

"What do you say to someone like famed Hollywood movie producer Peter Buckstein whose dream home was reduced to ashes Danny, a home he was building almost with his own hands?"

"I would remind Mr. Buckstein that as sad as his situation is, it's not in the same conversation as Imelda Vasquez's loss or that of the families of the dead students and firefighters. Tragedy followed Carl Tillson everywhere he went, it only differed by degree."

"You followed him too Danny. You went *willingly.*"

"And I always will for a good tip. It might make me vulnerable to hoaxes and weirdoes and stalkers but I make the effort because I might discover something important for the public. *And* law enforcement. If it's garbage or a hoax nobody but me has to know about it."

"Danny I literally wrote the book on weirdo stalkers. Literally wrote the book, you can buy it on Amazon. But this wasn't a hoax was it Danny?"

"It was not. Tillson didn't want to talk or tell me anything. He didn't say anything at all. Once I saw who it was I tried to get him to open up. I tried to get him to talk. All he wanted to do was ambush me and kill me, his way, with his flamethrower.

"We're going to see some of the video you took as well as the incredible portrait you drew of the arsonist and murderer Carl *Whine* Tillson after the break. Face to face with evil—Danny Kasho's incredible story continues after the break and you will not believe your eyes folks! Stay with us!"

The chat window turned blue as the show went to commercial.

The voice of Denise the producer advised, "Danny Kasho three minutes. Betsy MacFarlane stand by."

"Thank you," the former Betsy McBuff beamed with an uplifting trace of hope in her voice as long fingers caressed the cross hanging against her sweater.

Danny looped his headphones around his neck. He drank Sprite from a can and kept his eye on the time code ticking away at the bottom of the blue screen. Garrett had gone to get Chinese takeout from the place on the corner. The apartment was empty and especially quiet with the acoustical foam in place.

He gazed at the completed drawing of the Kasho house in Calendula. He'd fleshed out the texture of the tiles, the seaside sun reflecting gently on the upper windows, the shutters and the trim, and brought the garage more forward than it was in real life so you could see it from the street, which was the perspective he'd used. The garage door was up as it always was when Paul was upstairs, to help ventilate the workshop. The back end of the old Citroën peeked out from under the oil-stained drop cloth. Bicycles leaned together in the shadows beside it, and the tire pump too. Just one end of its pale T-bar handle catching a bit of sunlight, the way it had looked that morning. Danny was the last person to use it before the killer had and the pump vanished. The window in the workshop was open but there was no shadow of the man, no hint of his presence at all. His absence was like the unseen center of a black hole, detectable only by its affect on nearby objects. For a great many people Paul Kasho, like Carl Tillson, had made his existence permanent through pain.

His satisfaction when Lucy told him he was getting two full segments on Justine London tonight was like an adrenaline shot to his battered body. And that wasn't the only one—Lucy had to enlist CODA's intern for help handling the more TV appearances, radio interview requests, a half-dozen phoners, and sort through oodles of internet requests. Triple the amount he did after the Red Flag update about the Backbone Fire. Surfing the Pipeline.

She dispatched CODA contributor Jake Blumenthal to Van Nuys this morning. Jake was decent and decent was light years better than finance goon Patrick Dearing. He was among the first to post the expected news that Charlize Patron had indeed negotiated a plea deal over the long weekend—though the terms were not yet public. In return she agreed to testify against her former boyfriend and employer Nick Mendoza. Once again bonds formed in the heat of the moment proved the easiest to break.

On that note and every other one too Carrie Voelker had fallen silent, leaving Danny to ponder the lonely price of the game they played. He even missed the plasticky Japanese ideograms adorning her texts like neon signs in a back alley. At least Nick Mendoza and Charlize Patron might reunite them, if only for a little while. He heard the old witch Martha Simmons's curse: *Aren't you aiming a little high?*

He wondered how Ursula was doing. Wondered if she was wondering about him, or watching him, or just working through it on her own. Probably by working like him. She could be as pissed off as she pleased. They'd see each other sooner or later unless she quit, and Ursula wouldn't quit. She'd been shaken up but she'd rebound, at which she seemed adept. For him the terror in the cul-de-sac had come so soon after the terror at Decker Canyon that each had tempered the other and been more or less emotionally quarantined together. For now it was working.

Approximately 24 hours after the car bomb detonated the ringing in his ears had lessened but Danny could still clearly hear the screeching when it was quiet. So he'd filled the night and the day since the explosion with noise of one kind or another, staying too busy to dwell on the *what if's* again and thereby make a cozy place for post-traumatic stress to nestle in. Talking about it as if it was a story was easier and, he believed, acceptably therapeutic too which helped rationalize it.

Media wasn't his only obligation today. After three hours of deep prescription-assisted sleep he'd given his complete and updated statement at the West Hollywood sheriff's station, relieved he didn't have to ask Garrett to drive him all the way back to Agoura Hills. No license, no car, no phone. This was living, Middle Ages style.

Detectives Travis Salk and Igor Adjani, Tracy Orman, Pete Costner in a suit instead of a Hawaiian shirt, and the Ventura County detective De la Rocha were among the investigators crowded around a conference table cluttered with laptops and ethernet cables, phones and note pads, coffee cups, soda cans and water bottles. There were binders full of paper on the table. Records—the life of Carl Wayne Tillson distilled into data points to be disassembled and examined for clues to his violence, the red flags floating in all the blood. Danny thought he could still smell Ursula's perfume or shampoo or skin lotion in the room.

"Sixty seconds," advised Denise.

He showed them the pictures he took of Imelda's minivan right before it exploded. He told them he believed it was the vehicle Tillson drove to Decker Canyon and the one he used to kidnap and murder Jorge Ochoa. The detectives believed Ochoa had been killed where he stood. He'd walked into the lagoon on his own, unwitting to the end until Tillson raised the gun to his head. Perhaps he didn't even know then. Perhaps he spent his final second of cognizance trying to figure out the gringo's joke. Forensic specialists were going over the ruins of the minivan but nobody was expecting to recover much of anything with evidentiary value from it except for the chemical compositions of whatever he'd used.

"Mr. Kasho," Salk said when they finally finished up, "I would think being nearly murdered twice in as many days would scare anyone straight, but somehow I doubt it'll help you."

Danny almost said that it had helped scare him straight into the self-medicating embrace of Maker's Mark and Xanax, but he just smiled sheepishly in order to take the expedited no-contest route to the exit. His nightmares of Neil Weber and Imelda Vasquez and the blistering heat of Tillson's flamethrower licking his back were nobody's business but his.

"As flavorful as your website is for the moment," Salk continued, "I have a feeling we might see each other again. If we do I know you won't stay out of harm's way so just do us a favor and stay the hell out of ours from now on."

"Thirty seconds," said Denise.

Salk pointed to the photographs tacked to a board on the wall—pictures of the three dead firefighters, the five students, Imelda Vasquez's enlarged DMV photo and school portraits of her sons Mateo and Carlo. Imelda had succumbed to her injuries overnight, and so was spared both the pain of her injuries and the loss of her children. Jorge Ochoa's picture was fresh, taken at his autopsy this morning.

"Like it or not," Travis Salk said, "you are now part-owner of the space these people used to occupy."

That had bothered Danny ever since, as if the homicide detective had cursed him with the company of his own irascible ghosts. And now here he was, as the picture returned in the chat window and Denise counted him in, riding the news cycle and trying not to fall off.

The show returned with the now-familiar aerial shot of the two body bags being removed from the smoldering ruins of Imelda Vasquez's house. Firefighters stood in solemn lines on either side with their helmets off. The child-sized lumps inside barely bulged the industrial biohazard and blood-borne pathogen-resistant polyethylene, as if the awfulness of dead babies was communicable.

Justine London said "We are back," and the picture switched to the video taken from the first news helicopter over the cul-de-sac yesterday. Danny had watched it throughout the day between interviews, recap footage woven into live shots of the bomb techs working at Tillson's apartment in daylight today. Entering the structure and tackling the intricate traps that waited inside was not something you wanted to do in darkness, or with the slightest amount of fatigue. They had begun at sunup this morning.

"This was the incredible scene yesterday in Thousand Oaks, California," Justine said gravely. "Folks this is *unbelievable* footage. This is straight out of a Hollywood *nightmare.*"

The footage from the news chopper had been edited down to a harrowing sequence. The police airship circled below it at a lower altitude. Fresh smoke coiled up toward them from the exploded minivan. Danny and Ursula were two tiny figures bolting out of the street as the flamethrower's stream reached for them but fell short. He could still feel its heat enough to make him adjust his posture in his chair.

Justine London gaped, "My God, Danny you were *right there!* Who is that with you?"

"Just a friend, Ursula Ruda." All day he'd been mispronouncing it *Rudda* instead of *Rooda* just to piss her off and he didn't mention Crime Time at all. He hadn't seen any of her interviews but he was pretty sure he couldn't receive similar treatment—his name was already stamped all over the Angeles Arsonist's finale. Like a tightrope walker swaying over a gorge he was doing his best to keep things balanced in his favor.

Imelda Vasquez's agony was pixelated like a visual anomaly in the transmission of her death, her body blurred by the producers as she stumbled out of her house into the street, leaving her horror to the viewer's imagination until somebody inevitably posted the raw uncut footage online. They did not blur Carl Tillson's deliberate suicidal march toward the police. His flamethrower's long tongue of fire saturated the screen with a white flare when it erupted, then saturated it again during the fireball.

After an edit a dozen cops warily approached Tillson's smoking body, stepping around the blood, probing him with their feet. He moved, raised his hands, seemingly in surrender—the ACLU was going to make some righteous noise about that. The violence lacked any sound besides the helicopter's whine and one-sided remarks from the pilot answering questions from the on-air anchor back at the station and voicing fuel concerns offline, having just covered a high speed pursuit which ended nearby in Simi Valley.

"Was this suicide by cop, Danny?" Justine asked.

"It absolutely was. The chaparral landscape around Los Angeles burns in a crown fire regime which means when it burns, it burns all the way to the ground, consuming the whole ecosystem. That's a perfect metaphor for Carl Tillson and personalities like his. He didn't try to run or hide or take shelter, he just walked right at them, making sure he gave the police no choice but to kill him so he wouldn't have to do it himself. He was self-centered to the end."

Justine deadpanned into the camera, "I can think of a few more descriptive phrases than *self-centered* but we'd be fined by the FCC."

"He died one year to the day after setting the 80,000 acre Dillon Fire in Little Tujunga Canyon, which is when I first got onto the story. That was already the *seventh* major wildfire he'd set. By then he'd already burned over 150,000 acres of land."

The news helicopter camera zoomed in and out, trying to capture all the elements in play, and just happened to catch Tillson's pickup exploding a block away on Hillcrest. That you could hear over the helicopter, a muffled *whump* slightly delayed from the ejection of smoke which startled the pilot. Nobody but Danny and Ursula had video to match this.

Her cul-de-sac video wasn't as good as his, he had a better angle and you could see more, but she had crucial footage from Tillson's apartment that showed him grabbing the door knob, apparently about to enter the apartment before being interrupted—saved?—by Gandhi and the cops, all of them shouting over the bleating techno. If Danny's wrist had twisted and the door popped free of its housing he would have surely killed them all and everyone else within the potential blast radius and ensuing structural fire and collapse, and he'd be famous for an entirely different reason. The big first screw of it all.

But his hand hadn't moved. The tripwire hadn't been strained, hadn't snapped or pulled or whatever would have happened to initiate the complicated Rube Goldberg-like chain reaction Tillson had devised inside his apartment. Danny had imagined the big bear-like man crouching and ducking and stepping carefully as he moved around inside the cramped room with its hoarder-like conditions, a misstep away from prematurely initiating the disaster himself.

"Graphic ground-level footage from inside the cul-de-sac of *hell* shot by Danny Kasho, the LA crime blogger who tracked Carl Wayne Tillson aka the Angeles Arsonist to his *doorstep*. This is exclusive footage never seen before, folks. We have *three* videos to show you. Danny, set them up for us."

The exclusivity thing wasn't exactly true—this was the first time his videos were being shown on TV. CODA had already posted them as well as his Malibu Bowl interview with Tillson. He'd sent the three clips to Justine London's producer Denise but didn't know how they'd edit them for broadcast. He assumed severely.

He said, "I had just called the police after finding out where the still-unknown suspect was posting to my blog from."

"He was posting comments on your website is that right Danny?"

"Right, on Red Flag which I blog on CODA.com." He practically heard the slap of Lucy and Ronald Schiff high-fiving. "I'd gone to verify the address *after* I called the police and I saw a vehicle that looked like the one I saw the night before at Decker Canyon—the minivan driven by the arsonist which I had already described to police. That's when Tillson came into the cul-de-sac. He was coming straight toward me."

"Oh my good Lord, Danny."

"Imelda Vasquez's house was already burning so he must have started a fire in there first, maybe with a timed start for a delay, and then walked around through a neighbor's yard. We tried to hide behind a car but we couldn't, it wasn't safe, so we ran toward the houses at the end of the street."

"*Into* the dead end street Danny?"

"There was nowhere else to go Justine. I wasn't about to knock on someone's door and bring Tillson's fury into their home. Just then I heard gunshots, like automatic fire but way more, like a string of firecrackers popping off. At first I thought the police had arrived but the shots sounded like they were coming from *inside* the burning house. At that moment I realized we were trapped."

"Trapped between a lunatic intending to *burn you alive* and an unknown shooter *inside* a burning house! Barricaded suspect situations frequently end as burning structures and *dead* barricaded suspect situations don't they Danny? What happened next?"

"We were just starting to run toward the house next door to it because it was the closest thing to shelter, when the bomb went off in the minivan."

"The car you were nosed up to just *seconds* before?"

"Right. I was less than a hundred feet from it when it exploded."

"The fact that you're here tonight is a miracle isn't it Danny?"

"It's something, Justine."

"Then what did you do?"

"I ran back to the SUV we had tried to hide behind before, it was damaged by debris from the explosion, just because there was nowhere else to go at that point. Fortunately the police arrived and distracted Tillson, and that's when I was finally able to start videoing."

And with that Justine London's bright blue eyes narrowed to foreboding slits as she faced directly into her main camera. "Folks although this has been edited for content, viewer discretion is *strongly advised.* Leave the room *now* if you can't stand the sight of a murderous psychopath exercising his right to a speedy trip straight to *hell.* This is *America* folks. This is yesterday. This is *right here."*

The first video was 38 seconds long. Danny was proud of its graphic nakedness—on-scene video like this was as close as you could get without being there and was always engaging. But this being television they'd do what they thought they had to do to keep it accessible by their idea of what constituted a mainstream viewing audience.

The clip began with Tillson's march toward the initial responding police officers. The cops opened fire, thin-sounding snaps compared to the unearthly hoarse roar of the flamethrower. Ricochets hacked loudly into the Durango over Ursula's cries and Danny's bleeped-out expletives, his lips close to the mic of his camera. He narrated it today coolly and sparingly, distancing himself emotionally from the event by focusing on it editorially, as optimal frames, much as he'd learned to do with his childhood—Tillson down on one knee, Imelda Vasquez screaming horribly in the background. This footage could not have been in greater contrast to the news chopper's clinical distance.

Then Tillson stood up and resumed his death march into a fresh hail of police bullets. The two loud gunshots were clearly audible before the fuel tanks ruptured and Tillson was engulfed in the fireball.

The video abruptly ended.

Justine London gasped, "Oh my *God."*

Two shots. Loud and close to where he and Ursula had been. The police were massed at the entrance to the cul-de-sac and their gunfire sounded roughly the same—the same calibers at the same distance. Those two shots did not match the others and he hadn't solved their origin. One of those two shots, he believed, was the round that ignited the remaining fuel in Tillson's tanks, effectively ending the attack.

"Now folks," Justine London was saying, "this is the second clip, and hold on to your seats."

The second clip lasted 2:14 and was the eeriest. It was taken from behind the Durango but upright instead of in the limited view from underneath the vehicle so Danny captured a good view of the firefighters' entry into the smoke-filled street with fire extinguishers for Imelda. He panned over to get the smoking minivan door on top of the ruined Durango, then back out to the street. Tillson was disarmed and cuffed and his helmet and facemask removed. His camera's digital zoom didn't pixelate too badly and the close-up of Tillson's injured face was clearly visible—admittedly Ursula with her fancy camera got a better shot—though far from high definition. The producers left it as is. Tillson's lips were moving but you couldn't hear him.

"Danny what is he saying?" Justine London asked. "Could you hear him?"

"He was begging for help."

"For himself?"

"Right."

"Did someone tell him to take a number?"

Then Tillson saw Danny and looked right into the camera, which still gave Danny goosebumps, and started shouting.

Justine squinted as if it would help her discern his words. "What is he screaming at you Danny?"

He cleared his throat. "Kill Kasho, I think."

"Oh my God Danny."

In the background doors opened and neighbors crept out of their houses, stepping cautiously away from shelter as embers started to fall around the cul-de-sac. Even though he expected it the sight of the smoke a moment before the crack of the pickup exploding still gave him a jolt. Justine visibly flinched too. His excessive swearing was bleeped out again and his hands shook but his camera kept recording as firefighters and police ducked, then continued with their work.

"That was his own vehicle?" Justine asked. "The pickup truck he had modified to look like an official vehicle of some sort Danny?"

"Right. He wired up two car bombs as well as his apartment. The fire he started at Imelda's set off the arsenal he kept there. He weaponized everything he possibly could."

"All that remained was for him to kill innocent people," Justine flared her nostrils with finality, "and to die."

The producers blurred what portions of Imelda's burned body were visible through the firefighters tending to her but kept a clear view of Tillson, staring as long as he could into Danny's camera as he was moved out of the street by the cops, even closer so the severity of his head wound could be better seen. The ambulance for Imelda and the first fire engine rolled past behind them. The view of Carl Tillson's single eye fixed on the camera was interrupted by the cop. *Hey!* Pointing at the camera. *You two—get back inside!* The clip ended with a view of the chunks of the broken safety glass on the driveway. Ursula's video ended the same way.

Back to the two-shot.

"Do you feel he had a personal vendetta against you Danny?"

"I do, Justine, I really do. He pursued me, stalked me, coerced me into meeting him so he could ambush me. I came to talk, he came to kill."

"But why you?"

"We know he followed the news so he had to know about Red Flag. Maybe he didn't like the attention I was getting instead of him, or maybe that I didn't post the Malibu Bowl interview with him—before I knew who he was. Who knows. I can't answer that question. There's a lot of questions I can't answer Justine. All I know is if the police didn't get there when they did he'd have killed us. We had no place to go and his fuel tanks were still practically full at that point. Full enough to do the job anyway."

Justine said, "Now Danny the third clip is *fascinating.* Taken at the *bomb-filled apartment* moments before police evacuated the building. Did you have any idea you were standing inches away from certain *death?*"

"No idea at all. I was thinking maybe there could be another victim inside, someone who needed help, that was about it. Just my naturally helpful instinct taking over."

"If only there were more people like you Danny Kasho."

He almost said Amen.

The third clip was 1:08 long and began at the top of the stairs of the Shangri-La, looking down the row of open apartments toward the closed door of unit 27. The music was distorted into crackling white noise with percussive bursts on every downbeat as if Danny was tapping the camera's microphone with his finger. Nothing could be seen through his reflection in the window and the cracks in the Venetian blinds apart from a blurry texture that gave the appearance something had been pushed up against the window. He reached out and touched the door knob, held his hand there for agonizingly long seconds, and then Gandhi and the two cops arrived, very obviously busting them. *Who are you?* Unfortunately the show kept that part in.

Justine said, "Danny it looks like you were about to open the door. You grabbed the handle didn't you?" Circling back to tighten down that first screw.

"I did. The door looked unlocked and I thought there could be someone in there so there was that natural temptation to help. But then I thought—wait a minute, this guy's an engineer, he's an inventor, he's already blown up two cars, he could have done something here too."

"And thank God, Danny, thank *God* you had the presence of mind to do that."

He nodded somberly. "Yes."

"Incredible," Justine London said approvingly. "Now folks, take a look at *this.*"

His complete and colored drawing of Carl Tillson's Fireman666 costume appeared onscreen—also first published earlier today on CODA, about fifteen minutes after he finished and scanned it. Daylight had enabled him to add the details missing from his Decker Canyon sketch and listening to Justine London gush over it now on national TV gave him a ripple of guilty pride. After all his talent wasn't his at all but a going-away present from Killer Kasho. The seriously *ill* Killer Kasho. The commercial artist in Paul would have thought creating something "viral" just meant he had done his job, and dismissed the fleeting opportunity to brag. Paul had always encouraged his youngest son, and long after his champion's voice was silenced the act of drawing had become a kind of séance with the spirit of the father he should have had.

"This is the only rendering of the Angeles Arsonist's terrifying costume," Justine said. "This is incredible, folks. Danny—*wow.* This guy was a world-class *freakazoid.*"

"That is how Carl Tillson saw himself when he peeled back his façade, the false face he presented to the rest of us every day. When he looked at himself in the mirror, this is what he saw."

"The volunteer fire*fighter,*" Justine spat, then smacked her palm on her polished studio desk. "We will speak no more of the killer, the thief of lives, babies' lives, *precious* lives. Instead we will speak of the innocent, helpless *victims.* We will speak of the inexplicable, unnatural *loss,* the empty vacuum left by young lives snuffed out just as they were getting *started.* Death doesn't speak for them Danny—*we* have to. And so let's take a moment to hear the names, to acknowledge the loss we as a so-called *civilized* society suffer whenever we are robbed of the good and the decent and the *pure.*"

Danny bowed his head a little and hoped it didn't cause too much of a reflection off his forehead.

"Imelda Vasquez, her sons Mateo and Carlo, ages four and six, an entire young family *murdered* in their own home in Thousand Oaks. Katie Martyn, Lisa Higgins, Sondra Jaymes, Mario Sotillos, Neil Weber, college friends *murdered* in a Malibu cave. Captain Jason Hertzog and Specialist Brian Rollins, U.S. Forest Service firefighters *murdered* by the so-called Backbone wildfire raging across Malibu. Firefighter Specialist Richard Segers, LA County Fire Department, *murdered* last year fighting the devastating Chalk Fire in Stevenson Ranch. And last but not least, according to you Danny Kasho—an undocumented worker named Jorge

Ochoa, probably a father, certainly a brother and cousin, a supposed suicide, you say he was actually *murdered* and his body dumped in a lagoon wearing the arsonist's *boots?* His *boots*, Danny?"

"That hasn't been officially confirmed yet."

"But…?"

"But I think Tillson was coming apart mentally and when the existence of the boot prints he left by the cave was divulged he panicked. Jorge Ochoa was just in the wrong place at the wrong time."

"You had some harsh words for the DA about that didn't you?"

"She's a *deputy* DA and I still do have harsh words for her pivotal mishandling of privileged information. Critical details confidential to the investigators." He'd prepared with one of his favorite sayings: "Journalism isn't just the first rough draft of history, it comforts the afflicted and afflicts the comfortable. Jorge Ochoa might still be alive if not for Amy Childress." He knew that was going to cause a firestorm and he welcomed the fight—he was going to single-handedly position CODA's anti-Childress stance whether Lucy or Ronald Schiff or even William Craig agreed. Well maybe not Craig, but he'd go to blows with Ron and Lucy over it.

"Danny Kasho," Justine said in closing, "you have served your community well. I know we'll be seeing more of you in the future. When we come back, former adult *actress* Betsy MacFarlane aka Betsy McBuff, author of *Betsy MacFarlane Why Are You?* talks about being reborn after porn in our increasingly hedonistic world. And given the state of the world in Thousand Oaks, California today Danny, I say to her—I hope you had fun the first time."

"Me too," he said, but the show had gone to commercial and he was cut off.

CHAPTER 42

The primary blue sky over Pepperdine University was untarnished by smoke, the purity of its color challenged only by the emerald green of its vast lawn which boasted an even larger audience today than it did for the vigil three days ago.

The heat wave had broken. At 100 degrees the air changed, you could feel it without having to consult a thermometer, and today was appreciably cooler—all the way down to the mid-90s. An impossibly beautiful day to mourn the death of children, as if Nature itself was mocking the dead for missing out. Without the physical reminders of scorched earth and gutted families Carl Tillson's legacy of pain could be practically eradicated by the sunshine.

With milder weather crews battling the Backbone Fire had switched to direct attack. The stats of the blaze six days after ignition at 90% containment stood at 8800 total acres burned, 29 single and multiple family structures destroyed, 4 mobile homes destroyed, 21 vehicles damaged, 42 destroyed, 2 firefighters killed, over 200 injured. Estimated total private property value loss was already over a hundred million dollars.

Carl Wayne Tillson's preliminary autopsy findings were released this morning pending toxicology and results of DNA tests on the cup found at the Dillon Fire. Tillson had been shot 22 times by five different sheriff's deputies who fired a total of 53 rounds during the engagement. The cops' body cam footage had yet to be released to the irritation of the ACLU. Tillson's body lay in the street for nearly an hour but he was alive for approximately half that long before dying of blood loss—suggesting that had immediate medical attention been rendered his life might have been saved. Another point of disorder for ACLU lawyers to identify. Whatever the litigious denouement Danny's video clips were sure to figure prominently for both sides. Lucy said that William Craig was "aware of their significance." Lucy didn't volunteer anything more and he didn't pursue it.

He worked his way through the blue and orange sea of embraces and tears with his camera and a sympathetic face, roaming the crowd as stiffly as if he had a cane or a back brace, recording the grief of students expressing the wrenching transition from loss to remembrance like a pain collector filling his battered old valise full of sorrows. Even though he hardly used it anymore he already missed his old-fashioned but indefatigable Dictaphone. It was the audio equivalent of the courtroom sketch in the digital age of the omnipresent video camera but he'd had it ever since he started at CODA and was attached to its durable simplicity. There had undoubtedly been some old audio notes still embedded in its tiny cassette tape, distant echoes of forgotten things which had positively screamed their importance at the time.

In between getting a new phone and the obligatory calls to his bank and credit card companies he emailed Suge to thank him and to tell him the *federales* were so impressed by his work that they wanted to offer him the chance to put on a tie. Maybe he could get away with a clip-on. Suge replied, *Fight the power. Glad I could help. Nice work man.* His approval meant more than all the media requests combined. Credibility counted.

He posted the picture Tillson took of him outside his apartment building and he was working on the text of Code Four, the police code for no further assistance needed and his traditional title for the last entry of a piece, usually reserved for the sentencing and final thoughts. With Tillson's death it would likely be the last substantial update ever to Red Flag, a tangible separation after a whole year, as the case wound down into its denouement of damage assessments, blame assignation, and civil lawsuit cash-ins.

With two bothersome exceptions.

The gunshots Danny heard immediately before Tillson's tanks exploded, the two that were so clearly louder than the others on his first video clip. How different they sounded from the bristling police gunfire. How much nearer to he and Ursula, hiding behind the Durango, they had been fired. As close as the neighboring property. Closer maybe. It was impossible to tell conclusively from the video, but he was sure one of those two shots was the strike that caused the remaining fuel to erupt all at once. Tillson walked into a concentrated field of fire massed at the entrance to the cul-de-sac. But it was a shot from the *side* that effectively ended him.

Danny had already floated the "second shooter" theory—the cops being a cumulative "first shooter" for purposes of the argument—in an update to the post with the video. Now speculation was running rampant through the Red Flag comments community and far, far beyond. If two shots were fired and one bullet hit—then there was a missing bullet waiting to be found in the cul-de-sac, lodged in someone's house or car or tree, lost so far among the fire and explosion damage. Another shooter changed the complexion of the whole thing. But the cul-de-sac remained closed as police continued to work the scene and to discourage amateur detectives and looky-loos.

Just like his body Carl Tillson's life was being autopsied as the press went to work on his existence in tandem with the police and government agencies. Social media was the public's point of entry. His creepy Facebook page featured pictures of him dressed like a wildland firefighter, videos of firefighters in action, tributes to fallen firefighters. Lots of eye-wearying animated .gifs. It had been taken down but not before the contents were copied and disseminated across the web for posterity. There was no evidence Tillson did any actual firefighting—he'd applied to several different departments in Southern California and taken some classes, but in the end Carl Tillson was just a big man playing dress-up and threatening people because he could. Exposed in daylight without his Fireman666 costume and flamethrower he was a visually forgettable stranger, an overweight predator totally dependent on solitude when laying siege to a chaparral stand and surprise when attacking humans.

He had worked at Best Value in Malibu for nearly seven years. He'd never been promoted and had no known friends. He was typically scheduled to work Saturdays noon to nine, though he was habitually tardy, and usually had Tuesdays and Wednesdays off. Danny pictured him driving the forklift around the garden center with its open air and mesh screen like an aviary, the smell of Backbone's drifting smoke more intoxicating than the scent from the flats of flowers for sale. He'd probably been turned on the whole time. He'd used his employee discount liberally which had so far all but confirmed suspicions that it was how he assembled the bulk of his flamethrower. In fact there was every indication the device at the cul-de-sac wasn't his first, merely his most advanced—earlier models may have been used to start earlier fires, then discarded or cannibalized for successive models.

It took authorities until this morning to work through all the circuits and collapsing circuits wired inside Tillson's apartment once a robot disabled the initial tripwire. Bomb squad members then entered the apartment to begin disarming, photographing, removing and cataloguing the extensive contents. Once again Danny thought about Dennis Abner and Candrea Rooney. Surely with a scene this complex they'd been involved, helping to disassemble the puzzle to see the picture. He could still feel his fingertips on the unusually cool stainless steel doorknob of unit 27. Imelda's minivan had been a mere hundred feet away, but that room full of explosive chemical reactions and nails and ball bearings had been only a few feet away and potentially magnitudes more powerful. The knob had wiggled almost loosely in its housing, inviting just the slightest effort to turn it and apply weight and push it open enough to unleash the shrapnel-laced deflagration that would have ripped his body into unrecognizable half-vaporized pieces of gory biological lab specimens. And Rosario's twins in the apartment below, their tininess sure to vanish in the rubble and debris.

Inside unit 27 with the chemicals and wires and madness was the answer to what Tillson's last post on Red Flag meant, *Tell Mendes to kiss my ass.* There were three stacks each of 250 color photocopies apparently made on a machine in the Best Value office of the honorable Sam Mendes, the judge in Carl's divorce from his second wife Bonnie Tillson in Oxnard in 2016. Apparently Carl took umbrage with the amount of child support he was obligated to pay, and at his last court appearance became belligerent and had to be removed from the courtroom. Witnesses said he kept shouting that the system was out to get him. He'd since taken to hanging copy after copy of the picture on his walls to desecrate one after the other with sharp objects. Danny was unsurprised but unimpressed that Tillson's IQ had scored high on a court-mandated psych eval during the divorce proceedings.

Local NBC channel 17 in Bakersfield, a medium-sized gold rush way station of a town made permanent by the discovery of oil in a wide, diminishing agricultural valley a hundred miles north of LA, identified a woman whose badly burned body was found in a mobile home fire early Monday morning as Connie Tillson, 68, a reclusive longtime resident of the Royal Palms trailer park on Columbus Street. Connie was the mother of Carl Wayne, her sixth and youngest child. Witnesses at the trailer park said her son visited her regularly, usually driving his white pickup with the telltale red stripe down the side but sometimes another vehicle, a green minivan. Carl would have driven past Fort Tejon on the I-5 to and from Bakersfield. Danny wondered if finally setting a fire there—his second, two weeks after Hillcrest in Thousand Oaks behind Imelda Vasquez's house—had relieved stress going or coming from Connie Tillson's trailer.

A tantalizing anomaly in Carl Tillson's digital footprint had yet to be resolved—on Saturday he purchased an airline ticket online one-way to Des Moines for $278 using a credit card in Imelda's name. Authorities were trying to determine if he knew anyone there or had any connection to the city. Danny wondered if suicide by cop wasn't his original plan. Perhaps an ever-delusional survival instinct had been conning Carl into thinking maybe, just maybe, he could get away with everything he'd done and then hide like a war criminal among a civilian population.

Jorge Ochoa's autopsy could not determine if the head wound was self-inflicted or not, but there were no defensive wounds on his hands or arms and no water in his lungs, indicating Jorge wasn't breathing when his body went into the water of the lagoon. The Ruger .22 recovered at the scene was sold in 2016 to a man in Tennessee who had since died. A throw-away gun Tillson had bought somewhere.

Danny posted the photo he took of Jorge and Luis's Rosarito picture. There was no memorial for the day laborer except for a handful of immigrants' rights activists outside the federal building in Westwood, not far from where the remains of Pepperdine student Sondra Jaymes would be interred tomorrow at the famous Pierce Brothers cemetery, home to many entertainment industry legends. Then so on in succession until all five families had put their young loved ones in the ground. The body of Lisa Higgins had been flown back to Colorado accompanied by her bereaved family; she would be inserted into friendly soil instead of the dusty California dirt in which she'd died in terror. One funeral after the other to give fellow students and friends the chance to attend all four local services. Days and days of dead children.

In his blog Danny voiced passing support for immigration reform, whatever that really meant in practice, and didn't know if it came off as sympathetic or just an attempt to *look* sympathetic in the face of a loss as minor as an undocumented worker whose place on the sidewalk in front of Best Value hardware had already been filled with a fresh pair of boots. Murdered by a complete stranger who valued Jorge's life by the amount of time he thought ending it would buy him. Psycho logic, not criminal genius.

Danny culled Peter Buckstein's CV from the net but hadn't reached out to him for an interview yet. Hadn't even tried to. Now who was being a baby chicken.

Today the props from Sunday's vigil had been enhanced with larger crosses and bigger photographs of the Pepperdine Five. A solemn train of speakers—many friends but a few family members too—made stops at the podium. Danny got some good shots of the Reverend Randall with two L's Clarke in a pale suit the color of Katie Martyn's Acura after the paint had burned away, sermonizing with his finger upraised to the sky as if the blazing sun was his own shiny ring to wear. He couldn't help but wonder what kind of service Paul Kasho would warrant in prison. Or the prison hospital. What sort of memorial the man even deserved.

He spotted Ursula in the media encampment near the stage. He recognized most of the reporters with her too and took a deep breath, preparing to bluff, joke, and stall his way through the service. Reinforced by overdoses of ibuprofen and an Ace bandage around his ankle he threaded his way through the mourning students and entered the scrum of reporters and photographers. Reaction to him was muted because of the circumstances, expressions and murmurs a mix of congratulations and scorn. Most of them gave him a longer look than necessary to let him know that as soon as the memorial was over they'd each have a camera in *his* face.

He squeezed in beside Ursula and nudged her elbow. "Sorry I called you a powder-puff pastry chef."

She didn't acknowledge him. She was wearing different sunglasses, not her rectangular clip-ons over the prescription lenses. These were bigger, less practical and more fashionable, with an outsized logo on the hinges. Her hair was down, covering her ears. He assumed she had a back-up hearing aid in too, one that was probably bigger, more noticeable, less calibrated, like an old prescription. She wore the same goddamned safari vest over a white cotton t-shirt and was holding her fancy camera to her eye as if something remarkable was about to happen.

"How are you holding up?" he asked.

"Don't patronize me shithead," she said out of the side of her mouth.

Another reporter shushed them, one of the quasi-hot Fox girls who came and went with unremarkable regularity. This one was petite and sort of Polynesian-looking and teetering in Cirque du Soleil-high heels and would probably next appear in a small role during team coverage of a Hollywood awards show. Or an ill-fated mid-season reality show replacement program if she was truly endowed with good fortune.

Danny said to Ursula, "I was worried about you."

She lowered her camera but didn't look at him. She'd opted to go *au naturel* with the cut on her cheek instead of gauzed and taped. She'd camouflaged it with cover-up makeup, just subtly enough for a one-time deflection. The wound was serious enough to possibly scar, leaving her branded by the decisions she'd involuntarily revisit whenever someone's eyes fell to the mark on her right cheek. "I don't need your concern," she said, her words clipped like from one of Garrett's robot voice effects, "I need you to stay away from me."

"Like it or not we're sort of joined at the hip on this one."

"That's funny considering how far out of your stupid way you've been going to say my name wrong."

Justine London had been the start of it. Since then he'd done six more local, network and cable news shows, phoners with local and syndicated radio and satellite news channels. Lucy helped him settle on four video chats to do with select news websites; he still had two of those to do.

He said, "You've gotten press too and I didn't see my name. Oh wait, yes I did."

"I was the reason you were there in the first place and everyone's going to find out. You're a selfish, stupid shithead."

"GPS alone doesn't deal you in. You've got a long way to go before you're Betty Bernstein to my Woody Woodward."

"Seriously, *shut up,"* the Fox reporteress hissed. Her mouth was puffed up like Dalí's Mae West lips sofa and her eyelashes threatened to bat into the air and attack them both.

"Like it or not," he murmured to Ursula, "we're cross-promoting each other. We should make peace, work together for the good of our fellow man."

"Maybe when you get your facts straight and start being honest."

"You ought to get *your* facts straight, sweet cheeks—remember when I warned you to stay off my story? Maybe I wasn't talking into your good ear."

"You're going to look like the fraud you really are, mark my words."

"I'm going to look like an award-winning journalist, that's what I'm going to look like. Oh wait, I already do 'cause I already am. This is how hard I work for the money, honey. Now you know."

"You get by with a little help from your friends is more like it."

"Why can't we be friends?"

"'Cause you're a stupid selfish shithead that's why!"

The Fox reporter made a noise in the back of her throat and stamped a heel soundlessly into the grass. "Okay guys, seriously? For real? Are you kidding me? *Take it somewhere.*"

Five doves were suddenly released into the air, fluttering wildly around the lowest drones and up past the university's obelisk spearing the sky like a headstone at a mass grave. People gasped, applauded, wept, and concentrated on getting good video on their phones.

Danny leaned toward Ursula. "Is Dime Time happy you got a piece?"

She snatched up her bag at her feet. "A piece of what? The serial arsonist or the serial asshole who egged him on?" She wedged through the blue and orange crowd like a safari-colored torpedo.

Danny followed her. "Oh hey there Geronimo? Who egged who on? You wanted to see what happened as much as I did."

"If it wasn't for me you'd still be sitting in your car hoping your good story came back to find you," she shouted over her shoulder.

"Reprinting Amy Childress's speeches only goes so far. What are you anyway, her lobbyist? PR guru? You should thank me for giving you the gift of a good story for a change."

"If I hadn't written that Jorge Ochoa was a day laborer you'd have never found the boots. *My* readers will know that you're greedy and you're reckless and you don't care what you do or who you screw along the way as long as you get what you want. Stay away from me Danny, you're a shithead."

"Actually I'm a GEM—I Go the Extra Mile."

Ursula stopped so suddenly he ran into her. She shoved him back an arm's length and snarled, "You're a *mistake!* I don't want it to happen again! Ever! I don't want *you* to happen again! Keep doing what you're doing Danny, get yourself killed if that's what you want to do, but stay away from me. Understand? Stay away from me!"

"Fine, forget it—I just asked if you were okay, I wasn't looking for a dissertation on whatever it is you're talking about."

"You're hazardous waste!" she yelled.

He made a face. "Hazardous waste?"

Ursula stalked away a few steps, then turned around again, pushed her sunglasses up onto her forehead and said, "Imelda Vasquez's children shouldn't have been kept from living normal lives just because the son of Killer Kasho was." She glared at him long enough to make sure he saw her delivering the double-tap coolly and professionally, no hard feelings. Then she lowered her sunglasses, turned and kept walking.

Danny let her go. He'd think of a clever retort later, when he was by himself, but there was nothing right now. His mind was a frustrating blank.

In a few days the green alien head antenna ball he ordered online would arrive to her attention at Crime Time's Koreatown address. A note would be included with one word—*Geronimo.* Whether she tossed it or not didn't matter. Whether her new car even had an antenna to stick it on didn't matter. He felt better for doing it so he wrote off the donation with a heartfelt *whatever.*

Last night he'd Skyped with Cynthia. Victor was supposed to join them somehow but something had come up. Danny didn't ask what and was relieved anyway—it would be easier without him. He was drowning a Xanax in ice cold sake and was as mellow and calm as he'd been in days.

Cynthia's hair was scrunched up in a clip on top of her head and she looked tired, like she'd just finished the last of the chores before bed. "Will said with all the trouble you went through you should write a book."

"About the trouble or the story?"

"Can't you use one to explain the other? Danny I appreciate what you do—we both do—and I know you can't choose what you're good at in life, but we'd like you to live it long enough to visit us." Cynthia rubbed her belly through her t-shirt. "All four of us. Geez Danny—Celia's already *six* and she's never even met you. And you're going to be an uncle again."

"I promise I'll visit soon. I want to see you guys too."

He told her about Paul's move to CDF from Solano and what it likely meant. CDF was full of seriously ill, aged and terminal prisoners. You went in a person and came out as the contents of an urn, about five pounds. They recycled the wheelchairs. That's where dad was now. Dying in prison at the old age of sixty-eight.

"But he wasn't given a life sentence," Cynthia said, dabbing with a Kleenex at the tears welling in her eyes. "He shouldn't still *be* there."

"Has he ever come up for parole?"

"How should I know?"

"Did Vanessa ever mention anything?"

"No, you know that. I'd have told you." She blew her nose. "But I think I know who might know."

"Who?"

"Remember dad's lawyer? Bernie Ehrenpreiss? He still lives here. I got his number for you."

"For me?"

"You know what I mean. He might know someone. Ready?"

Frowning, Danny grabbed a pen and wrote it down. Same old area code. He knew the lawyer's name of course but had no recollection of ever meeting the man he'd heard sometimes referred to as a family friend. And there weren't many of those.

"Maybe he knows Gary Calder too," Cynthia suggested.

"Guess we'll see."

"I'm glad you're giving us the chance to, Danny."

Maybe Gina the actress would give *him* a chance of some kind, but even Holiest of Holies Michelle seemed like a long shot today. He took a couple pictures of Ursula but the digital zoom on his camera wasn't great at that distance. He needed to get close.

And so he had, and so he would again.

He took a few more pictures of the student memorial, others of nothing in particular just to dissipate his irritation.

Hazardous waste?

He heard birds for the first time in days and felt very small here between the ocean and the hills burned bare, on lush green grass aimed only at the sun and not at an arsonist's point of origin.

CHAPTER 43

The iron handrails flanking the six stone steps were presumably designed to inspire the sense of welcoming arms offering encouragement and support to the visitor come to call. Terracotta pots overflowing with flowers that looked like out of season poinsettias blooming colorfully and compactly squeezed the approach up the steps which tapered as they rose to the arched front door, made of heavy wood and partially shaded by a decorative nylon awning. The outside light and mailbox were to the right on the wall which rose around to the second story of the house. The doorbell was inlaid to the left of the door, on the same side as the bay window of the living room.

He pressed the flat of his thumb onto the doorbell and held it there for a couple seconds. He heard nothing from inside. He took the knocker which no longer sported a plastic pineapple and banged it onto the door three times, firmly. It was a spacious house, no telling where someone was or if anyone was even home. He thought there was though—the news vans had gone and things had returned to apparent normal on the street.

A true friend was the one who answered the distress call no matter the hour and Danny was deeply comforted knowing he had one in Garrett, who had been watching the unfolding coverage from Thousand Oaks on TV, unaware that Danny was right in the middle of it. He arrived to pick him up at the edge of the police perimeter Monday night like salvation itself, bringing water, some almonds and a Valium, whatever he could grab on his way out the door. Danny gratefully devoured it all.

The last thing he had asked of his stalwart amigo was to drive him back to Thousand Oaks yesterday to retrieve his car yet again. Even without a temporary license he was determined to get his wheels back. His messenger bag and the contents of his J-kit had to be replaced, but they could be. Maybe the Louis Vuitton couldn't, but everything else could—even the expensive as hell Sony camcorder, which was a write-off but still came out of pocket. The official media parking permit on the other hand was of such singular value that he wasn't finally free of the anxious knot in his belly until he unlocked his scratched and dirty Accord with his spare key and found it safe and sound in the glovebox.

After all these years he knew exactly how much of the Killer Kasho story he'd told Garrett, keeping track was second nature to him, living the great omission. He felt like an imposter living in the pockets of space he'd elbowed out between truth and revelation. It wasn't fair to Garrett. It wasn't fair to him either, he'd just learned to live with it, but he realized after all this that he didn't know how best to thank Garrett—more Maker's Mark? More Xanax? What was a fitting appreciation of how far above and beyond his roommate had gone for him?

"Danny, you are the most consistently interesting person I know," Garrett had said on their way across the Valley with another drive-through bonanza of greasy fried goodness spread across wax paper in their laps. "But dial it down man, dial it *down*. Who's that reporter you're all up into?"

"Carrie Voelker. There may have been a minor setback with that."

"Like Inglewood minor? I am truly sorry to hear that Casanova, but she *is* a little above your pay grade."

Danny grunted.

"And I'm not just saying that because I'm pissed over the whole stealing my gun and almost getting yourself killed twice in two days thing," Garrett said. "Put all that aside for a moment if you will. My point is that what Carrie Voelker does is *reporting*—wrap the news up with red lips and great tits and sing me all the woes of the world. What *you* do my friend is kamikaze journalism. Like those kooks who go live in the wilderness because they think bears are cool and then they get eaten by them. You think the end doesn't come as a surprise to them too? And then we have to shoot the bear like it's the bear's fault lunch wore Levis that day. *Report,* Danny—that's your job, to do more of Carrie's kind of reporting."

"I wish I could do more of her anything but I think that ship has sailed."

"Then start swimming brother. You got a halo around your heart that totally undercuts your efforts to come across as a steely-eyed bad ass. You ain't no Lee Van Cleef."

Danny grunted again.

"And if you didn't know it before, you do now—when you dance with the devil in the pale moonlight you wind up in line at the DMV." Garrett took his eyes off the road to look at him sternly over his sunglasses. "Don't make us have to shoot the bear."

Maker's Mark, Danny decided.

He pressed the doorbell for another three-count and banged the knocker into the wood again.

After a moment the door was unlocked and unlatched and it opened inward a few inches. A young man with messy brown hair, disc-shaped plugs stretching his ear lobes, a bushy goatee and a hostile frown glared out at him.

"Good morning," Danny said.

The guy blinked twice at him. "I don't believe this."

"I'd like to talk to Mike please."

"I don't believe my eyes! Are you really standing here? Is it really *you* on my doorstep?"

The door swung open all the way and the guy stepped out onto the stoop. He was in his mid-20s, barefoot in black shorts and a purple and gold Lakers tank top, shorter than Danny but with a muscular wrestler's physique. He crossed tattooed arms across his chest and looked Danny up and down as if trying to decide which part of his body to grapple first to twist into a fleshy pretzel accompanied by the muted pops of a percussion section of dislocated bones.

"I just want to talk to Mike for a minute," Danny said. "No questions. I'm not working."

"Is that what you call what you do? You pretty much false advertise the business you're in, asshole. The answer's no. The answer's fuck off. The answer's I should beat your fucking face in."

"We both know that wouldn't do you—or Mike—any good." But still, Danny wanted answers and an exit, not bleeding lips and missing teeth.

The guy took a step forward. "You know I've about had it with your threats."

Danny held up his hands. "I'm just here to talk."

"Who *cares* that you're here? So what that you're here? A whole lot of better people than you aren't here anymore, you're just taking up space and I'm done with you taking it up at my house with my family. Get out of here. Get off my property or I'll beat your fucking face in *before* I call the cops. I don't care."

"Look, I just want to—"

The guy took another step toward him and Danny backed down a couple steps. "Get out of here!" he screamed.

The door opened wider and Mike Cruz appeared behind him. He put his hand on the guy's shoulder as if stabilizing a wobbly washing machine. "I'll take care of this Jack, thank you."

His stepson shifted his weight from foot to foot and snarled at Danny, "Whatever service you think you provide, you don't. You're a leech, that's all you are."

Cruz squeezed Jack's shoulder, gently but firmly, and the young man stomped inside. Danny thought Jack Cruz was not so unlike Victor Kasho, whose anger was like a wildfire spotting ahead of itself to stay alive.

Mike Cruz left the door open a crack and stepped out onto the landing. Danny could hear the TV on in the background, live coverage of the walking procession for the two fallen LA County firefighters from City Hall to the Cathedral of Our Lady of the Angels downtown. There were an estimated six thousand mourners in attendance including the governor and local politicians and firefighters from across the state. Danny thought it would make a good time to drive over to Pasadena and pay his own respects.

"What can I do for you now Mr. Cash Oh?"

Cruz towered over Danny who stood down on the second step between the flower pots. Cruz wore sandals, thigh-length athletic shorts and a cardinal USC t-shirt that looked new. His hair was uncombed and his cheeks had a dusting of white stubble. His eyes were red-rimmed and a little runny and he looked like he'd aged ten years since Danny last saw him on Monday.

"I wanted to see how you were doing," he said.

Cruz stood with his hands behind his back and his face shaded by the nylon canopy over his door.

Danny cleared his throat. "And I wanted to apologize."

"To me? Whatever for?" Cruz leaned forward. "Where would you even begin?"

Danny felt like he was being upbraided by a vice principal, the kind that needed to see a certain amount of contrition before granting clemency. "For breaking my code of ethics."

"Faithless men have no ethics."

"As a devotee of Doubting Thomas, patron saint of reporters, I should have kicked the tip's tires before I drove it around. I have to live with that."

"At least you have the chance to." Cruz took a half-step forward. "You are apologizing for being a thief and a liar and an opportunist. You are a merchant of misery and your currency is the pain and suffering of others. You pretend a camera gives you legitimacy but all it gives you is an excuse."

"An excuse to try." He hated how weak his retort sounded.

"*Try harder*. People like you start wildfires too—of slander and misinformation. You get drunk on every victory 'cause overall you're on a losing streak. You can't take shortcuts with people's lives. It may just be a keystroke to you but it is real life on the other end of it. It is actual flesh and actual blood and actual reputations. The enemy within is the ease with which something can be done superseding the question of whether it *should* be. Nobody even asks the question anymore—*should* we? Just *can* we? And you think your great moral quandary is over a shortfall in *ethics?* You think you can *apologize* your way out of everything? Apologies aren't good enough anymore. They *don't suffice.*"

Danny stared at his shoes. He hated having to apologize. The whole ritual of contrition made him want to double over and puke which is why he tried to avoid putting himself in the position of having to. Fuck Mark Pavelko and the rabbit he rode in on.

Cruz glared at him reproachfully in silence for a minute more then said, "Why are you really here?"

"I told you why."

"Amplify your answer."

Danny lifted his eyes and met his. "I just have a couple questions."

Cruz raised his head like a hound acquiring a scent. "That's more like it."

The garage workshop looked as if someone had come in solely with the intention of fucking with the owner's OCD—things weren't out of place so much as out of the *right* place. Equipment and tools which had been so neatly bundled when Danny was in here Saturday night had since been separated and rearranged. Drawers protruded at differing fractions of inches from shelves and cabinets he hadn't noticed.

He got the sense there were fewer things in the room too, as if some items had been taken away instead of put away—for instance the broadband scanner was still there but the laptop and spiral notebooks were gone. Nothing a stranger to the workshop would notice but he figured to Cruz it probably looked like a blind man had tried to reassemble his elephant.

Instead of welding supplies and the face shield and goggles, the only thing remaining on the work table was the black binder. It had been there when they entered the workshop after he followed Cruz up the driveway—he wouldn't allow him in his house—as if Cruz had left it out on purpose.

Cruz leaned against the table with his arms folded across his chest and sandals crossed at the ankles, watching Danny who stood awkwardly in an empty space of open concrete floor, trying not to touch anything as he looked at the annotated USGS maps and photos on the wall-mounted dry-erase boards, all those red and yellow pushpins with their tiny sticker labels placed like electrodes on a troubled brain, a CIA remote viewer's efforts to see through eyes that weren't his own.

And the flamethrower schematics like encoded battle plans.

"Go ahead and ask," Cruz said.

"Did you build it?"

"I tried to design the device, as I explained to you, to see what parts I'd need and where I could get them."

"If you were him."

"Yes, if I was him."

"Looks like you got pretty far with the plans."

"You're qualified to render that opinion?"

"How many pins are there? It looks like all the Angeles Arsonist fires are there."

"It *looks* like they are? From where you're standing? Tremendous eyesight runs in your family does it?"

"There's way more than seventeen pins."

"Are there?"

"How many?" Danny asked. "How many red ones?"

"Forty-five."

"And yellow?"

"Twenty-one."

"So…like, sixty fires?"

Cruz grimaced.

"I can't do long division either," Danny admitted.

"Sixty-six."

"How did you get from seventeen fires to sixty-six? How do you know?"

"I don't. No one does. No one ever will now."

Danny glanced at the black binder and Cruz followed his eyes. He figured Cruz was a good investigator the way he was a hunter—watching where his prey wanted to escape and closing off the avenue. As skilled a trapper as Carl Tillson almost was at Imelda Vasquez's cul-de-sac. "When did Carl Tillson become known to the task force?"

"Someone said he was?"

"Someone will."

"Who? Your benefactor?"

"My what?"

"Where is Mark Pavelko today?" Cruz asked.

"I believe he went back to San Francisco."

"I believe he had to."

"The old man of the mountain hears everything."

"Because I know my job better than you know yours. And as soon as you and people like you are no longer curious about me I can get back to doing it. Where will you go back to?"

"Work too."

"While you still can."

"As long as our society values bullets more than babies I'll always have something to write about."

"We value quality targets above all so I don't wish to keep you from making yourself one. People like you always do."

Danny nodded at the binder, pretending not to recognize it and eager to change the subject. "What is that?"

"It's alphabetical, that's what it is." Cruz watched him intently. "Help yourself?"

Posing that as a question convinced him at once that Cruz knew he'd been in here. Saturday night during the fundraiser he'd seen the lights on and blamed hapless helmeted Larry from Gold's Gym, but since then he'd learned the truth and now here they were, alone together with Cruz's angry stepson fuming nearby.

Danny opened the stiff cover and looked again at the face of angry white Marvin Akon. He thumbed through the plastic sleeves in time with his accelerating heart rate and descended through the last names and nondescript faces of all these men who never knew they were in Captain Mike Cruz's special book, until he reached the last entry. There was no discounting marker strike through the dark eyes and flat nose, the chunky face that looked more like the person he'd met at Malibu Bowl than the shaved, feral animal at Best Value Hardware.

Tillson, Carl, DOB 10/15/78.

There were a lot of handwritten notes in the margins of Tillson's priors, which amounted to exactly none, words underlined and asterisked—white

Toyota pickup, a license plate highlighted in yellow, combinations of letters and numbers penciled in around it.

Danny looked up at Cruz. "You had him."

"I did not."

"How'd you find him?"

"There was a witness at the Channel Fire."

Ten days before the massive Chalk Fire erupted on Saturday September 29 the Channel Fire burned 30 unremarkable acres on the east side of the 5 freeway near Castaic in the Santa Clarita Valley north of LA. Until this moment the low-level blaze, lacking in destructive power to anything but indigenous wildlife, had been overshadowed in the way victims of a prolific killer could be by Tillson's major successes—Box, Dillon, Chalk, and Backbone. Danny had never heard of any witnesses to any of his fires before—any. Part of the mystery of the Angeles Arsonist was that no one had ever seen him. A man carrying a flamethrower torching national forests and subdivisions and he'd been invisible the whole time.

But of course he hadn't been.

"The witness reported seeing a white pickup leaving the scene," Cruz said, "and was able to provide a partial tag."

"Was it registered to Tillson?"

"At the address you tried so hard not to verify when I asked you for it. Once again wasting precious time in a situation where time is as much the enemy as the suspect himself."

Danny almost apologized but knew it would just wind Cruz up again so he said nothing and stared at the blank space where Tillson's priors were supposed to be and thought again about sharks moving underwater, less than shadows until the strike. There was the inaudible sound of a fuse connecting in his head. "You knew where Imelda Vasquez lived?"

"We did."

"Did you talk to her?"

"She vouched for him."

"For what?"

"For his whereabouts on and around September 19 2018 when the Channel Fire was started."

As he said that Danny picked Imelda's name out of the handwritten notes. There were more sheets tucked in the plastic sleeve behind the one with the photograph but he didn't think he had the privilege to remove them despite Cruz's invitation to help himself. It was probably the second visit by the cops Jesse Lynne Jr. had mentioned. Imelda had called the police on Tillson once—but the second time they'd come all on their own, because of Mike Cruz. "She must have been convincing," he said.

"I don't recall her convincing anyone of anything, she simply refused to supply us with enough reasons for some people to stay on him."

"You thought you should?"

"I did."

"But you couldn't convince the other investigators?"

"One in particular seemed resistant to the idea. Evidently they had someone else in mind already." Cruz showed his teeth. "And so Carl Tillson was buried beneath the deluge of information an investigation like this inevitably develops. Even with a task force supposedly managing the flow of information."

Danny closed the cover of the binder. "He wasn't entirely buried. You knew."

"In the end it doesn't matter."

"Sure it does."

"I'm not surprised you think it does, I expect you to think it does, you'd surprise me if you didn't and you're incapable of surprising me, but it doesn't."

"Truth is truth whether anyone knows it or not."

Cruz frowned. "That's ridiculous."

"Truth will out then, is that more your vintage?"

"That's naïve, which is what I expect from you."

"Every secret gets blown eventually. Every one of them. It may take a lifetime or a generation, but nowadays we end up knowing pretty much everything eventually, like it or not."

Cruz barked a single derisive laugh. "Leave it to you to say something like that. I don't know when your generation is going to grow up or what it's going to take. Maybe all the grief your self-centeredness causes coming back on you tenfold will do it."

"Maybe the four horsemen of our fathers' apocalypse will too. If so I hope I'm there and have WiFi."

"Careful what you wish for, Mr. Cash Oh. Can you see yourself out or do you need assistance?"

"I can do it myself." Danny turned to go, then stopped. "Oh yeah—there is one more thing."

Cruz sighed and shook his head like someone unable to dislodge a tenacious salesman.

Danny said, "You and I have a secret."

The fireman raised his eyebrows. "Do we?"

"We do."

"And what do you suppose that is?"

"Where'd you go after you left us in Thousand Oaks? I didn't see you again until after everything had happened."

"I went to the address just like you—after you were expressly told not to."

"You wanted to see if I was right."

"I wanted to make sure you weren't wrong again."

"I think you can amplify your answer."

Cruz stared at him. He pushed himself off the table and stood up straight, probably wishing he had more of a height advantage over Danny. "What do you think you're getting at Mr. Cash Oh?"

"The two gunshots."

"What?"

"On my video. There are two gunshots that clearly weren't fired by the police. You can hear them clear as day. One of them made Tillson's fuel tanks erupt. In effect it was the kill shot. And it didn't come from the cops."

Cruz said nothing.

"So the question is," Danny continued, "who fired the shots? If there were two shots and one of them hit, then one shot missed—and that bullet's still somewhere in the cul-de-sac just waiting to be found. On the east side of the street I think, probably embedded in the front of someone's house. Could be in good enough shape for a ballistics exam to confirm it wasn't fired by the cops. And if they didn't fire it, then the question is who *else* was in the street on Monday? With a gun?"

Cruz's eyes had noticeably darkened. "This is your theory?"

"I call it the Second Shooter Theory. Catchy huh?"

"It's as clever as it is unsubstantiated."

"The shots are right there in the video. Everyone's talking about them. Sooner or later someone's going to go look for it."

"The police closed the street so the professionals can do exactly that."

"They aren't looking in the right place. They don't know what to look for."

"And you think you do?" Cruz spat. "You and whoever you tell on the internet? You're going to get somebody arrested for trespassing."

"Someone else was there, Mike." Danny could see that the fire captain didn't like his using his first name, as if they were chums. Worse—equals. "When they find the bullet they'll look for the gun that fired it. When they find the gun the owner of it's going to have a lot of explaining to do." He smiled grimly. "Surprise."

Cruz was silent for a long moment. "You're suggesting I was there?"

"I'm not suggesting. I saw you there. Plenty of people did. You said yourself you were there."

"With a gun? That I used to murder Carl Tillson?"

"What were you banging on the side of the car?"

Cruz snapped his fingers, a dull pop that might have sounded like the gunshot that ended Jorge Ochoa's life. "I get it—you couldn't get me for the Angeles Arsonist so now you're trying this? Accusing me of what—assassinating Carl Tillson in front of twenty cops? None of whom saw anything?"

"The cops saw the person they were aiming at. They weren't looking anywhere but down the barrels of their guns."

"And a good thing they were too, or are you the sort of person who prefers the sanctity of a murderer's bill of rights to the safety the rest of us should be able to take for granted?"

Cruz's stepdaughter Julia appeared in the doorway of the storage room. She was the spitting image of her mother Jackie Waller but as a blonde, tall and lean with an athletic build and a skin tone accustomed to unrelenting California sunshine. She wore a new-looking USC shirt too and held a cell phone in one hand and was crazy beautiful. "Come back inside daddy."

She shot a tight-lipped look of undiluted hatred at Danny who suddenly felt embarrassed on top of unworthy. He cleared his throat and said to Cruz, "I just wanted to apologize to you and I wanted to do it in person. I'll be on my way."

"There is one more thing," Cruz said.

He took a step toward Danny and Julia came into the workshop on long brown legs and touched his arm. "Come inside daddy."

"Fame isn't permanent. A dead child is." Cruz let the words hang in the air like bodies of the hanged before he gestured at the door.

Julia glared a chain gun stream of disgust at Danny. "Get out of here. Don't come back or I'll call the police. And I'm serious."

Danny glanced at Cruz on his way to the door. Cruz's stare made him feel like a deer or elk or rare white rhino moments before drawing its last unknowing breath. He headed down the driveway past Cruz's truck as leggy Julia led her stepfather back inside the house, closing the sliding glass door in the back yard firmly, without slamming it.

Danny put on his sunglasses and doffed his new black CODA baseball cap and walked to his car, passing reporters' debris trapped in the curb, paper cups, tape, bits of plastic. He'd stopped by the swag closet at work this morning for a replacement cap, ducking manager Ronald Schiff who had a bounty on him should he show himself in the office. He didn't see Lucy either but carried her cool with him like a charm bracelet. *Good work Danny.* Lucy could be like a situational *digestif* sometimes.

He thumbed his new phone which was already synced up, its contents a duplicate of what had been on his broken one, and scrolled down to Gary Calder's number. Scrolled further to the number for lawyer Bernie Ehrenpreiss. Back up to Calder. Toggled between them as he drove south to the freeway with the windows down and the air off, purging Red Flag in the windy heat gusting through the cabin. The what-ifs scattered like ravens from the shoulders of a scarecrow.

He still hadn't found the little leather book with the brass clips his dad gave him from the house fire. Worst case scenario it was gone. Next-to-worst case it was buried in an unmarked box in Vanessa's garage in Calendula. *If* the boxes were even still there. If she hadn't given them away to her self-help group along with her car.

Over the past week he'd been called a parasite, ambulance-chaser, leech, thief, liar, merchant of misery, opportunist, hazardous waste. He was a jack of all torments and yet a flamethrower and a car bomb couldn't kill him.

What he *was* was seeing Holiest of Holies Michelle tonight for drinks, late. It was a diversion for today and an investment in tomorrow. Then he'd start on the Chinatown tip. Between Travis Salk's irascible ghosts and Mike Cruz's curses of careless wishes and tenfold grief he wouldn't be lacking for company.

Wu and Fong NOT strangers Huan market.

Strands of webby connections plucked like muted piano strings.

Plenty of ghosts to come.

If you enjoyed this book please return to your point of purchase and rate it.

ABOUT THE AUTHOR

Steve McManus was born in Brampton, Ontario in 1970 and grew up in Calgary, Alberta. He wrote his first mystery novel while attending the University of Missouri-Columbia as a music major, and continued writing after he moved to Los Angeles where he became the drummer for rock band Darling Violetta, who released three CD's, appeared on *Buffy the Vampire Slayer,* and performed the theme song to the hit spinoff series *Angel.*

For more information, news, and offers please visit:
stevemcmanus.com
facebook.com/SteveMcManusBooks
twitter.com/SMlit

www.ingramcontent.com/pod-product-compliance
Lightning Source LLC
Chambersburg PA
CBHW030822310726
48980CB00006B/599/J

* 9 7 8 0 9 9 6 4 4 8 5 0 5 *